Glancing sideways at Cornish as they rode down
the valley she was not at all surprised to see the
customary scowl on his face.

'Look on the bright side, Colonel,' she said, a
barely suppressed chuckle in her soft voice. 'How
much worse if I couldn't ride at all!'

'That's a thought that's been exercising my mind
for the last half hour,' he admitted with a twisted
smile. 'I was so surprised when I found you were
the mapmaker Jo had recommended – '

'Horrified might be more accurate.'

'Horrified,' he agreed. 'So horrified, it never
occurred to me to ask whether you could ride. And
there are no tracks up-valley for even the toughest
carts.'

'Lucky for you then,' she observed drily.
'Y'know, I can't help wondering . . .'

'What?'

'You dislike females so much and I know you're
not really convinced I can make you a decent map
so – ' She raised her eyebrows. 'So why did you
take me on?'

About the Author

June Wyndham Davies was born in Liverpool and brought up in North London. After studying German at university she embarked upon a varied career, working as, amongst other things, a translator, a travel guide, a teacher and an actress.

She now lives with her son and daughter in South Buckinghamshire, where she enjoys being a member of her local theatre group and furthering her ambitions as an author. She has written fiction for a woman's magazine and has also published two previous novels.

JUNE WYNDHAM DAVIES

FOOL'S GOLD

CORONET BOOKS
Hodder and Stoughton

British Library CIP

A CIP catalogue record for this title is available from the British Library

ISBN 0-340-58491-2

Printed and bound in Great Britain for Hodder and Stoughton Paperbacks, a division of Hodder and Stoughton Ltd, Mill Road, Dunton Green, Sevenoaks, Kent TN13 2YA. (Editorial Office: 47 Bedford Square, London WC1B 3DP) by Clays Ltd, St Ives plc.

For Owain and Angharad
for love and support and cups of tea

and in memory of John

ACKNOWLEDGEMENTS:

Many thanks to the staff, past and present, of Bourne End Library, the Historical Society of Sacramento, California and my family and friends.

Prologue

The normally bustling heart of San Francisco was deserted. On every shop or saloon doorway hung a notice: 'Gone to see the hanging'.

Down on Sacramento Street the powerful late spring sun burnt away the sea mists round the former Mills and Vantine warehouse, the Vigilantes' new Fort Gunnybags. There was an air of tense expectation as men, women and children in their thousands jostled for position beyond the eight-foot high protective wall of sandbags. Shopkeepers and tradesmen mingled with bankers, gamblers, miners and saloon girls in the vast swaying and murmuring crowd. They had come to see Cora and Casey hang.

On the roof of the Fort between cannon and field artillery pieces stood the old fire bell which had summoned the Committee of Vigilance of 1856 to bring belated justice to San Francisco; watchful men with rifles at the ready scanned the nearby rooftops and the crowd below, on the alert for a last-minute attempt by Casey's friends to stop his execution for the murder of James King, the crusading newspaper editor. Three thousand Vigilance troops in the town would ensure that Casey and Cora would not this time escape the hangman's noose. It was Cora's acquittal of cold-blooded murder after a mockery of a trial rigged by his brothel-keeper mistress's money that had led the citizens of San Francisco to take the administration of justice into their own hands and they would not be baulked again.

Boos and catcalls echoed around the broad street as Casey, politician and County Supervisor until King revealed him as a former inmate of Sing-Sing, made his last speech to the crowd.

At last the two men were led out on to hinged platforms built outside the second floor windows. A noose was put around each neck, a white cap slipped over each head.

A Vigilante soldier leaned out of each window, knife in hand, ready to cut the ropes supporting the traps as soon as King's funeral cortege was sighted. All eyes swivelled to the Union Street junction to await the signal.

A man, hat pulled down over his eyes, collar turned up despite the sweltering heat, slipped around the corner to the rear of the Fort, shielding the small child by his side from the gruesome scene.

Round the back, where the cavalry and artillery horses were stabled, a man clad in the black frockcoat and top hat of the doctor lounged against a hitching rail. At the far end of the yard was a dusty farm cart with an elderly carthorse hitched to it.

'Here child!' The doctor held out a red, shiny apple. 'Go sit under that tree while we talk.'

The child, clutching to her a rag doll, looked briefly up at her companion for confirmation. He forced a smile and nodded. She took the apple and trotted off with her prize.

'Dead?' he asked in a fearful whisper.

The doctor mopped his sweating forehead. 'No, not dead,' he replied in the clipped tones of the New Englander. 'Despite that fearful Chinese concoction you tricked the jailers into giving her.' He caught the look of consternation on the other man's face. 'Don't think I didn't know what caused the miscarriage,' he growled in exasperation, running skeletal fingers through prematurely white hair. 'But there's a greater danger now. The Vigilantes have taken all the prisoners from the jail; they're for trial. Those charged with murder first.'

'And one hanging only whets the appetite for another.'

'The mood the mob's in today, they won't care about justice.' The doctor shrugged. 'I'm no judge, but I can't believe she deserves to hang.'

'What can I do?' It was a despairing whisper.

2

'Already done it!' the doctor announced with glee, then had to turn away to stifle a racking cough. 'They knew she was sick — I told 'em so. Weren't too surprised when I told them she'd died. Jailer's seen the corpse, seen the grave, signed for her.'

'But —'

'Don't worry. I paid him off. He won't talk. Now you've got to get her out of here. Help her forget. I'm sure you got another concoction for that,' he said with a rueful smile. 'Get her clear away from San Francisco, up into the hills where the air's better. Try and get work up on one of the *ranchos* — they're always looking for servants and hands.' He drew out a handful of letters. 'I already got some from the agencies.'

'How can we thank you?'

'Ain't no need.' He limped across to the cart and raised the horse blanket a fraction. 'See, she's fine for a few hours yet on the laudanum. Take the cart out to Murphy's on the stage road, and leave it there. Get on the stage and then I don't want to know where you go from there. Savvy?'

'Why are you doing this for us?'

The black-clad figure shrugged again. 'The kid, maybe.' He looked across gravely to the skinny child, playing in the dust with her rag doll. 'Or one last good deed before I die.' He gave an unpleasant laugh, devoid of all humour. 'Look at me!' He pointed to his yellow face and bloodshot eyes. 'My cough, my skin. I'm yellower'n you are! You know as well as I do 'bout these things. A few months, mebbe even a year — depends whether my liver gives out first or my lungs. And I didn't get neither from porin' over my books. Guess I'd like to make up to the Lord for some of the things I've done I ain't too proud of ...'

A bell tolled, mournful, solitary. Then all the bells of San Francisco answered.

'Don't stand here gossiping!' urged the doctor. 'Soon as they cut those ropes, there'll be all Hell let loose. Get outa here and hightail it to the stage road!'

On Sacramento Street, one of the watchers on the roof spotted King's funeral cortege leaving the Unitarian Church a block away and gave the signal. Two men reached out and

3

cut the ropes of the traps and a great roar went up from the crowds below.

As the bodies of the hanged men swung in the gentle breeze that came off the ocean, the little cart drew out of the town and headed north.

Chapter One

It was an unusually hot day, a promise of the hot summer still to come. Down in the Sacramento Valley, a distant view through the clumps of ancient oaks, the heat haze already hung over the mighty river and above it the distant jagged peaks of the Sierras reared up, snow-topped, against a shimmering backdrop of dazzling blue sky.

The group of men who stood on the *portal*, the verandah which ran the length of the old Spanish-style building, had the air of men who had fulfilled a distasteful but unavoidable task and were all relieved to be done with it.

Under normal circumstances, the minister would never have considered riding out all this way to perform the last rites for one who, when all was said and done, had been a foul-mouthed scoundrel who had made himself obnoxious to everyone from Sonoma to Sacramento and had, in all likelihood, never set foot inside a house of God in his life, but, as the minister's sister had wisely pointed out, these were not normal circumstances, nor was California, the newest of the United States of America, in any way a normal place. The Spanish influence still lingered on, even seven years after the Mexicans had ceded the territory, and Protestants were decidedly in the minority.

Besides, he had nothing against the Colonel, apart from the fact that he had left the ranch in such unworthy hands while he wasted his time and money in San Francisco. And it had been the Colonel who had sent for the minister to perform the burial. Some cock and bull story there had been that said the dead man was in some way related to the

5

Colonel, but the minister could not believe that. There was no further resemblance between them than that they were both dark and both spoke English with the same accent. But there it ended : the Colonel was a tall, quiet man of whom he had heard no ill spoken, whereas Jem had been a paltry man, loud-mouthed, immoral and too ready with a gun. In less than a year, he had brought the splendid ranch the Colonel had entrusted to him to a sorry state, despite one of the best years since the state was settled.

What the Colonel thought of his deputy's achievements it was hard to tell; his face was curiously immobile, apparently unmoved by the loss. Apart from a few curt words to Kerhouan in that peculiarly liquid speech that only they seemed to understand, he had said very little throughout the mercifully brief service or the scratch funeral meal that had followed.

Reverend Cooper sighed in relief as he saw Kerhouan, the Breton foreman, bringing his horses and buggy around the corner from the stables. The ranchhouse was in such a dreadful state that he preferred, despite the heat, to drive back to Sacramento, to eat one of Letitia's excellent suppers and sleep in his own clean bed.

The young boy Manuel called out something in Spanish and gestured down the dusty track. Toiling up it in the heat of the afternoon came a woman and a tall man with a child on his back. From the thick layer of dust on the woman's skirts, they had come some distance that day. Against the sun's rays, they wore the wide, half-domed, plaited straw hats of the Chinese coolie.

'Mr Cornish?' The woman approached them hesitantly while the man lowered the child from his tired shoulders and stood aloof.

The rancher nodded. One did not insist on titles out here in the wilds.

'I am the new housekeeper.' Her voice was harsh and low, edged with fatigue.

Cornish drew his brows together in a frown. By her voice she was too old for a housekeeper, too old to travel half across the county for work. The wide coolie's hat shaded her face, making it difficult for him to make out the features, but by her dress and accent she was not Oriental, which the man, despite his height, clearly was.

'I answered the advertisement.' She was speaking rapidly now, an edge of anxiety overlaying the exhaustion. 'We sent references.'

He looked at her with a heavy frown creasing his forehead, but still he did not answer. She began to rummage desperately in the canvas bag that hung from her thin, stooped shoulders. 'Here!' She thrust the letter into his unwilling hands.

He opened it with reluctance, for at the sight of the handwriting he realised what he would find there.

In a scrawl barely legible and hardly literate, Jem Cornish of the Tresco Ranch offered the applicant the post of housekeeper on bed and board terms, wages to be discussed later 'if satesfaktry'. Wordlessly he handed the letter to the Reverend Cooper, who glanced over it and could barely suppress a grim smile. Jem Cornish had been finely misled, he concluded. If he had survived, it would have been just retribution on him to have this gaunt, stooped creature for housekeeper; retribution for the local Indian and Mexican girls he had abused and ill-treated and estranged from their own people. Bed and board indeed!

'Is something amiss?' The woman's voice, raw with fatigue, drew the minister sharply back to the present.

'Jem Cornish — the man who wrote you this letter — is dead,' he said gently. 'And Colonel Cornish —'

'— has no need of a housekeeper,' said the rancher harshly.

'I can work well,' she replied, her voice staccato in her eagerness to convince him. 'I can cook and mend, keep house, work in the fields.' Then, as he made no reply, she turned back to the minister. 'I'm stronger than I look, really I am. I can work in the fields if you need extra hands for the harvest. And Chen Kai is a good worker too. We would well earn our keep.' She did not mention the child, who sat silently on the lush green grass, blue eyes wide in her grubby face.

Cornish turned to the woman's companion, standing quietly to one side.

'And the child — is it yours?' he demanded, and was rewarded with a scornful look.

7

'The child is of your race,' came the brusque answer.

'Which company holds your indentures?'

'No company has claim on me,' said the man proudly, holding his head high. 'I am a free man. I go where I please and work for whom I please.'

Cornish raised his eyebrows in surprise. Virtually every Chinese who came over to California was an immigrant indentured to whichever merchant company had paid for his passage.

'Chen Kai-Tsu is a well-educated man,' said the woman, anxious to please. 'He speaks excellent English ...'

'So I hear.' The rancher folded the letter and handed it back to her. 'There's no need here for a housekeeper, but an extra hand's always useful. He can cook for the men while we get Tresco working again.'

Ever since the first Chinese had come in '49, the myth had grown that they were good cooks and launderers. The truth was that, in a land starved of women, the Chinese, ever mindful of their debts to the merchant companies, would turn their hands to whatever work they could get. So they ended up with the jobs that the Spanish-Americans, jealously guarding their pride and masculinity, would not consider even if they were starving.

'Sir, I assure you, the lady is a far better cook than I,' he said anxiously.

'Standard of cooking don't bother me. I need a man who can turn his hand to anything. No place here for women and children. You take the job, I'll pay her fare back and something for her trouble.'

'But, Corr-onel, I promise you, she is strong enough to take on anything when she has had enough to eat. See, we've just walked all the way from One Horse Town ...'

The rancher shook his head and turned away.

The woman clutched her companion's hand. 'Take it, Kai,' she begged him. 'Please! Or we'll all starve. At least this way you'll have a place.'

'No!'

'You must.' She looked scornfully at the rancher, his back turned as he spoke to the minister. 'He'll never take a woman on. But we're far enough away now to be safe. I'll find

8

something in Sacramento: it's booming since they named it the capital. There'll be shops and stores ... I'll manage. Colonel Cornish?' She moved away before her companion could argue any further. 'Thank you, Colonel. Chen Kai will be happy to take the position.'

He raised his eyebrows at her elegant speech. Was she a lady's maid? he wondered. What was she doing out west with a young child? Of course, there might have been employment for her if Bella had married him instead of ... He closed his mind firmly to that train of thought.

'I'll pay your fare,' he offered stiffly. 'San Francisco is ...'

'No! No, never again!'

Such vehemence. Were they running from the law or the Vigilantes? he wondered. And was it the woman or the man? In this wild and comparatively lawless society the one was as likely as the other; gambling, women and drink always proved a lethal combination.

'Try Sacramento then,' suggested Cornish indifferently. 'Plenty of work there. Or Washington on the other bank. Old James McDowell's widow runs the place. Plenty of saloons,' he said casually, 'so they always need women.' Even worn-out husks like this one, so great was the shortage.

He glanced across at her as he spoke and was surprised to receive a piercing, almost contemptuous glare from beneath the brim of that battered straw hat.

He turned away, uncomfortable, speaking more brusquely than he had intended. 'Better make up your mind. Reverend Cooper'll give you a ride there, but the horses are getting restless in this heat.'

Cornish stood back and watched the Chinaman hand the woman into the gig and swing the child easily on to her lap. He held on to the woman's thin hand, reinforcing his earlier impression that she was his woman.

Unexpectedly embarrassed by their touching farewell, he turned away sharply. Striding into the ranch house, he swept the last remnants of the funeral meal into a leather satchel that hung behind the door.

The Chinaman was still standing by the gig as he emerged. 'Send me your location as soon as you can,' he said in that

9

curiously correct, almost unaccented English he spoke. 'I will get in to see you as soon as I can. There will be supplies to be fetched from the city, be sure. But if you or the child need me, or if there is any trouble, you send here for me.' As she hesitated, his voice grew harsh. 'Swear it,' he insisted.

'Oh, Chen Kai! Better for you to forget all about us. I have only ever brought you trouble.'

'Swear it!' he commanded sternly.

She muttered something too low for Cornish to make out, but it seemed to satisfy her companion.

He stepped forward to shake the minister's hand and dropped the leather bag alongside her shabby bundle on the boards of the gig. A flick of the whip and they were off, along the winding, dusty track that led down into the bottom of the valley.

The Chinaman watched until they disappeared from sight through the stand of trees. Then, face expressionless, he turned back and picked up his pack.

'Kerhouan will show you where you sleep,' said the rancher. 'It'll be a shakedown in the barn at first. Then you can start clearing up in the house. There's a deal of hard work needed to get this farm back on its feet again. If you're planning on staying, best show what you're worth.'

Chapter Two

The minister's gig bumped its way down the dusty track,
rocking from side to side over the uneven surface. Alicia
held the child clasped firmly to her side; she was desperately
tired and anxious, terrified at the thought of coping without
Kai for the first time in four years, but she knew she must
hide her fears.

The first few miles were covered in silence. No doubt the
minister was misreading the situation as so many before him
had done, and feeling morally outraged at having to take
such a woman into his gig.

Strange how much more indignant the Anglo-Americans
were at the idea of one of their own women as mistress to
what they regarded as the lesser races: French 'keskeydees',
Spanish-American 'greasers' or, worst of all, the 'Chinees'.
And yet she had known ministers in the larger mining camps
and small townships who had accorded the mistress of a
leading Anglo citizen all the dignity of a wife, however
infamous she or her man might be. To Alicia, however,
the nationality was the least aspect: to be a kept woman
was the deepest degradation she could imagine.

When the track levelled out on the valley floor, she eased
her arm from Tamsin's side and opened the bag the Colonel
had handed her; the sight of the food made her mouth water!
On top of the food was a small purse. She untied it and could
hardly restrain a cry of surprise at the stream of dollars that
poured out into her hand.

'But this is far more than the fare to Sacramento!' she
exclaimed.

'The Colonel has always been a generous man,' replied the minister drily. 'Perhaps he hopes you'll have the sense to get back east again. California's no fit home for a woman with a small child, protected only by a Chinee. What fools you immigrants are! Like lemmings. Some fool shouts "Gold!" and you all run ...'

Odd to hear herself described as an immigrant. And yet, if one wanted to be pedantic, they were all immigrants except the native Indians, and few enough of them had survived the great influx of the white man. But she regarded herself as a Californian, bred if not born, for she had grown up here with the first settlers, the Spanish-Americans; certainly she had more right to call herself Californian than most.

And how shocked her New England mother would have been, she thought inconsequentially, to hear her strictly brought-up daughter call herself Californian!

It was almost fourteen years since they had first set foot on Californian soil in '42 after an appalling voyage round the Horn – the Connecticut lady all fear and foreboding, the eleven-year-old child all restless curiosity. They had settled among the Spanish ranchers, Russian fur traders, American whalers and hide and tallow dealers in the little village on the Bay, called Yerba Buena for the medicinal herbs that grew in abundance on its many hills.

She could barely remember her birthplace: the handsome New England estate with its gentle, undulating hills and valleys, the elegant classical mansion looking across the Hudson towards West Point was only a collection of fugitive memories now. And lost to her for ever.

She had been eager for the new life in this vast empty country where everyone spoke Spanish and all the other children had black hair and fiery dark eyes, and soon grew impatient with a mother pining for the niceties of Connecticut Society. Papa had to come to the new lands of California and Oregon to make his maps and surveys, so it was folly to yearn to be anywhere else.

Only later, some time after her mother's death, married herself and walled in by the miseries of her own circumstances, could she understand how her mother had felt, uprooted from a settled society and replanted in an alien

12

land where, of the four hundred and fifty inhabitants, barely half were American and of these only a handful female. It was a society in which Judith Jameson's rigid upbringing and innate pride did not allow her to take a part; she had withdrawn firmly behind the shuttered windows of the wooden house which looked down Pleasant Valley to the waters of the bay, there to brood on the sad chance which had brought her to this miserable and wretched corner of the continent.

She had married Major Owens when he was an officer instructor at the West Point Academy, and had never come to terms with the footloose, adventurous mapmaker he had become, ever eager to join one of the mad expeditions to Oregon or the Mexican borderlands, to the Platte or the Sweetwater River with Frémont, or up the Pacific Coast with Commander Wilkes.

She would not accept any invitations from the Spanish-speaking ladies in the little settlement by the Bay, or even from the wives of the American whaler captains. One group she stigmatised as heathens, the other she regarded as so very far beneath her that to notice them would be mutually insulting. She withdrew like a snail into her shell and, before long, the invitations ceased. Her only joy in life was the constant scheming to get her daughter back east to prepare for the inheritance which would eventually come her way as the last of the Jamesons.

But Alicia had been quite uninterested in the glowing future held out to her as the chatelaine of Valley Hall and its wide acres: she was far happier if she could escape, with the connivance of the Mexican maids, to ride with the daughters of the Mexican governor, the *Alcalde*, with only their black-robed confessor as chaperon. And escape became far easier as her mother lapsed into imagined invalidity, hardly ever leaving her bedchamber.

The most exciting moments in Alicia's monotonous life were when her father and his companions made a rare return to base. Most of the Army Corps of Topographical Engineers were former West Point men, like her father, selected not only for their qualities of leadership and adventurousness but also for their specialised knowledge.

The United States wanted to purchase California from Mexico. The planned surveys were part of the American strategy to acquire the vast area before the British moved in from British Columbia and Vancouver Island, or the Russians – already established just north of Yerba Buena at Fort Ross – from Alaska, to annexe California from the weak and inefficient Mexican governors for the sake of its flourishing fur trade.

Travelling with each survey were geologists, map-makers, guides, topographers, mountaineers and artists, as well as the necessary military support. They surveyed new routes for possible future emigration overland, for improved communication, from the frontiers of Missouri to the mouth of the Columbia, even making a rash crossing of the Sierra Nevada in the middle of the winter and nearly losing some important scientists en route.

When they did have the chance of leave in Yerba Buena, they took it enthusiastically and the young girl, playing hostess during her mother's illness, was for all of them a fond reminder of the homes they had left behind. As she grew up, she had no difficulty coaxing her father's colleagues to initiate her into the mysteries of geology, cartography, or daguerrotyping, for which exacting science she soon showed a remarkable aptitude. On a few memorable occasions, they even took her up into the mountains with them, to make maps and take photographic plates. She rode the mountains, swam in the icy streams and gloried in the freedom of the empty valleys and the splendour of nature unsullied by any human presence but their own.

Then they would be off, gone as swiftly as they had come, leaving her to the stifling, enclosed atmosphere of the unhappy house. In the empty days that followed their departure, she would sit at the open window, oblivious to the sea fogs blowing in from the bay and drifting up the valley, oblivious to the boom of Borica's shore batteries sending the flocks of startled pelicans to wheel in a screaming mass over Alcatraz Island, and dream of the day when she would be old enough to travel up into the mountains with her father and his companions, surveying, mapping, photographing new scenes, strange Indians, mountains that no white man

14

had ever seen, until her mother sent the servant to bid her come and read to her from some improving volume or play for an hour on the inlaid piano which had come round the Horn with them.

Apart from her father's all too infrequent visits, little else happened in the small settlement as Alicia Owens was growing up. In '42, the Russians withdrew from Fort Ross and returned to Alaska; they sold their stock to Sutter, a Swiss immigrant, for his new ranch up on the Sacramento which he called New Helvetia, though travellers called it Sutter's Fort. More immigrants arrived, many of them in wagon trains over routes mapped out by her father. In '46, the *Brooklyn* deposited over two hundred Mormons on the shore, which vastly increased the numbers in the small settlement, as well as the racial and religious variety! The Mexicans began selling off to the newcomers the land which the Spanish had originally assigned to the Missions; private ranches began to spring up from the coast to the Pacific Ranges, north and south of the great bay. By her fifteenth year, relations between the new, mainly Anglo-American immigrants and the Mexican government had deteriorated and the *Alcalde*, prophesying war, left for Monterey, taking his daughters with him.

'Washington or Sacramento?' asked the minister curtly, his voice bringing her back to the present with a jolt.

'I — I beg your pardon?' She tightened her arm around the child, sleeping peacefully between them, her face buried in the woman's lap.

'Will I put you down in Washington or Sacramento?' He gestured to the river ferry tied up at the levée, embarking a flood of passengers, on foot and on horseback, from the teeming river front.

She looked around her at the garish saloons and the raucous passers-by.

'Sacramento, if you will be so kind,' she said firmly.

'Stay in the gig then, or they'll charge you extra for the crossing,' he said, negotiating the horse and cart through the lounging crowds and across the rumbling gangway onto the ferry.

15

'I can pay for my own passage,' she replied sharply. She drew out the purse and tried to pass one of the gold coins over to the minister.

He turned to her in exasperation. 'Let me give you some advice, ma'am which I hope you'll take for the sake of my calling, if for naught else: if you're too good for Washington, then you'll need every last red cent of that money to find a lodging in Sacramento that'll come up to your requirements. Accept a kindness when it's offered with the best of intentions; pride is a vice, ma'am, and one you can't afford in your situation, if I may say so.'

The ferry cast off and worked its way across the broad brown river between a number of skiffs and sailing ships and past a huge white-painted sidewheeler, taller above the water than anything she had ever seen before.

At the far bank, she stepped down out of the gig, unassisted, and lifted the child down.

'Thank you for driving us this far,' she said primly. 'It was very — Christian of you.'

Before he could stop her, she had slipped away down the gangplank and disappeared among the loafers on the quayside.

Sacramento: a hustling, bustling city. Alicia had last been here in '48 when there was barely more than the white-washed adobe buildings of Sutter's Fort, just beginning to gather around it the tents and shanties of the first goldminers in the American River Valley. The fort was still there, on the bluff where the American River poured its swirling waters into the mighty Sacramento, but now it was dwarfed by the spreading streets of Sacramento City. The town had been laid out by Sutter's son in an attempt to bring some order to the sprawling mass of tents and shacks that had sprung up almost overnight. In spite of fires, floods and cholera, the town had continued to grow and in 1854, mindful of its proximity to the gold that provided the wealth of the new State, the politicians had designated it state capital. More permanent buildings had sprung up along the grid system and the town was pushing the surrounding forest back a little further each year as it expanded.

Alicia looked around her in confusion, almost regretting

16

the instinct which had made her give the minister the slip. Even this late in the afternoon the town was full of men from the mines and ranches that spread out along the Sacramento Valley and up the length of its many tributaries. Sacks and bales were stacked along the broad Embarcadero and the levée, waiting to be loaded on to the numerous ships berthed alongside. The labourers shouted and hollered as they worked, but few took any notice of the stooped woman who stood bewildered in front of the warehouses, her face hidden by the domed straw hat.

'Lisha,' whispered the child. 'I'm very tired.'

Resolutely, she turned her back on the bustling riverside, forcing her tired legs to carry her deeper into the heart of the town. The main street was alive with crowds of men, walking, lounging, exchanging news on street corners, despite the heat. Although a hundred and twenty-five miles from the Pacific Ocean and well on the way to the high mountains of the Sierra Nevada, Sacramento itself was only thirty feet above sea-level and the heat could climb to 110 in the shade at the height of summer. The unmade roads and constant coming and going of horsemen, carriages and carts combined to stir up a stifling blanket of fine white dust that hung like a pall over the town, irritating the eyes and burning the throat.

The crowds that passed behind them were a motley selection: Negroes from the Southern states, mulattoes from Jamaica, Kanakas from Hawaii, Peruvians, Chileans, Mexicans, French, German, Italians, even Australians.

On every corner thimble-riggers, French monte-dealers and string-game tricksters were vying to part the miner in search of entertainment from his hard-earned gold. 'Three ounces no man can turn up the jack!' or 'Six ounces no one knows where the little joker is!'

An auctioneer was calling his goods from a canvas booth. 'All at a bargain! Splendid double-soled triple-pegged waterproof boots! Fit your road-smashers exactly — yours for only four and a half ounces, sir!'

Although Sacramento was a thriving city, the gold boom was tailing off somewhat and the ships tying up at the wharves with wares that they could once have sold for up to ten times their real worth, often found that the market had dried up on them. Gone were the days when cornering the market in pans or shovels could make the seller's fortune quicker than a bonanza strike. Nowadays the man who cornered the market in cast-iron stoves was more likely to have to sell below cost to cover his shipping costs, or in the more extreme cases, see his undertaking go bust and his iron stoves, chamber pots or kegs of nails dumped into the mud pits or dustholes of the big towns to become the foundations of some of the major thoroughfares.

With a sigh of relief she lowered herself on to an upturned barrel on the dusty sidewalk and opened the bag, listening to the auctioneer while she and the child finished the food. After the boots, the auctioneer began to sell off lamps and candles, before moving on to a stock of old-fashioned clothes, male and female, that some shipper back east had had the happy thought of unloading on the ignorant westerners. Eagerly, Alicia fished out the purse she had concealed in the skirts of her old black dress. There were no ladies out on the streets that dusty afternoon and she was able to buy a dove grey silk dress with the old style leg o'mutton sleeves and rather over-ornate trimmings, two bonnets and a couple of pretty shawls and a petticoat for the expenditure of only one of the quarter eagles she had had from the man at Tresco. The rest, over and above the fare to Sacramento, she was determined to send back.

Nothing else in Sacramento proved as good a bargain as the clothes, however. After trailing around the town for a couple of hours, she was forced to take a room in a far from salubrious building behind the Embarcadero warehouses. All the decent lodging houses were far beyond her means until she could get work and earn. She was forced to concede the justice of the minister's remarks.

She was no more successful with her attempts to find work. As she emerged from the third milliner's to turn her down, she suddenly caught sight of herself in the plate glass window. She stopped in her tracks and passed her hand wearily across her brow.

'What is it, 'Lisha?' asked the child tiredly.

'Good God!' she said under her breath. It was hardly

surprising no one would take her on. She had barely recognised her own reflection. This shabby, stooped figure was
not Alicia Langdon! Wearily she abandoned the search.

The first night in Sacramento, she was too tired to do
more than wash and fall into bed, but her landlady, the
Widow Grey, made up in other respects for her lack of home
comforts : she knew just what work there was available in
the Golden City and promised to give Alicia the names of
several stores that were short-handed.

She woke next day feeling well rested. It was many weeks
since she had slept a night through, despite all Kai's concoctions. It had taken weeks to get the drugs out of her system,
weeks when she had been so unnerved by the silence of the
wide open spaces after the raucousness of the claustrophobic
prison cell that she had turned to drink for comfort, stolen
and lied to Kai to get her hands on a bottle. But now she
was over the worst and as each day passed, she felt a little
more able to face the world.

Remembering the shock of that reflection, she took the
time to wash herself from head to foot and clean the thick
dust out of her hair. She dried it and brushed it till it shone.
She put on her spare black skirt and the brighter of the
acquired shawls and, with one of the gay new bonnets
swinging by the ribbons from her fingers, looked at herself
gravely in the fly-blown mirror.

She drew herself up and straightened her shoulders. It was
as if she had peeled off the old layers acquired in prison and
drawn on a new personality. Behind her Tamsin bounced on
the bed.

'Now you looks like my Lisha again!' she exclaimed
excitedly.

Alicia hugged the child, but when she turned away again
her face was grim. If only she felt like the old Alicia, she
thought. But there was no turning the clock back. What was
done was done and she could never be the same girl again;
recent events had only finished what Robert had begun.

Robert.

Robert had been so handsome. He had been on board
Catesby's flag-ship when it put into Yerba Buena − or San
Francisco, as she was learning to call it − to take possession

19

of California for the United States at the end of the Mexican war in '48.

Grieving for her dead mother, hope fast fading for her father, officially posted missing with a lost expedition into the interior, she had hurried down to the harbour hoping for a letter from her grandfather, enclosing a ticket for her return to Connecticut, where she could make her home with him at Valley Hall.

Seventeen years old, bereaved, cut off from the world in the little house with the mourning blinds drawn against the yellow sea-fogs, she was ripe for love. Blue eyes crinkled in a tanned face, long legs braced against the slight swell that rocked the deck, the fair-haired young Lieutenant seemed to her a giant, a hero.

The servants had returned to Mexico with the *Alcalde* and his daughters at the outbreak of war and she had no one to advise her. She was swept on board the flagship and off her feet by Lieutenant Robert J. Langdon. Within a week they were wed.

Her wedding night was a disaster, an unsatisfactory, fumbling night with Robert rendered too drunk by his fellow-officers to fulfil his desires, but she was young and optimistic, and she knew it was just a hiccup in their love affair. But the next morning Robert was posted 80 miles north to New Helvetia, to carry news to the settlers up by Sutter's Fort of their new status as citizens of the United States.

Robert came back a changed man. Outwardly still the handsome young officer she had fallen in love with, but with a feverish gleam in his eyes, a slight tremor in his hands. At first she thought he was drunk again and her heart sank at the prospect of another night of inconclusive humiliation, but he was not drunk. He was far sicker than that: he had caught gold-fever.

He had led his little party of Marines without mishap through the heavily wooded valleys up to Sutter's Fort. It was normally crowded with newly arrived emigrants and those Californian Indians who had survived the white man's diseases and now clustered around the trading posts or the Catholic missions, but Robert's party found the normally bustling fort almost empty. Gradually, in cryptic whispers and muttered clues, the story came out. James Marshall had found some curious deposits in the tide-race of the new sawmill his Indian labourers had built on the American River and the resulting exodus among his workers had left poor Johann Sutter with fields of sown crops and no prospect of any to harvest them; virtually every fit man, Indian and white, had gone upriver in search of the elusive gold.

Barely half of Robert's marines returned from the American River with him, and he made little attempt to coerce them. Within hours of their return, before the word could spread, he sold the wooden house and plot which had been her home for six years, and bought himself out of the Navy.

'But it's not my home to sell!' she protested weakly. 'It's my father's!'

'If he's still alive, which I doubt,' he replied brutally. 'Any reasonable man would say it's yours, and your property became mine on our marriage, so I can do as I like with it.'

He must have seen her look of shock, for now he became wheedling, sliding his arm around her waist and kissing her cold cheek. 'Sweetheart, how else am I to get the money to start up? I have to buy out my commission, buy some transport and tools, and still have enough for a good stake. Don't you see, my darling, we're in at the beginning! We'll be in and make our fortune before anyone else knows about it! A fortune for us and our children! Why, we'll be able to buy up the whole of San Francisco Bay by the time we've finished! A little hardship now, that's all. You won't mind living in a wagon or a tent, will you? Like a real pioneer!'

The picture he painted for her bore very little resemblance to reality. The ox-drawn wagon took them and their supplies up as far as Sutter's Fort, but from there on, the trail to the diggings was up narrow defiles, alongside roaring torrents which flowed down to the American or Feather Rivers, and only pack-mules or horses could get through.

The first night in the diggings, she carefully hid the drink outside the tent and, despite the mountain cold, arrayed herself in the silk nightgown she had had made with

21

her wedding dress; shyly she averted her eyes as Robert undressed, sliding across beneath the rough blanket to make space for her husband, blushing as she remembered how she had reacted to the feel of his powerful, demanding body urgent against hers as he kissed her a reluctant farewell before returning to his ship.

Seventeen and ignorant, she was not prepared for what followed. She caught her breath in a startled gasp as her husband reached out and ripped her robe deliberately from neck to hem. Frozen with fear she screamed in pain as his strong fingers dug agonisingly into her soft breasts. Before she could move he rolled heavily on top of her, tearing at the remnants of her robe and knocking the breath out of her.

'Robert! You're hurting!' she whispered hoarsely, the warmth draining from her body to be replaced by a cold terror she had never before experienced.

He growled deep in his throat and transferred his cruel grip from her sore breasts to her wrists, pinning her on her back as she struggled to pull away from him. He was breathing heavily, grunting as he butted his hips violently against hers. She didn't know what was happening, she only knew that she was alone here with a man she hardly recognised as her husband, miles from another human being, and he was hurting her. She began to struggle again and he let go of her wrists and closed his hand slowly round her throat.

'No, Robert!' she gasped hoarsely.

'Damn you to Hell, you bitch!' he cried. Then the pressure seemed to lighten a little and he rolled off her. Eyes wide with fear, she backed away on all fours, until she tangled in the shredded remnants of her silk robe and fell in a painful heap on the earth floor. A rough hand grabbed her hair and jerked her head up, then Robert swore again and threw her violently back down on the floor, shouting at her words she hardly understood. When the mists of pain cleared from behind her eyes, she looked up and saw in the flickering light of the lamp the sweat standing out on his brow.

'Robert?' she moaned. 'Please, I —'

Then his open hand landed on the side of her .head and she saw no more.

She grew up swiftly that early summer of 1848. Miles away

from civilisation, friendless, penniless, with everything she had ever owned now Robert's, there was nowhere for her to turn. She became increasingly a stranger to the violent man who called himself her husband. After the first few weeks of brutal, failed attempts at consummation, he did not attempt to come near her again in what she mentally thought of as *that* way. And she was glad.

Chapter Three

'You come for them directions?' demanded Widow Grey, not looking up from the vast tub of washing in the yard. 'Aggie! C'm'ere and take over!' When Aggie at last came stomping across the rotting verandah, an assortment of grubby children in her wake, she turned around, drying her huge hands on her apron.

'My, my!' said Widow Grey admiringly. 'There's a change in a night!' She stepped round Alicia, looking her critically up and down. 'Lot younger'n I thought,' she said consideringly. 'Be a waste to send you to the stores. You want to go make your fortune in the saloons! All them *hungry* miners!'

It was the way she said 'hungry' that did it, threatening to break through the fragile mental barriers Alicia had erected to preserve her sanity. Tendrils of panic began to lick at the edge of her mind like little flames. A brief image – one moment there, the next gone – etched briefly on the back of her eyes like a print emerging from a negative. A small body in a corner, like a rag doll tossed carelessly aside; a man in a pool of blood; terror palpable in the very air. She squeezed her eyes tightly shut and the image was gone as swiftly as it had come. If she let the memory unwind – but that way lay madness.

'You all right, dearie?' The voice intruded, rough but solicitous. 'Here, sit down. Don't look like you've been eatin' enough recently.' Alicia opened her eyes to see the arch smile. 'Have to fatten yourself up a bit. Miners like their women well-covered. Now there's the White Horse, the Missouri ... or you could try the Green Tree or the Elephant.'

'Thank you, ma'am,' she said firmly, 'but I'll start off with the stores, if you don't mind.'

'Too fine for the saloons, are we?' mocked Aggie. 'Well, there ain't no room for airs or graces this end of town, I can tell you! An' if you're reckonin' on findin' a position, better leave the brat behind with us and that'll be three dollars extra.'

She could feel the sidewalk loungers watching her as she walked out down the street, eyes cast down, but she forced herself to pay no heed. She found Carson's Stores down near the waterfront without too much difficulty and within minutes had been taken on by Missus Carson, a short, rather angular woman with a sour expression.

'You'll help in the shop and the stores out back,' she told her. 'Hours as necessary — I never close when there's folk to buy. Sundays are your own; wages as good as you'll get anywhere.'

Alicia took what was offered gratefully. She knew she hadn't the strength to go on looking.

It was hard work and none of the people she worked with particularly congenial, but it was a living. When she was fitter and stronger, she would look again. Sometimes when she was heaving sacks of flour and barrels of bacon under Missus Carson's eagle eye she thought longingly of the pretty little milliner's shops. But there too there'd be floors to scrub, windows to clean and back yards to scour!

By the end of the first week, she knew why Missus Carson found it so difficult to keep help in the store. Not only was there her sharp tongue to contend with, but there were two other drawbacks. One was the saloon which her brother, Ned Sullivan, ran. The saloon was attached to the store and Missus Carson stayed open much longer hours than the other stores in the hope of catching as much trade as possible from miners made more expansive by Sullivan's rot-gut whiskey. While they bought more drunk than sober, some of them tried to be as familiar with the shop girl as they were with the bar girls, but Alicia's years in the mining camps helped her turn off such approaches with a smile and a joke. The other problem was Mr Carson, and he was not so easily dealt with.

25

He must have been a handsome man once, but he had long since run to seed on his brother-in-law's whiskey and his own weak nature. His sandy hair was thinning and what was left he plastered across his freckled pate with a strong-smelling oil which seemed to permeate him entirely. Whenever she looked up in the store, she would find his watery blue eyes fixed on her; she didn't much like the expression in them. He was always about the store, without, as far as Alicia could see, contributing much to its prosperity. At first she thought it just coincidence that he was always in the back room when she was fetching in stores, but by the end of her first week she knew it was not.

She began to wonder whether she would not be safer in the saloon where at least Sullivan had promised that, if she would try out behind the bar, he would keep her safe from any unwanted attentions. 'What the girls do after we close is their business,' he explained. 'I'll pay you for servin' in the bar, and that's all you have to do 'less you wants. And I'd like ter see the feller that'd force hisself on you when I'm around!'

The other two employees worked exclusively in the livery stable and smithy behind the store. It was one of the biggest in Sacramento and she found Jim, the liveryman, an old Cockney sailor thrown on shore by a lame leg, and Sam, his half-Indian assistant, better company than the proprietors. Part of her duties was to take them out their dinner each day and keep the livery books up to date. Early in the week she found an order for a new plough horse for Tresco and persuaded Sam to take a note out to Chen Kai-Tsu with her directions.

A week after her arrival in Sacramento, she was crossing the yard at midday, carrying a heavy tray which she almost dropped when Chen Kai stepped out of the shadows.

'Kai!' She pushed the tray unceremoniously at Sam and hugged her friend enthusiastically under Jim's interested gaze. 'Oh, I'm so glad to see you!' she exclaimed.

'How is it with you, Alicia?' he asked softly, taking her hands in his and holding them tightly. Jim, clearing his throat, turned away to polish saddles.

'Better,' she murmured. 'Much better.'

26

'This is not what I'd have chosen for you,' he said rather bitterly, looking at the tray. 'Why do you have to eat in the stables?'

'I choose to,' she replied with a smile. 'Better company.'

He looked her over closely. 'You look much better.' He was relieved to see the grey shade had gone from her unnaturally pale skin and the hollows in her cheeks were beginning slowly to fill out again. 'Tell me how Tamsin is.'

They stood in the shade of the livery stables while she told him of the arrangements she had made for Tamsin, but all the time she was looking back over her shoulder, listening for the shout that would summon her back to the counter.

'I can't stay much longer,' she apologised.

'They work you too hard!' he said accusingly, swift concern in his eyes.

'You know I was never afraid of hard work,' she said with a shrug. 'It would have been better if I could have got a living-in job, to have Tamsin with me, but there are very few jobs like that. The hours are rather long, to be sure, but the money is good. I could get more if I took up Sullivan's offer to work in the saloon in the evenings ...'

'No! We don't need money that bad. I still hope Corr-onel Cornish may be persuaded to take you on. And you working as a bar girl would hardly help my case!'

'Poisoned him already?' she asked tartly.

'Not yet,' he confessed ruefully. 'But give me time.' The smile faded and he looked a little anxious. 'Till now, there has only been the Corr-onel and a few hands to feed and none of them much notice what they eat. Besides, I could always blame it on the poor supplies. But new hands will demand better chow than I can manage. Next week, we go up-country with Ker-hwan and all the new hands Corr-onel is hiring. We are going to build a cabin and corral for Pedro the shepherd and his new wife. I will have to cook for them all — and I have to buy supplies myself — today!'

She laughed at the woeful expression on his face. 'Take prepared meat that only needs slicing up or frying up at the most — hams, tongues, pickled beef. And if it goes wrong, those marvellous herbs of yours will cover up a multitude of sins! As for the supplies, you just leave it to me.'

27

A shrill voice called out, angrily demanding to know where that 'dratted girl' was.

'Missus Carson – I'll have to go. Kai, when you come in, don't forget to make it clear you're purchasing for Tresco.'

'Or they'll throw me out?'

'They don't exactly practise what they preach here in Sacramento. But Missus Carson is very anxious to get the big ranch accounts. It's her only chance to compete with Hopkins and Huntington.' She picked up her skirts and turned to run. 'Oh, don't touch the bacon, whatever you do. It's ex-Army, and rotten.'

It was not Missus Carson but her husband who was waiting for her in the gloomy corridor that connected the livery yard to the store. She drew back to let him pass, but he stayed where he was, blocking her way.

'Who you meetin' out thar?' he asked, his little eyes darting past her.

'Meeting?' She looked at him blankly. 'Only Jim and Sam. I took their food to the livery stables as I have done every day since I began working for you – for Missus Carson.' She'd given Kai time enough to get away. 'I can hear Missus Carson calling me,' she said. Still he did not stir. 'Coming, ma'am!' she called out in a carrying voice.

Carson stepped back in alarm, but as she slipped past him, she felt his sweaty hands linger on her waist. It was all she could do not to scream and she had to fight to drive away all the horrors that tried to push their way into her consciousness at his touch. She wanted to slap his stupid, leering face, but she repressed the urge before it got out of hand. For the foreseeable future at least she needed the security of the Carsons' job to keep her and Tamsin from starvation. Just pray that Carson's fear of his shrewish wife and her hulking brother would stop him short at the roving hand.

She bustled about the shop, tidying up. It was a large store, thriving under Missus Carson's vigorous leadership. In the front shop they stocked staple provisions: meat, bread, molasses, salt, preserved fruits, meat and vegetables, cheeses and hams, sides of beef and so on. In the second room, they had beds and bedding, overcoats, guernsey frocks and flannel shirts and drawers, boots and shoes, rubber waders and anything else the miners might be tempted to buy for their comfort in the hills. To one side, off the corridor that led to the saloon bar, was a third chamber full of mining tools and equipment, gold scales and medicine chests, the province of Missus Carson's brother.

She looked around the room at all the equipment, running her hand down the smooth handle of a miner's pick. Even now, she had only to close her eyes and she could once more hear the sounds of those early mining camps and smell the overpowering stench of the primitive diggings. Men worked from morning till night, waist-deep in the icy streams, digging the dirt out, sorting it, panning the more promising material to let the water separate out the gold – if gold there were – from the heavy alluvial sand. It was hard, back-breaking work and they retired only when the light failed, to lie shivering in their inadequate tents, soaked by the heavy mountain dews, until it was time to rise and start the weary work once more. They had to be constantly alert to guard their claim, and look to their mules or their tools which they always had to leave on the claim to establish possession. There was little time to wash clothes or sweaty bodies, or dig proper latrines, and the camps looked and smelt worse than the most appalling slums of the most overcrowded cities of Europe.

In that first hot summer and autumn, the Langdons found barely enough gold to live on. Food had to be bought at highly inflated prices from the camp chandlers who had organised a supply chain from San Francisco. Bread which sold for five cents in the east cost fifty cents in San Francisco and over a dollar by the time it reached the diggings. At least eight dollars worth of gold a day was needed just for enough bread and beans to stay alive and, more often than not, they did not make that much. The level of gold in the little marked jar rarely reached pork, let alone beef, and only the merchants seemed to be making that elusive fortune. Inevitably, they had to use up what was left of the money from the house just to survive.

Those miners who had the sense to group together were a deal better off, for they could send one of their members off to the nearest town — Sonora in the southern mines or Sacramento in the north — for fresh supplies. If they trusted each other sufficiently, he could even convert their gold into currency and bank it for safety while he was there, and the rest of the group would carry on digging, with the absent member receiving his fair share of any gold struck in his absence.

Robert, however, would have none of this. No one else was trustworthy; besides, tomorrow or the day after they would make the big break, find the mother lode, make their fortune. Why bring others in to share the big strike?

Then he would go into Angel's Camp or Hangville for supplies and hear tell of another big strike somewhere. Someone would tell him of a man who had heard another say he knew a fellow who had met a man who was in a party shovelling up the big chunks. Lump fever would strike again and they would pack their meagre belongings on to the old mule and trek across the rough foothills of the Sierras to yet another wild and desolate spot. They left Bidwell's Bar just before the big strike, then Old Dry Diggings, then Bullard's Bar where they had seen miners paying at the store with lumps of gold.

They spent the winter in a miserable shack at the Fork of the Yuba. When an adventurer named Stoddart reeled into the camp with a tale of a lake whose shores and bottoms were studded with gold, it was inevitable that Robert would join the expedition to find the Golden Lake. It was all a tale, of course, and soon they were all referring to it as the Great Goose Lake Hunt. Stoddart fled and the disconsolate parties returned to the Yuba. Three Germans, becoming detached from the main party, returned to Downieville by a roundabout route, further north-east than had previously been prospected, and, on the east branch of the north fork of the Feather, they found some rocks riven with cracks packed with gold they could pry out with their knives. Rich Bar and the many bars that were discovered around it were soon overrun with thousands of miners. Robert, failing to

30

make the quick strike he had hoped for, soon abandoned his claim and moved on.

When they came down from the mountains, he went into San Francisco for supplies. There was a letter for her, brought round the Horn on the new Pacific Mail : Grandfather Jameson was dead and Valley Hall was hers. After a few superficial words of sympathy, Robert loaded up the mule and they set off back to the camps. There was no point, he said, in giving up now, just as they were about to make the big strike. Connecticut could wait a little longer.

She gritted her teeth and continued to cook and wash and mend for Robert, struggling to make a home for them out of the disgusting shacks and tents and lean-tos they lived in, even standing beside him, panning the soil they had dug.

She had absorbed a great deal of information from her father and the books he had left in Yerba Buena and occasionally she would venture, when they were staking a claim in virgin territory, to suggest those parts of the terrain where the easily accessible 'placer' gold might be. Robert invariably treated her suggestions with deep scorn and she had to endure the chagrin of seeing other, later miners, move in to 'her' spots and walk off with the prizes.

In the first year, when placers were rich and pickings easy, there was a deal of cameraderie among the miners, and though the shortage of women was acute, she never had anything but the most civil of treatment from the rough men of all nationalities who crowded into the foothills of the Sierras and it eased the pain of her unhappy marriage. But as the gold became harder to find and more and more men poured into the hills to find it, envy and greed, sharp practice and suspicion began to creep in. The awesome splendour of the rocky gorges and tree-covered slopes of the Sierras began to be eroded by the misery and squalor of the men who pillaged them.

The miners, always superstitious and willing to put their success, or lack of it, on any back but their own, began sarcastically to call Robert 'Lucky Langdon' and to regard him as an ill-omen.

31

She was stacking a barrel of pickled tongues in the front of the shop, for it was nearing the end of its life and needed to be sold if it were not to be written off as a dead loss, and studiously ignoring the lascivious comments of two miners lounging in the doorway, when she saw Kai out of the corner of her eye.

Before she could straighten her aching back and speak, Missus Carson shot out of the shadows, a broom held before her as if she would sweep him back out on to the sidewalks.

'Git outa here, you heathen! Don't serve no furriners in here. You git along to Chinatown, along with the rest of your kind!'

'I have the order for Tresco supplies,' said Chen Kai, hands together, bowing courteously, but not too low.

'Want we should throw'm out, lady?' asked one of the loungers, a rough, heavily bearded man who looked as if he had missed out on the pre-celebration bath even the dirtiest miner generally took as soon as he got into town. 'Or shall we just cut off his pig-tail, huh?'

Kai did not wear his hair in a pigtail, but cut as much in the Western style as thick, straight black hair could be. Apart from his straw hat, his clothes were entirely the same as those of any Westerner.

Missus Carson was nobody's fool. The mention of Tresco had worked on her like a charm, exactly as Alicia had known it would.

'Tresco? Whyever didn't you say so before?' she snapped. Then she turned on the miners. 'Dratted men! Git outa here if'n you ain't buyin' anythin'!' she ordered. 'And you, mister,' she turned on Chen Kai-Tsu, 'give the girl your order. And mind it's collected by tonight — don't hold with no Sabbath opening!'

It didn't take too long to give the order and Kai allowed 'the girl' to make suggestions here and there. To placate her mistress, who, in between serving the other customers, hovered attentively at the other end of the counter, she tried to persuade him to take a few sides of bacon.

'Thank you, missee, no bacon. We have bacon already to use. Next time we buy bacon.'

32

'Very well.' She had to turn away to hide a smile. 'The order will be ready for collection any time after three.'

'Thank you, missee. I will be here then.'

A bow to Missus Carson in the shadows and he was gone.

'Pretty much time you spent on that Chinee,' grumbled the storekeeper, aggrieved that she had had to serve the few miners who had come in herself, when she knew full well that half of them only came in to look the girl over. 'Few enough young women about, even now Sacramento's so settled,' her brother had observed. 'Attractive wench like her, bound to bring 'em in, just to look at her, and if you can't sell to them once they're in, you're not the woman I took ye for, Millie! Aye, one our rivals can't match, that one.'

Missus Carson had agreed, even rooting out one of the blouses she had foolishly bought in early on in the business. It was old-fashioned, of course, but so was the girl. Perversely, that only seemed to increase her attraction. The blouse was only loaned, like the large holland apron with which the girl protected her skirt in the front shop and the storerooms out back. After all, who knew how long she might stay? She could remember the time when a woman could bury her husband one day and marry the chief mourner the next. Not quite so frantic now, of course, but the shortage of unattached women was still acute. With twelve men to every woman, even the worst fright or shrew could have her pick; for a handsome and still youthful woman, even a widow with a young child, the choice was more like a hundred.

'Too much time, ma'am?' queried Alicia, raising her eyebrows. 'I'm sorry, I must have been mistaken. I thought you were eager for the Tresco account, and it seemed to me that a little encouragement and assistance might bear fruit in the future.'

'Don't she talk beautiful?' came a voice from the doorway. 'Cain't never hear enough of it.' It was Ned Sullivan, a huge bear of a man who ran the saloon and the miners' stores. More intelligent than either his sister or his brother-in-law, he was the driving force behind the enterprise. He made no secret of his admiration for Alicia, but he was more open than Carson and never attempted to take advantage

33

of his position. He was loud-mouthed and uncouth, but she respected him for his politeness towards her.

'An' that's sense she's talking there, so 'tis,' he boomed. 'You were sour enough when Hopkins took the Vincent account, weren't you? Well, if'n you don't want the other big ranches to go to them, you got to butter 'em up a bit. Time's gone now when you could pick and choose who you served and when, times when miners would offer you bags of gold to sell them the last loaf of bread instead of some other poor starving devil. Gold's runnin' out, Millie, leastways for the small miner. Now it's all the companies and the ranches, thass where you got to look for business. An' there's not many others besides us and Hopkins can hold big enough stocks. And, tarnation, if'n Tresco chooses to send a Chinee or a three-headed black man in to buy, then them's the ones you got to butter up some. Ain't that so, sweetheart?' He turned to Alicia for her support.

He was right, but she doubted that many would see his point of view. California had floated for almost six years now on a sea of gold and most of the State's inhabitants saw no reason why they should not continue to do so. But the placer gold, the easily accessible gold found on river-banks, or in old river beds and sand bars, had almost all been dug out and only the seams that ran deep into the mountains still remained. Only the big mining companies could get at this with hydraulic mining, washing the mountains away with jets of high-powered water that came out of the flumes so fast they could kill a man. The day of the prospector was coming to an end, but few were willing to believe it so long as there were still unexpected discoveries. While one miner could still make his fortune by a lucky find, so, they believed, could all of them.

'And no matter what happens to the gold, there'll always be a call for a bottle or two of whiskey and a pretty girl!' he chuckled. 'How about it, eh, girl? You could do well in the saloon, much better than in here. Why not just come through for a few hours each evening, since you're so short on money? Always tips and extras to be picked up.'

'Thank you, but no.'

'If you're worried about the kid, well, dammit, you and

her could move in here. Millie's got plenty of rooms, and then I guess you'd rest easier. Aw, c'mon, why not give it a try?' He had the grace to smile as she shook her head. 'Ah, well, if you've set your mind against it ... Pity. Great pity. I'm that desperate for new faces in there since Mollie and Jennie left, and you'd be a prime attraction.'

Chapter Four

Until she was nineteen, she'd never thought she could be an attraction to anyone.

The Langdons had left the northern fields and arrived in San Francisco en route for the southern mines. It was her birthday, and almost two years since she had married Robert. The town had changed beyond recognition in that time; the little fishing village was now a roistering, rowdy, good-time town. Unlike the miners with pay dirt to spend – and the streets were full of them – they had difficulty finding a room they could afford. Not for them the night on the town, the restaurant, one of the flourishing new theatres. Robert, apparently oblivious to the date, left her behind in the scruffy rooming house while he went to see a man 'about some business'.

'Brought his woman with him, did he?' she asked unwisely, wrinkling her nose at the stink of whiskey and cheap perfume clouding him on his return. 'Or did you finish your business early?'

'Thass right,' he slurred. 'Bought myself a woman. Whaddya think abou' tha', eh?'

She shrugged. 'I trust you had a successful evening.'

'Succesful! You laughing at me?'

'No, I –'

'Met up with Fisher, I did. Thought I'd get even with him over that trouble at Little Rich Bar.'

Alicia shivered. She'd taken against Fisher from their very first encounter. He had staked a claim near them at Little Rich Bar up at Hangtown, in the very dry ravine that she had suggested on their arrival, and which Robert, naturally, had turned down with open scorn. Within a week, Fisher had dug out a fortune while the Langdons had made barely enough to buy food for the mule. Far from treating her with the respect the other men gave her, Fisher was forever leering at her, making suggestive remarks and trying to catch her alone. He would often come up behind her when she was washing clothes in the stream and just stand there, thumbs hooked into his pants pockets, licking his full lips and stripping her with his hot, greedy eyes.

'And did you?'

'Challenged him. Three card monte.'

Her heart sank. Robert had not the stomach for a gambler.

'I'd have won, too,' he boasted, 'cept he put Vasquez up against me. All the greasers are good at three card monte.'

'Then why did you play?'

He looked at her shiftily. 'Matter of honour,' he said, slurring his words.

'Honour? You! Oh God, how much did you lose?'

He shrugged. 'Everything.'

'The last of the gold?' she shouted angrily. 'You've lost it all? Oh, how *could* you, you fool!'

She paid dearly for her outburst, for he had drunk too much to contain his impotent rage and lashed out at her with his fists. For once she didn't scream as his knuckles smacked into her flesh, throwing her against the wall. Her last thought as she fell to the floor was that she would bear it no longer.

The next morning when he awoke, heavy-eyed and fuzzy-headed, she was sitting quietly by the door, her meagre belongings packed in a small bundle, holding a piece of blood-stained linen to her forehead.

'I'm leaving you Robert,' she said softly. 'I can't go on like this.'

'And what does your ladyship intend to live on, pray?' he sneered.

'I shall go back to Connecticut,' she said calmly through swollen lips.

'And what will you use for the passage money? Shirt buttons?'

'Give me the directions of the lawyer. I'm taking out a loan against Valley Hall.'

He struggled out of bed and crossed the room to loom over her. 'Won't take you as far as the harbour,' he laughed mirthlessly. 'I sold Valley Hall last fall. The last of the estate followed the gold last evening. Fisher has it all now. An' y'know what? Lusts after you, does Fisher.' He nodded his head foolishly. 'Asked me to throw you in with the stake, but more fool me, I had qualms. Told him he'd have to wait till I'm gone. Then she's all yours, I said. Fair and square. God knows why; I'd have been well rid of you.'

After that, they'd gone south, to Sonora, the town that the Mexicans from Sonora State had set up to supply the mines along the Southern tributaries, the Merced, Tuolumne, Mokelumne. Their luck did not improve, but at least Alicia had company, for the Mexicans had brought their wives and mistresses with them, which had attracted other miners with women to settle there.

It was a colourful little town, retaining some of the wild beauty that was being eroded further north. Surrounded still by trees, the town was a mixture of adobe mud-baked buildings and tents hung with gaudy silks and flags, brightly dyed shawls or multi-coloured Mexican blankets known as *zarapes*.

She and Robert led increasingly estranged lives but the fact that she continued to share his roof – or canvas – when he was in Sonora protected her from other, unwanted attentions. As long as she was seen to be associated with 'Lucky Langdon', the most foolhardy and boastful buck would steer clear, for fear the ill-fortune might rub off.

She made a modest living helping Angelina, the fat Mexican woman who ran the cookhouse. The food was not as bad as in the advance camps, where even those miners 'digging up the lumps' had to settle for appalling food because there was simply nothing else available. At least in Sonora one of the Mexicans would occasionally take a day off to hunt venison or game. Now and then there would be a cow from Southern California or a nearby ranch and that would mean fresh beef, but usually it was pork. Alicia learned how to cook pork, pickled or cured but mostly fried, as that was about all it was good for. They fried it for breakfast and supper, boiled it with the beans and soaked bread in the grease and then fried that.

'I've lived on swine till I grunt and squeal' ran one popular miner's song, and Alicia found herself in heartfelt agreement. She often thought back to the early days when the carcasses of the Longhorn cattle, slaughtered and stripped of their hides and fat for tallow, had been left to rot in the sun on the shores of San Francisco Bay. What they could have done with only half that wasted meat!

In Angelina's busy *cantina*, Alicia learnt how to make sourdough bread, flapjacks and hotcakes, and she and Angelina cultivated a little truck garden out back so that the miners – and their cooks – had some vegetables and fruit and managed to avoid the land scurvy that struck down so many.

Alicia's twentieth birthday passed unnoticed. With decent food her thin frame filled out with womanly curves and she alone seemed unaware that she had blossomed from gawky girlhood into a glowingly attractive young woman. She was not happy, but she had learnt to come to terms with her situation. She saw Robert only rarely, usually only when he needed supplies. She had learnt not to try to hold back any of the money she had scrimped and saved: he was stronger than she and would take it anyway. Better to give it him with a smile than have him wrest it from her and give her a black eye or a split lip in the process.

Someone was watching her.

It was a sensation she had become accustomed to, working with Angelina in the *cantina*. Usually it was the miners, who seasoned their gaze with a kind word or a joke, but sometimes it was the men who passed through the mining camps with the travelling whorehouses, the 'hell-on-wheels' that traipsed from camp to camp, parting the miners from their hard-earned cash – and often their health as well. Not one passed through without the man in charge trying to tempt her away from the *cantina* with the offer of untold wealth – and a pretty dress.

39

It was late afternoon, and she was taking advantage of a momentary lull in the tide of Carson's customers to make up an order to go up to Folsom on the new Sacramento Valley Railroad. As she turned to lift a box of candles down off the shelf, she looked across covertly out of the corner of her eye.

She nearly dropped the candles. Neatly attired in a jacket and smart waistcoat suitable for a visit to town, Colonel Cornish stood in the doorway, hat in hand, looking at her with frank admiration.

She took a deep breath to subdue the rising tide of panic and forced herself to serve the next miner who had lounged through from the saloon.

She looked again as she gave Jedediah Barrett his change. The rancher was still there.

'Thank 'ee, Miss' Owens.' Jedediah touched his hat as he scooped up his supplies.

Fortunate that she had thought to change her name! Emboldened, she looked again at the Colonel and saw not a trace of recognition. But of course there was little resemblance between the smiling shop assistant and the worn-out wreck of a woman who had presented herself at Tresco. The broad sun hat had shaded her face then and the halfway decent clothes she wore now made a difference. She could consign the worn, sad and ragged figure of Mrs Langdon to the past.

'Can I be of assistance, sir?' she asked, purposely lifting her voice to change its timbre.

'Collecting the provisions for Tresco,' he said with an attractive smile. 'No hurry.' He cast his eye over the list she had drawn up with Chen Kai and added a few items for his own use. 'And there's a quantity of ale and spirits from Sullivan. And the oil.'

She came out from behind the counter to go into the stores.

'Don't stir,' he bade her easily. 'The boy will bring the bills through.'

As he spoke, a lad of about fifteen brought through a sheaf of papers with Sullivan's barely legible scrawl wildly all over it. Cornish bent forward to help her decipher it, so that she could price up the items —

something Sullivan always left to the front shop –
and she took the opportunity to have a good look
at him.

He had a rather long oval face with fine features that might
once, in his youth, have been delicate, but which now simply
gave a balance to the lines etched on his face. His hair was a
dark brown that verged on black and his eyes were a curious
shade of green, very penetrating. He was clean-shaven and
his wide mouth above the pointed chin could, she guessed,
as easily thin in fury as smile. The hand moving over the bills
was long and slim, but his shoulders were rather hunched,
throwing his body out of line.

She realised she was staring. 'Cash or account?' she asked
hastily.

'I'd as soon pay cash,' he said, drawing out a purse full of
double eagles. 'And if there's anything on account for Tresco
run up over the last year while – while I was away?'

'I'll check before you come in again,' she promised. 'Next
month, I guess.' A whole month before she would see Kai
again.

'Oh, I don't know about that,' he grinned. 'Sacramento has
improved so much since I was last here, wild horses won't stop
me coming in at least once a week.'

Alicia's astonishment was mirrored in the open-mouthed
expression of the young lad.

'Wagon's – uh – all loaded up, Colonel,' he stammered.
'Ready – when you are.'

The Colonel flashed her a lop-sided grin, bowed briefly to
her, and was gone.

The Colonel cursed fluently as the horses were backed in and
hitched to the wagon.

'Hold them steady!' he snapped at Manuel.

'They're very fresh!' the boy replied mildly.

'And I'm being sour for no cause,' grinned the older man,
ruffling the lad's hair as he hitched them up. 'I'm sorry,
Manuel.'

'It pains?' queried the lad, cocking a knowing eyebrow in
his dark, mobile face.

The man shrugged fatalistically and, as if to deny it, vaulted easily, one-handed, up on to the buckboard, settled himself and drove off.

With a conscious effort, he smoothed the frown between his eyes and rested his left arm on his knee, feeling the relief course through every vein, through every nerve in his body.

Yes, it pained. With every movement of a finger, with every shrug of a shoulder, it pained. He thought he had learned to live with it, but there were some days when he cursed himself for not having let them take it off and be done, days when he could cheerfully have picked up the axe and finished the surgeon's work for him.

Today was one of those days. But not as bad as the day they had buried Jem. With only Manuel, Pedro and Kerhouan on the ranch — he did not count the minister, of course — he had insisted on bearing his part in carrying the coffin and as a consequence had jarred his bad arm most villainously. Just one more element of disaster on that disastrous day.

He had been, he knew, very short with Jo Chen's woman: after all, she had come in all good faith, on the strength of the letter from Jem. He had tried to salve his conscience with the money, but the obstinate female had sent it back again with a message that she had kept 'only as much as was justified for the inconvenience of the wasted journey'.

'For God's sake, man!' he had shouted at Jo Chen. 'I can well afford it! And she — with that child to feed ...'

'To have insisted would have been to offend her deeply, Corr-onel. She has found employment and can support herself and the child.'

He shrugged. 'In her situation, that kind of pride can prove costly.'

He had done all he could to offset any harm Jem's actions might have caused and his conscience was clear. He turned his mind back to Tresco and building the new house for Pedro and his future wife. The new hands he had hired on would all be out at Tresco in the next few days. He'd set Jo Chen to clearing up the old barn for a bunkhouse. Maybe Pedro's girl could be persuaded to cook up some fresh bread for them ...

As the carriage breasted the last slope on the drive up to the ranchhouse, he stopped for a moment to sit and savour the clear, warm air.

From these gentle slopes he could no longer see the dust haze
that hung over Sacramento, just Tresco Valley's green acres as
far as the eye could see, blurring into the wood-fringed slopes
of the Vaca mountains. A beautiful spot. The river, the valley
and the ranch had been named for the green and flowering
Tresco Abbey Gardens in the Scillies where he had spent a
few happy months in his youth, working with his gardener
uncle. And if he looked over to his left, across the Sacramento
Valley, he could see the jagged peaks of the Sierra Nevada,
where it had all begun.

What a fool he had been to waste his time running after
Bella in San Francisco, when he could have been here, building
his dream! But even Jem had not been able to wreck it; thanks
to Kerhouan there would be crops to harvest this year. Soon
the hands he had hired would be here in the Valley and the task
of turning Tresco into a successful working ranch, profitable
and above all self-supporting, would move on another stage.
And as for Bella ... he suddenly realised that not only was
this the first time he'd thought of her in a week, but he'd also
spent a fair part of the afternoon paying attention to another
woman! There was hope for him yet, he thought wryly, as he
clicked his tongue at the horses and moved on to Tresco.

Tresco was one of the big new ranches that were appearing
throughout the Central Valley of California, between the
Sierra Nevada on the east and the Pacific Coast Ranges in
the West. Unlike the other ranches, however, Tresco land did
not confine itself to the valley of the Sacramento. To be sure,
he held thousands of acres of lush fields down in the fertile
valley bottom, where summer temperatures that never sank
below 100 ensured bumper crops, but the major part of Tresco
land lay on both sides of the tributary once known as the Santa
Caterina, from the saint's day on which its Spanish explorers
had first sailed up it. The Tresco river took its head waters
from a crystal clear lake in the foothills of the Coast Range
and bubbled down over the rough hillside until it reached the
broad valley bottom. A few miles before its junction with the
Sacramento, it deepened to become navigable.

To the get-rich-quick men of the gold boom time, it
seemed like madness not to choose the acres that had
been up for grabbing down along the Valley of the

43

Sacramento, where grain ripened more rapidly and cattle fattened fast.

But Cornish had his reasons.

There was a sudden rush of late-comers to be served that evening, for Carson's never shut shop until the saloons were well and truly full. It was well past nine before the shutters were finally put up and by that time the noise from the saloon was almost overwhelming. One of the last customers was an elderly clerk from the Sacramento office of the California Steam Navigation Company, whose steamboat fleets dominated the river traffic from San Francisco up to the furthest navigable reaches of the Sacramento Valley rivers. A strict teetotaller and a lay preacher, he was only too delighted to offer her his escort back through the rowdy streets to the lodging house.

Sacramento on a Saturday night was no place for a woman to be out alone. Sacramento had not quite the brawling reputation of its wilder neighbour San Francisco, nor was it as wild as some of the earlier mining camps where two and three day binges were commonplace. The story was still told of the traveller who had arrived at Rich Bar at three o'clock in the morning, found a bed in the hotel, but been kept awake all night by the carousing miners.

'Your customers are up rather late tonight,' the traveller had commented.

'Lord bless you, no,' the proprietor had replied. 'The boys of Rich Bar generally keep going for forty-eight hours. It's a little late in the morning for the night before last, but for last night, why, bless you, it's only just the shank of the evening.'

Rich Bar had long since been worked out and abandoned, a ghost town with no inhabitants to carouse, but the memory of such nights lived on and miners came in every Saturday night from the surrounding camps to gamble, whore and drink themselves senseless into the Sabbath.

As they progressed down the waterfront, the old Embarcadero for Sutter's Fort, to Widow Grey's boarding house between the Folsom Road and the wharves, they passed the Tehàma Theatre, formerly the Eagle, where Lola Montez

44

had recently tried, and failed, to redeem her reputation as an actress.

As they rounded the corner, they came face to face with a group of miners fresh into town.

'Oh, pretty lady,' cried one with a flourishing bow. 'Won't you take pity on these lonely gentlemen? Can we not implore you to join us for dinner?'

'We've come all the way in from Rough and Ready Camp just to find you!' exclaimed another.

'Thank you, no,' she replied with a smile. 'My little girl is waiting for me.'

The first man bowed again. 'Let us not delay you!' he cried, with the theatricality of a man well on in drink. 'Hurry away to your little child; leave us with the memory of devoted motherhood.'

'Le'sh shpeed the lady on her way with a shalute!' said another, and they all lined up and insisted, much to Mr Jones's embarrassment, on discharging their shotguns into the air in salute, causing not inconsiderable alarm in the neighbourhood.

At every saloon they passed the evening was already in full force, and at Madame Charlot's, the painted women in their startling finery were hanging out of the upper windows, anticipating a busy evening. She was very glad to have the elderly clerk's escort, particularly when they reached the end of the Embarcadero and narrowly avoided being knocked over by a bearded miner in a filthy red shirt being hurled unceremoniously out on to the sidewalk from one of the saloons as they passed.

Tamsin was in bed when she arrived, but, as the landlady informed her, not asleep.

'Had one of her screaming fits, she did,' said the Widow Grey with her usual air of gloomy satisfaction. 'Fine all day, ate her supper with nary a peep, went to sleep, then all Hell let loose.'

Alicia's heart sank as she made her apologies mechanically and hurried up the rickety stairs to the cramped and shabby room. Halfway up the stairs she began to shake. She made it to the landing where, leaning against the wall, she took out the phial of Kai's mixture and poured it down her throat. She took a few deep breaths, opened the door and turned up the oil lamp which guttered in the corner, casting giant shadows over the uneven wooden walls. Tamsin was sitting bolt upright in bed, clutching the rag doll that Alicia had made her in better days, her eyes still wide with terror.

Alicia fought down the instinct to rush across the room and wrap the frightened child close in her arms. She dealt with the lamp, crossed to the bed and, keeping her voice deliberately normal and everyday, said: 'Hello, my lovely. Did you stay awake to see me?' She kissed the child warmly, an arm casually round her shoulders, but her heart was wrenched by the rigid self-control she could feel in the thin body.

'Oh, Lisha! Beatrice thought that the nasty man had come back!' She was close to tears again, but bit her lip to stop the show of what Chen Kai called baby behaviour, projecting it instead on to the doll. 'Beatrice cried,' she concluded sadly.

Close your mind. Shut it out. Force your voice to stay calm. 'Tell Beatrice we're in Sacramento now; we can all be happy again.'

As she said it, she felt a shiver run up her spine. Kai would have said she was tempting fate to speak so, but then Kai, despite his mission upbringing, had no faith. About her own she was not so sure.

As if she had followed her thoughts, Tamsin wriggled closer and put her head on Alicia's shoulder.

'Kai isn't here any more,' she said sadly, her head drooping until she nestled her cheek against Beatrice. 'I do miss him.'

'He isn't far away, darling,' she said bracingly. 'He's still in Sacramento, really. And he's got a good job with people who treat him well. We must be glad for him.'

'Am glad,' said the child with a trembling lip. 'But Beatrice wants him here.'

Alicia had no more comfort to offer, so she drew her back down the bed, stroking her hair back out of her eyes.

'Lie down now, my sweet, and tell Beatrice to go to sleep. It's past her bedtime.' A thought struck her and she passed her hand beneath the thin quilt.

'It's all right,' said the child with quiet dignity. 'It's dry. Beatrice doesn't wet her bed any more. But she wishes you'd take that sticky sheet away now she doesn't need it any more.'

In truth, Alicia had wrapped the mattress in her rubberised canvas cape more to stop anything inside Widow Grey's mattress getting to them than to keep the mattress safe from Tamsin.

Gradually she felt the tension ebb out of the thin frame as Tamsin settled down with Beatrice beneath the quilt. Alicia sang her some of her favourite songs in a soft voice, trying to ignore the shouts and raucous laughter and slamming of doors coming from other parts of the establishment. She preferred to close her mind to what went on behind the other doors. At least three of the other female residents of the Widow's lodging house would not have been out of place at Madame Charlot's, and Aggie Grey's own brood of assorted half-castes owed much to their proximity to the docks. She couldn't have picked a worse place to try and forget the past, she thought with a shudder.

At last Tamsin grew calm, though she still did not fall asleep. Alicia rose and poured the ewer of water into the basin which stood on the chest and stripped off her dusty dress to wash herself in the tepid water. Night and morning, summer and winter, she never failed to wash herself and the child from head to foot, even if she had to break the ice to do it. To this ritual she ascribed the fact that, throughout the years in the filthy mining camps, she had never succumbed to the countless virulent illnesses or infestations that hundreds of others had fallen prey to.

Kai had shown her the herbs to scatter in the sheets to keep the fleas at bay, and which ones to distil to wash Tamsin with when she was in unavoidable contact with sick or verminous children; Alicia made a mental note to find time to go out into the surrounding countryside to pick some more. She listened to the whine of the mosquitoes pinging against the shutters; thanks to the aromatic liquid which stood in bowls on every surface, their lodging, despite its proximity to Sutter's Slough, had none of the monstrous insects which made life so hideous elsewhere in Sacramento.

She picked up a brush and uncoiled her luxuriant hair. It was a pretty but undistinguished shade of light brown, except where the sun had picked out streaks more golden-red than fair. Thank God the doctor had not cut it off when she was in the fever. Twenty times on the right she brushed it, then twenty times on the left, before she laid aside the brush and braided it softly into a slim plait over each shoulder. She tied the ribbons at the neck of the long, worn nightdress and looked solemnly at her reflection in the cracked glass on the wall.

Soft brown eyes gazed back at her, shadowed still by the dark circles of those last dreadful days in San Francisco. Both she and Tamsin could do with some good fresh air. Perhaps tomorrow they would walk out from town, along the river-bank. She passed a tired hand across her forehead as if to erase the frown lines there.

As she snuffed the lamp out and groped her way to the bed – not a difficult task, since the room was barely larger than the bed – she heard Tamsin murmuring to Beatrice.

'It'll be all right, Beatrice, you'll see,' she whispered. 'We'll find the wagon again and make all the pictures for ev'rybody and you shall sleep in your own little bunk. An' ev'ry night we'll find somewhere nice and green like that pretty place where Chen Kai is, and we'll pitch camp there. And Chen Kai'll tell us stories while we girls all cook us the food and ...'

A deep sigh, then the heavy breathing told Alicia she was asleep. As she lay in the bed and let the exhaustion of her body overtake her, tears ran down her cheeks. Let Tamsin have her dreams, for children needed hope, but for herself there could be no delusion. The days when they had roamed the countryside, staying in the mining camps or the towns as the feeling took them, making a more than comfortable living from the photographs that they took of the miners or the prosperous tradesmen and their families, were gone. They had lost the wagon for good and with it had gone the only freedom she had ever known.

Chapter Five

Sleep was a long time coming that night, despite her physical exhaustion, and, lying between sleep and consciousness, she found herself thinking back to the time when Chen Kai-Tsu had come into her life.

The autumn of 1852 had been an unusually hot one. On the main street of Sonora, Mr Stiles, the proprietor of the stationery store, the miner's 'intelligence' centre, was passing buckets of water up to his apprentice to line up on the flat roof of the store; the fire risk was high after such a long hot summer. As she passed on by Bertin's Exchange and Banking House, she heard someone hailing her.

She turned, shading her eyes, and saw a German miner who'd been out at Angel's Camp at the same time as the Langdons, when Bennager Raspberry the storekeeper had thrown out a keg of brandied peaches that had spoiled on the Cape voyage and all the pigs in Angel's Camp had stayed squealing drunk for four days and nights.

'You Missus Langdon, *nicht*?'

'I am,' she replied cautiously.

'Your man, he very sick up by Sierra City,' said the German, spitting skilfully out into the road. 'Pretty soon, you be vidow. Go stake your claims, before men he owes comes for his tools and his mule.'

'You are a fool!' Angelina told her roundly. 'Madness to go up there. You think Lucky Langdon gonna leave you anythin' worth risking your health for?'

'That's not why I'm going,' she said quietly, packing her few belongings into a saddlebag.

'What for then? Love?'

'I married him for better or for worse, Angelina.'

'And he kept his vows so well, huh?'

'No. But — '

'Alicia, think! Could be cholera, smallpox, spotted fever, anything.'

'Angelina, I have to go.'

'Then take the mule.' The cook gave her a piercing glance out of her normally placid eyes. 'You come back?'

'I — I don't know, Angelina, really I don't. It depends on so many things . . .'

'Like if he dies?'

'I'll make sure the mule gets back safely, whatever happens.'

'God watch over you, child. You sure deserve some good fortune.'

Within the hour, she was on her way. She tried to persuade Doctor Walker to accompany her up to Sierra City, but he was too far gone in drink to be of any use to anyone. She bought a bag of medicines from his wife, took Angelina's mule and set off up into the hills.

She looked about her with wonderment, half-convinced that she had taken the wrong road through the forest. She had expected to see a thriving township: all she saw before her was the crumbling remains of one. Since she had last been in Sierra city, the buildings that had risen so proudly and swiftly from the forest had been abandoned and the luxuriant growth of summer made it look as though they would soon return whence they had come.

The saloon was a burnt-out shell; the church at the head of Main Street stood as the inhabitants had left it, half-built, its roof timbers bared to the sky like the ribs of some primeval skeleton. Those sidewalks that had survived the fire lay under a heap of rotting leaves and Main Street itself was full of mud holes.

The stench of decaying waste hung over the little stream that had once gurgled down the mountainside; now it trickled sluggishly behind the empty buildings, around the heaps of mouldering rubbish that lay along its course.

She remembered the cocky little miner they had elected as the Mayor of Sierra City, the grandiose plans he had spoken of at the patriotic parades, the sanitation engineers and the volunteer fire company he had pledged in the *Sierra Gazette* — too late, by the look of the charred buildings up at the east end of Main Street — and the Opera House and the dance hall the local merchants had proposed. And in the end Sierra City had suffered the fate of so many other townships in the goldfields: the rich placer gold had been worked out and the miners had moved on. What the fire had not consumed, the forest would soon engulf. Before long, it would be as if Sierra City had never been.

Strange, though, that there was no sign of life. Usually at least one old miner stayed on, obstinately convinced in the face of all reason that right here where they had started was where the Mother Lode would be found. But in Sierra City there was no one. If the fire had not driven them away, then perhaps fear of the sickness had.

She turned her mule back down the Main Street, back to the dusty, rutted forest road again.

There had been a rumour, she remembered, of rich diggings up in Dry Gulch, way above the town, farther yet into the mountains. No doubt Robert would have gone there, following the rest of the sheep. She mopped her forehead, gritted her teeth and set the mule at the mountain track.

The sun had dipped below the rim of the distant mountains when at last she emerged from the gloom of the forest. In front of her was Dry Gulch, but in all the tangle of tents and lean-tos, there was no sign of human life. The fire in the centre of the gulch was cold and had been so for at least a day and no smoke rose from among the clumps of fir trees that hung precariously to the rocks above the gulch.

Something moved in the trees and she started violently, thinking fearfully of grizzly bears.

'Missie lost her way?' came a voice from behind her.

She whirled in the saddle to see a Chinaman, face hidden beneath the brim of his large straw hat, bowing obsequiously to her.

'No one here, missie. Much sickness. Better go back.'

As he spoke, she saw a thin thread of smoke rising over to

51

her right and before he could stop her, she dug in her heels and rode the mule over to the clearing. She dismounted in front of a large tent.

The Chinaman rushed to bar her way.

'Missie not go in,' he said urgently. 'Is much sickness here. Cholera.'

Her heart turned over. In his weakened state, brought about by too little good wholesome food and far too much strong drink, Robert would stand but little chance of fighting the dread killer.

'I must go in,' she said with a calm which she did not feel. 'My husband may be in there.'

He raised his hands, palms upwards in a gesture of resignation. 'Then first you tie this round you neck, missie.'

'This' was a pungent resinous lump of asafoetida on a string.

'Then you rub this round you face and hands.' He produced a phial of equally pungent liquid and she did his bidding without a murmur.

Even the pungency could not overcome the stench of the tent into which the Chinaman showed her. A primitive oil lamp in the centre of the tent, no more than a rag dipped in a dish of perfumed oil, illumined the pallets around the canvas walls. One of the occupants was tossing and turning feverishly and the Chinaman hurried across to his side and bathed his face, then held him while he writhed, screaming, racked by terrible spasms.

'Here, missie!' He summoned her urgently to his side. 'You give him drink. I hold him still.'

It took their combined efforts to get the water past his cracked lips, then he fell back on the hard boards in an exhausted sleep − or was it stupor?

'What hope for him?' she whispered to the Chinaman.

He shook his head slowly.

Slowly she looked around the tent until she found Robert. She took the few steps to his side and the Chinaman followed her.

One glance at Robert and she knew the worst. He lay in the same stupor as the first man, but already the flesh had wasted away from his face, and he did not look as though

52

he would emerge again from that deep sleep. She had come too late.

She knelt by his pallet all that evening, bathing his face, trying to squeeze a few drops of water from a sponge against those black, cracked lips. Towards midnight, he stirred and opened his eyes. She leaned forward, brushing the lank hair from his eyes.

With a great effort he raised his head.

She felt, rather than saw, the Chinaman, Chen, come up behind her with a cup of some herbal mixture, and tensed. Robert might be pleased to see her, but it was just as likely that he would insult her. He had never hesitated to humiliate her in public: he frequently came into the cook house in Sonora roaring drunk and if she was not quick enough to set food before him and hand over what he deemed to be sufficient money, often struck her in front of the terrified women. Only Angelina was not frightened of him and his reputation: once when he had laid Alicia's forehead open with his fists, the cook had come in upon the scene of mayhem and gone for him with the carving knife.

'Well,' he breathed in a hoarse whisper, 'if it isn't my saintly Alicia.' Her heart plummeted. 'Ministering angel, eh? Left the wifely concern a little late, haven't you? But then, you never did quite fit into that role, did you?'

She flinched away. Even now he could still hurt her. She glanced back over her shoulder, but Chen had moved away and was busying himself on the far side of the tent — or pretending to do so. She did not much care which.

'Drink some of this, Robert,' she murmured, holding the cup to his lips.

With the last ounce of energy he would ever summon, he knocked it out of her hand to spill half on him, half on her.

'Poison me now, would you?' he snarled. 'Bury me and marry one of the other curs who're always sniffing round your heels? Be in for a shock, wouldn't they? Don't know what a frigid bitch you really are, do they?' He paused for a painful, panting breath and a cunning look came over his face. 'Anyway, Fisher staked for you, didn't he? When I go — you'll be his. He'll have it all then. You and Valley Hall.'

53

She began to shake as she always had done under his tongue-lashings. Even when he fell back and lay panting for breath, grey-lipped, she could not speak.

Gentle hands drew her up from her knees.

'Missie go out for a moment, breathe some fresh air,' said Chen softly. 'I take over here.'

Blindly she held the cup out to him and stumbled out of the tent to breathe in great lungfuls of pine-scented air in the chill night until she was calmer. She had to force herself to go back in: Robert or no Robert, she could not leave the Chinaman to look after them all alone.

But Robert would never hurt her again, with his tongue or his fists. He had sunk back into the stupor from which there was no awakening. A few hours later, just as dawn was beginning to lighten the shadows in the gulch, he died.

She put on the odorous muslin mask Chen handed her. Wordlessly they wrapped him in his bedroll and lifted the board on which he lay. There was no weight left to his body and they carried him, without much difficulty, down a path through the forest to where a digging had already been turned into a grave.

'You go now, missie,' he urged her. 'Back to camp. I finish here. Not good sight.'

She shivered. 'How many?'

'Eight already. You go now please.'

What matter if the prayers were said here or at the tent? At least there she could ease the last hours of the other three wretches.

Two more died in the early hours of the next day; masks over their faces they carried them again to that hideous pit. The fourth fought long and hard to survive. To Alicia's surprise it turned out to be a woman.

'Wife of picture man,' said the Chinaman enigmatically, and Alicia was too tired to demand an explanation.

'Wife of picture man' lasted another thirty-six hours, then she too died. For the first time Alicia saw some emotion cross her companion's face. 'All so unnecessary,' he said, or so she thought, yet how should he speak such good English all of a sudden? 'If only she had listened ...'

'She fought hard,' said Alicia as they trudged wearily back

from the communal grave. 'I thought she might have pulled through.'

'Sick as others. But better reason to live.'

'What reason?'

'Missie see. Later I show.'

Later. But first they had to burn the tent, the tents of the sick miners, all their possessions.

'Now your clothes, missie, please.'

Again that obsequious bow which accorded so ill with those knowing eyes.

'No trouble, missie. I smoke 'em only. Burn off any infection. You go behind they tree. I behind they. Put clothes in my tent and burn special herbs. You see.'

It was a little late to think about her situation, isolated up in the mountains, miles from anywhere – and anyone – alone with a total stranger. Instinctively she knew that he meant her no harm and did as he bade her.

It was soon done and the clothes no worse for the experience.

'Now, missie, now I show.'

In a clearing not far from the camp a small wagon, a little like a shed on wheels, stood incongruously among the trees. A pair of mules cropped the grass nearby. Beside the wagon, a little spring bubbled out of the ground and plashed its way across the clearing to run down the hill until it found the Stanislaus itself, a mile or two further on.

Mystified, she followed the Chinaman up the steps. As he opened the door, a baby of about a year gazed up from the drawer in which it lay, reached out its arms and smiled at them.

'Her baby?'

He nodded and then she cried: for the baby, for the mother who would never again hold it in her arms, for Robert and his wasted life and for the baby they had never had. She cried and cried until she felt a tentative hand on her arm.

'No more cry, missie, please! Need help now.'

Gradually the racking sobs stopped and she took the baby in her arms and held it tight.

'Please, missie. Help me?' he pleaded. 'If Chen take this

55

Anglo baby down into town and tell the people her parents died in my tent ...'

'They'll string you up.'

'I could have saved them if they'd let me. I have skills with herbs.'

'They won't care about that.' Prejudice against the Chinese was so strong that no one would listen to his explanation.

'I'll help you, of course.' She passed a weary hand across her eyes. 'But ...'

'Plenty time think, missie. Have to wait anyway.'

'Of course. To be sure we don't carry the infection.'

They stayed in the camp for three days, she with the baby in the wagon and he in his tent farther away across the gulch. They lived on the food she had brought up with her and the little that he had left. There was no milk for the baby, but he brewed up a strange gruel out of ground beans and some herbs that he picked. It seemed to agree with little Tamsin.

The first day they did little but sleep and eat, for if Alicia was tired, then the Chinaman, Chen Kai-Tsu, was exhausted.

On the afternoon of the second day, she sat on the steps of the wagon, the baby on her knee, trying to work out a tale for the folk of Sonora which would not involve Chen Kai-Tsu.

'I could take the child to Angelina — she'll know a Mexican woman who'll take her in.'

A shadow passed across Chen's face. 'In Sonora? Picture lady not like them there. Think they all her-et-ic.' He struggled with the word. 'She a Batt-Batt ...'

'Baptist?'

'So.' He nodded. 'She believe her God protect her.' He laughed scornfully. 'She better have trusted my herbs against the cholera!' She had never heard him speak so freely and rather suspected he had been drinking. Soon after, he fell asleep, leaning against the slender tree-trunk.

He did not stir for hours. Then, as the sun began to dip below the rim of the hills behind them, the baby cried and he stirred in his sleep. Quite clearly she heard him say: 'Even the pigs don't foul their own troughs, but Anglos, they foul their own wells!'

She fed the baby, put her in the wagon to sleep and when

he awoke she was sitting in front of him, watching him with a puzzled frown.

'Missie?' His eyes were alert and wary.

'Chen Kai-Tsu, I think you should drop this "missie" nonsense. This act of the meek Chinese coolie simply will not do. Twice now when you have been off your guard, I have heard you speak perfect English!'

He jerked his head up and for the first time she saw the shadow of fear in his eyes.

'An opinion I would prefer you to keep to yourself, ma'am,' he said coolly. 'With the general run of Americans in the mines, it pays to be what they expect: a meek, ignorant Chinese coolie. Exceptions are liable to be subjected to even worse treatment than the rule. Twice I have set up a small drug store, a *botega*, to sell simple medical supplies to the miners. Twice they have burnt me out. They think it unsuitable that a Chinee should claim medical knowledge, even the most basic. The last time, three of my people died.'

'Then why stay?'

'Like most of us here, I guess. Where else would I go?'

'Is your family here in California?'

'Never had a family. I'm a foundling, picked up on the banks of the Pearl River. Maybe the son of peasants who died in one of our endless famines, or maybe I was the unwanted product of one of the western missionaries or traders.'

'You're certainly taller than the average Chinese!' she agreed. 'Who found you?'

'A very kind, very good old man who took me in and raised me.'

'A doctor?' she hazarded.

'Not a doctor as you would imagine a doctor to be!' he laughed. 'But a healer, yes. He was a follower of K'ung Fu Tzu – Confucius – what you in the West call a philosopher, a wise man. He taught me much. But he was old and he died.'

'What happened to you then?'

'I went to Canton and tried to get work there, but I was still young and not strong enough. I was handed over to the British – you understand they have had great power there since the Opium Wars – and they sent me to a Mission in

Hong Kong. They fed me, educated me — on their terms! Because of a shortage of western doctors, I was eventually allowed to work in the Mission Hospital. A marvellous opportunity; I could compare European medicine with traditional Chinese healing and select what is best from each. If I could have stayed there and worked with my own people, I would have been happy. But I was a *native* and could not qualify and so I had to leave.' He chuckled reminiscently. 'I fell out with the Crown authorities and the Mission, then I compounded my crime by telling the local overlord that I thought no more highly of his ancestor worship than I did of the Anglicans! The one action they ever agreed upon was that the colony could dispense with my presence. They found me a ship on which I could work my passage to Hawaii. I stayed there awhile — there is a large colony of Chinese among the Kanakas in the Sandwich Islands — but my appetite for travel had been whetted and so I joined another ship and came here to Gum Shan, the land of the Golden Mountain.'

He picked up a long twig and snapped it in half and half again until it was no more than a pile of bark and fibre.

'That's another reason why the Americans don't like me — I'm still a free man. I worked my own passage and owe no allegiance to the companies. The democratic Californians find it easier to deal with Chinese immigrants who know their place — even though that place is virtual slavery.'

'So you came to make your fortune in the gold fields?'

'One man's fortune is a hundred men's disappointment,' he said drily. 'No, I don't really know why I came. Sometimes I think it is worse here than in China. No matter how hard the Chinese work, how much trouble we go to not to vex the Anglos, they despise us. If they are drinkers, they despise the Chinese who smoke opium — yet what difference is there? They will stake a whole mine on the turn of a card or roll of a dice, and still despise the Chinese for gambling at Mah Jongg — yet what difference is there? They despise the white who does no work — yet they despise the Chinese more because they will work the abandoned claims and tailings a white man will not look at; they drive them from the mines, and they must become cooks or launderers to pay off the debts to the Companies. They pin their faith in a drunkard like Doctor

Walker and his ilk, but they won't let me nurse them because I am a "Chinee".' He hunched his long body forward and stared down at his hands for a moment.

When he looked up again, a smile crinkled the edge of his almond shaped eyes. 'And now I am becoming maudlin, like the best drunken American.' He reached behind the tree and swung a half-empty whiskey bottle in front of him. 'If you are brought up among the *yang-kuei-tsu*, the foreign devils, it is easy to pick up their bad habits,' he laughed.

Alicia woke early the next morning. Tamsin was still sleeping peacefully in her straw-filled drawer. Outside, the birds were singing and she felt, for the first time in years, hope stir afresh within her. It was a new day. Without Robert, a new life.

She rose quietly and stretched. She washed in the little brook that ran down from the spring and fetched more fresh water from the source, ready to mix with the ground beans for when Tamsin woke.

She had a sudden longing for a warming cup of the sage tea that Chen Kai brewed, for the autumn air was chill this morning. But there was no sign of her companion. She suspected that he had drunk rather more than he was accustomed to and overslept.

She skipped up the steps and began to explore the cupboards inside the wagon. After all, Tamsin's family had lived here: there must be utensils and stores. And some fresh clothes for Tamsin. So far, Chen Kai had always changed the child's bindings, but it was surely time that she pulled her weight.

The inside of the wagon was lined with cupboards. In the first, she found some cups and pitchers, rough plates and bowls and some knives and spoons, but it was what she found in the locker behind the seat that caused her to let out a whoop of triumph.

In a large latched box were sheets of polished glass in a variety of sizes. Battened tightly on the shelf above were a number of large bottles of ether and alcohol, nitrated cotton, silver nitrate, hyposulphite of soda.

She looked wildly around her, then gently lifted the baby out of the cot. Beneath the quilt and straw on which she lay was a further locker. In it, nestling in a quilted box, wrapped

59

in black cloth, was a Talbot camera with the wide aperture lens necessary for portraiture, a tripod to support it and a case of delicate tints for hand colouring. Underneath she found a box marked 'patent albumenized paper' and a pamphlet: 'All you need to know about the new collodion process, as devised by Mr. Frederick Scott Archer'. The 'picture man', unlike so many other daguerrotypers, had believed in keeping abreast of progress. He had moved on from Daguerre's 'mirror with a memory' to the new glass plates for the wet collodion method, which Alicia had only read about, which allowed faster exposures than before and claimed to give better, clearer images even in poor lighting. And paper to print on, in the negative-positive process devised by Fox Talbot — more popular with miners who wished to send their calotypes home, to grieving parents or pining fiancées!

Chen Kai found her still standing there, in a daze. He picked up the baby from the floor where she was wailing.

'Something is wrong?'

She turned to him, eyes aglow.

'Chen Kai! How would you like to leave Dry Gulch — and Sierra City — and never have to go down into Sonora again? Make a completely new start!'

'How? Have you struck gold?'

'In a way!' she said excitedly. Then, suddenly, her face fell and the animation drained away. 'But ... the wagon isn't ours and nor is the equipment.' She sighed heavily. 'And yet it did seem such a tempting idea.'

'If the wagon belongs to anyone, it beongs to Tamsin, and she won't want to get up on the box and drive away yet awhile. Can't be mine: Chinese can't hold property.' He looked at her curiously. 'Were you thinking of selling it? I've not heard of any other picture men about the place might be interested in it — leastways, no closer than Auburn one way and San Francisco the other. This one was the only picture man I'd ever seen round the Southern mines.'

'Was there much work for them roundabouts?'

'Plenty. Can't be more than a dozen men in the whole of California who know how to operate the picture machines. And like the storekeepers and the saloon-keepers: it's the men who supply the miner's needs who make the money, not the

60

miners. But this wagon is about as much use as fool's gold! We have no picture man.'

'Yes we have!' He looked at her in blank amazement. 'I can make daguerrotypes. *I* am the picture man, you must be my assistant – my picture lady!'

She knew a momentary qualm as she said it. It was, after all, some years since Nuñes Carvalho had shown her how to take and fix the image, and techniques had improved rapidly since then.

'It – it was all a long time ago,' she stammered.

'If you did it once you can surely do it again.'

She must. She could not turn her back on this chance of independence – a chance to escape the memory of Robert and the stigma of being Lucky Langdon's woman.

And then there was Tamsin. Could she hand her over to some stranger and walk away, never to know how she was being cared for, whether she was loved?

'Everything must be here,' he said softly. 'All you have to do is remember what order it goes in. Start practising now; teach me what I must do.'

Still she hesitated.

'Think of all those rich miners out there in the hills, desperate to get themselves pictured off, to show their families back east how well they are doing.' He reached out gently and touched her arm. 'We have both suffered ill fortune in the past: now the Fates are smiling on us at last. It does not do to turn your back on them.' She looked from him to the baby and back to the camera again. 'They may not give a second chance,' he said sombrely.

She handed him down a coarse apron of duck and selected two bottles from the shelf.

'Mix some of that with twice the amount of this one,' she instructed. 'Don't breathe in the fumes! I'll set up the tripod.'

He put his hands together and bowed. 'Velly good missie!' he said gravely. And as he raised his head, she saw that he was beaming from ear to ear.

So they had set out, full of confidence, on the road that led inexorably to San Francisco ... and the shadow of the gallows.

61

Chapter Six

After another hard week labouring at the Carsons', Sunday did not turn out to be the day of rest that Alicia had hoped for, as she had decided to go to church — the church the Carsons attended. Not that she was going to suit them, of course, but she had learnt from Mr Jones that the minister's sister ran a sort of Dame School for the younger girls of the town whose parents could not or would not send them back east to Young Ladies' Academies.

It was, she admitted guiltily to herself, pure self-interest that was taking her to God's House this fine summer's morning — but then, of how many others could the same not be said?

It did not take her long to wash and dress them both. She took time to pretty up Tamsin, brushing out her thick fair hair and weaving through it blue ribbons to match her eyes.

She was a curiously biddable child, had been so ever since that dreadful time up at Coloma. If only Alicia had more time to devote to her, she knew she could bring her out, turn her once again into the bright, vivacious little girl she had once been. But a biddable child was so much easier.

She hoped she might be able to persuade the minister's sister to take Tamsin into her Dame School. It would cost money, of course, but not much more than she already paid the rapacious Aggie Grey for her casual supervision. And this time it would be money well spent, for Tamsin would be continuing the education that Alicia had started in better days and receiving more attention than the careless, slipshod Aggie lavished on the entire brood. She had had to close her mind to the question of Tamsin's safety and well-being during the day; it was a worry, but she could see no cure for it.

The streets were almost as bustling and busy on this Sabbath as on any weekday. With the scattered population of the outlying ranches and the mining camps, Sacramento had never concerned itself overmuch about Sunday travel and the streets were full of carts and carriages and riders on horseback.

She walked resolutely down towards the Main Street, with Tamsin at her side, looking neither to right nor left. She wore her bonnet at a demure angle, shading her face from the dust and the heat of the sun. The pale grey silk dress she had bought at the knock-down street corner auction that first day in Sacramento had been thoroughly washed and the sleeves restyled more in the modern manner; the over-ornate trimmings around the neck and hem had been ruthlessly removed and the decolletage filled with a muslin fichu. Now, with a Paisley shawl around her shoulders, more for modesty than warmth, she made a pleasant enough picture, attracting admiring glances from the gentlemen as they passed in their carriages on their way to church, and occasional warm comments from the miners hanging around on the street corners and sidewalks.

She had never rated her looks very highly, right from the earliest days in California when her only ambition had been to have olive skin, dark eyes and luxuriant black locks like the *Alcalde's* daughters. Robert – handsome, dashing Robert – had always called her plain and, as in so many other matters, she had accepted his judgement.

In a crowded city, London, Paris or New York, she might not have rated a second look, for she was attractive rather than stunning. But she was young and she was beginning, in spite of everything, to regain that joy in life that had been so strong in her. In California women were still very scarce and Sacramento thought her beautiful.

It was pleasantly cool in the newly finished stone church, even though the place was packed to the doors with the upright citizens of Sacramento and their families and a seething mass of miners.

She realised guiltily that she had not been in a church since

63

that fateful day in Yerba Buena when the ship's chaplain had married her and Robert in the little clapboard church down by the Presidio.

So often she had meant to slip into a church and give thanks for the three blessings that had come into her life that autumn up at Dry Gulch: Chen Kai, Tamsin and the picture wagon, but Sunday had never been for them a day of rest. Whether in the mining camps or San Francisco, Sunday had been the only day for cleaning out the studio, polishing up the plates with acid and powdered pumice, developing and printing out the last boxes of exposed plates and replenishing the chemicals.

She settled Tamsin into the pew and gazed around with fascination at the cross-section of Sacramento society. To the right of them, in the centre aisles, the occupants of the main pews exchanged polite bows with one another. Their shawls and waistcoats were of brighter hue than might have been acceptable on a Sunday back east, but this was California, the Gold State, and here it was the fashion to show your wealth in your dress.

She listened in fascination to the elderly lady in the pew in front of her who was impressing her out of town companion by pointing out in the piercing whisper of the hard of hearing just who was acknowledging whom and, equally diligently, who was ignoring whom.

'There's Collis Huntington and his nephew. Look. Dressed very plain, in black. And that tall, gangling fellow, that's Mark Hopkins. The fashionable woman next to him, that's his wife. See, she's smiling at Huntington. There's a rumour Huntington and Hopkins are going to combine their stores.'

In that case, thought Alicia grimly, Hopkins' store on K Street would cease to be one of Carson's main rivals and would, in all likelihood, drive them right out of business.

'I thought Hopkins was settled in San Francisco?' objected her companion.

'They're here to discuss the new railroad with Theodore Judah. He wants them to finance it.'

'Is he here?'

'Yes, there he is.'

'Not very handsome, to be sure, though they say he'll go far.'

64

'Crazy Judah, they call him up here. I prefer to ride on the stage coach, myself.'

'And who is that ravishing creature across the aisle?'

'That brazen creature all decked out in Chinese silks? What dear Henry refers to as one of our "soiled doves". That's Yuba Jenny.'

'How shocking to see such a creature in the House of God!' said her companion in a horrified whisper.

The deaf lady shrugged. 'What would you?' she hissed. 'She provided most of the funds to build the church!'

So enthralled was Alicia by this recounting that she had not noticed that the preacher had come in until other members of the congregation began to shush the elderly lady, whose habits were clearly known and tolerated.

She rose with the rest of the congregation and turned to the pulpit. Suddenly the church was no longer cool and she was sure she was about to swoon with the heat. Looking down benignly on the assembled congregation was the Reverend Cooper.

By the time they rose to sing the first hymn, she had recollected herself and was able to sing, albeit rather quaveringly, with the rest of the faithful. The Reverend Cooper was, she chided herself, unlikely to condemn her from the pulpit. And half way through the mercifully short sermon she realised he was almost certainly not going to recognise her anyway. The Colonel had not recognised her in the store and he'd been standing much closer; the minister had had his attention always with his horses on the rough road and had scarce paid her any heed. And of course, the straw hats would have hidden their faces. She allowed herself to relax a little.

She realised that in dismissing him as a dry old stick, she had done the Reverend Cooper a disservice. He knew to a nicety how to hold the wayward interest of the miners clustered at the back of the church and, without insulting anyone's intelligence, explained his beliefs and his sermon in simple terms. The hymn singing was rousing, the homilies and readings brief, and she came out of the church with a feeling of well-being she had not known for the last miserable six months.

65

Her heart lurched as she realised that the Reverend Cooper and his sister were waiting to greet every churchgoer individually as they came out.

Miss Letitia Cooper was a lady in her late forties, still smooth of face and with the most delightful cornflower blue eyes. Her voice had a musical lilt to it and she fluttered her hands as she spoke, like a failed opera singer, thought Alicia wickedly. But there was no mistaking the sincerity of her greeting when Mrs Carson scurried across to introduce them.

'Mrs Owens, you say? My dear, how delightful to meet you. Our little society here can always do with some more ladies. We are so few, and out in the wilderness still, as far as civilisation is concerned, State Capital or no State Capital. And all alone with the little girl to care for. How do you do, my dear. What's your name?'

'Tamsin, ma'am.' She dropped a little bob and blue eyes looked into blue and seemed to like what they saw, for a little natural smile, the first for many months, curved the child's soft mouth.

'What a beautiful name. In honour of the heroine of the Donner tragedy, is it not?' She did not wait for an answer, but addressed herself again to Alicia. 'And so you are being so good as to assist Mrs Carson in the store?' This was a novel way of putting it and one that didn't seem to appeal much to the Carsons. 'I should have visited you before this, but I understand you live out of town?'

'A little way,' confessed Alicia, who had no intention whatever of mentioning that she lived at Widow Grey's, which she was beginning more and more to think of as a house of dubious, if not ill, repute.

'You must be very busy during the week, but there is not a great deal for respectable ladies to do here on the Sabbath. Apart from the services, of course,' she said, with a wry smile at her brother who was discussing parochial affairs with one of his wardens. 'I hold a sort of ladies' party every Sunday when Octavius goes up to Perkins to preach. We sew for others and have a little chat and some tea and cakes and so on.' She turned to Tamsin. 'Now do you think you could bring your mama along, say about half after three?'

Tamsin giggled at the thought that she would be in charge of the party. 'Oh yes, ma'am!' she agreed.

In a distant room, a mantel clock struck three.

'The lady said there would be tea and cakes, Lisha,' ventured Tamsin. It was nearly a year since all the trouble had started and at least that long since she had eaten a cake. Her eyes grew dreamy at the prospect.

Alicia was in a quandary. She had always tried to avoid too much contact with the other females in the towns and camps, either because they were not ladies at all, or because she had not wished to provide a juicy subject for their gossip.

But surely by changing her name she had left Lucky Langdon's shade behind? And the social contact would be welcome, she had to admit, for she was missing Chen Kai more than ever; Tamsin was normally asleep by the time she returned from her day's drudgery at Carson's and the Greys, mother and daughter, had not two ideas in their heads to rub together.

'There will be a lot of other ladies there,' warned Alicia. 'All watching to see how well we behave.'

'Then we can go?' She could not suppress the excitement in her voice. 'I'll be very good, Lisha, really I will!' Alicia could not resist the appeal in the child's eyes.

'Of course you will, my lovely!' she said with a laugh. 'And we shall both have tea and cakes!'

A warm welcome awaited them that afternoon at the smart house on L Street, just a block away from the Stage Depot. The house was from the outside neat and trim, just like Miss Letitia.

Inside, however, Letitia Cooper had been unable to resist the current fashion for clutter. The windows, endowed with attractively simple shutters in the Federal style, were festooned inside with deep wine-coloured curtains heavily fringed to match the covers on the chairs and couches. The walls were panelled in a rich dark wood, heavily overcarved and topped with moulded leaves and urns. In the centre of the longest wall stood a marble-faced fireplace, its three tiers supported by sculpted columns and topped by a mantel draped in rich purple velvet. In the centre of the room stood

67

a vast table on massively carved legs, half hidden by fringed drapes, over which had been cast a linen cloth for the sewing. At the far end of the room, the panelled wall was interrupted by heavily carved doors which could, at need, be opened to throw the two adjacent rooms into one.

The floor space was almost entirely taken up by spindly chairs, delicately carved and inlaid, small desks, a secretaire and a side table. Wherever there was a space, however small, there was either a spool-turned whatnot crammed with little china ornaments, cups and plates, silver compotes and urns, or potted palms and aspidistras set in huge floor vases or hip-level wicker planters. On the walls hung tinted lithographs of bucolic scenes and recent disasters in home-made frames adorned with the cylindrical pods of the cattail reeds, and what were presumably family portraits in more elaborate gilt frames. On the floor was spread a rich Chinese rug, and the elaborate patterns struggled to emerge from their ruby red background into the few unfurnished spaces.

The overall effect was overwhelming; at Alicia's side, Tamsin stood wide-eyed, her thumb in her mouth, drinking in the spectacle.

'My dear Mrs Owens, so pleased to see you,' fluttered Miss Cooper. 'As you see we are all hard at work.'

A group of women sat around the table, their work baskets, some lined in patchwork, some in quilted satin, in front of them.

The bell pealed again. 'And here's another arrival. You must excuse me. Mrs Revel, I rely on you to introduce Mrs Owens to our little group.'

Mrs Revel smiled rather grimly at the newcomers and proceeded to make the introductions. There were a dozen or so at various tables and others still arriving. The majority were elderly, although one middle-aged lady turned up with four of her eight daughters in tow.

'Mrs Pikeman and her invaluable young ladies,' commented Miss Cooper as she fluttered past. 'Without them, I would not be able to run my little school.'

They were working on an exquisite patchwork quilt.

'For Hester. She's to marry an attorney from New York

State. So handsome,' said young Gertrude dreamily. 'Fortunate Hester!'

She earned herself a reproving glance from her mother. 'We also do some plain sewing for the poor,' Edith Pikeman informed her gravely, drawing the attention from her blushing sister. 'We have merely put it aside for a week or two while we finish the quilt for Hester's wedding.'

As an unknown quantity, Alicia was at first allowed to do no more than trim the edges of the strips under the eagle eye of Mrs Sharples, the wife of one of the Steamship Company's captains, but when she broke off to stitch a little shawl from a scrap of material for Tamsin's doll, and it was seen that her stitches were as small, neat and even as Edith's or Gertrude's, they were swift to draw her in to stitch at the quilt.

All around her fingers were flying busily — but not as busily as the tongues. Miss Cooper's parlour was for these woman the social centre of Sacramento. Many of them had come in from the surrounding country, from the ranches or the local river stations, to go to church in the morning and then to dine with their husbands at one of the few respectable hotels now to be found in the Capital. Afterwards, their husbands would forgather in bars and smoking rooms to discuss the price of beef, grain or gold, or the shortcomings of the Governor or President, and in such establishments there was no place for women — no place for ladies, at any rate.

Others, such as Mrs Revel, lived in Sacramento itself, but the shortage of polite female society was so acute still that they were only too pleased to leave their own four walls, or the stores or warehouses where they worked alongside their husbands throughout the week, and come to this oasis of civilisation.

They gave Alicia a warm welcome, although they were inclined to make a fuss of little Tamsin, which put Alicia on edge, for fear she might cause offence — or let something fall about their past.

Something of this Miss Cooper must have sensed, for when she came in with the last of the guests, she gently extricated Tamsin from the circle of cooing ladies and dispatched her, kindly but firmly, to a little antechamber that opened off the main parlour. A group of boys and girls were seated around a large nursery style table playing pencil and paper games. Miss Cooper entrusted Tamsin to the care of a dark-haired, dark-eyed girl, gawky and clumsy as only twelve-year-old girls can be, who glowed with pride at being given such a responsibility.

Alicia had braced herself for a stream of questions about herself – where she had come from, who her husband had been – but she was relieved to find that the ladies were more interested in what she was doing now than in her past. So many Californians had originally travelled west to avoid something in their past, whether situation of birth, brushes with the law or bankruptcies and business losses, that it was not considered polite to enquire too closely.

'Miss Cooper tells me that you are assisting in the Carsons' store, my dear Mrs Owens,' said Mrs Spalding. 'Have you heard the rumour that the Hopkins and the Huntingtons are planning to combine? Does Mrs Carson think that it will affect her trade?'

'Sacramento is growing so rapidly now, ma'am, that I should imagine there would be room for any number of stores.'

'Thank Heavens they chose us for the Capital,' said another lady with iron grey hair neatly coiffed. 'At least we know we'll still be here in ten years time and can plan some civilising influences, such as schools and libraries and opera houses, without having to leave them to rot when the seams run out! No one who has not lived in as many mining camps as I have can fully appreciate the joys of a settled life!'

There were murmurs of agreement from around the room.

'What schools are there in Sacramento?' Alicia enquired, glad to find that the topic of conversation had moved away from her.

'Oh, my dear ma'am!' fluted Mrs Revel, a tall, angular lady who spoke as much as possible without fully opening her mouth, which possessed two rows of blackened stumps. 'It really is too dreadful! Of course, my husband insisted on sending the boys back to my sister in Saint Louis to be educated, but for the poor girls ...! Either you must swallow your prejudices and send them to the Catholic convent schools, where the education is very well but they are exposed to all the Romish influences at such an impressionable age, or they must make do with study at home.'

'My own daughters, all of them, were educated out here,' said Mrs Pikeman proudly. 'At home at first, then they followed a course of study laid down by Miss Cooper while they helped out with the younger ones. And I don't think they could have turned out better if I'd sent them back east to one of these fancy Young Ladies' Academies. And what's more,' she went on in the tones of one who will not brook any argument, 'both Agnes and Matilda have determined to do the same with their boys when they come to be old enough. Why, if we keep on sending our young people back east to be educated, stands to reason they'll be educated for life back east and there they'll stay, when what we want is to educate them for life in California.'

'I have great hopes of Mr Tukey,' offered one lady nervously.

'Tukey!' exclaimed Mrs Sharples scornfully. 'Who's to say he won't run out of funds, just as Harkness did? They called on him to begin high school teaching months ago and all he can say is "he hopes to commence shortly"! Oh, for teaching wagon drivers to write their name and reckon up, he will do very well, but can we base the prosperity of the state on that?'

'And he has over a hundred more applicants than places,' added Mrs Spalding. 'So he don't take anyone under ten ...'

'I think you'd go far to find a better teacher than Miss Cooper,' insisted Mrs Pikeman. 'As for sending your child to the *public* schools. Well! It's just asking for 'em to catch smallpox and cholera and – and – infestations! More teachers like Miss Cooper is what we need.'

'Kind of you to say so, Mrs Pikeman, but we can't get away from the fact that I have no qualifications to teach the older ones. I can't help thinking that it would be better if we had some good Protestant educators here in Sacramento for them.'

'There's always the new college in Benicia,' sniffed one lady.

71

'True. And I believe that Miss Atkins is establishing her Seminary along all the best principles of modern education, but we should have one here! After all, are we not the Capital? We should be giving the lead!'

The conversation began to turn on what constituted a good education for girls, but when Mrs Pikeman and Mrs Revel, to no one's particular surprise, began to bicker in a rather more personal manner, Miss Cooper intervened to bring the discussion to a close.

'Perhaps Mrs Owens would read to us while we finish off our sewing for today,' she suggested in her soft musical voice. 'Gertrude, would you look after the children? And ask Louisa to fetch the *Pilgrim's Progress* for Mrs Owens, if you please?'

She turned back to Alicia who had laid her sewing aside obediently. 'We read Sir Walter Scott at our Wednesday meeting, but I think Bunyan more suitable for the Sabbath. The children learn a verse or two from the Bible each week.' She gestured towards the antechamber where the smaller children were listening to Gertrude reading to them from a large leather-bound Bible. 'But of course, not Tamsin, dear child. I don't expect she can read small print yet.'

'Oh, indeed, ma'am. I taught her some time ago and she is ever eager to learn more.'

'Excellent!' exclaimed Miss Cooper. 'Perhaps when she is a little older, she will join our classes.'

'The moment you can find a place for her, ma'am, she will be there.' She had sown the seed; now she'd have to wait and see if it struck.

Louisa stood at her side with the book. 'We had just left the Slough of Despond, ma'am,' she offered shyly, pointing out the relevant paragraph with a none too clean forefinger. Alicia began to read.

They had almost finished the chapter when an impatient knocking was heard.

'A little early for the gentlemen,' said Miss Cooper with a puzzled frown.

The maid appeared at the door after a moment. 'Mrs Lamarr,' she announced, and in swept the most beautifully dressed woman Alicia had ever seen. The woman herself was

72

quite a handsome blonde, but so showily was she clad that one noticed the clothes first.

An extremely close-fitting pale blue bodice, elaborately trimmed with French lace, tapered down to a narrow waist whence it flared out into a wide billowing skirt of darker blue, flounced with lace and ribbons, which only emphasised its width, a width that could not possibly have been produced by the usual layers of starched and quilted petticoats.

Miss Cooper stood quite overwhelmed by the sight, her usual polite greetings dying on her lips.

'My dear Letitia, I can see you are quite *bouleversée* by my new *toilette*,' cooed the newcomer before Miss Cooper could recollect herself. 'Splendid, is it not?' She posed just inside the door, the focus of all attention.

'Quite – splendid,' faltered Miss Cooper.

'But my dear Letitia, you must – yes, positively you must – have your doorways altered. One can scarcely pass through them. In San Francisco, *everyone* is having double doors put in.'

'It seems a little extravagant!' murmured Miss Cooper faintly.

'But it is *de rigueur*, my dear, positively it is! For the crinoline, you know, is become all the rage. It will sweep from San Francisco even to this benighted backwater, I promise you.'

'But ... but ... dear Mrs Lamarr ... it is so wide,' protested Miss Cooper. 'However do you sit down?'

'Certainly not in one of those antiquated armchairs of yours, my dear Letitia,' said the newcomer crushingly. 'But if Agnes or Gertrude or whichever of the dear Pikeman girls it is would be so kind as to exchange, I do believe I shall make do with her chair.'

Overwhelmed by the confidence of Mrs Lamarr and unheeding of her mother tugging at her sleeve to try to keep her in her seat, Edith Pikeman stumbled to her feet and held the chair for the newcomer who subsided with a rustle of expensive silks on and all around the vacated chair.

With a sniff that spoke more than any words, Mrs Pikeman rescued the quilt from beneath the sea of blue.

'What, ladies, still at your endless stitching?' enquired Mrs

73

Lamarr, raising her eyebrows at the assembled group.

Several of them looked daggers at her, but only Mrs Revel responded.

'Indeed. And we were reading *Pilgrim's Progress*.' She didn't say 'Until you were so rude as to interrupt' but it was implicit in her tone.

Mrs Lamarr raised her eyes eloquently to the ceiling and folded her hands demurely in her lap. 'Then, pray, continue.'

Chapter Seven

The gentlemen soon after began arriving in twos and threes, but Alicia read steadily on to the end of the chapter. Then she laid the book aside and helped Edith collect up the pins and needles while the sewing was carefully folded away.

The maids brought in the tea trays and the connecting doors were thrown open to reveal buffets and side tables laden with vast arrays of some of the most mouthwatering little cakes and biscuits, cold meats and relishes, sweets and titbits that Alicia had seen for some time. Waffle cake, hoe cake, johnny cake and dodger cake all vied for her attention and out of the corner of her eye she could see Tamsin staring open-mouthed at the spread.

The arrival of the tea was a signal for the little groupings of ladies to break up and circulate, exchanging greetings and news with the gentlemen who had arrived to join their wives and daughters. Miss Cooper's receptions were unusual in that the entertainment was not planned to suit the gentlemen. There was no separate room set aside for them to talk of elections, governors and the price of produce while the ladies were reduced to look at each other's toilettes till they knew each pin by heart, or talk of Parson Somebody's last sermon on the day of judgement or Doctor T'otherbody's latest cure until tea came to relieve their boredom. Here they could play their part in the conversations, which made it much more lively.

Some of the men Alicia had already met, for a number of them had made a point of coming into Carsons' store to cast an eye over the new assistant, but they greeted her politely enough now, under the watchful eye of the Reverend's sister.

Miss Cooper drew Alicia across the room to stand with her and hand out the tea she was dispensing. 'An excellent way to get to know our little society,' she murmured.

Alicia handed out the delicate cups and saucers and exchanged pleasantries until she suddenly caught sight of Mr Jones, the elderly clerk from the California Steamboat Company who had escorted her home the previous Saturday. She hoped that he would not let drop where she lived, for she was quite sure that it would not be favourably looked on by the assembled company. Folly to have come here, she told herself angrily. Better to have stayed aloof; she still had some pride left.

She was relieved when Mr Jones caught her eye and merely bowed politely. Besides, it was too late to be uninvolved: standing beside Miss Cooper, handing round the cups of fragrant tea, she was introduced to the manager of Wells, Fargo & Company, the Sacramento manager of the California Steam and two of his captains, the two Crocker brothers, Charles, the store manager, up from San Francisco to discuss the railroad, and his brother Edwin, a leading attorney and tipped soon to be a judge.

It was a motley assortment of people to be collected under one minister's roof. At any gathering west of the Mississippi, the men far outnumbered the ladies and while some of them were polished ladies' men, looking well at their ease sipping tea and eating dainty rout cakes, others like Captain Sharples – a giant of a man who looked as though he could, with one wide gesture, bring the walls of the minister's house crashing around their ears like Samson in the temple – looked as though they had rather be anywhere else but here.

Inevitably, much of the discussion centred on events in San Francisco, and when Alicia heard someone mention the Vigilantes, she found she was quite relieved to be confined to the tea table.

'If you'll excuse me a moment, dear Mrs Owens,' began Miss Cooper. 'I must just have a word with Mrs Crocker – Mrs Edwin Crocker, of course – about our plans. You'd

76

never guess, as she's so quiet, but she is the prime mover in the State campaign to found good schools for this flood of young people we have. And charities — you'd be surprised how much money she manages to raise for our Asylums and Orphanages, just by a little gentle persuasion.'

Mr Spalding brought his cup back to be refilled.

'Thank you, ma'am. I wonder, ma'am,' he coloured up under his tight starched collar, 'you may have heard tell of Miss Letitia's musical evenings? Do you sing?'

'Well I —'

'Would you permit me to escort you on Saturday?' He mopped his damp forehead with a colourful kerchief. 'With my mother, of course!'

Before she could answer him, there was a stir behind them.

'Why, Jack Cornish!' purred a seductive and silken voice. 'I had not thought this was *at all* the kind of gathering to attract *you*!'

It was Mrs Lamarr. She had effectively barred the Colonel's way with a swish of broad skirts and he did not look to be in the least pleased about it.

'Mrs Lamarr.' He nodded in acknowledgement, his manner cool and offhand while hers was openly flirtatious.

'But of course you'd heard that we were back from San Francisco?' She ended on a teasing note, peeping up at him through darkened lashes enviously long.

'On the contrary, ma'am. What Sacramento heard of your stay in San Francisco led everyone to believe that your honeymoon would be an unusually extended one.' His voice grated. Alicia wondered that the blonde did not stand aside and let him pass, to bring the uncomfortable exchange to an end, but Mrs Lamarr was made of sterner stuff.

'Oh, cruel, Jack,' she whispered. Then she made a little moue of disgust. 'And so we should have stayed, but Mr Lamarr, the naughty man, declared that he positively could not stay away from his ranch any longer. Really, he was quite rustic about it.'

'Indeed, ma'am? One would have thought that his duties in the legislature might have brought him back even sooner.'

A ripple of amusement ran through the room, and there

was even a hastily smothered giggle. Alicia, finding herself staring, turned her attention hastily back to the tea table, but she need not have worried: every eye in the room was fixed on this oddly contrasting couple.

Miss Cooper, recovering her composure, stepped into the breach.

'My dear Mrs Lamarr, you must excuse us. Colonel Cornish and I have a great deal to discuss and I know he has to leave shortly if he is to conclude all his business and still reach Tresco before it is quite dark.'

The smile that the Colonel gave Miss Cooper was quite dazzling, transforming his whole face. Just as she whisked him away from Mrs Lamarr, a thick-set man appeared in the doorway, a heavy scowl on his rather podgy face.

'Cornish.'

'Lamarr.' The acknowledgement was glacial. The Colonel stepped aside to allow the newcomer to enter and then proceeded to turn his back on the room while he entered into a deep discussion with Miss Cooper.

'If looks could kill . . .' crowed one of the ladies.

'The way she threw herself at him, what could one expect?' came the sour reply.

Alicia continued to dispense the tea, wishing she could make out what Miss Cooper and the Colonel were saying. What they had in common she could not imagine, and at the same time, she despised herself for wanting to know.

The Lamarrs interrupted them rather unceremoniously to take their leave, giving the cue as they left for the party to split up into groups and gossip in corners.

'Oh dear! I do so dislike it when people start chin-wagging at someone else's expense!' regretted Miss Cooper, moving across with the Colonel towards the tea-table.

'Don't fret about it, m'dear,' Cornish consoled her. 'If Bella thought they *weren't* talking about her, she'd feel she'd failed.'

'It's very naughty of you to say so,' scolded Miss Cooper. 'After all, if you had not been here, I daresay there might not have been all this gossip and speculation. And with all that upset, I quite forgot to introduce you to Mrs Owens, a newcomer to our little community. Mrs Owens, this is Colonel

78

Cornish of the Tresco Ranch just outside Sacramento, one of our biggest landowners and a great help in the campaign to set up schools and a library.'

'Indeed?' Alicia could feel her eyebrows raising in disbelief at this unlikely aspect of the Colonel's character.

'I have already had the pleasure of making Mrs Owens' acquaintance at Carsons',' he said, an unexpected warmth in his deep voice. 'And really, to introduce me thus on a day when I'm having all my old follies thrown in my face will give Mrs Owens a very strange notion of me.'

The Sharples were taking their leave and Miss Cooper scuttled off to remind them of next Saturday's musical soirée.

Alicia swallowed nervously. If Tamsin saw the Colonel, she might approach him with a demand to know where Chen Kai was. A swift glance reassured her: Tamsin was still in the antechamber, drawing under the close supervision of Edith Pikeman, who had retired there when Mrs Lamarr had so unceremoniously deprived her of her chair.

She looked back to find the Colonel looking down at her with a smile on his face. She racked her brain for something to say, but inspiration had deserted her. To cover her confusion, she turned away and poured the rancher a cup of tea, quite forgetting to ask first whether he wanted one or not.

'Miss Cooper said you were campaigning for schools and — and a library,' she said as she poured. 'Are all the Senators in favour?'

'I doubt it. Anyway, I'm not in the Senate.'

'Oh! I see. Only I thought ...'

'I leave politics to the hot air merchants, such as Lamarr. There are many better ways of getting a State on its feet than by talking about it endlessly.' He propped his shoulders against the wall and folded his arms, looking down at her with a cynical expression on his face. 'Congregate a hundred Americans anywhere, they immediately lay out a city, draw up a State Constitution and apply for admission to the Union, while twenty-five of them become candidates for the United States Senate, so they can go back east and set Washington to rights. Just as Gwin did. But none of that benefits the people

79

who *live* in that new State! Action, that's what we need. Not words!'

'I agree with you, Colonel,' she said with a smile. 'Then you have a personal interest in the outcome ... for your own children's education?'

'I have no children. Nor a wife, thank God!' he replied bluntly as he took the cup. 'A new state is the last place in the world for pampered women and children. Let them stay back east until all is settled.'

'Then why the schools?'

'Because not everyone thinks like me, unfortunately. If we must have women and children, then let the children at least be educated here, not back east where they are taught to be fit for nothing!' he said roundly, unconsciously echoing Mrs Pikeman's earlier words.

'I think you overstate your case. Times have changed. After all, California has been a state now for nearly five years and here we are in the capital, surely as civilised a town as we are like to find?'

'Oh, I grant you, San Francisco will soon have every vice of any city back east, and Sacramento is never far behind, but I believe that the cities have little to say to our future. The prosperity of California lies in its fertile lands and few of your San Francisco or Sacramento ladies have anything to contribute there.'

'Then Mrs Crocker and Miss Cooper are wasting their time?'

'Oh, they do their best and do it very well, I take nothing away from them, but neither of them can stand up to the vested eastern interests. And the hot air spouters will insist that the schools – our schools! – are set up on eastern lines, in order that we may appear civilised to the effete Easterners!' he exploded angrily. 'Latin primers and Greek gobbledegook! California has a much greater need for a mining college – and for an agricultural college!'

'One to teach the gold-grubbers more scientific ways of tearing the land apart and the other to teach 'em how to put it together again,' she agreed gravely.

'A woman with a sense of humour, by God! And a brain!' The frown vanished from between his eyes to be

80

replaced by a broad grin. 'Mr Owens is a lucky man indeed!'

'Don't take the Lord's name in vain, Colonel,' scolded Miss Cooper. 'Mrs Owens, here's Mr Jones wants to know whether he may offer you his escort home again.'

'I'd be pleased to offer Mrs Owens my escort if Mr Owens isn't available,' said the Colonel sternly, trying to freeze the clerk out.

Alicia flushed at the thought of the Colonel's reaction to Widow Grey's rooming house. 'Thank you Mr Jones,' said Alicia with a calmness she did not feel. 'You are very kind, Colonel, but indeed it is on Mr Jones's way and quite out of yours.'

She turned to pass out of the hall and was very relieved to see the Colonel detained by Edwin Crocker. Once in the hall she hurried Tamsin into her shawl and tried to whip her away before the Colonel could see her – or she him. He had not associated her with Mrs Langdon yet – but the presence of the child might speed him to make the connection and she had no wish to see herself pilloried in the eyes of the assembled company as the destitute beggar she must have seemed that day out at Tresco.

'Lisha?' demanded Tamsin with a little frown. 'Don't we know that man?'

'No, my dear. Now say your goodbyes to Miss Cooper.'

'Goodbye, Miss Cooper,' said Tamsin with an obedient curtsey. 'And thank you for a pleasant afternoon.'

'You must come again, dear child,' said Miss Cooper with a soft smile. 'Perhaps your mama will bring you again next Sunday. Now, run along with Gertrude and fetch the fruit Rachel has put out for you in the kitchen while I have a word with your mama.'

Tamsin and Gertrude skipped out of the hall just as Colonel Cornish re-emerged from the saloon.

'I do so hope you will come to our little soirée on Saturday,' she pressed Alicia. 'An excellent way to get to know people – nothing too formal, you understand. Saturday at nine.' She seemed to take Alicia's acceptance for granted. 'I am sure that Mrs Carson will let you leave a little early if I ask her.'

'Oh, but ma'am, I really think not ...' There was a note

81

of panic in her voice. Sewing afternoons were one thing, but a full evening in society was quite another!

'Nonsense, my dear Mrs Owens. It will do you a world of good to see a little more company,' insisted Miss Cooper.

'I — I do not go into society ...' she began.

'Why not?' demanded Cornish, reappearing at her elbow. 'Do you have some dread secret?'

'No, of course not! But ...'

'Colonel, really! Mrs Owens is a widow,' chided Miss Cooper.

'But not still in strict mourning, or she wouldn't be here,' he went on relentlessly.

'No indeed,' said Miss Cooper. 'I'm sure Mrs Owens will give us the pleasure of her company.' She was struck by a happy thought. 'Colonel Cornish, you can escort her!' she announced.

From the look on the rancher's face Alicia doubted whether he had had any intention of attending the soirée, but he swiftly suppressed the look of annoyance and bowed politely.

'At a quarter before nine, Mrs Owens. At the store.'

Before she could protest any further, he was gone.

The first day's logging went well. On a little bluff, close to the stream that ran down the hillside, but high enough above it not to be in danger of floods in the spring thaw, the foundations of Pedro's house could just be seen in the silver moonlight. Away from the bottom of the valley the nights were much cooler, and the men welcomed the hot chow that Chen had prepared for them. It was not exactly what they had expected, however, for the pickled tongues were very salty and Alicia had forgotten to tell him to soak them. The beans were tastier than usual and the bread was good, but the men drank a great quantity of coffee that night.

As the stars came out, twinkling above the massive trees, and the moonlight spilled on to the grassy slopes of the Vaca foothills, the men wrapped themselves in their bed-rolls against the chill and gathered around the camp fire. The boss, as the new hands called him, opted for the first watch. He had little interest in tall stories and whiskey drinking and relied on Kerhouan to keep it under control.

Watch was not too arduous up here: there was more danger of wolves coming down from the high timber-line after the sheep than of rustlers or Indians. Once the pen was built, Pedro and his Julia would have a peaceful, idyllic place up here. He knew a brief pang at the thought of what might have been, but he shrugged it off, walked away from the fire and sat himself down on a rock where he could keep a good eye on the sheep, temporarily penned in a bowl-shaped depression just beyond the house.

Back at the campfire, the conversation had turned, inevitably, to women. One of the men was reminiscing about a saloon girl he had met in Coloma, while another grumbled about the lack of decent women who were not too proud to be seen with a ranch hand.

'Say, Jo,' chimed Jos Evans, one of the older hands, a rough but skilled horse-wrangler. 'Didn't I hear tell you brought a woman overland with you? White woman?'

Chen Kai gave a grunt that might have been a yea or a nay.

'Whatever happened to her? For sure the boss didn't want no woman out on the ranch!'

Kai threw the dregs of his coffee onto the fire where they spat and sizzled.

'She went to work in Sacramento,' he said curtly.

'Must look her up,' said Jos with an evil grin. 'What saloon she work in?'

'No saloon!' snapped the cook. 'She is not that kind of woman!'

'Huh! If I had a dollar for every time a man said that 'bout a woman ...'

With a hiss Chen Kai sprang up from his bedroll; his knife was at Evans's throat before the other man had realised what was happening.

Kerhouan's soft commanding voice cut through the simmering tension.

'Don't do it, Jo,' he called softly. Unseen by the others, his hand had gone to his gun under the bedroll. He would not hesitate to use it: that was his duty as foreman of the hands, but he hoped he would not have to. The dour Breton had grown to like the cook. Perhaps the fact that they had

83

both been brought up by nuns, he in Brittany, Chen in Hong Kong, had provided a common thread in the two disparate lives. Certainly he appreciated the Chinaman's wry sense of humour, if not his cooking.

'Then he will apologise!' snarled the cook. 'Or I kill him!'

'Apologise, Evans,' said Kerhouan, still in the same level tones. 'And if you want to stay working at Tresco, lay your tongue off his woman.'

'*Not* my woman!' growled Chen. 'If he want to stay *breathing*, he will keep his foul tongue off my friend!'

'Here!' protested Evans, rolling his eyes to see whether the knife had been withdrawn. 'I never meant no offence, not to you nor her, I swear it!' The sweat gathered on his brow and rolled down into his eyes as he looked up into the implacable face above him. 'If'n I've offended, sure I'm sorry!'

Chen Kai let out his breath in one long hiss, then rocked back on his heels and sheathed his knife in one rapid movement.

'Is good,' he said, his precise English deserting him momentarily. 'Will do.'

Later next day Cornish found himself working alongside Chen Kai, trimming the logs with adzes while the others hauled them across to set on the foundations to form the front and back main timbers.

He pushed his hat to the back of his head and leaned against a tree.

'You know, Jo, you're a good worker,' he observed, 'but no one's indispensable.'

He looked up to see what effect his comment had had. Chen lowered his adze and stood before him, stony-faced.

'Ker-hwan told you,' he said heavily.

'Had to. It was his duty as foreman. He also told me Evans provoked you. But that's no reason for knives. If you have any grievances with the men, settle them with your fists.' He threw his adze down and brushed his dark hair out of his eyes. 'I need to build up a good team of men if I'm to put this ranch to rights. And if I have dissension and feuds, then I don't have a reliable team.' He paused and looked long and hard at the cook. 'There'll be no guns or knives between the men. Those are my terms, Jo, and if you'll accept them, we'll be happy to have you.'

Chen looked the other man straight in the eye. 'It will not happen again, Corr-onel,' he said gravely.

Later that evening, Cornish left the rest of the group by the campfire and crossed to the cook pot to fill his tin mug.

'My God! This coffee's thick enough to float a pistol!' he muttered. He took a cautious sip. 'Still, least it's not salty! Mind if I join you, Jo?'

'Please.'

'This woman you had the fight over,' he began carefully, 'I guess she means a great deal to you.'

'She is my friend,' answered Chen with simple dignity. 'My good friend. We have been together for more than four years now.'

'In San Francisco?'

'No, not there!' he answered, rather too quickly. 'All round. Everywhere. We − er − travelled a great deal through the mining camps.'

'Selling?'

'Just doing − well − this and that, you know ...'

'Uh-huh. Why d'you give it up?'

'It − ah − it gradually became less profitable,' stammered Chen Kai, looking down into his coffee. 'And − and − she felt we should be more settled − for the child's sake. That was why we looked for housekeeping posts ...'

'She would not have enjoyed working for Jem,' said Cornish, picking up a stone and pitching it viciously into the stream below. 'But you: surely you could always find work?'

'In Chinatown, you would say?' He laughed, but there was no mirth in the sound. 'No. My roots are not there. I have no wish to get on over the backs of my fellows and I will not get involved with the *tongs* or the Six Companies. Besides, many Chinese would not accept me: I reject their ancestor worship and superstition. I think my chances of reincarnation are the same whether I'm buried here or have my bones shipped back to China! One land is much like another, except that here in Gum Shan there is no famine.'

The Six Companies were merchant companies who paid a

man's ticket over from the impoverished Middle Kingdom to America and then hired his services out to mining companies, road and railroad builders, thus holding him in a kind of perpetual debt bondage, where his labour never improved his lot. The Six Companies kept the largest part of his earnings, a small part went to keep the individual alive, another fraction back to his family left behind in China, and the last part was kept by the Company to ship his coffin home in the event, disastrous for most Chinese, that he should die in Gum Shan, far from home and far from his ancestors.

'No,' sighed Chen. 'I do not belong there. They think me a heathen, I think them gullible fools. And they would never accept her — or the child.'

'California is no place for a woman,' growled Cornish. 'Women are never anything but trouble.'

'Not to me,' said Chen quietly. 'She was my strength when I had almost given up. She made me proud of what I am. And now I must be strong for her and for the child ... It is the least I can do.'

'You saw the child when you were in town?' The thought of the child had weighed more heavily on his conscience than the woman.

'Not this time,' he chuckled. 'She is boarded out and not everyone welcomes a Chinee on the doorstep. Or treats him like a human as you and Ker-hwan have done.'

'Kerhouan and I have travelled the world some,' said Cornish with a wry grin that made him seem much younger. 'We see a man as a man. Most forty-niners never went further than the next street before they made the great trek to the mines. And once gold fever grabs 'em, they just see everyone else as a rival for that elusive fortune. Anyways, you've clearly been better educated than the rest of 'em: that'd put their backs up from the start!'

'True!' Again he laughed that harsh, untuneful laugh. 'I have much to thank the mission for: with one stroke they made me — and unmade me!'

Chapter Eight

Mrs Carson had tried in vain to attract the 'society' trade and she didn't know whether to be more pleased or exasperated when the Sacramento ladies began to call at the store. It was Ned Sullivan who revealed that the new assistant had made quite a hit at one of the gatherings that the Reverend Cooper's sister held. Mrs Carson herself had gone once to an afternoon 'At Home', but she had not felt comfortable and had never gone again, though that did not stop her strongly resenting their interest in the Owens woman! When Miss Cooper herself came into the store and asked if the assistant might finish work early on Saturday to attend the soirée, she resented it every bit as much as Alicia had known she would.

'Got another gel to help in the store then, have ye?' demanded Sullivan thrusting his face pugnaciously in his sister's.

'You know I ain't!' she snapped back.

'Then don't push her the way you are!' he told her. 'She's enough to do in the store without sending her to heave the barrels and sacks about. You'll make her ill, you will. Or she'll up and quit and then you'll be in trouble.'

'Thinks herself too proud to help in the storeroom, do she?' sneered Missus Carson. 'Just because she's found some high-falutin' friends don't make her any more'n just the hired help around here. An' don't think I didn't see you carrying those barrels for her, fool that you are! Think she'll thank you for it? Anyways, if she don't do it, who will? Hey? You oughta be in the store or the bar, not runnin' around like a dog arter a bitch. And I'll not do it for her. Why should I? What do I pay her for, eh?'

'Neither you nor her should be doin' it,' he insisted. 'What's wrong with that lazy husband of yours doin' some work, eh? Whiles we're talking about dogs.'

Alicia was in two minds as to whether she should go to the Cooper house again. If the musical soirée was anything like the ones they used to hold in Yerba Buena, each of them would be expected to contribute something to the entertainment and the only songs she knew were either in Spanish or the popular songs of the mining camps! If she did go, she'd better confine herself to accompaniment on the pianoforte — if her fingers had not stiffened up too much since those endless hours of practice with Mama.

She was discovering that Sacramento was seething with more social activities than she had thought possible. Now she was known to be not only a widow but one not averse to appearing in society, a number of unmarried men — clerks, ranch foremen, the tongue-tied manager of the Express Office, an actor from Forrest's Theatre, a doctor, two attorneys and the undertaker — drifted into the store in the course of the week to persuade her to accompany them to lectures, concerts, barn-raising dances, or a debate on phrenology and philosophy between Professor Buchanan and Doctor Rice. She declined all the invitations politely, even though she was pining for adult company and it appeared that single women in Sacramento did not go to interesting things like lectures by themselves. First let her overcome the hurdle of the musical soirée, she told herself, and then she would see. Meanwhile there were barrels to move and stores to clear out. Time and Missus Carson waited for no man.

Out at Tresco the hands were just coming in from the fields down valley where Kerhouan's crops were growing tall and lush, promising a decent harvest despite the recent neglect.

They cleaned up in the bunkhouse and then sat down at the long table in the centre of the room, their faces grim and set. They ate their chow pretty much in silence, in contrast to the usual good-humoured ribaldry that accompanied Jo

Chen's tough cornbread or overdone hotcakes, because word had got around – nobody quite knew how – that bad news had come to the boss, all to do with the ranch, and each man was wondering to himself whether having fallen into such a comfortable berth, he might not be about to be tipped out of it again.

Most of the hands were former miners who had either failed to make the big strike or had frittered their gold away on high living and ended up poorer than when they had arrived. Nearly all of them – whether European, Mexican or eastern Americans – lacked either the desire or the finance to return; for better or for worse, they were now the new Californians. There was not a great deal of choice of work in the new state for men such as them: either you signed on with the big mining companies that were tearing the landscape apart to get the less easily accessible gold out – quite a different proposition for the miner who had previously only worked with a pick and shovel and pan – or you went as a ranch hand, turning the wilderness into good agricultural land to feed the teeming population of San Francisco and the other communities that were springing up all around.

There were plenty of ranches where a man could find work, although few of them were crying out for workers as they had in the early days of the gold rush, when high wages were offered to tempt men down from the Sierras to the farms in the valleys, but good employers were few and far between. Tresco offered year round work for good men, not just seasonal employment and hunger in the off season; more to the point it offered a man great opportunities. Within the fort there were any number of buildings that the boss was having cleaned up; he planned to have proper bunkhouses for the hands, where other ranchers took advantage of the climate and left men to sleep out throughout the year, a good cookhouse, stables, a smithy. To men who had seen mining towns spring up overnight, the potential of Tresco was clear. And there was always the example of Pedro to tempt them: set up in his own little establishment with his wife and her brother, to all intents and purposes his own man, in charge of the sheeprun up-valley. Yes, a wise man would stick around Tresco and see what happened. But they'd all be glad to know what it was that had maddened the boss so.

Chen Kai-Tsu left the two young lads whom Kerhouan had delegated to help him scrubbing out the pans and took a dish of the stew and a heap of the hotcakes into the ranch house.

He looked around in disapproval at the mess in the house which never failed to vex him. The fellow they had been burying the day of his arrival had left the house a veritable pigsty and it revolted him to see the Colonel living in such chaos. He had allowed Chen to clean out one end of the kitchen and one of the rooms upstairs where he slept, but there had been no time to do any more, for more often than not they were all out on the ranch every day, seeing to the herds, overseeing the planting of the second crop and checking the boundaries down in the valley to make sure that no squatters had damaged the fences or taken any of the animals.

The Colonel and his foreman were sitting at a table covered with paper, old documents curling at the corners mixed in with scraps of paper sacks covered with scrawling figures. Chen was at a loss to find a place to put the dishes down.

'Leave it,' said Kerhouan tiredly. 'Eat, then we'll see if we have any better ideas.'

'What better ideas?' demanded the Colonel, sweeping the papers aside angrily. 'There are no better ideas, dammit! If I sell my land to pay the lawyers to fight, he's got us. If I don't fight he's got us. Either way Lamarr can't lose.'

Chen hovered around while the men ate, fetching salt, filling glasses, stacking the dishes. When the table was clear, he recovered the papers from the floor and attempted to put them in some sort of order.

'Leave that!' snapped Cornish.

'Very good, sir.' His heavy lids hooded his eyes, hiding the expression there. He bowed to the Colonel and turned to go.

'Hell, Jo, I didn't mean to snap.' Cornish passed his hand over his eyes. 'Bring us some of your appalling coffee – and a cup for yourself. I don't see why we should be the only ones to suffer it!'

He had regained his customary self-control by the time Chen Kai came back with the coffee can and the three mugs, and Kerhouan had produced a bottle of whiskey.

They sat together occasionally in the evenings, the boss, the Breton foreman and the Chinese cook, trying to sort through the piles of unpaid bills and unanswered letters which lay in dusty heaps all over the house. Chen had some skills in accounting which Kerhouan lacked and between them they had managed to solve a few of the problems which had been Jem Cornish's legacy. Chen sat impassively, sipping his whiskey, waiting. Across the table from him, Cornish drank glass after glass as if it were water.

'Heard of Sutter?' demanded the Colonel at last.

'Sure. The man who started all the gold rush. Used to own all the land north of Sacramento and up along the American River.'

'That's right. *Used to*. Used to own all of Sacramento too. But his land grants were suspect and he had to mortgage his holdings to pay lawyers to fight his claims for him. Lost almost all of it.'

'Remember also the Indian girls and him three parts drunk every day on *aguardiente*!' protested Kerhouan. 'And he could have raised money from his harvest if he had not been too mean to pay top dollar to get workers.'

'Nevertheless, he went from the ruler of a virtual kingdom to poverty in a few years. He had gold, cattle, grain, land — and what has he now? Six hundred acres of Hock Farm on the Feather. All because the lawyers disputed his boundaries and his land grants.'

He reached out an unsteady hand and slopped some more whiskey into his glass, wincing at the movement.

'Another bottle!' he demanded. Kerhouan looked at him steadily, his eyes narrowed, making no move.

'Another bottle, dammit!' he repeated.

Kerhouan shrugged and rose from the table, returning after a moment with more whiskey.

'And now that bastard Lamarr wants to see me off the same way!' He ground his teeth. 'Four years the Land Commission's been sitting and next month it's supposed to

91

close and now − *now*, by God! − he says that my boundaries have never been "satisfactorily fixed"!'

'Are your boundaries not then laid down in the title deeds, Corr-onel?' Chen's face was as impassive as ever, but his eyes were bright with interest.

'Oh, yes, they are all described − in Spanish, which the Land Commissioners do not speak! But will they be satisfied that "the large oak by the third waterfall from the source", or "the three cairns" is where I say it is, and not where Lamarr says it is? If he had put in his claim even three months ago, I could have had a surveyor out to draw up the disputed areas − but less than a month! It's impossible. Even if I could find one that Lamarr hadn't got to first, I doubt he could draw up the relevant points in time.'

'Is that all that's needed? A representation of the points Lamarr disputes?'

'Yes. Then we swear their accuracy in front of a lawyer − I know one in San Francisco who is honest enough − and it is then up to Lamarr to disprove their validity.'

'I can find you a good mapmaker,' said Chen Kai casually. 'In Sacramento.'

The rancher looked up from his glass with a startled expression on his face.

'Trustworthy?'

'Completely.'

'Able?'

'Competent and intelligent.'

'My God.' Cornish tossed down another glass. 'And will he work for me?'

'This ... mapmaker ... needs a good position,' replied the cook carefully. 'And will do whatever you require in as short a time as is practicable.'

'Jo,' enunciated the Colonel solemnly, 'if this fellow is all you say, then perhaps we can beat Lamarr after all! I'll ride in first thing in the morning!'

'I'll give you the directions,' promised Chen Kai.

'Then, gentlemen, adieu until the morrow.' He staggered to his feet and picked up the almost full bottle of whiskey by the neck, swaying slightly. He bowed mockingly. 'So, I bid you goodnight.'

Kerhouan watched his unsteady progress across the floor and listened to the crash of his booted feet on the wooden stairs, then turned to Chen with a wry grin.

'Don't count on seeing 'im until Sunday at soonest.'

'Who then is this Lamarr?' asked Chen, a frown wrinkling his smooth forehead. 'He has much of his own land. Why does he want Corr-onel's?'

'It's personal between them two. Ever see Mrs Lamarr? No? Belle Kingsley she was when Jack first met 'er. Daughter of one of the California Steam men. Rich and spoilt. "*La belle Belle*" they called her here in Sacramento. But Sacramento not good enough for 'er. 'Er father take 'er to San Francisco.' His English was becoming more fractured as his narrative progressed: he too had been drinking freely. 'Only the best for Belle: balls, soirées, theatre outings – and 'im, *mordieu*! Like the lap-dog. She whistle, 'e run after 'er. I think it was still the bang on the 'ead, make 'im stupid. They was engaged, but it was one day on, one day off. Then she begin to play 'im off against Lamarr. Quiet rivalry was no good to 'er, it 'ave to be all in public. I think she like them to fight over her; in the end, it nearly come to a duel between them.'

'What happened?'

'Overnight, just like that –' he snapped his fingers '– Colonel Jack come to 'is senses. Tells Lamarr he can 'ave 'er and welcome. Lamarr is pleased, but I think she never forgive Jack. I think she is behind all this – or maybe Lamarr too 'as come to 'is senses, who can tell?' He drained his glass and set it down with a heavy sigh. 'Anyways, soon after, Colonel Jack receive news that this Jem –' he said the name with unmistakable loathing '– 'e is sick, so he come back 'ere, and find Tresco like this.'

'This Jem – he was Corr-onel Jack's brother?'

'*Non!*' Kerhouan was emphatic. 'He never 'ave no brother. But they both are coming from Cornwall, you understand, and out 'ere, they call all the Cornish miners "Brother Jack". This *laer*, this thief, this Jem, 'e was there when the mine cave in and they all think Colonel Jack is dead when they pull 'im out. He sees way to 'ave all the gold the others have dug out. When Colonel 'ave 'is senses back, Jem tell 'im 'e save 'im from the mine. So when Colonel leaves, 'e leave Jem in charge of Tresco.'

'But when he regained his memory ...?'

'That I cannot tell you, for I do not know.' He shrugged. ''E must 'ave known the truth, but I think while 'e was in San Francisco, 'e do not care much what happened at Tresco.'

'Does he often drink this heavily?'

'It is when his arm pains him badly, you understand,' said Kerhouan loyally. 'Otherwise, no, not even in San Francisco ...'

'I had noticed the arm,' nodded Chen thoughtfully. 'But I could give him something better than whiskey to take away the pain. You tell him that ...'

'When 'e is sober,' warned Kerhouan. 'When 'e drink this much, 'e is like the bear with the sore 'ead, you leave 'im alone.'

Saturday dawned and with it the decision to go to the soirée. Alicia dared not chance offending Miss Cooper and losing the place for Tamsin in her school. She spent the entire day convincing herself that she was far enough away from San Francisco to be safe from accidental discovery.

Before she left early on the Saturday morning she explained carefully to Tamsin where she was going and the child promised to be good for Mrs Grey. Alicia could only hope that the promise of future Sunday afternoons with cakes and tea would suffice to hold off the dreaded nightmares.

The day seemed endless, but at last came the grudging dismissal.

'I suppose you can go and tidy yourself up, if'n you're so set on goin',' muttered her employer.

She took the bag with her silk dress in it into the back store. Surrounded by barrels of flour, she began to unbutton her blouse, but stopped as a sudden thought struck her. She crossed the room and heaved a barrel of flour in front of the door. Sure enough, just as she was slipping into the dove-grey dress, she heard the handle turn and the door rattle against the barrel. She smiled triumphantly to herself as she heard the muttered cursing.

She rebraided her hair to her satisfaction, coiling it into the nape of her neck and teasing a few curls forward to cluster round her face, then she took out a flask of Kai's herbal medicine and swallowed it down. When she felt she could face the world, she rolled the barrel aside and stepped out.

'Good night, Mr Carson,' she said coolly.

When she got to the front of the store, she did not find the Colonel on the sidewalk, however, but the Reverend Cooper.

He raised his hat, an old-fashioned low beaver, and bowed slightly to her.

'I am the bearer of Colonel Cornish's apologies, ma'am. He has been detained on his ranch and will not be able to join us this evening. Letitia hopes that you will not object to my escort instead.'

'It's most kind of your sister to concern herself.'

And yet, perversely, she *was* disappointed by the Colonel's absence, even though she held him at least partly responsible for her present situation!

The company at the soirée was sufficiently varied to make up for his absence, although baritones and tenors far outnumbered sopranos and altos. The general standard of musical performance was not, however, such as to deter even the most amateur of performers. Apart from Mr and Mrs Revel and their pallid-faced son, not one of the others could hit a note accurately and hold it true.

And there was a piano — a rare sight still in California.

'Do you play, Mrs Owens?' enquired Miss Cooper.

'I did — a long time ago,' she admitted. She thought back to the endless hours of practice her mother had decreed. Robert had sold her piano for a good price to a saloon bar. 'My fingers are very stiff.'

There was a wider variety of people here than there had been at the sewing bee, including the ministers of the Episcopalian and Methodist congregations and a number of Spanish-Americans, who she was sure must be Catholics. When it came to a social life, there was apparently more willingness to put aside religious and sectarian differences here than in equivalent gatherings in more populous regions. And class differences too, she reflected as she was introduced to a prominent politician — although she wondered whether the greeting would have been so warm if she had still been working with Chen Kai and living under the same roof!

The refreshments too were of a different nature, although just as lavish. The sight of the cold meats, jellies, salads and fruits laid out for the delectation of the guests made Alicia's mouth water so that she could hardly bear to turn her back on the table and concentrate on the music and general conversation. So little did the Carsons pay her and so much did she pay the Greys for lodging and looking after Tamsin that very little was left over and in the middle of this land of plenty, she often did not have enough to eat. She had been mad to send the money back to Tresco.

The conversation in between the musical items was all about the situation in San Francisco. While her fingers moved obediently, though a little stiffly, over the keys to accompany Mrs Revel's rendition of 'Where'er you walk', selected from Miss Cooper's wide range of music books, Alicia listened avidly to the gossip and speculation, but no one seemed to have any certain knowledge, each condemning the other's opinion as 'mere rumour'.

She was glad to accept the offer of a drink from young Mr Revel when at last she was released from the piano where she had ended by murdering 'I Dreamt I Dwelt in Marble Halls' from *The Bohemian Girl* with the enthusiastic but totally untalented Edith Pikeman.

'A brave effort, Mrs Owens,' he said softly. 'I think you might just have saved the honour of Messrs Bunn and Balfe!'

'Barely, I think,' she replied with a chuckle.

'May I offer you a glass of this excellent punch?' he went on. 'Octavius Cooper is a dab hand at the blending.'

The guest were all helping themselves liberally to this potation, a glowing bowl of fragrant ruby red liquid with the crystalline snows of the Sierra Nevada floating on its surface. Alicia accepted a glass and sipped at it delicately, savouring the glow of it as it seemed to spread through her veins, dispelling the feeling of tiredness that had filled her body ever since she had started heaving the barrels and sacks that morning.

There was a stir at the door and a portly Spanish-American

96

entered, a stunningly beautiful woman at his side. They were rapidly enveloped by a crowd.

'The Leons,' murmured Mr Revel in her ear. 'Just back from San Francisco.'

'What news from San Francisco?' demanded Mrs Revel almost immediately. 'Does the Vigilance Committee still govern the town, or have Sheriff Scannell and Mayor Van Ness come out of their bolthole and taken the reins of government back again?'

'For myself,' interrupted Mrs Bryant, her colour high, 'I'm all in favour of the Vigilantes if City Hall is too cowardly to enforce law and order!'

'And corrupt!' growled Mr Revel Senior. 'While the like of Belle Ryan can buy a jury with her ill-gotten money ...'

'The gamblers and the harlots run the city like their own private kingdom!' objected another. 'More than time they were stopped! All power to the Vigilantes, say I!'

'Hang the lot of them!' said one.

'Hanging's too good for some of those villains!' cried another.

'Ladies! Gentlemen!' The Reverend Cooper was deeply shocked. 'Let us not fall out over the matter. Let us rather thank God that we in Sacramento have not been visited with the misfortunes that afflict our neighbours on the coast, and pray that He may bring a just and fitting end to this sad episode.'

'Amen!' said the beautiful Señora Leon fervently. 'We imitate San Francisco in so many ways. In this, let us hope not.'

'They have hanged four more of the murderers, Andrews among them,' said Leon. Only sharp-eyed Miss Cooper saw the sheet of music slip from Mrs Owens's fingers and flutter gently to the floor. One glance at her dead-white face and she stepped wordlessly between her and the rest, effectively blocking her from their view.

'Now they've moved on to other crimes – corruption and so on ...' Leon went on.

'That'll keep 'em going the next five years!' muttered Captain Sharples with grim humour.

'They were to disband this month. A lot of the petty

criminals had the sense to get out before the warrants came, and the Vigilance Committee are providing tickets to help them on their way. Governor Johnson has finally stood up and said 'enough', but I don't think anyone's taking any notice. He's declared a state of insurrection, but both General Wool at Benicia and Captain Farragut at Mare Island have refused to send in troops.'

'Perhaps they think reform was long overdue,' commented Mr Reese.

'Perhaps,' agreed Señor Leon. 'But matters are going from bad to worse. I shan't be going near San Francisco again — and I don't recommend anyone else here to do so.' He paused and scanned the expectant faces around him. 'You see, they sent Sterling Hopkins out with an arrest warrant for James Moloney, and there was a brawl, and David Terry —'

'The Supreme Court Justice?'

'The same. Governor Johnson's hot-headed friend. Stabbed Hopkins in the neck. He's not expected to live. They've thrown Terry into prison at Fort Gunnybags and are threatening to hang him.'

'But — but — they can't hang a Justice of the state court!' exclaimed Mr. Barrington angrily.

'If they don't — then it means he's above the law,' reasoned Señor Leon. 'Not exactly what the Vigilance Committee has been fighting for. But maybe they've overreached themselves this time? The Captain of the *John Adams* has demanded the Vigilantes hand Terry over.'

'And what have they to say to that?' asked Mrs Revel eagerly.

'They've abandoned their plan to disband,' he said sombrely. 'And if Hopkins dies, I think they will hang Terry and that will put them against the Governor himself.'

'The Navy against the Vigilantes,' began Miss Cooper in a horrified whisper.

'It would be open warfare,' agreed Señor Leon sombrely. 'And both the Vigilantes and the Governor are sending to Sacramento for support.'

There was a short thoughtful silence, broken at last by Captain Sharples.

'I see Colonel Cornish is not here tonight,' he observed.

'And what of that?' demanded Miss Cooper aggressively.

Captain Sharples shrugged. 'Perhaps he felt it was his duty to rejoin the Vigilantes,' he speculated.

Alicia shivered. Someone had walked over her grave.

'Another glass of punch, Mrs Owens?' offered Mr Revel, returning to her side as the gathering broke up into small groups.

'No, I thank you,' she declined the offer. She had scarcely eaten anything today, for Missus Carson had not allowed her a break, to make up for her early departure. 'Perhaps later on.'

Miss Cooper was bewailing the lack of a good violinist. 'Here we are with a violin, a harp, a piano, and we can't play any duets. What a pity Colonel Cornish could not come!'

She assumed that this was one of Miss Cooper's usual butterfly changes of subject until Revel assured her that the Colonel was one of the best exponents of the violin, or, as he insisted on calling it, the fiddle, that California had ever seen.

'But come, Mrs Owens,' he rallied her. 'A well brought up young lady like yourself surely had some lessons on the harp? Enough to play a simple duet with me and satisfy Miss Letitia?'

'I'm afraid not, Mr Revel. My mother taught me to play the pianoforte, but there it ended, I fear.'

He sorted through the various bound volumes of songs until he found a book of Scottish ballads and persuaded Alicia to sing one of Robert Burns' beautiful songs with him. Her voice was not big, but it was sweet and true and blended well with his pleasing tenor, so that when the last note died away the applause for the first time that evening was more genuine than polite.

The cold collation was eaten, to the accompaniment of much speculation about the situation in San Francisco, which Alicia managed to avoid, and at last, to her relief, the evening drew to an end. This time, Mr Jones, the elderly clerk, was not present to help her out of her dilemma and she stood by helplessly while it was decided that the Revels would see her safely home. Her only consolation was that the older Revels decided to go with their married daughter and her husband, leaving their son to escort her.

'My God!' he said softly as the gig drew up alongside the crumbling sidewalk outside the Widow's Grey's.

'It is ... only temporary.' she began to stammer. 'Until we can establish ourselves ...'

'This is no fit place for a lady,' he said firmly. 'Whatever are the Coopers thinking of?'

'They don't know where I live ...'

'But – they could surely help you to a better place!'

'I don't want their damned charity – or yours!' she burst out angrily.

'My dear Mrs Owens!'

Seeing the shocked expression on his face, she bit her lip and tried to control her anger. 'If I am to amend my situation – as I fully intend – then it will be by my efforts and mine alone! If I'm not good enough for your circle because I work in a store and live in a place like this, then I can relieve you all of the embarrassment of my presence!'

He caught her hands in his and pressed them. 'I meant no offence, you know. Indeed I admire your independence of spirit. But pride is not the only consideration; friendship must surely be allowed to take its place. There are better jobs and better places for someone of your abilities. The Reverend Cooper and I know them all.'

'Really?'

'I am deputy editor of the *Tribune*: our offices are used as a sort of employment agency. And the Coopers always know the best lodgings before they come on the market! I'll let you know if I hear of anything suitable,' he assured her. 'It would be a pity to lose the company of the only woman beside my mother who can sing a true note!'

She laughed. 'I'm sure you are right – but I would still prefer that you did not tell everyone where I live.'

'Your wish is my command,' he said gravely, his thin, bony face lightening with a smile. 'May I have the pleasure of escorting you next week? No need to commit yourself now. I hope we shall meet again before then.'

She thought he was going to kiss her, and had a fleeting return of that nightmare feeling of panic, the memories she had buried and shut out of her mind by the iron control she had enforced to save her sanity. She almost sighed with relief when he merely bent to kiss her hand.

'Until next week, Mrs Owens,' he said.

But fate had other plans in mind for her and it was to be some time before she returned to Letitia Cooper's parlour.

Chapter Nine

Next morning she slept late and there was barely time to wash and snatch a hasty breakfast before it was time for church. Tamsin was very tired and Alicia was inclined to be a little impatient with her, an impatience she regretted when, despite the hardness of the pew, the child fell asleep in the middle of the service.

Perhaps she was finding Aggie Grey's boisterous brood too much for her, she thought, stroking the little girl's golden hair out of her eyes. Avoiding Miss Cooper's anxious enquiries after the service, she hurried her home and put her back to bed. But within an hour, the child was awake again, bouncing impatiently up and down on the bed, demanding to know why she had to sleep in the middle of the day.

'I want to go out in the sunshine, Lisha,' she complained vigorously. 'Why cannot we go for a walk? We could pick flowers on the riverbank. You'd like that, Lisha, wouldn't you?'

'Yes, my sweet. It's probably just what we both need,' admitted Alicia with a chuckle. 'Perhaps you're like me — nothing wrong with you but the blue devils!'

And so it seemed. They walked upstream of the Embarcadero and across the rickety trestle bridge to the little tree-covered spit of land that jutted out into the inlet or slough that Sacramento rather grandiosely called Lake Sutter. In the distance the chimneys of the Californian Steam Engine Works pointed heavenwards, but today no steam or smoke rose from them. They crossed the spit, swinging along hand in hand, their worries for once put aside, revelling in the

102

peace and the warmth of the sunshine, pausing now and again to pick some more herbs until Alicia had quite an armful.

On the steep bank just below the turnpike road they found a fallen tree and sat down on it to eat the last bits of bread and cheese in the hot golden afternoon sunshine. Beatrice, the rag doll, had been tucked into the bag with the food and she sat beside Tamsin on the log, listening to the birds calling and watching the fish jumping in the sparkling waters of the inlet below.

'No cakes today, Lisha?' asked Tamsin rather forlornly, head on one side.

'I don't think so, my lovely,' answered Alicia ruefully. 'Just in case ...'

And yet, watching Tamsin running about the clearing, chasing butterflies, it was hard to believe there was anything wrong with her. More likely she was, like Alicia herself, just tired out. The peace and quiet of the clearing was beginning to have its effect on her and she could feel her eyes closing in spite of herself.

'Come on, my lovely.' She began to collect up her shawl and her bag. 'Time we were going back.'

'Ohhh!' The child's face began to pucker. 'Don't want to go back to that house ...' She had never referred to Widow Grey's as home. 'Just a little while longer, Lisha, *please!* Beatrice wants to watch the butterflies!'

Alicia turned her head to watch the jewelled butterflies flashing in and out of the sunbeams. The sun was warm on her skin and there was no noise but the birds and the occasional clatter of hooves as riders passed behind them on the turnpike road. It was very tempting.

'Just a few minutes longer. But stay close. That water's running quite fast.'

She must have dozed off in the hot sunshine, for she woke with a start to a piercing scream from Tamsin.

'Beatrice!' Tamsin stood a few yards in front of her, her body rigid as she watched the rag doll fall down the steep bank towards the Lake, then in a flash she had thrown herself after her doll.

Alicia moved instinctively, as quickly as she could, but for one dreadful moment it seemed she would be too late. After

103

the first mad dash to save Beatrice, Tamsin seemed suddenly to become aware of the danger into which she had flung herself. She stopped in panic on the brink of the drop, but the impetus of that first mad dash had carried her too far and she slithered, staggered and slipped over the edge. Throwing herself full-length on the ground, Alicia just managed to catch her hand in the waist of the child's dress. With a calmness she did not feel, she commanded Tamsin to stop wriggling.

'Hold still!' she panted. 'Now – one arm up to me ... slowly!' The child flung her arm up suddenly and almost jerked them both into the deep water, but Alicia just managed to grab her frail wrist.

Her back hurt her, her shoulders were burning, feeling as though they were about to be pulled out of their sockets. She tried to summon up a last great surge of energy to draw the sobbing child back up the bank, but in her heart she knew she could not do it; the strength simply was not there.

'Hold still, Tamsin,' she panted. 'Keep still. I'm just going to shout someone on the turnpike ...' If there was anyone there, she thought despairingly.

Then, before she could raise her head to call, a black shadow fell across her face and she turned her head to see someone standing between her and the sun. He looked to be at least eight feet tall.

Whatever his height he appeared at least to be quick of comprehension. No exclamations or questions – he simply threw himself down alongside her, pinned her shoulders to the ground with one strong arm and reached down the bank to grip Tamsin's other wrist.

'Now, pull hard!' he commanded and, painstakingly slowly, Tamsin's tear-stained face appeared over the top of the bank.

She would have liked to lie there on the cool damp grass for ever till the burning, wrenched muscles in her arms stopped aching and her back stopped shooting agonised pains to her terrified brain, but it was impossible. Tamsin was sobbing for Beatrice, her unknown rescuer was saying something she could not distinguish, and another, vaguely familiar voice was exclaiming somewhere behind her.

Catching her breath in great gulps, she rolled over and

looked up into quite the most handsome face she had seen since Robert's death. Blue, blue eyes were gazing down with lively concern from a lightly tanned face beneath a mop of fair curls. As he reached down to draw her gently to her feet, she saw that her unknown rescuer was not quite the eight foot giant he had seemed from her worm's eye view, but he must have been a good six, broad-shouldered, slim hipped, like one of the Greek gods in her school primer.

And good-mannered into the bargain. As she stammered out her thanks, he bowed over her hand and kissed it.

'A pleasure, ma'am, to be of service to you — and your little girl,' he said gravely.

She sought for words suitable to express her feelings, but could find none. 'Tamsin,' she said inadequately, 'say thank you to the gentleman.'

But Tamsin's normally perfect manners had completely deserted her.

'Beatrice is going to get drownded!' she wailed.

'Who's Beatrice?' enquired the other voice. She whirled to see Clive Revel standing patiently holding the two horses, his own and his companion's.

'Her doll,' she replied anxiously.

He looped the reins round a low branch and stepped forward to the edge of the bank. 'Ah! I can see Beatrice!' he exclaimed exultantly. 'Not too far down — caught on a thorn bush.' He broke off a whippy stem from a nearby clump of young saplings. 'Brenchley! Hold onto my legs, there's a good fellow.'

'But Mr Revel ... you'll spoil your clothes!' she protested as he flung himself full-length on the mossy bank.

'Nothing compared to the safety of Beatrice,' he said with a grin. 'My father once had to row out to a boat in 'Frisco harbour that was just about to sail back round the Horn, just because my sister had left her rag doll on board! Mathilda she was called, I remember.' He wriggled forward until he was right on the edge, hanging over, secured only by his friend's weight on his legs. 'Ah! I have her now!'

Tamsin was jumping up and down with excitement, barely held back by Alicia. Revel hooked the whippy stick into the sash of the doll's dress and eased it slowly up the bank until it came within his reach. He stood up, the doll firmly in one hand, dusted himself down with the other, then turned to Tamsin. He bowed to her with a great flourish. 'Beatrice!' he said solemnly. With a shriek, the child took the doll and hugged her to her heart.

'Oh, thank you, *thank you!*' she cried ecstatically. As Revel bent over her with a smile on his pale face, she flung her little arms around his neck and kissed him enthusiastically, causing him to blush furiously.

'Clearly I should have rescued the doll and abandoned the child!' said the fair man with a rueful smile.

'I'm sorry,' apologised Alicia with a rueful smile. 'But you see, Beatrice is the most important person in her life.'

'After you, surely, ma'am?'

'Perhaps,' she agreed gravely, but in her heart she knew it was not true. Beatrice was constant. Alicia had abandoned the child when she needed her most.

She could feel her legs beginning to tremble as reaction set in and she was grateful when Brenchley pushed her gently back down on to the log.

She looked up, sudden tears filling her eyes.

'I cannot find the words to thank you enough. Both of you. God knows what I would have done had you not been by.'

'Only too delighted, ma'am,' responded the tall man, bowing gracefully over her hand. 'May I introduce myself? Augustus Brenchley, ma'am, always at your service.'

'I thank you, sir, and you, Mr Revel, for rescuing us from the results of my unforgivable carelessness.'

The fair giant smiled sweetly down at her. 'Not carelessness, ma'am. You were simply overcome by the heat of the day. Too many late nights, I daresay. I confess, I have been pleasantly surprised at the variety of entertainment offered by Sacramento society.'

She had to suppress a bubble of hysterical laughter at the suggestion that her social life had caused her exhaustion! Heaving the sacks and the barrels from early morning to late at night had left her barely enough strength to walk back to the Greys and crawl into bed. The thought of dancing the night away was in itself quite exhausting!

'Mrs Owens is not able to give Sacramento society the

pleasure of her company as much as Sacramento would like,' commented Revel smoothly. 'But you may meet her again at the Coopers' soirée on Saturday.'

He pressed her to join them at the Orleans Hotel, where they were to meet some friends later that afternoon, but much as she would have welcomed a good slug of whiskey — an unladylike habit she had got into with Angelina in times of stress — she knew all they would offer her would be a cup of coffee.

'You are very kind, gentlemen, but Tamsin has had an uncomfortable afternoon and the best place for her is bed,' she replied firmly.

Mr Brenchley took Tamsin up before him on his horse and, Alicia having declined Revel's horse, they walked back across the trestle bridge and along the edge of town to the Greys. They picked their way through the stagnant pools and she grew hot with embarrassment as Aggie Grey and a handful of mucky children leaned over the rickety garden fence to watch them lift a sleepy Tamsin down, but she was too tired and anxious about the girl to care what Brenchley thought.

She refused to let either of the men carry Tamsin upstairs, although it was no easy task for her to do it herself, for the child was heavy and her long skirts and full petticoats hampered her on the rickety staircase; she could not bear them to see the squalor of the house or the bareness of their room.

She sat up all evening, sponging the little girl's head as she tossed and turned, berating herself for her folly in taking her to the lake. How could she ever face Kai again after betraying his trust?

Towards midnight, Tamsin seemed to grow a little quieter. Her own eyelids were heavy as lead, so she slipped into the bed, cradling the child in her arms. She was soon asleep, but that night, for the first time in weeks, she dreamed once more of prison. 'They will hang you, of course,' said the voice gloatingly. She could not see the face but she knew it was evil, evil. 'I'll make sure of that.' She woke up in a sweat, hands clutching her throat. Shaking, she groped for Kai's herbal draught and hoped for oblivion.

Tamsin grew steadily worse the next morning. Alicia sent

apologies to Missus Carson and, swallowing her pride, a note to beg Miss Cooper's help. But Miss Cooper was out of town with her brother, and Aggie took one look at the feverish child and commanded her mother to throw the two of them out.

'I ain't risking none o'mine taking the fever!' she shrieked. 'An' I ain't having no sassy notes from Ma Carson telling me to nurse the brat whiles my fine lady goes back to work!'

Before Alicia could draw breath, they were out on the muddy sidewalk, their traps bundled up beside them. Once more she had to swallow her pride. She sent a lad to hire a cart with her last few coins and deposited herself, the child and the bundles on Sullivan's doorstep. Even if it meant that she had to work in the saloon, she had to have a roof over their heads at least until Tamsin recovered.

The Colonel did not appear again until early on Monday morning and then he looked so grey that it was a wonder to the men that he had managed to get out of bed at all.

Chen crossed the room without a sound and set a mug of acrid green liquid down in front of him.

'Drink this, if you please. Then you will feel like new.'

Cornish sniffed it suspiciously, looked sideways at the cook, then came to a swift decision and drank it in one gulp.

'My God!' he gasped from a burning throat.

'Now water,' said Chen soothingly. 'Better?'

The Colonel's eyes stopped watering; he caught his breath again, and nodded weakly. 'I could even manage some of your coffee and hotcakes, I think,' he said resolutely. 'But no bacon,' he added hastily.

When the cook put the plate in front of him, he looked at it in some trepidation. 'Tell me, Jo, how come you can make so many exotic concoctions and yet you can't cook to make a dog hungry?'

Chen shrugged. 'Just luck, I guess,' he grinned.

After a few mouthfuls of coffee he put the mug down abruptly. 'What day is it?' he asked.

'Monday,' replied Kerhouan.

'Hell and the Devil!' exclaimed the rancher wrathfully. 'I was supposed to be at a soirée on Saturday evening!'

'I sent one of the lads in with your apologies,' explained Kerhouan smoothly.

'More to the point if you'd stopped me getting drunk in the first place!' he snapped.

'I want to pick a fight, I'll pick me better odds than that!' answered Kerhouan with a laugh.

'What? Can you get better odds than a one-armed drunk?' demanded the Colonel bitterly.

'Half a Cornish wrestler is still more than I can cope with.'

The Colonel munched morosely at the food on his plate, then pushed it abruptly to one side.

'Jo!' he called. 'I'm off to Sacramento now. Give me the directions for this here mapmaker of yours.'

'Here it is, Colonel Jack,' said Chen Kai softly, handing him a scrap of paper.

'Right. And what stores do we ...' He broke off abruptly. 'Is this your idea of a joke?' he demanded wrathfully. 'Because if it is, you've picked a mighty fine time for it! Mrs Langdon? Isn't that the poor woman who came here with you?'

'That's her,' replied the cook calmly.

'I need a mapmaker, not a bloody housekeeper!' he exploded.

'She'll make you as good a map as anyone, Colonel, I promise you.'

'But she's a woman!'

'She's a good mapmaker. Talented. Army-trained, virtually. And honest.'

'I don't want a woman on Tresco!'

'Do you have any choice, *mon ami?*' asked Kerhouan reasonably. 'Why not try her out? After all, there is no one else you can trust. And if she's no good, pay her off and send her on her way.'

'I'll give her a trial,' he said grudgingly. 'But only for as long as the survey lasts — if she's good enough to last *that* long! Don't imagine I'll keep her here just to suit you, Jo!' he snapped. 'That's out of the question.'

Chen Kai bowed impassively and said nothing at all.

Not until he was on the ferry did the Colonel think to

look at the scrap of paper for directions and he suffered another shock when he saw that her address was given as Carson's Stores! Strange that he had not seen her there. Still, he reasoned, if you had an attractive young woman like Mrs Owens to serve in the front, you could afford to keep a worn-out, bad-tempered old husk of a woman like Mrs Langdon out back in the store rooms.

He would have had to call into the stores anyway, to see Mrs Owens and offer his apologies for failing to appear on Saturday. He began to run suitable phrases through his mind — called away urgently — unexpected emergency — desolated to have been unable to keep so pleasant an appointment ...

He was still mulling over the best approach when he stepped up on to the sidewalk and in through the front door of the store. The bell jangled musically as he closed the door but no one responded to its summons, for all the occupants of the rear of the store were indulging in a vociferous exchange of insults and abuse at the top of their voices and the Colonel walked straight into it.

The giant Sullivan was standing in the archway that led to the saloon, remonstrating with someone just out of his line of vision.

'Look now, me darlin', would you ever put that thing away before she starts in with the hysterics again?' he implored. 'I'll give you me word he'll not touch you more.'

'She's mad. I tell you, insane! She should be locked up!' screeched Missus Carson shrilly. 'We should never have taken her on, a slut like her. Just look at her. A daughter and no wedding ring to her name! The Jezebel! She's been tempting him to damnation since she arrived here. Well, she'll not get her hands on him again, I swear!'

'*My* hands on *him?*' The young woman's voice was incredulous. 'My God! I wouldn't touch him if I was drowning in quicksand!'

She stepped out into the shaft of sunlight that slanted across the main store from the window above the door, driving Samuel Carson before her. The wretched man cringed behind his brother-in-law, shifty eyes fixed on the broad carving-knife which Mrs Owens was waving under his nose.

110

'Lay a finger on me just *once more,* I'll cut your balls off!' she hissed, emphasising each word with a slash of the knife.

Cornish blinked in astonishment, hardly able to credit what he was seeing and hearing.

'Throw her out! Throw her out!' screeched Missus Carson.

With a gesture of disdain Mrs Owens flung the knife down on the counter. 'Believe me, if I had the choice, I wouldn't stay here a moment longer than I needed!' she said scornfully.

'Go then, you – you Jezebel!'

'Don't be a fool now, Millie. Lose her and you lose a deal of custom. All the carriage trade, fer a start. Better you try to give that husband of yourn a deal more work to do out back and keep him out of the store!'

Cornish decided the comedy had come to an end. He picked up the bell on the counter and shook it vigorously.

Seeing the women distracted, Sullivan jerked his head towards the back door and Carson took the hint and fled.

'*So* sorry, Colonel Cornish,' gushed Missus Carson. 'A little difficulty with the staff. So difficult to get good hired help these days, don't you agree?'

He didn't, but this was scarcely the time or the place to say so. Now that the message was finally getting through to even the most inveterate optimist that the easy placer gold was played out, there had been a steady influx of men into Sacramento and San Francisco, together with all those for whom life at the camps was no longer providing a living wage: camp followers, cooks, storekeepers who could no longer afford the credit needed to keep their heads above water. He had had no difficulty in hiring hands by the dozen even for such an out of the way place as Tresco; if only stores payed living wages, assistants should not be too hard to come by.

'Just a few items, ma'am,' he said, passing her a short list. He had more sense than to ask for Mrs Owens or Mrs Langdon by name: only get Missus Carson out of the store and he could make his own arrangements. Deliberately, he picked up a copy of the *Tribune* that lay on the counter and leant against the wall to start reading it.

Missus Carson called shrilly for the girl to come out and

111

get the Colonel's order together and stalked off out to the back where she could be heard haranguing her husband.

The Colonel lowered his paper and looked gravely at Mrs Owens as she hurried in, list in hand, and reached up to one of the top shelves to fetch down a box of tea.

'Here, let me get that down for you,' he offered swiftly. His greater height made it easier for him to reach it, although she noticed that he did not use his left arm and consequently had to inch the container forward with just one hand.

He set it down on the mahogany counter top and turned back to her.

'Allow me to say, Mrs Owens, how very sorry I was to be unable to escort you to the soirée on Saturday,' he began.

She looked at him through narrowed eyes. 'It makes no odds, Colonel,' she replied coolly, with the tiniest inclination of her head. 'The minister was a worthy escort.'

He bowed, barely suppressing a chuckle. So she wasn't impressed by his position in society! That made a pleasing change.

'Will you take your order with you, Colonel?' she asked as she assembled the last few items. 'Or have it collected?'

'I'll take it with me,' he replied. 'Tell me, m'dear, is the other lady working out back today?'

'Missus Carson?'

'No, no. The older woman. With the child.' Still she looked blankly at him. 'Dammit, what was her name?' He consulted the scrap of paper. 'Langdon. That's it. Mrs Langdon.'

She felt as though an icy hand were squeezing her heart. Her throat went dry and she could hardly get the words out. 'There ... there ... is ... no Mrs Langdon working here.'

'But there has to be. Unless she has recently changed posts.' He thought a moment. 'In confidence, Mrs Owens, I need to find her fast. I hear she can make maps and one of the hands told me she worked here ...'

'Chen Kai ...'

'Yes, but how ...' His eyes widened as the truth began slowly to dawn on him. 'It can't be ... You're not ... Good God, she was *old!*'

'Not old, Colonel Cornish. Just sick and exhausted.'

He saw the flash of contempt in her eyes and there was

no longer any doubt in his mind that he had found Mrs Langdon.

'Your goods are ready, Colonel,' she said coldly, pushing his order across the counter at him. 'Good day.'

'No. Wait.' He placed himself between her and the door. 'I still need a mapmaker.' He thought of Tresco and swallowed his pride. 'To be honest, I'm desperate.'

She looked him straight in the eye. 'Good,' she said deliberately. 'So now you know how it feels.'

'But ...'

'Damn you, Colonel,' she said angrily. 'And damn your job.'

A child's thin wail echoed through the back of the store.

'Go see to your brat!' yelled Missus Carson from the doorway to the saloon. 'And mind, if she's not any better by tomorrow, to the Asylum she goes!'

Her eyes widened in fear and she gathered up her skirts and ran down the corridor.

Tamsin was lying in the corner of the windowless store room which had been allotted to Alicia. A truckle bed had been dragged across to the door to catch any breeze there might be, but the child was hot and feverish, blonde hair clinging damply to the flushed cheeks.

'Oh, Lisha! Beatrice thought you'd gone!' she wailed in a thin thread of a voice.

'No, my sweet,' she said in a cracking voice. 'Tell Beatrice I'll always be here when you need me.' She wrung out a cloth in a cracked basin of fragrant liquid and mopped the child's face with it. 'Now, Tamsin, drink up some more of Chen Kai's lovely drink to make you better.' She held a chipped mug to the child's lips, but she kept turning her head from side to side and spilling the amber liquid on the bedroll.

'Not lovely!' she wailed. 'It's hobbable! And Beatrice wants Chen Kai ...'

'Chen will be very offended if you say that about his medicine,' came a deep voice from the doorway.

Alicia whirled in fury to see the Colonel standing in the doorway, his broad shoulders propped against the frame.

Before she could speak the angry words that sprang to her lips, he had crossed to the bedside and taken the cup from her

113

nerveless fingers. 'Come,' he commanded. 'If you drink this up, Tamsin, I'll take you to see your friend Jo Chen. Would you like that?'

Tamsin's eyes opened very wide and she looked at him in some trepidation, but she did as she was bid, drinking down the liquid in noisy gulps. She coughed on the last few drops, but he still tilted it down her throat.

Alicia lay her back down on the bed and smoothed the curls out of her eyes. In a moment, she was asleep and Alicia stalked out of the room into the corridor, followed by her unwelcome visitor. Carefully she closed the door behind her before turning on him.

'How dare you say that to her!' she demanded indignantly. 'I don't want your job – or your charity!'

There was a swift footfall and he stepped back into the shadows as Missus Carson's head came round the door. 'If you can spare us some of your time, Mrs Owens,' said the storekeeper sarcastically, 'there are customers waiting ...'

She would have gone, but his hand shot out to detain her.

'If you stay here, she'll have the child in the Asylum tomorrow – and how much chance d'you think she'll stand there? Come with me, you'll have a well-paid job for the month at least. And the child can have a decent roof over her head and proper fresh air. By the looks of it, the fever still has a day or two to run. Jo Chen will probably have a cure for it. I can't think why you haven't sent for him.'

'I couldn't – he'd have left his post, with or without leave . . . And the town is full of men eager to step into his shoes.'

He put out his hand gently to turn her round to look at him, holding her gaze with his own. 'You know there's no choice,' he told her softly.

She knew it. Her own life she might take chances with, but not the child's. She had seen too many children die since her early years in Yerba Buena. Not just children had died, of course; men and women by the hundreds had perished in the mining camps, and not just of cholera or typhoid. In camps where milk was scarce many had died from milk poisoned by a weed the cattle occasionally ate, or from contaminated food.

114

Many after the long sea-voyages had been so weakened that they had died of something as simple as land scurvy because they had not the knowledge or the strength to seek out the native berries which would have saved them. But somehow it was always the children whose death seemed the most tragic: the hope of the future, dragged around the Horn or across the vast prairies and deserts, only to die in the Promised Land.

It did not take her long to pack up the few things that they had managed to bring from the Greys' with them and while Cornish bought the surveying equipment she would need from Sullivan, she slipped her bundles out with the Colonel's order and gave them to Jim. Then she carried Tamsin out into the livery yard.

'Goodbye, Jim,' she said softly. 'Don't tell them where we've gone. It will be easier for everyone this way.'

'Goodbye, missie. Gawd bless yer — and the li'l 'un,' said the old sailor. 'An' let's 'ope you lands in a better billet next time.'

Chapter Ten

Alicia breathed in deep lungfuls of the crystal clear air and listened to the tap-tap of the acorn woodpecker; at the approach of the carriage deer slipped away into the shadows of the oak wood.

It was a hot summer's day, but once they had left the broad brown Sacramento behind them and begun to climb up out of the valley, it became a different, more bearable, temperate heat. The sky was still blue but the metallic glare that hurt the eyes in the capital had gone and without the constant haze of dust that hung over the town the air was much fresher.

Half an hour after leaving Washington, they breasted a broad hill and she could hardly suppress an exclamation of delight : the valley of the Tresco lay at their feet, its sides scored by numerous small streams sparkling in the bright sun as they bubbled down to the Tresco, meandering through the lush green meadows in the valley bottom. The entire valley floor, as far as the eye could see, was covered with colourful summer flowers.

'It's beautiful!' she whispered in awe.

It was a view she had not seen before, for when she had been driven away in the Reverend Cooper's gig, she had not dared to look back.

It took them nearly an hour to cross the valley, clattering over the new bridge at one of the narrower points of the Tresco, and drive up to the green plateau above the river where the ranch house stood.

Near the bridge was a scatter of adobe houses with the desolate and blank appearance of houses long unlived in.

One of them had a rudimentary bell-tower on the roof.

'Mission buildings,' he explained curtly.

'But the missions never came this far, surely!'

'No. Nearest one's at Sonoma, I reckon. Mateo, who sold out to me, reckoned this was some sort of an outpost. Didn't last long. Legend is the Holy Brothers brought in some illness, wiped out all the converts. That's why there are no Indians in this valley.'

The entire upper plateau where the main house stood was surrounded by one of the great prickly nopal pear hedges that the Franciscans had planted to protect their orchards and gardens. She remembered Father Dominic at Mission San Francisco showing her how to eat the *tuna*, the fruit that grew on the great prickly hedges, and avoid the numerous tiny thorns on the skin. This hedge was high and dense, sure sign that it had been there for years.

He climbed down to open the massive gate let into the nopal hedge and she saw again how he favoured one arm as he carefully pushed the gate aside. Inside the great hedge, she could see a riot of vegetation, lilies and roses that had run wild, tangled with ancient trees, some still in blossom.

They passed beneath an archway into a large stableyard where one of the hands came to take the rig into the cool of the stables. The buildings round the back of the house were very extensive.

Cornish handed her down, then scooped Tamsin effortlessly up into his arms and strode off towards a further small archway with a curt 'This way!' to Alicia.

They passed into what had once been the garden. Various articles of farm equipment, old harrows and twisted ploughshares, cluttered it up now, but to Alicia, who had often visited the missions with her Mexican friends, the outlines of the flower beds and the herb and vegetable garden were quite clear. It was a large area, for it would have needed to supply all of the requirements of the mission – or fort – in the event of supplies not coming through from the coast, and it was all entirely surrounded by a high adobe wall that was almost completely obscured by a rampant tangle of green and purple vines.

Cornish turned sharp right and went in through a jumble

of cluttered rooms into the back of the house. Carefully he laid the sweating child down on an old high-backed carved bench.

'Guess Jo must be out in the yard,' he muttered. 'I'll go see.'

Left alone, Alicia looked around her in amazement. From the outside, there was no hint that the house was so large.

The room she was in now, which must once have been the *sala*, the main refectory hall of the mission, was about thirty feet long. On one side unglazed arched openings with folded back wooden shutters faced into the inner courtyard, empty but for a basin with a bubbling and sparkling fountain. On the other side two rougher openings had been hacked out of the adobe wall to give a look out up and down the valley. The walls themselves were badly in need of fresh whitewash and the smoke-blackened beams were thick with dust and cobwebs. More recent occupants had left behind a quantity of ornately carved dark oak furniture, but that too was dry and cracked and filthy. Later residents had not been as concerned by defensive considerations, for a herringbone pattern of poles and split juniper had been laid between the massive roof beams, and split boards laid above them to form a second storey, access to which was up an exquisitely ornate staircase set against the centre of the inner wall.

'Alicia?'

As usual, she had not heard Kai come in. She whirled, her face lightened by a delighted smile.

'Kai! Oh, it is so *good* to see you again!' she exclaimed, rushing across to grasp his hands.

They stood for a moment, hands locked tightly, while he scanned her face. 'Corr-onel tells me there was trouble at Carsons' store,' he said anxiously.

'Trouble?' Her eyes took on that blank look he dreaded so much. He wondered if he had not done more harm than good by giving her those herbs in San Francisco. They had helped then, hazing her memory of what had happened, but he had never intended her to go on taking them for so long.

With a smile, he patted her cheek softly. 'No matter. You look better now,' he murmured.

'Hardly surprising!' she replied wryly. 'Even the little I

had to eat at Carsons' was better than — before.' Her voice cracked on the words. 'You never told me how dreadful I looked, Kai. Colonel Cornish thought I was an old woman.'

'You must have come as something of a surprise to him!'

'More than you might think! You see, he'd already met me — but knew me as Mrs Owens.'

'A good thought,' he agreed gravely. 'But the little one, Alicia? Corr-onel tells me she is sick.'

'A fever,' she replied abruptly, willing him not to ask why she had not kept her promise and sent for him. 'I tried to get a doctor, but I hadn't enough money. He said to wait until she was in the Asylum, then the Town Council would pay him to treat her.'

'Doctor!' He almost spat the word out in disgust. 'Most of them would not know a childhood fever from the plague, even when they are sober — and that's not often.'

He crossed to where Tamsin lay, very still, wrapped in the Colonel's travelling cape; he felt her forehead and smelt her breath.

'It is well, Alicia,' he pronounced with a sigh of relief. 'Something she has taken from other children, no doubt. But not serious. I will give her a draught. She will sleep perhaps one more day and then she will be better.'

'Thank God!' She sat down abruptly, and quite unexpectedly burst into tears. 'I was so worried!' she sobbed. 'If anything had happened to her, it would have been my fault!'

'But it did not,' soothed Chen Kai. 'And now you are here she will have fresh air and good food. And so will you.' He raised his head. 'Hush now! Corr-onel is coming and it will not do for him to find you weeping.'

When Cornish came back into the room, she was gazing out of one of the windows, up the valley to the road they had travelled along that hot, dusty day when they had first come to Tresco from One Horse Town.

'There's a shortage of clean rooms, Jo,' he said, 'so they'd better bed down in your room tonight. Then tomorrow you can find something better. Get a couple of the boys to help you. There won't be much chow to prepare: I want as many of

119

the hands as possible out riding the boundaries. I wouldn't put it past Lamarr to use the old trick with professional squatters, even if it risked a repeat of the '50 War!'

In 1850, squatters, some genuine, some hired by ambitious men, had taken over what they considered still to be public land. The Squatter's War that followed the eviction had resulted in the shooting of the Mayor and the murder of Sheriff McKinney, but the practice of hiring a 'professional' squatter and encouraging him to stake a claim on a rival's land had still not died out.

It did not take Chen long to clear his traps out of the room he had been occupying up to now, a high and airy chamber which seemed to have been tacked on between the kitchens and the courtyard almost as an afterthought, and a rope bed was soon knocked together for Tamsin.

She woke as they carried her through the kitchen. Her eyelids flickered and then she opened her eyes wide and looked up into the face of the man who was carrying her. The fear on her face turned swiftly to joy.

'Chen Kai!' she whispered in tones of wonder. 'Oh, Chen Kai, you didn't forget us! You came for us, like Lisha said!'

She clung to him and would not let him go.

The shadows were lengthening before Chen was able to slip his hand out of Tamsin's loosened grip and head for the kitchens.

'I regret, Corr-onel, chow will be a little late tonight,' apologised Chen as he met his employer in the garden.

The rancher laid aside the knife he had been sharpening on the whetstone and sniffed the air.

'If that ain't chow, I don't know what it is. Smells good,' he said appreciatively. 'Should have known it wasn't yours! Let's go see.'

A pot of savoury stew was bubbling away over the fire and at the side the griddle was heating to cook the hotcakes to serve with it.

'My! That's the best smell this kitchen's known since the Holy Brothers moved out!' exclaimed the Colonel.

'Some of the smells in this kitchen have been here ever since they left!' she replied drily, jerking her head to the piles of

120

papers and accumulated rubbish at the far end of the kitchen. 'I'm surprised at you, Chen Kai! How you could cook in such a mess, let alone have people eat in the middle of it!'

'That's down to me, I guess,' said Cornish. 'Some of those papers are important, but they're so mixed in with the rubbish that I can't move anything till I've had a chance to sort through.'

'Papers would be much safer in one of the inner rooms, away from the fire,' she said decisively. 'Leave them much longer and you'll have rats in here.'

'Anything else you'd care to reorganise for me?' asked the Colonel sardonically, propping his shoulders against the wall and surveying her through narrowed eyes. 'I'd remind you, Mrs Langdon − or do you prefer Mrs Owens? − that you were hired on to make a map for me. That's all I require of you. I'd advise you to take a leaf out of Jo's book and confine yourself to your proper duties.'

She returned him look for look for a brief moment, then deliberately took off the old flour sack that she had tied over her dress for an apron and handed it to Kai.

'I'll be with Tamsin until my services are required.'

She nodded coolly and strode out of the room, forcing him to step aside. Outside the door stood Kerhouan.

'Damned arrogant woman!' growled Cornish, looking angrily after her. 'I knew it was a mistake! Trying to organise me before she's even got her foot in the door ...'

Kerhouan saw the mutinous look in Chen's face and hurried into the breach. '*Eh bien*, most people who clash with strong-minded women end up eating humble pie − we just end up eating Jo's terrible cooking again!'

'Hah!' It was as much a bark as a laugh, but the confrontation was avoided.

It took Cornish nearly an hour to sort out what he wanted from the untidy pile of papers in the corner, but by the time the food had been carried out to the barn, now a bunkhouse for the hands, he thought he had got most of it ready.

He strode back across the courtyard to the kitchen, just in time to see the woman heading towards the outbuildings.

'Hey! Where are you off to?' he called. 'Jo's just serving up!'

She turned to look at him, surprise on her face.

'To the bunkhouse,' she replied. 'I'm told that's where the hired hands eat.'

'Serve you right if I let you go ahead and eat there!' he snapped. 'That'd sure be an eye-opener for you!'

'You think so?' she enquired, eyebrows raised demurely.

'Field hands eat in the bunkhouse,' he said brusquely. 'House hands eat in the kitchen, unless the boss invites them to eat with him.'

She made no move to answer, but stooped to smell one of the flowering vines that clambered up the old adobe wall that ran around the garden.

'So I'm inviting you,' he went on, in tones that sounded churlish even to him.

She looked at him measuringly, then abruptly nodded her head. 'I accept your invitation.'

When they'd eaten, Chen Kai went to take a sleeping draught to Tamsin. Alicia rose and started to clear the dishes.

'Leave them, leave them,' said Cornish impatiently. He pulled a dog-eared map out of the vast pile at his elbow. 'This is the map we worked on when I bought out Mateo — there's Lamarr's section to the north, over as far as Washington. And this one —' he pulled out an even more tattered parchment ' — is the one Mateo worked on when he bought from Carillo. Then this is the Bidwell map of '44 that Larkin reprinted in '50; we based the confirmation of the land grants on that. This is the document from Micheltorena confirming the first land grant, and this is the one from Alvarado confirming it again after Micheltorena had been overthrown — or that's what I'm told for I don't read Spanish — at least, not this kind of legal mumbo-jumbo. Only thing all these maps have in common, to my untrained eye at least, is that they are all different and all equally inaccurate.'

'Of course they are! No one had then properly surveyed the area. That was not done until my —' She paused and bit her lip. 'I believe,' she continued in deliberately controlled tones, 'that no accurate map was available until '54 when the army released the Wilkes map.'

122

'None of which helps me.'

'Except that no one can possibly produce anything more accurate. And the intention of the contracts is all we can hope to prove, surely?'

He did not answer her but continued to stare at the maps as if he would wrest the truth from them. Then, with a sudden movement that made her jump, he rolled the maps up together and laid them firmly on one side.

'Lamarr'd give a lot to get his hands on those,' muttered Kerhouan.

'You know where to keep them,' replied the rancher gravely. 'They're your responsibility when I'm not here.'

'*Soit!* I will not let you down.' He reached out for the bottle and poured himself another whiskey, gazing down into the amber liquid as if it held the answer to all their problems.

Cornish turned back to Alicia.

'Can you be ready to leave at first light?' he demanded.

'Whenever you wish. But — forgive me — should we not take the maps with us? How else can we check the boundaries?'

'I know each one like the back of my hand,' he grinned. 'We'll take one of the hands with us. He'll read you out the bits in the contract where the boundaries are described.'

'But wouldn't it be better if ...'

'Until the morning, Mrs Owens, good night.' He turned away deliberately and refilled his glass.

It was a rebuff, a dismissal. She had tried to help and he had not even waited to hear her out. She rose and pushed the chair back angrily. She turned away and saw Kai standing in the doorway.

'How is she?' demanded Alicia anxiously.

'She sleeps. No more need for worry.'

'Good.' She stepped away from the table and shook out her crushed skirts. 'I'll sit with her tonight.'

'No, you won't!' snapped the rancher. 'I'll need you fresh in the morning.'

123

'Do not worry, Corr-onel,' said Chen reassuringly. 'The child will sleep.'

'Pah!' Kerhouan, who had been drinking morosely, suddenly slammed his glass down on the table, making them all jump. 'Lamarr uses the best lawyers, the best Spanish-speaking clerks in Sacramento to drive you out!' he exclaimed in disgust. 'And you – you go to rely on a half-educated Mexican who speaks worse English than me!'

'Not to fret, Kerhouan!' chuckled Chen. 'Mrs Owens learnt the best Castilian Spanish from the *Alcalde's* confessor and Mexican Spanish from her servants. You have no need of any of the hands.'

He took Alicia firmly by the arm and guided her out of the room before anyone could say anything more. In silence they walked across the yard to Chen's room. There, out of earshot of the others, she turned on her friend.

'Kai!' She looked at him wide-eyed with fear. 'You shouldn't have told them! Now they could find out who I am – perhaps about San Francisco!' Her voice was rising in panic.

'I think not.' He shrugged fatalistically. 'I think they are too busy with their own problems to care who we are, where we are from. But think: if Corr-onel loses Tresco, then we will be back on the road again.' He looked at her consideringly, his head on one side. 'And you are not yet strong enough for that. So – we do all we can to help him keep Tresco. You make him his maps for one month, more if we are lucky. I can work here maybe six months or more. Corr-onel Jack has great plans for Tresco once he has dealt with Lamarr. He pays well and we can save much – perhaps you can go back east, if you want, leave it all behind you.' He paused and grinned at her. 'Anyway, I like him.'

'Like him? That ill-mannered arrogant woman-hater! Kai, how can you?'

He smiled gently. 'Perhaps because I am not a woman! Now, sleep well, Alicia. I will call you before first light.

There is a potion on the table in case Tamsin wakes. And here — this is for you.'

A wild dove cooing on the roof of the *portal* outside her window woke her with the dawn. Rising quietly so as not to disturb Tamsin, she stretched, picked up the ewer on the table, threw a shawl around her shoulders and slipped out of the door and into the garden.

She drew the bucket up quietly from the well in the middle of the deserted stableyard and filled the ewer. The dove had settled back into its nest again and the silence was total. Above her, the sapphire sky was lightening to a pale azure as the sun rose above the Sierras. She wandered across to the archway and gazed down the valley, watching as the early sun caught the sparkling waters of the Tresco down below, dispersed the tule fog that hung over the distant valley of the Sacramento and tipped the far towering peaks of the Sierras with rose.

She became aware of another presence in the yard and turned, expecting to see Kai. It was Colonel Cornish. She drew nervously back into the shadows in the lea of the wall and pulled her shawl more closely around her, poised for flight.

His hand shot out to take her arm in a surprisingly strong grip.

'Don't go,' he said softly, dropping his hand. 'Five minutes will make no difference. This is my favourite time of the day — not to be rushed.'

They stood there, side by side, not speaking, for no words were necessary, just watching as the land, the beautiful, fertile, magnificent land reawoke in the warmth of the sun.

A door slammed on the far side of the yard and the mood was broken.

'I — I had better hurry,' she smiled weakly. 'Chen Kai will be sounding the iron for chow ...'

'You must be the only one who hurries for Jo's chow!' he chuckled. 'Go on — off you go. Time to see to the child before we leave.'

A different man from the night before!

They lost their early start while a suitable rig was found for her, for the only sidesaddle in the stables was of such antiquated design and so worn that she flatly refused to use it. She marched into the stables, to the surprise of the men working there, and selected for herself one of the smaller saddles with a high cantle and pommel.

'I don't need sidebars and footboards,' she said crisply. 'If one of your men can put plain stirrups and *mochilas* on this, I will do very well.'

Not one of the men on Tresco was without experience with horses and all to do with them and several hurried forward to help, taking the opportunity at the same time to have a surreptitious look at the newcomer. Within twenty minutes, it was done. Kerhouan threw an extra saddle blanket over the top and at last they were off.

Glancing sideways at Cornish as they rode down the valley she was not at all surprised to see the customary scowl on his face.

'Look on the bright side, Colonel,' she said, a barely suppressed chuckle in her soft voice. 'How much worse if I couldn't ride at all!'

'That's a thought that's been exercising my mind for the last half hour,' he admitted with a twisted smile. 'I was so surprised when I found you were the mapmaker Jo had recommended —'

'Horrified might be more accurate.'

'Horrified,' he agreed. 'So horrified, it never occurred to me to ask whether you could ride. And there are no tracks up-valley for even the toughest carts.'

'Lucky for you then,' she observed drily. 'Y'know, I can't help wondering ...'

'What?'

'You dislike females so much and I know you're not really convinced I can make you a decent map so —' She raised her eyebrows. 'So why did you take me on?'

'What else could I do?' he asked in disgust.

She looked around her at the broad fertile fields of the valley bottom, the cattle grazing in the distance. 'Tresco is rich. Why not simply pay the Land Commission officials whatever they want to put the judgement in your favour? Outbribe Lamarr.'

His face darkened, marred by a black scowl.

'You wouldn't understand.'

She shrugged. 'Then explain it to me.'

He looked at her through narrowed eyes. 'I didn't need to explain it to Chen. He understood. But then,' he shrugged, 'he's a man.'

She said nothing.

'If I did as you suggest, then Lamarr would have won. Tresco would always be tarnished and I'd always be beholden to the men I'd bribed.'

'I admire you for your honesty and principles.'

'I didn't bring you to Tresco to discuss my principles!' he growled. 'You're the lesser of the two evils and that's all there is to it.'

'So polite!'

'I don't have time for the sort of namby-pamby society talk you ladies require!' he snapped.

'I'm not a lady!' she snapped back. 'I work for my living like any paid hand!' She put her heels to her horse. 'So let's get on with it!' she called back over her shoulder.

The first day's surveying took them through the fertile acres of Tresco's holdings down in the valley of the Sacramento — little chance of argument there, since the river itself formed the boundary, with rights of navigation automatically ceded to the holder — but once they moved away from the river, accuracy became more important, for this was the border with Lamarr's lands.

Cornish had been sceptical about the army training Chen had claimed for her, but when he watched her map out with a practised eye and hand every natural landmark exactly as it occurred in the land grant documents, he had to admit, grudgingly, that she knew her job.

'Your husband train you?' he asked as he set out her chalks for her at the head of the dry gulch that she was mapping.

'No.'

'Who?'

'A — a relative. He made maps — in the Army.'

'Back east?'

127

'No.'

'Don't give much away, do you?'

'I've never been required to give my life history to an employer before,' she replied curtly.

'You're not required now,' he conceded. 'I was just curious. You must admit, you and the child and Jo Chen — it's a strange set up. Enough to make anyone curious.'

'See that cairn?' she interrupted him. 'That's the kind of boundary mark you've got to look out for. Rivers and gulches, they're no real problem. They don't usually shift — or if they do, the whole world knows of it. But a cairn can be shifted overnight — and then who's to say it was ever anywhere else?'

She put her drawing pad aside, kilted up her skirts and stepped forward to the edge of the gully. To his astonishment, she dropped down on to her stomach and wriggled even further forward, holding her pencil out before her and squinting along it.

'Whatever are you doing?' he demanded.

'Triangulating,' she responded absently. 'Fix that cairn against three fixed points — hills, mountains, tall trees, whatever — and you've fixed its position. Of course, there's only us to say it's where we say it is but ...'

He had been about to offer her his hand to help her up, but she froze and stared straight past him.

'What's the matter?'

'Make a photographic plate of it! Of course! Why didn't anyone think of that before?'

'Photograph the scenery?' He shook his head in despair. 'If that isn't just like a woman!' He looked out across the gulch and back down towards the valley with a jaundiced eye. 'Daresay it's a good vista, but it'll still be there next year. Which is more than Tresco will be if I don't get that map made.'

'If you'd just stop regarding me as an empty-headed idiot, you and I might get on a little better and progress a little faster!' she said crisply. 'I am no more interested in the vista than you! But if we took plates of all the boundary markers — from three points, if necessary — then we have a permanent record, don't you see?'

128

'By God, you're right!' he exclaimed, his eyes wide. 'And if we had copies made, we could send them to the Federal Land Office, here and in Washington!'

'We'd still need the map,' she cautioned.

'Oh, of course,' he agreed. 'The map may prove to be sufficient in itself – but the photographs! They would put paid to any nonsense Lamarr might think up about moving markers or putting squatters in in the future.'

He reached down and jerked her to her feet. Holding on to her wrist he grinned down at her, eyes sparkling. Then suddenly the light died out of his eyes. 'Damnation!' he swore softly.

'What is it?'

'That brings us back to our starting-point!' he said angrily. 'Where can I find a photographer who can keep his mouth shut and who hasn't already been got at by Lamarr? Virtually impossible, without alerting the whole of Sacramento to what we're doing!'

'Don't fret, Colonel Cornish,' she reassured him. 'You see, that was our trade.'

He frowned. 'Daguerrotyping? *That* was what you did round the camps?'

She nodded.

'Mrs Owens! I may live to bless the day when you persuaded Jo Chen to stay on at Tresco!'

She smiled a wicked smile and slowly shook her head. 'Not him,' she murmured.

'Not . . .? Oh no, don't tell me . . .' His face was a picture, as conflicting emotions warred for supremacy.

'Chen Kai has many talents and skills which I could never hope to master,' she laughed, 'but he cannot take a decent plate to save his life!'

He was quiet for the rest of the morning, holding the surveying stick while she adjusted the theodolite, carrying her board for her and generally keeping out of her way when he was not needed.

In the afternoon they came up with a couple of the ranch hands riding patrol along the boundary, which at that point followed a small creek.

'Any sign of trouble?' asked Cornish anxiously.

129

'Not a sniff of it,' replied the older man, who spoke in a strong Scottish accent with overtones of Georgia. 'Just being here'll be enough to keep them off, for you could see them coming for miles.' He gestured across to the open land on the far side of the creek. 'Lachie was about to pour some coffee, if you'd join us ...?' His voice trailed off as he took in the sight of the woman behind the Colonel.

Cornish dismounted. 'I'm sure Mrs Owens would appreciate a rest as much as I would,' he replied heartily, hoping she would not think herself above sitting with the hands.

'More!' exclaimed Alicia, urging her mare forward. 'I'd forgotten just how long it was since I'd been on horseback!'

She winced as she tried to bring her leg over the pommel to dismount. Impeded by the heavy skirts and with the mare restless under the unaccustomed handling, she looked as though she might end up on the dusty ground. Cornish swiftly crossed to her side, picked her up easily by the waist and lifted her down to the ground.

She bit her lip in annoyance.

'I can usually manage by myself,' she protested.

'I know it.' He spoke softly and his eyes, when he looked down at her, were gentle and understanding.

'Thank you, Colonel,' she murmured — and meant it.

Sitting in the sunshine on a small rocky outcrop while the coffee bubbled on the fire, looking across the drifts of blue ookow lilies and the clumps of yellow rock roses to the Sierras, she thought how happy she could be in such a peaceful place. Sharply she shook her head to dispel such foolish thoughts. She could not afford to grow sentimental. Within a month, two at most, she would be back in Sacramento again, trailing around the milliners and dressmakers, looking for another position to support her and Tamsin. She took a heartening sip of the strong hot coffee.

The younger man, Lachie, was speaking to her.

'I beg your pardon?'

'I was asking, ma'am, if you hailed from San Francisco? I've a notion your face is familiar.'

'Not San Francisco, no,' she replied hurriedly. 'We always lived further north — much further north.'

'Shasta, would that be?' enquired Calum Mackechnie.

'We were there for some time,' she said airily. 'All round the northern mines.'

'Owens,' mused Mackechnie. 'Don't rightly remember that name though.'

She glanced up from her coffee to find Cornish's cool gaze on her. She looked away again swiftly; she could only hope he thought the matter of the name not worth bothering about.

By the end of the day they had surveyed and mapped all the way along from the Sacramento to the border with Lamarr's territory and were heading towards what had been McDowell's and was now the little town of Washington. As the sun began to dip towards the peaks of the Coast Range, they packed their gear and turned back to Tresco. It had been a long day.

Chapter Eleven

Chen Kai hurried out to help her down from the saddle with the little girl close on his heels.

'Tamsin!' she exclaimed in surprise, holding out her arms to hug the child warmly.

'Hello, Lisha!' she said with a grin. 'Chen Kai let me get up after lunch and we fed the doves. Look, aren't they pretty?' She pointed up to the roof where the white doves sat gently cooing, picturesque against the warm red tiles. 'Chen Kai says there's an old dovecote on the other side of the fort, but he wouldn't take me there today . . .'

'Tamsin,' she chided the child gently. 'Colonel Cornish will think you have forgotten your manners.'

The child put her hand up to her mouth with a little giggle. 'I'm sorry, Lisha!' She turned to Cornish, who was unbuckling the saddle from the powerful stallion he rode before handing him over to Luis to take to the stables. She crossed to stand in front of the rancher and held out her hand. 'How do you do, Colonel Cornish?'

He bent down to take her hand, smiling at such formality from so small a child. 'I am very well, I thank you. The better for seeing you recovered.'

'Oh, I'm *much* better now,' she said enthusiastically. 'And I'm glad you let Lisha and me come and see Chen Kai again. I *did* miss him so much!' Then, disconcertingly, 'I've seen you before, haven't I?' She tilted her head to one side to look up at him curiously.

'When Jo Chen came to work at Tresco,' he replied gravely. 'And I think I saw you at Miss Cooper's house, though I didn't realise then that you were Jo's friend.'

'Oh, yes! I liked it there. I hope Lisha will take me there again.'

'I'm sure Miss Cooper would be delighted to see you again. Perhaps next Sunday ...' he began, then pulled himself up short, aghast.

Alicia saw the sudden change of expression on his face.

'Come, Tamsin,' she commanded, in a voice that brooked no discussion. 'We must not trouble the Colonel. I am here to do a job, not go a-visiting.'

Chen Kai had exceeded his instructions and, instead of preparing one of the upstairs rooms, had cleaned out two rooms which opened on to the verandah which ran round the courtyard, so that she would be by the main house and yet independent of the household.

When she entered the outer room, her eye first took in the bright Mexican rug that covered the earth floor, then the motley collection of furniture that Kai had gathered together. She was too tired to do more than murmur thanks to him, but he had seen her eyes light up with pleasure as she walked in and that was sufficient reward for him.

Half an hour later Cornish wandered into the kitchen to find Chen gazing anxiously into the cauldron.

'Mrs Owens joining us later?' he asked casually.

'I think not, Corr-onel,' replied the cook. 'She is tired. Not that the work was too hard for her,' he hastened to assure him, 'but it is long since she sat a horse and she is stiff. What she needs is a hot bath. I gave her some stew. She may already be asleep.'

'Damnation!'

'I am very sorry, Corr-onel. If we had known ...'

'Not your fault, Jo. Nor hers. I suppose it was only to be expected she'd be saddlesore. But I'd hoped to discuss this idea of hers to buy a camera. Still, you can advise me on that, no doubt.'

'She ... wants ... you ... to ... buy ... a ... camera?' asked Chen carefully.

'Yes. Great idea of hers. Make plates showing the boundary

133

markers in their proper place, to submit to the Land Register ...'

'She is mad!' Chen's face had gone the colour of old ivory.

'Oh, I don't know. If she can do it at the same time as the mapping, I don't see it will slow us down any. When you've got got that stew sorted out, perhaps we can discuss equipment ...'

'*So* sorry, Corr-onel,' said Chen, bowing submissively. 'Would help, but I was only humble assistant. I know nothing of such matters.'

Cornish narrowed his eyes suspiciously, but Chen only gazed back at him impassively.

'Oh, damn you, get on with the cooking!' he growled in exasperation, and turned on his heel and stormed out.

Cornish and Kerhouan dined together in the overheated kitchen and then, after the strong-flavoured mess had been cleared away, Cornish resolutely sat down to sort through some more of the papers.

Leaving Luis and Xavier to clear away in the bunkhouse and clean the dishes, Chen Kai hurried across the courtyard to knock urgently on the door of Alicia's room.

'Who is it?' came a sleepy voice at last.

'Me. Kai.'

She opened the door in her nightdress, drawing a shawl around her shoulders, barely managing to suppress a yawn.

'Corr-onel speaks of a camera,' he snapped.

'Yes. Isn't it a good idea? If we can fix the positions of the boundary markers, it will give added weight to the map.'

'And of course it was your suggestion? A good way to show Corr-onel you are not the witless person he holds all women to be?'

'You don't think I did it just for that? Chen Kai! Just for my own pride? Of course it's not essential as the map is. But it will help his claim, really it will!'

'And who will go into Sacramento and buy this camera?' he demanded angrily. 'Corr-onel Cornish?'

'Of course not!' She furrowed her brow at his slowness of understanding. 'He knows nothing of cameras!'

'So you or I will go into Sacramento and walk into King's or

Beal's Daguerrean Gallery and select one?' he hissed. 'Alicia, I think you left your brains behind when you came out of prison!'

'I — I — never thought ... but nobody cares in Sacramento ... we're far enough away from San Francisco.'

'Do you think that there are so many cameras bought in California that news of a lady or a Chinaman buying one will not filter through, back to San Francisco, where Beal or King go to collect their supplies? And if it comes to Fisher's ears? Do you think he can no longer put two and two together? Or do you think he will look in his mirror and tell himself that it no longer matters?'

'What can we do?' she whispered.

'We have to explain to Corr-onel Jack —'

'No! Not all of it, Kai? I — I couldn't bear it! I just couldn't!'

He heard the rising hysteria in her voice. 'Alicia! Stop it!' He grasped her shoulders and shook her roughly.

She caught her breath on a shuddering sob. Pressing her hands to her mouth as if she could force the sobs back, she looked round the little room with wide, tragic eyes.

'I felt safe here,' she said tragically. ' "The pretty green place" Tamsin calls it. A refuge, an oasis. And now I've put it all at risk with one thoughtless, boastful remark.' The tears were streaming unheeded down her pale cheeks. 'Must we go on the road again, Kai?' she whispered brokenly.

'No! We haven't come through all this just to be beaten by that bastard!' His voice hardened. 'Dry your eyes, Alicia. Leave this to me.'

'Then you'll tell him ...'

'As much as I have to,' he said with a shrug. 'And as little as I can get away with.'

She didn't expect to sleep again that night, but the exhaustion of her body overcame the turmoil of her mind and she was soon asleep, to dream of wide open spaces and green hills, of prison bars and the hangman's noose.

As Chen Kai closed the door noiselessly behind him, he saw a movement across by the stable entrance and whipped out his knife.

'Who's there?' he hissed.

A light flared and Colonel Cornish stepped out of the shadows.

'It's me, Jo,' he declared, a trifle impatiently. 'Who in Hell did you think it was?' As he turned the lantern on the other man, he saw the flash of the knife in his hand. 'I've told you before about that damned knife of yours — you're a deal too ready with it. What would you have done if it had been one of the hands? Stuck the blade in him?'

'I — I thought it was someone listening ...' stammered Chen lamely.

'Listening to what, for God's sake?' he demanded irritably.

'I think I have to talk to you,' responded Chen softly, putting the knife away as he spoke.

When they were seated at the table in the kitchen, he sat and gazed down at his hands for a few moments.

'Corr-onel, I believe you are an honourable man. What I say to you now, let it go no further. Tell no one, not even Ker-hwan. In this I trust you.'

Cornish nodded.

'You remember, Corr-onel, I told you Alicia — Mrs Owens — and I, we travelled round the mining camps? You have realised by now that Alicia took daguerrotypes.'

'A talented woman. But why give it up? Lack of customers?'

'No. We didn't give up willingly, I assure you!' He laughed harshly. 'We were very successful!' It was not a boast, but a statement of fact. 'We had our own wagon, and in time also our own studio in San Francisco. They flocked to it: the traders, the miners on the town, the saloon girls, the gamblers ... Ay me, the gamblers!' He sighed heavily. 'And that was our undoing.'

'How so?'

'A man — I spit on the grave of his ancestors! — a man came to the studio with one of his whores. A bad man, an evil man, but in San Francisco very powerful. My friend had come across him before I knew her. He was, it seems, obsessed with her. They had words. Very foolish.' He shook his head over the folly of it. 'From that day on our fortunes changed. Small things at first. Thefts of chemicals. And then the props.'

'Props? The only props I know are pit props – and what would they be doing in a daguerrotyper's studio?'

'Properties. It is, I believe, a theatrical term. In our business, you do not just need a camera and tripod. Many of the miners who come to have their likeness taken want to impress their families back east with their prosperity. We lend them – lent them – a fancy coat, a top hat, a gold watch chain; in the studio we had velvet curtains for them to be photographed against, an elegant little antique table with a tasteful plant ...'

'Good God!'

'It is as important as the skill of the photographer,' agreed Chen solemnly. 'Mrs Langdon – Alicia – often said that the gilt on the frame of the photograph was the nearest most of them ever got to gold.'

'A perceptive woman,' he assented gravely. 'And so these – er – props went astray?'

'We did not despair. We had savings. We bought more. Then one day a miner came in – blind drunk – stumbled against the tripod and smashed the camera. By accident, it was said. And suddenly, no one could sell us a new camera. Three days later, our studio burnt down.'

'There are many fires in San Francisco ...'

'On a damp day in autumn? No. It was no accident. I smelt the oil myself.' And heard the child's screams, he remembered, reliving for a moment the horror of the realisation that Tamsin was still in there.

'But you still had the wagon?' The rancher's voice brought him sharply back to the present.

'Yes. We were in Coloma, trying to persuade an old man to sell us his camera, when our enemy finally sprang the trap on us. A note signed by her husband, pledging the wagon to this man against a gambling debt. And a sheriff's man to enforce it.' He sighed. 'It was a lie, of course, for there *was* no wagon until after her husband's death. But they took it!' He banged his fist on the table in sheer frustration at the memory. 'Although they had no use for it, they took it.'

'But some of it was your share. Surely he had no claim to that part?'

'For the sake of your ranch, Corr-onel, I hope you are not really so ignorant of the laws regarding property. Not only can a Chinee not give evidence in court, he cannot hold property. Any claims I might have had had no standing in California law.'

'So what did you do?'

Chen hesitated a moment, biting his lip, and Cornish wondered if he would hear any more.

'There was much trouble – much. And so we had to leave.'

'No wonder the poor woman looked so worn,' said the rancher sympathetically. 'But who is this enemy?'

'Better you do not know. I only tell you this so you understand that it is out of the question for either Alicia or me to buy a camera. We have finished with that life – this must be a new start.'

'You surely don't think this enemy is still looking for you?' he demanded incredulously.

Chen rose to his feet. 'Corr-onel, I bid you goodnight,' he stated.

'So be it,' agreed the rancher reluctantly. 'Then we'll stick to the maps.'

When Alicia awoke the next morning, she found a note pushed under the door.

'No more worry', wrote Chen Kai in his customary scrawl. 'All is settled. Say nothing. Colonel is an honourable man'.

'Good morning, Mrs Owens,' said Cornish with the hearty air of a man who had already been up some hours. 'Ready to leave shortly?'

'Whenever you wish, Colonel.' She reached over to straighten Tamsin's apron.

'Lisha's legs are hurting her from the horse riding,' piped up Tamsin.

'Tamsin!' snapped Alicia angrily. 'Little girls should speak when they are spoken to!' She felt herself colouring furiously under the rancher's keen scrutiny. 'Now eat your bread and

138

be quiet.' She poured some more coffee into her mug. 'Pray take no notice of the child, Colonel Cornish. I shall be ready as soon as you require.'

'At your convenience, Mrs Owens,' he said with a slight inclination of the head. 'Another hot day, by the looks of it. Today we will survey the lower land grant section.' He paused as though struck by a pleasing notion. 'The lower land grant section,' he repeated, then turned sharply on his heel and out into the yard, shouting for Jo Chen.

In a few moments he was back.

'I'll just fetch my equipment,' she said hastily, rising from the chair with a wince that did not go unnoticed.

'Jo's in the yard collecting up all the linen for a washing day,' the Colonel informed her casually. 'Anything you or the child want washed, get it for him now.'

He saw her hesitation. 'No room on a ranch for false modesty, ma'am,' he said laconically. 'I doubt you'll have any time for laundry these next three or four weeks.'

When she finally tracked Chen Kai down she was surprised to see him outside the stables, loading baskets of washing into an old-fashioned solid wheel cart, the like of which she had not seen since her first years in California.

'Kai! Whatever is going on?'

'Corr-onel Jack says we go into the foothills to do the washing.'

'But who will look after Tamsin?'

'Tamsin is coming with us,' came Cornish's voice from the doorway. Alicia turned swiftly to see him emerge from the shadows with Tamsin perched on his shoulders, held up by one hand, chuckling as they jogged along.

'In you go, young lady,' he ordered, swinging her down easily and depositing her in the back of the cart. 'Get in, Mrs Owens. Luis! Xavier! Come on, you rascals! Where's that basket?'

The two young lads, no more than thirteen or fourteen, came puffing across the yard, carrying a large wicker basket between them.

Their father Juan hitched two riding horses to the back of the wagon, then climbed up to the front of the carriage and clicked his tongue at the great heavy carthorses harnessed in

139

tandem to the shafts. They headed away from the river, along a barely visible track which led up into the lower hills.

A questioning look at Kai brought nothing but a shrug of the shoulders. Exasperated, Alicia leant back in the chariot and, as the warmth of the early morning sun soothed her, she determined to let the day take care of itself.

The broad beautiful valley was unfenced and dotted with browsing wild horses and longhorn cattle. After an hour of bumping and jolting which no spoked cart wheel could ever have stood up to, the chariot turned into a smaller canyon and among the oaks she could see plumes of smoke rising.

'*Agua caliente*, Mrs Owens,' announced the Colonel, drawing his horse alongside.

Hot springs! Not smoke, then, but steam!

The chariot drew up at the foot of a gentle slope and everyone climbed out. Above them twin streams tumbled down the hillside, cascading through two series of pools marked by columns of steam; water, strong with minerals, flowed over the rim of one crusted basin to the next until at last they ran together at the foot of the slope and flowed down a worn channel to the broader stream at the end of the canyon. The whole hillside was thickly covered with ancient oaks and patches of willow which screened each basin from the next.

The horses were released from the shafts and turned loose to eat the wild oats that grew so profusely at the lower end of the canyon, while Luis and Xavier, no strangers to the *agua caliente*, began to carry the sacks of linen to the lower basin. They rubbed soap on the linen and then jumped into the basin to trample the laundry on the rocks until it was clean. To high spirited lads, the splashing and leaping was as much play as work and Chen Kai had to do no more than supervise.

Cornish cleared a patch of ground away from the open breezy grassland and built a fire. He set a pot to boil for coffee, then wandered across to Alicia, still standing by the cart.

'Now, Mrs Owens, if you and Tamsin would care to take the first dip in the top basin?' He laughed at the look of doubt on her face. 'It is very well screened, Juan is down with the horses, the boys are under Jo's watchful eye and I have a

140

feast to prepare.' He picked up a saddlebag and passed it to her. 'I think you will find all you need in there. Believe me, you'll feel much better for it: the hot springs are better than ordinary water for aches and pains and we must have you back in the saddle by this afternoon.'

Alicia closed her eyes and lay back in the hot water of the mineral spring pool, letting the warmth seep into her tired limbs and draw out the chafings and aches that the day in the saddle had brought about. Tamsin sat in the shallows, splashing and chuckling, singing one of her little songs to herself.

In the lower cascades she could hear the two young boys calling and whistling in high spirits, with the occasional deeper voice of Juan or Chen Kai calling them to order when they got a little too carried away. The upper cascade was well sheltered from below by a tangled screen of goat willow and alder trees in which the birds were singing merrily to one another. The sun beat down on their faces and Alicia had to make a great effort to stop herself falling asleep as the little waves caused by Tamsin's splashing slapped at her body.

At last she dragged herself out of her torpor and began to wash Tamsin vigorously with the hunk of soap she had found in the saddlebag, together with a couple of huckaback towels and clean linen for herself and Tamsin. She could only hope it had been Chen Kai who had put it there!

Tamsin was fidgety and rather cross about being taken away from her splashing games and she wriggled energetically under Alicia's hands until at last the soap went into her eyes and she howled.

'Hush, Tamsin,' chided Alicia. 'The men will hear you,' The last thing she wanted to do was remind the Colonel of the 'burden' of the child. Why, this day of all days, could she not behave?

'Don't care!' screamed the child defiantly. 'My eyes hurt!'

Impatiently Alicia splashed clean water in Tamsin's eyes. 'There now, it's gone!' she snapped. 'Now for goodness' sake, hush that noise. Get out and dry yourself!'

Tamsin's bottom lip stuck out mutinously but Alicia

ignored it. She had caught the smell of fish cooking and realised guiltily that she had been here for far too long. Swiftly she soaped herself and sank once more up to her neck in the warm water to rinse off the residue, then, with a quick glance around, stood up into the warm sunlit air, shaking her hair out and making the drops sparkle in the brightness as they scattered around her.

She reached down to the saddlebag, only to find that it was empty. Tamsin had dried herself and pulled on her drawers and chemise, and now she was wandering past the little thicket and down the path to the lower cascades. One towel was wrapped around her head in a rather lopsided imitation of the turban Alicia usually wound her wet hair into, the other was trailing behind her in the dust.

'Tamsin!' she hissed in panic. 'Bring those towels back here *at once!*'

She realised her mistake as the child whirled about, her eyes lit up with mischief.

'You come catch me!' she cried gleefully, quite convinced that this was a repeat of the bath time romps that she and Alicia had enjoyed in those far-off good times when they had had the wagon and the nice house in the big city. 'I keep it till you catch me!'

'Not here, Tamsin!' she pleaded desperately. 'We can't play here!' Her voice grew stern as she tried to suppress the rising panic. 'Tamsin! Give me that towel *now!* You are a naughty girl!'

'*You* naughty!' cried Tamsin. 'You won't play! So I won't give you the towel! So there!'

Down below she heard the clanging of iron on iron, calling them to eat. And she had not even begun to dry her hair! Whatever would the Colonel think?'

In despair, she grabbed her chemise and held it across her middle as she tried to grab the towel, but Tamsin, content now that she had persuaded Lisha to play, darted just out of reach.

'Tamsin!' she cried in desperation as she darted back around the corner of the alders.

'What in tarnation's keeping you, Mrs ... Owens ...'

Cornish's voice died in his throat as he came sharply round

the corner of the thicket and face to face with Alicia. They both stood rooted to the spot.

He knew he should have looked away, turned his back on her to save her embarrassment, but he was quite unable to move.

How did I ever think her old?

She looked absurdly youthful, her rich hair dripping round her face, each drop of water shining like a crystal in the strong sun. The chemise she held in front of her could not conceal the slimness of her shapely legs, the swell of her firm breasts and her soft, pale, sloping shoulders.

I want to reach out and touch that beautiful body. But if I do, would I stop at touching?

They seemed to have been standing there an age, eyes locked together, when Tamsin broke in on them. 'Lisha?' she said hesitantly.

The spell was broken and he turned wrathfully on the child.

'Give your mother the towel, child, and get yourself down the hill *pronto!*' he snapped. The little girl looked at him wide-eyed, thrust the towel wordlessly into his hands, put her thumb into her mouth and fled.

His eyes fell to the towel in his hands; he cleared his throat, suddenly embarrassed. Alicia could not take it from him without dropping the chemise, so he strode across to her side and draped it around her shoulders. As he wound it around her, he caught a brief tantalising glimpse of rivulets of water chasing each other down a narrow creamy-pale porcelain smooth back towards small, firm buttocks. He hesitated a moment longer, breathing faster, sweat beading his upper lip; he thrust the ends of the towel at her, turned sharply on his heel and headed back down the path.

In five minutes she was down by the campfire, her hair plaited damply over one shoulder. Xavier handed round delicious grilled fish freshly caught that morning in the brook.

Cornish was grateful to see that she did not blush or simper as he passed her a hunk of rough bread to mop up her plate. They had to go on working together and he knew he must force himself to put out of his mind that arousing glimpse of her half naked body.

143

While the boys packed up the linen that was dry and spread the heavier sheets out on the bushes to dry, Cornish went up to bathe and she lay down under the trees in the shade while Kai played at pitch and toss with a very subdued Tamsin.

Checking her equipment in the saddlebag, she became aware of Tamsin at her side, looking rather doleful. On an impulse she bent down and gave her a swift hug, to be rewarded by a big beaming smile.

'Be good for Chen Kai? Promise?'

The child nodded.

'And stay with Juan while Chen Kai has his bath?'

'I think I will leave that.' Chen ruffled the child's hair and watched her skip away to play. 'She has the imp of mischief in her today . . .'

'She'll be good,' insisted Alicia confidently. 'And it's an experience not to be missed! It's the first time I've felt really clean since I came out of pris –'

Her voice trailed off as a tall shadow fell across them. She looked up at the Colonel with wide scared eyes.

'Since I left the city,' she ended lamely.

'If you're ready, Mrs Owens?' Cornish held her horse while Chen helped her up into the saddle.

'About Tamsin . . .' she said to Chen as he handed her the reins.

'You worry too much, Alicia,' was all Chen would say.

It was cool in the trees and she was glad to be out of the fierce afternoon sun, but before long they emerged again above the tree-line where they could no longer see the smoke of the campfire or the jets of steam from the *agua caliente*.

'How far till we reach the boundary?' she asked as they paused to let the horses drink from a little spring that trickled out of the bare hillside.

'About ten minutes' ride,' he replied, mopping his forehead with a dampened kerchief and replacing his hat. 'Still worried about the child?'

'Of course not!' she snapped.

'Don't lie. You've done nothing but gaze back since we started out.'

'I'm sorry.' She compressed her lips angrily at the implied criticism.

'Don't be. I'm sure you won't let it interfere with your work. And I'm equally sure that Jo can cope with her.'

'But what if she is naughty for Juan?' She was betrayed into speaking her fears aloud.

'Juan? He's had five children and every one of them ten times more mischievous than your little girl. How old is she? Seven?'

'Five,' she corrected.

'Good God! Then a little mischief is only to be expected. Though I was sorely tempted to dust her seat for her when you didn't.

'I — I couldn't.'

He gave a sudden loud crack of laughter. 'Don't tell me I've saddled myself with a Quaker!'

'Not at all. Just because I won't smack Tamsin ...'

'Why not?'

'For reasons — for reasons that are none of your affair!' she said with a sudden flash of spirit.

'True. And I don't intend to discuss that young lady all day. Come on.' He urged the horse on up the increasingly steep trail.

They surveyed and mapped up both sides of one small peak that afternoon and Alicia soon found that the sweat was pouring off her body, exposed as they were to the burning sun.

'So much hotter up here than I expected,' she panted as she clambered down a little scree to line up an angle.

'Here,' he said brusquely, 'take some of this.' He held out a flask to her and she drank greedily from it in great gulps.

'Hey! Not like that! You'll make yourself ill!' He took it back from her and corked it again. 'Didn't your mapmaker ever tell you to drink sparingly in a hot sun?'

'It's so long ago, I'd almost forgotten,' she admitted with a wry face. 'It's so much cooler down in — down in — San Francisco.'

He looked at her with narrowed eyes and made as if to speak, but then thought better of it, clamped his mouth shut, picked up the surveying stick and marched across the scree away from her.

145

Chapter Twelve

They rose, as they always did, before the dawn. Today would see the last of the mapping of the boundary line up in the Vaca hills and they hoped to get as much as possible done before the onset of the exhausting midday heat. Tamsin was, for once, still asleep and Chen Kai and Alicia stood in the stableyard, packing the equipment into the saddlebags and talking softly.

'It will be a hard day, Alicia — long and hot,' warned Kai, tightening up the girths. 'Be sure to take your broad-brimmed hat — and keep it on!' He narrowed his eyes and squinted up towards the hills. 'There's a storm brewing up — are you sure that you can cope? The horse is already becoming restless.'

She laughed softly. 'Kai, don't fuss! I swear you're turning into a venerable Chinese grandmother!'

He chuckled wryly. 'Perhaps you're right. But I do worry ... I do not like to see you doing so much. All this hard riding — and helping me out too. I wish that I could come with you and help you. It is too much for you.'

'Kai, *look* at me! How long is it since I looked so well, eh?'

'It is true,' he conceded gravely. 'Not since ...'

'Not since before all the trouble ... And as for hard riding, I love it!' she exulted.

'It suits you well,' he admitted. 'You are like one of those little sand lizards in the Sandwich Islands: put you down anywhere and you instantly blend in with your background.'

'But Kai, you forget, this *is* my background. My happiest memories are of the days when I managed to slip away to go riding with my father and his company up in the hills.'

'But remember — it is only for the month,' he reminded her sombrely.

'A month of this and I shall be like a new woman,' she exulted. Kai helped her up into the saddle, smiling indulgently at her, happy to see the sparkle in her eyes once more. 'Fresh air, hard riding, interesting work and good food ...'

'I trust you refer to my campfire efforts,' came Cornish's voice from close behind them. '*Good food* is not exactly the phrase that springs to mind when I dwell on Jo's concoctions!'

Alicia started nervously, jibbing at the horse's mouth and making her prance restlessly.

In an instant the rancher was at her side, reaching up to take the reins firmly above the bit and control the horse.

'Didn't mean to startle you ...' he began.

'Of course you startled me!' she said wrathfully, as she brought her mount swiftly under control once more. 'It's bad enough Kai gliding around and materialising out of nowhere, without you doing it too! And don't call him Jo!' she went on with a flash of pure anger. 'He has a proper name! He's Chen Kai-Tsu, not Jo Chinaman!'

He narrowed his eyes and looked at her consideringly. 'If you are ready, ma'am?' He checked his girths, climbed into the saddle and set out, without a backward glance to see whether she was following him.

'Keep an eye on Tamsin if you can, Kai,' she murmured. 'Don't let her get under anyone's feet except yours!'

'She'll be fine. But you be careful — and remember, we're dependent entirely on the Colonel's good will, so try to mind your tongue!'

She wrinkled her nose in disgust and screwed up her face in a very childish way, then set her heels gently to the mare and cantered off in Cornish's wake.

It took them more than an hour to reach the hills and once the sun was up, the heat was almost unbearable.

'Never known it so hot up in the hills!' he exclaimed as he handed her the flask of water.

'Chen Kai said there would be a storm,' she ventured, but he did not answer.

147

The heat was becoming oppressive and the constant staring into the heat-hazed distance was beginning to make her eyes water and her head ache. Lack of rain had laid the mountains under a thick mantle of reddish dust and as they rode on, the fine grains penetrated their sweat-soaked clothes to irritate their skin, redden their eyes and clog their mouths. The elation of the morning was evaporating from her with the sweat, but she certainly wasn't going to be the first one to suggest that they turn back.

They paused briefly during the worst of the midday heat to rest and eat some skillet bread and meat.

'I take back all I said about Jo — I mean Chen Kai-Tsu's cooking,' said Cornish, chewing the fragrant bread appreciatively.

Alicia, who had mixed the dough late the night before, and risen early to bake it, said nothing.

They shared out the last of the water in the flask and then, as she made to get up and continue with the work, he reached out lazily and drew her back into the shelter of the little bluff, out of the direct sun.

'The Mexicans have a habit that I normally frown upon, but it's just made for a day like this,' he said slowly. 'The *siesta*. I'm going to indulge in it. I suggest you do the same. It was an early start.'

With that he tipped his hat over his eyes and leant back.

He was right, she thought. It was really too hot to move. Better to sit awhile and wait for the light breeze of the afternoon to spring up. Not that she would sleep, of course, but it would be pleasant to rest her eyes.

Someone was shaking her arm. She forced her eyes open with some difficulty to see Cornish looking down at her with an unfathomable expression in his uncomfortably penetrating green eyes.

'I would have let you sleep on,' he said bluntly. 'But the weather's moving on apace and it's time we headed for home.'

High in the sky thunder heads were building up over the distant mountains, blotting out the higher peaks completely.

Each thunder head was edged with leaden yellow and the sun cast a strange unearthly glow.

'Sorry. Hadn't meant to sleep,' she said thickly. 'My eyes were tired ...'

'My sheep man, Pedro, rode in and out without disturbing you at all!'

She looked around her uncertainly. 'But you can't run sheep up here!' she exclaimed.

'Of course not. But over the next shoulder is a small high valley, just perfect for sheep. Pedro saw us from the other side while he was scouting out strays and came over to check us out. He reckons there's a storm brewing.'

She rubbed her gritty eyes.

'There's a cave just round the bluff here with a spring in it. I've tasted it: it seems good.'

She found the cave without too much difficulty and located the spring bubbling up at the back by listening. She washed away the dust and returned to find Cornish packing the equipment away in the saddlebags.

'There's not much more to do,' she objected. 'It seems a shame to come all this way and leave the job unfinished.'

He sniffed the air and shook his head reluctantly. 'Not worth the risk,' he decided. 'These Pacific storms can be worse than anything I've ever known in the Sierras. Best place to be is down in the valleys, not exposed up on the hills.'

They set off at a fairly brisk pace, but the terrain, and the nervousness of the horses as they sensed the coming storm, was against them. They were still slithering down the brush-covered lower slopes when the storm broke above them with tremendous ferocity.

At first there was no rain, just ominous rolls of thunder that seemed to shake the mountains, and violent jagged flashes of lightning that played over the flanks of the hills with a ghastly orange radiance.

The third flash of lightning struck the ground about a quarter of a mile ahead of them, consuming a live oak in its path in a spectacular, crackling sheet of flame.

It was too much for Alicia's mare. She bucked and reared, whinnying with fear as she tried to unseat her rider and bolt. It took all of her skill and strength to keep her under control,

149

but nothing would induce her to go forward another step and she stood, trembling, her head hung low.

'It's no good,' the Colonel ground out between his teeth after another futile attempt. 'We'll have to take shelter some place. There's a little canyon over to our left, aways back a bit. As I remember, there's a fair massive overhang there that'll provide some shelter.'

They dismounted and with much coaxing persuaded Alicia's mare to follow Cornish's rangy chestnut stallion into the canyon. Tethered to a low bush under the overhang, away from the fury of the storm, she soon quietened. The riders, barely dampened by the rain which had just begun to fall, pulled their blankets from behind the saddle and settled themselves down, backs against the rock face, to wait for the storm to blow itself out.

'How long do you think it will last?' she demanded, shaking the raindrops out of the brim of her leather hat.

'Half a day, a day, two days, who can tell?'

The rain began to fall in real earnest as he spoke, drumming on the rocks overhead and forming little cascades that sprang off the edge of the overhang as great torrents of water fell from the skies. Thunder crashed and lightning played evilly around the tops of the mountains.

He moved away and started to gather twigs and dry brush from the rear of the overhang.

'Surely we won't need a fire?' she muttered irritably, pushing a strand of hair off her face. 'Wet or no, it's still quite warm enough.'

'It's not to warm us,' he replied. 'I just want to dissuade any four-footed refugees from the storm from joining us. Unless you fancy supper with a grizzly?'

She shivered. 'No thank you!' She laid aside her blanket and, ignoring his scornful laugh, helped him collect more wood.

'Who did Pedro think we were?' she asked suddenly. 'Squatters?'

'Yes.'

'This far out?'

'Pedro was in Sacramento a few days ago and all the talk in the saloons was of the unknown − but obviously wealthy −

man who was trying to buy the Briones place and the part of Soto's that butts on to mine.'

'Lamarr?'

'If not him, then one of his cronies. So it's as important to get the boundaries clear here as up Sacramento way.'

There was silence for a while, then he looked sideways at her and stated casually : 'Pity about the camera.'

'It was not possible,' she declared stiffly.

A few moments later he tried again. 'We could be here for some time,' he said conversationally. 'What shall we talk about?'

'I — I'll get on with my mapping,' she said, crossing to her saddlebag to draw out the board and chalks. Instead her fingers closed on something in there that she had forgotten. She drew it out to look at it more closely.

'What's that?' he asked.

'Bit of rock I picked up by the spring in the cave.' She held a small misshapen rock up to what little light was penetrating the curtain of rain. 'Did you know you had cinnabar on your land?'

'Cinnabar?'

'Yes. You smelt mercury from it. You could get a good price for it — the big mining companies can't get their hands on enough of it and they need it to refine the gold. I remember my father and I found some up north and . . .'

'You always pick up stray rocks?' He crossed to her side and took the stone from her.

'Habit of a lifetime.'

'Gives us something to talk about,' he approved. 'I thought after Jo's warning — I beg his pardon, Chen Kai's warning — that I wouldn't get more than an aye, yes or no out of you today.'

She threw him a fulminating glance; she could not trust herself to answer.

'Just what do you have to mind your tongue about?' he asked curiously. 'After all, Jo — Chen Kai! — told me a fair amount about the trouble you had. You're not alone in that. I guess half California must want to leave their past behind. Men who've been in trouble with the law, women who've been camp-followers or saloon prostitutes . . . hey!'

151

He flung his hand up to fend off a swinging open-handed blow from Alicia.

'What the Hell's got into you?' he demanded angrily, seizing her wrist. 'Oh, you thought I was implying that you ... Oh no, ma'am,' he said mockingly. 'You may have *half* the attributes, but you're too cold by far!'

She turned away, ashamed to have let her feelings show so clearly.

They'd always made her shake with fright, the men with the leering faces who came to Sonora with the 'hell-on-wheels', the strings of wagons which moved tirelessly from advance camp to advance camp, supplying the men with red-eye whiskey, high-stake gambling and women.

Change the subject quickly. Wipe the memory before ...

'And you?' she demanded with a sudden spurt of anger. 'What did you come to California to escape?' She lay back against the saddle and watched through half-closed eyes the waterfall that ran off the front of the overhang. 'This military title of yours, for instance. I don't imagine that's American.'

'In a way. I was in the American militia ... Vigilantes.' He saw her try, and fail, to suppress a shudder. 'Of course that was the first time round. In '51, when bands of criminals roamed the streets,' he went on. 'The worst were the Sydney Ducks: one and all former guests of her Britannic Majesty's penal colonies.' He looked at her consideringly.

'Yes, but – Vigilantes!' she exclaimed with loathing.

'The Vigilantes did some good before they got above themselves and confused justice with the lynch mob.'

'Couldn't you have controlled them?'

'We ran many criminals out of town, but no one was ever lynched when I was in charge. Mind you, I was only promoted to Colonel once it was all over.'

'Promoted?'

'I was already a captain; *sea* captain, but they could never see the distinction,' he chuckled. 'In the end I gave up trying. It's like being called Brother Jack, or Cornish, in the mines. In the end it's easier to go along with it than argue. Besides, it suited me at the time.'

'You had a past to forget too?' she demanded, with renewed interest.

He tipped his hat back from over his eyes and gave her a long, hard look which she found rather unnerving.

'Don't tell me if you'd rather not,' she said hastily.

He shrugged. 'Let's just say I left Cornwall in a hurry,' he said frankly.

'So where did you go? America?'

'Brittany at first.'

'Hence Kerhouan?'

'Hence Kerhouan. I knew that part of Brittany well, since we did a fair bit of trade with them. And I knew the sea, so we joined an Atlantic packet as crewmen.'

'And how did the fleeing seaman become the owner of Tresco?' she asked with interest.

'Not all at once,' he grinned reminiscently. 'Gradually worked my way up until I had my own ship – "a small thing, but mine own". We used to trade up and down the eastern seaboard. Then we carried a shipment around the Horn and no sooner had we delivered the goods than the rumour of gold reached the harbour and suddenly I had no crew.'

'So you went to the mines too and made your fortune,' she concluded.

'We saw which way the wind was blowing. Kerhouan and I sailed the brig back to Panama City two-handed, and picked up a crowd of would-be gold-rushers. With them as crew, we picked up supplies and landed them all safely at Yerba Buena. The profit from that little venture saw us through the first year; after that, we realised we could make more profit selling my expertise to the bigger mining companies and conglomerates that were springing up than standing all hours waist-deep in a stream.'

'What expertise? What earthly good could your knowledge of seamanship do them up in the hills?'

'I only knew the sea as every Cornish lad knows the sea; I'd never made a living from it. My parents had greater plans for me.' There was a bitterness in his voice at odds with the smile on his face. 'But it was not to be and when we fell on hard times, which coincided with one of the regular slumps in the fishing, I was sent down the mines. I made use of the education I had received and when I left Cornwall, I was well on the way to becoming a good mining engineer.

'When the forty-niners moved on from panning to burrowing in the hillsides for the veins, I designed 'em pumping engines and improved pit props. And spent every spare minute looking for a likely spot to dig out my own fortune. I bought my mine from an easterner who was heading back home, poorer, sicker and tireder than he came.

''Course he'd driven his shaft in quite the wrong direction: I saw the potential and sank all my money into the mine. Kerhouan and a few other Cornishmen, Brother Jacks, worked with me. And that's where I got the money for Tresco.'

'That was the mine that collapsed?' she asked softly.

'I suppose Kerhouan told Chen Kai?' He closed his eyes and for a moment she thought he wasn't going to go on. 'Not that it matters. We lined our new shaft in the proper manner, but we could not afford to reline his; the day after we dug out a fortune in gold, the tunnel collapsed. Only three of us survived. Kerhouan was away fetching supplies and Jem pulled me out. Only because he didn't know where the gold had been stored.' He grinned. ''Course, he planned to take off with the gold before Kerhouan returned. But I confounded him by surviving.'

'And the mine?' Her gentle voice broke in on his bitter memories.

'We never reopened it. And never will.' His eyes were hard as pebbles. 'I lay there for weeks, thinking of the men who'd died. I saw how we had destroyed that beautiful valley, scarred it with spoil heaps and desolate canyons which we'd dug out, defaced and abandoned. All for greed, the greed that had killed my partners and sent me back underground when I so hated and loathed it.'

'But you had been brought up with mining ...'

'I'd always hated it. I remember my first day down the copper mine as if it were yesterday. We spent the day waist deep in water, hacking away at the rock face, looking for colour. The only time we climbed up out of the mire was to eat. I put my pastie down on my kerchief and a rat ran alongside me and began to gnaw at it. From that day on I thought of nothing but getting out of the mines — and yet I let my greed draw me back. When I was fit again, I blew up the entrance to the mine and took my share of the gold to buy Tresco. The rest – the rest is just fool's gold as far as I'm concerned. And I won't care if I never see another nugget as long as I live. So the cinnabar can stay where it is: I won't help the mining companies to ravage the land any more than it is.'

'Why buy these hills if not for mining? Why not more fertile valley land?'

'You've seen what man can do to the land,' he said bitterly. 'Polluting and blocking the rivers. I control my own water supply. All the Tresco, from the source at Clearwater Lake down to where it runs into the Sacramento, is on my land.

'Tresco is a living memorial to Tregorran, Humphries, Jespor and Freestone – the Brother Jacks who didn't make it.' He gazed blindly into the distance as if he were seeing their faces again, then, very quietly and with an earnestness that made Alicia shiver, he went on: 'And if Lamarr tries to take it from me, I'll kill him.'

At last the thunder and lightning ceased, although the curtain of rain still hung over the landscape. Alicia shivered. Soon, if they were to stay, they would have to light the fire.

'Can you saddle your own horse?' he asked abruptly, rising to his feet and sniffing the air. 'The worst of the storm has passed so you shouldn't have any trouble with the mare.'

'Yes. But surely we can't make it back to Tresco in this light?' The driving rain had so overcast the mid-afternoon sky that it was more like dusk than day.

'Not Tresco, no. Although perhaps alone I could have made it.' He raised his hand to forestall her protest. 'I know, I know, it's not you — it's that dratted horse. She's been eating her head off for far too long in the stables with no one to ride her.'

And that 'dratted horse', having stood docilely to have her saddle put on flatly refused to budge from beneath the overhang and no amount of coaxing could move her.

'There's nothing else for it,' he concluded through gritted teeth. 'I'm damned if I'll freeze for an obstinate mare. You'll have to get up before me. It's not too far — no more than half an hour normally.'

'But your poor horse!'

'He's carried heavier loads, haven't you, Ross?' he drawled, patting the stallion's neck. 'He's sure-footed and he knows the trail to Pedro's house very well.' He reached his hand down to her. 'Come on!' he ordered impatiently. 'Or we'll be here all night.'

'But what about Rosita?' she asked.

'Rosita? She'll either stay here and sulk or follow us.' He drew her up with some difficulty, impeded as she was by damp skirts that had dried clammy on her, and held the mettlesome stallion tightly in check while she settled herself in front of him.

It was a long, wet and weary journey, but as he had said, Ross knew the way well. He skirted the sagebrush, almost invisible in the grey light, and minced daintily across the unexpected cascades that tumbled down the hillside. And when she looked around after a few minutes, Rosita was trotting obediently behind Ross, ears flattened in the torrential rain, the picture of equine misery.

'Lean back!' growled Cornish. 'Makes my arms ache reaching round you!' Unwillingly she relaxed her tense muscles and forced herself to lean back against him. As the warmth seeped from his body into hers she began to shake. It was a long time since she had been so aware of a man's body. She had travelled for years with a man — but this was not Chen Kai.

She was not the only one to suffer. The feel of her waist under his hand brought back vividly to him the sight of her half-dressed body shimmering in the sunlight at the *agua caliente*. He wanted to press her closer to him, to bury his face in her neck and breathe in the fragrance of her hair; it took an iron control not to do so.

Working with women was the very Devil! he told himself grimly. But his innate honesty forced him to qualify that: working with *this* woman.

Once the solution would have been easy: a trip to town, preferably San Francisco, where he was not quite so well known, and a visit to one of the more discreet brothels.

156

He had done that before, most recently after the break with Belle, but on that occasion he had induced in himself such a feeling of self-disgust that he was not eager to repeat the experience.

It was a close question which of them was the more relieved when the light appeared over the brow of the hill.

The welcome they received from Pedro and Julia was as warm as the glow from the blazing fire that lit up the main room of the log cabin and they were swiftly installed in rocking chairs on either side of the fire, Alicia in a borrowed robe of Julia's and Cornish in a dry shirt with a blanket round his waist, Pedro's pants having proved too small. Their clothes steamed on one side of the fire while to the other a coffee pot hissed and bubbled merrily.

Julia, a merry and sociable girl of eighteen or nineteen, was delighted to have their company and plied them with delicious food which soon warmed them through. Her brother Manuel was rather more serious, modelling himself on his brother-in-law Pedro, a more taciturn man, though no less genuine in his welcome.

'We get so few visitors this far from Sacramento,' prattled Julia gaily as she handed round the plates of deliciously savoury meat and vegetables, concoctions of beans flavoured with hot spices, and delicate sweet pancakes. 'You should come to see us more often, Colonel Jack!' she scolded. 'I'll wager you don't get fed like this at Tresco!'

Cornish looked across the table at Alicia and gave her a broad wink. 'Depends who's doing the cooking!' he said deliberately.

Alicia looked at him in stunned silence. Had he been aware all the time that she was helping Kai?

Over supper, there were the usual polite questions, not too probing, about her arrival at Tresco, where she had come from, how long she had been in California.

She managed to answer most of them with a light touch — and without giving too much away.

'You wouldn't have liked working for that Jem though,' said Julia with an expressive shudder. 'Be happy you didn't come to Tresco until he was gone.'

'Ever been in Mokelumne?' asked Pedro curiously, as he

157

handed the sweet cakes across the table. 'Or Sonora? Your face looks kinda familiar.'

The fact that she had had the same feeling of déja-vu about Pedro did nothing to stop the familiar sinking feeling in her stomach.

'Years ago,' she responded swiftly, conscious of the rancher's eyes fixed on her. Adroitly she turned the conversation back to Pedro and Julia, asking them how long they had been in California, where they had met? By the time Julia had recounted the story, with many giggles and blushes and sidelong glances at Pedro, the difficult moment had passed.

After supper, Pedro and Manuel took the lantern and went out to check on the sheep fold, while Julia and Alicia cleared away and washed up the dishes and Cornish discarded the blanket for his dry pants.

On their return, Manuel, much to his disgust, was sent bleary-eyed to bed while Pedro picked up his guitar and began to strum a gentle tune. Alicia, in the place of honour in the rocking chair, felt a strange contentment creeping over her, and a pang of envy too of this serene little family. She let her eyes close and imagined them in a few years' time, with children on their knees, secure in their valley, well-fed and content, while she — she might be on the road again, drifting from town to town, struggling to earn an honest living.

She suddenly became aware that the music had stopped. She opened her tired eyes. Cornish was sitting on the other side of the fire, regarding her closely with a frown between his eyes.

'What is it?' he demanded sharply.

'What?'

'You looked as though you were about to burst into tears.'

'I — I was just thinking about Tamsin,' she lied. 'Hoping she won't worry when we don't return.'

'Chen's not a fool,' he replied shortly. 'He only has to look at the weather to realise we could never have made it back to Tresco. And Kerhouan knows we're near Pedro's cabin.'

She glanced around her, barely suppressing a yawn. 'Where are Julia and Pedro?' she asked.

'They rise early and retire early,' he explained. 'I told them not to wait up. You've been dozing for over an hour,' he added drily.

'Sorry.'

'You've been burning the candle at both ends for too long,' he observed. 'I should have realised ...' He rose and stretched. 'Bed,' he pronounced.

'Where?'

He nodded to the two bedrolls in front of the fire, side by side on the brightly coloured Mexican rugs. Her eyes widened.

'I can't sleep in the same room as you!' she exclaimed hotly.

'There isn't that much choice.'

'You and Pedro ... me and Julia ...' she suggested.

'I'm not going to disturb them now.'

'But why didn't Julia think of that? Oh!' She coloured furiously. 'She thinks that you ... and I ...'

He shrugged indifferently. 'Isn't it a little late for modesty?'

'What the Hell is that supposed to mean?'

'Not much modesty in a saloon,' he sneered.

She narrowed her eyes in fury as the import of his words hit her. Obviously Julia was not the only one to have got the wrong impression. Well then, let him think that. What did she care? Any reputation she might have had had been blown away that day up at Coloma.

'Many people come to California to start again,' she said with a forced laugh. 'You included. Why should a saloon girl be any different? And who are you to play God?'

In the kitchen she washed her hands and face perfunctorily, ran her fingers through her hair until her eyes watered and then braided it. No comb, no clean linen. Her stomach lurched. No sleeping draught.

She was angry: with Cornish for bringing her here, with Chen Kai whose meticulous care in doling out the herbal drink so exactly had left her stranded here without support, but within seconds of the thought she had turned the blame where it belonged: fairly and squarely on her own shoulders. That she, who had always thought herself so independent, should think she could not manage without drugs! Was she really that pathetic?

Buoyed up by her own anger, she marched back into the living room. Unceremoniously she dragged her bedroll and blanket into the farthest corner and turned the lamp down. She turned her back on Cornish in his bedroll and stripped down to her chemise, unaware that the flickering firelight lit her figure up in silhouette much more than the lamp would have done.

As she drew the blanket up around her ears, she heard an amused chuckle from her unwelcome room mate. 'Goodnight!' he called softly. She rolled over and did not answer.

In the small hours of the morning, she was regretting her move. This corner was in direct line of the door and cold draughts were whistling through the gaps. Strange to remember that in Sacramento the air was hot as in a furnace; even in Tresco the huge fireplaces would not often be needed, but this high up in the mountains, the night temperature dropped quite rapidly.

'Come back to the fire,' came a low voice. But pride and stubbornness sustained her and she turned once more on her side and tried to sleep.

Julia, rising early to stoke the fire and cook breakfast before the men rode out, was shocked to find Alicia curled up in the corner. In the kitchen she exclaimed volubly over her guest's cold and pinched face.

'So stupid!' she exclaimed. 'I had not realised — I had thought — '

'That I was his woman?' flashed Alicia bitterly. 'I don't suppose you're alone in that. Seems you can't work for a man here without being thought a kept woman.'

The storm had passed. Outside the sky was clearing. Over the valley the cloud was beginning to break up and a fugitive ray of watery sunshine shone down on the sheltered valley. Alicia would have liked to stay there for ever.

While Pedro and the Colonel walked around the yard to see the improvements Pedro was making, Alicia and Julia fed the chickens and then prepared food to take with them.

'Come up and see us again as soon as you can,' insisted Julia.

'There's still a lot of work to be done,' said Alicia weakly.

'Promise you will come when it's finished,' urged Julia. 'We have so few visitors — and there's not another woman within miles.'

Alicia fobbed her off. 'I don't know what we shall be doing next,' she told her with forced cheerfulness. 'We may go back to Sacramento when this job is finished, or we may try our luck further afield.'

She turned to pack the food in the saddlebags and found Cornish standing in the doorway, regarding her curiously.

When they rode off up-valley Alicia's spirits were as low as the grey cloud which still masked the tops of the mountains.

Chapter Thirteen

While Alicia was clambering up hillsides and down canyons, mapping the course of foaming torrents and delicate waterfalls that arched down verdant hillsides, Chen Kai was not idle.

Each morning, after the Colonel and Alicia had set off to survey and Kerhouan and the hands to ride the boundaries or check on the livestock in the far valleys, he would set Tamsin at the long table in the kitchen with the Bible, McGuffey's First Reader and her slate and slate pencil. Perched on a rolled up bedroll to bring her up to the level of the table, she would copy out her letters and spell out the story in the primer until Chen Kai, summoned from his scrubbing and cleaning, was satisfied with her progress.

She would often be joined at her task by Jorge and Josefa, sturdy children, older than her, the younger children of Juan. Although their older brothers, Xavier and Luis, earned their keep by helping around the ranch, the younger two, until her recent death in the care of an aged aunt in Sacramento, had been left very much to their own devices. Alicia, when she discovered their existence, had been appalled.

'Señora – what else can I do?' Juan had demanded helplessly. 'Colonel Jack, he does not like the women and children on the ranch. Until they can work like Xavier and Luis, they must keep out of his way.'

'They are so young!' protested Alicia. 'Surely they need a mother.'

'Señora! For every woman in California, there are a

hundred men. What woman in her right mind is going to take on four children?'

'But they can't stay hidden away indoors for the next four years! You must speak to the Colonel about them!'

'I cannot.' He shook his head at her lack of understanding. 'I have a good job here. I dare not risk losing it all by angering the Colonel.'

'To be kept hidden away — it isn't right!'

'Better than the orphanage, I think,' he said sombrely.

'The Devil finds work for idle hands,' muttered Kai grimly when he heard of this. 'They are too young to work, but not too old to learn.' And he sat them alongside little Tamsin at the table and set them copying and reckoning.

When the lessons had been done to his satisfaction — and his standards were as high as his expectations — he would take all three children out into the overgrown kitchen garden. Together they cleared away years of weeds and neglect to reveal straggling rows of squash plants, everlasting spinach and Indian corn, self-seeded year after neglected year from the original plants that the Holy Brothers had brought overland with them from the coastal missions nearly a century before.

Chen Kai taught them how to recognise the seedlings and plant them out in neat rows in the freshly turned earth. They even found a herb garden hidden beneath a riot of flowering vine. Chen Kai and Jorge ran lengths of wire along the old adobe wall and fastened the vine to it, careful not to disturb the ancient fruit trees that clung to the wall, while an excited Tamsin identified the herbs to Josefa and told her gravely what each was used for.

It was not all work, however, and in the heat of the day the children would sit in the courtyard and take a *siesta*. In the cooler hours, they would teach Tamsin their songs and games, but at the first warning of the return of the riders, they would scuttle back to their shack behind the stables.

One hot and dusty afternoon, the Colonel and Alicia arrived back at the ranch to find Kerhouan, who had just ridden in from the southern boundary, standing in the stable yard with a large covered basket in his arms which he was

163

regarding with a baffled expression. Agitated high-pitched noises were coming from within.

'What in Hades have you got there?' demanded Cornish in some amusement.

Kerhouan pushed his hat back on his head, said something in Breton that didn't sound too polite but made the Colonel smile.

'For Chen, ma'am,' he said as he caught sight of Alicia. 'From Pedro's wife.'

As he spoke, Chen Kai came round the corner of the yard with Tamsin at his heels.

'Ah, Ker-hwan! From Mrs Santana?' He took the basket from him eagerly.

'Come and see, Lisha!' cried Tamsin, tugging at her arm.

Mystified, they all followed Chen Kai around the corner, to be pulled up short at the sight of a fenced grassy run and a neat shed built at the back of the stable.

Tamsin opened the gate to the run and Kai unfastened the basket. Out tumbled two vociferously indignant hens and seven or eight fluffy chicks.

'Chickens!' exclaimed Cornish.

'Ohé, Chen Kai!' called Kerhouan over the fence. 'Now we have tough burnt chicken for when we tire of tough burnt beef!'

Chen Kai, who had never had any illusions about his cooking, took the comment in good part and joined in the laughter, but Tamsin scooped up one of the cheeping balls of fluff in her little hand and hurried over to the picket fence.

'They're not for eating!' she said anxiously. 'These are from Mrs Santana's best layers. They'll give us lots of eggs!'

One of the two broody mother hens came clucking anxiously around Tamsin's ankles.

'You don't give her back her chick, Mrs Santana's best layer going to have your toes for her tea!' chuckled Kerhouan.

Tamsin handed the chick carefully back to Chen Kai, who shooed them all into the shed for the night.

'Now, *belle demoiselle*,' Kerhouan went on gruffly. 'Would you like a ride back to the rancho? Perhaps we can even catch our supper before it goes up in flames!' he jested.

He caught the little girl by her hands, scooped her out of the chicken run up on to his shoulders and carried her back to the house.

Not until later when they were sorting through some more papers did Cornish refer again to the new arrivals.

'I've been watching that kitchen garden coming back to life, Jo — Chen Kai,' he commented. 'A deal of work's gone into it all. You've done well.'

'I did not do it all by myself,' said Chen Kai-Tsu gravely. 'Jorge helped me build the shed and dig the garden. Josefa and Tamsin did the planting and the chickens were their idea ...'

'Just hold on there! Who is Jorge? And Josefa?'

'Juan's two younger children,' replied the cook imperturbably. 'Just as bright as their brothers. Jorge is as good with plants as with horses and young Josefa has a great talent with figures.'

'I heard his two youngest were in Sacramento!' objected Cornish, banging the papers down with more force than absolutely necessary and causing clouds of choking dust to fly out.

'The great-aunt who looked after them died,' said Chen Kai precisely. 'She was very old.'

'So he holed them up here and hoped I wouldn't notice?'

'What else could he do?'

The Colonel looked at the three hopeful faces turned towards him — it seemed even Kerhouan had known of the children's presence.

He ran his fingers through his hair.

'Kerhouan!' he grated. 'Have one of the hands put up a sign out front tomorrow.'

'A sign?' demanded Kerhouan, one eyebrow raised in surprise.

Cornish looked Alicia straight in the eye. 'Write on the sign: "Tresco. Home for Waifs and Strays"!' he growled.

One evening Alicia came out on to the verandah to find Tamsin sitting with Kerhouan on the bench, listening wide-eyed to a story.

'I hope Tamsin isn't being a nuisance to you,' she said anxiously. 'I know you're very busy — please don't let her get under your feet.'

He looked up from the wood he was whittling, a warm smile crinkling his dark eyes. 'You worry too much,' he chuckled. 'Me, I enjoy to sit with the child.' He sighed and his eyes clouded over for a moment. 'When I left Brittany, I had a little sister of about her age.'

'What was her name, Kerhouan?' asked Tamsin.

'Marivonne,' he said with a reminiscent smile. 'Like you, she had no fear of the horses. But she had darker hair than you and darker eyes too.'

'Did you used to take her rides on your big horse too? And tell her the stories about the mermaids and the fairies?' asked Tamsin eagerly. 'D'you know, Lisha, where Kerhouan comes from, they have elves and fairies and mermaids! And before they knowed America was here, Brittany was the end of the earth?'

'Nonsense.' Cornish must have been standing behind them for some time. 'Cornwall is the end of the world. Everyone knows that.'

Kerhouan chuckled, but Tamsin looked up at the rancher, eyes wide and mouth open. 'Oh!' she gasped. 'And what about all the fairies and mermaids then?' She put her head on one side as though seeing him with new eyes. 'And what about the Kingdom that drownded beneath the sea?'

'All stolen from the Cornish, m'dear,' declared the rancher with a mischievous smile. 'Now close your mouth before a fly pops in.' He bent down and swung her up on his shoulder with his good arm. 'Would you like to come to the stables with me and give Ross an apple?'

'Yes, please!' she exclaimed. 'Only — may I have one for Gwalarn too? Or he'll be jealous ...'

'Gwalarn?' queried Alicia as Tamsin jogged across the yard high up on Cornish's shoulders. 'An unusual name.'

'It is a wind that blows to Brittany from the north-west,' replied Kerhouan. 'Whatever good or bad comes to fishermen in Brittany comes from that wind — but we Bretons are fishers and sailors, not horsemen, and so when I came on dry land, whatever good or evil came to me, depended on my horse. So Gwalarn he became.'

166

Tamsin perched on top of the pile of hay in the stable watching Colonel Jack grooming his horse. Ross and Gwalarn had each taken an apple from her hand and now she sat contentedly munching one herself, asking him questions between mouthfuls.

He told her of piskies who played tricks on Cornish folk, milking their cows in the morning if they lay too long abed; he told her of King Arthur, sleeping in a cave beneath his mighty castle of Tintagel till he and his heroes would be called again. She listened to him round-eyed.

'When we go into Sacramento, we shall have to buy you a storybook for your mama to read to you,' he suggested, bending down to clean Ross's hooves.

'I can read myself,' she boasted.

'Oh, can you, madam?' he teased.

She reached behind her and picked up a scrap of old paper that had caught on one of the partitions. 'I can! Really I can!' she insisted, and proceeded to read out a report from the *Sacramento Transcript* on the plans for the California State Fair. She stumbled over the occasional word, but read it through to the end.

'Lisha teached me ages ago,' she confided, 'but I like the pictures better. They're not as good as Lisha's pictures though. I wonder what equipment they use?'

'Why do you call your mother Lisha?' queried the Colonel. But the child was down from the haypile and out of the door before he realised she was moving. He stood there a moment, hoof-pick in his hands, then slowly he turned back to the haypile and picked up the scrap of paper. 'Yes,' he breathed. 'I wonder what equipment they use? Now whyever didn't I think of that before?'

'It wasn't something I could discuss with you at the Hotel,' explained Cornish casting an anxious look over his shoulder as Revel closed the door to his private office.

'Lamarr has been going the rounds of Sacramento boasting he'll have your lands off you before the year is out,' said the sub-editor, carefully arranging his pens and pencils in a neat row. 'The chief has been carrying editorials warning of the dangers of a renewal of the old land and squatter problem if people can't keep a rein on their greed. But – ah – I'm not sure he'd want us to take sides ...' he ended delicately.

'I've no desire to endanger the *Tribune's* independence,' Cornish reassured him. 'This is something quite different. See, I've found a better way of beating Lamarr's land-grabbing – strictly between you and me, of course!'

'That goes without saying,' Revel assured him. 'Do tell. I'm intrigued!'

'A survey,' Cornish informed him. 'The boundaries as they stand in the old documents surveyed, mapped and sworn out, every last landmark given a map reference that even Lamarr and his gang of corrupt lawyers cannot dispute. Only it all takes time and that's something we haven't got. D'you know what triangulation is?' he demanded unexpectedly.

The sub-editor raised his eyebrows and shook his head.

'Well, thank God for that! I began to think I was the only man in California who didn't!' Cornish laughed. 'It's matching a given site against three fixed points in order to establish its position ... And if you can photograph it against, say, a waterfall or a mountain peak, or even a stand of trees,' the Colonel continued, 'then you have proof incontrovertible that it is where you say it is. Now I have the surveyor but he could work better with a camera.'

'Then I'd recommend King's – or Beal's Daguerrean Gallery is very good if he's not too sure what equipment he needs ...'

'A compact English-style field camera, to take Talbotypes or Calotypes, *not* the heavy plates. Also a folding dark room and the relevant chemicals and equipment,' Cornish read from the list he had drawn out of his breast pocket.

'Daguerrotypes give more detail,' objected Revel.

'I'm told that's balanced out by the superior portability of the calotype,' replied the Colonel with a wry grin. 'Anyway, don't ask me, I'm just the errand boy. Now, the important thing is, can you buy it for me?'

'I can, of course ...'

'Will you? I can't go myself. Apart from the fact that I don't know what I'm talking about, I can't risk it getting to Lamarr's ears before we've completed the work.'

'That's as may be,' said Revel cynically, 'But I swear

there's a hell of a lot more to this than meets the eye.'

'Very likely. But will you do it?'

'Call by later this afternoon, on your way back to Tresco, and there'll be a couple of anonymous-looking boxes for you to load up,' said Revel with a long-suffering sigh. 'And I don't think I want to know anything more about it until you get confirmation of title from the Land Commission.'

'On that day, I'll stand you the best dinner Sacramento can provide!' promised the Colonel, picking up his hat and preparing to depart. 'Anything else happening in town?'

'As you'd know if you came to Letitia's more regularly, the town is positively humming with gossip on two points.'

Cornish raised his eyebrows enquiringly.

'One: Hester Bryant has broken off the engagement to Augustus Brenchley – no, I don't think you ever met him. He's a friend of mine from back east – I introduced them – and he's only been out here a week or two. Neither of them will say why, so the gossips are having a prime time. Two: more seriously, there's a positive hue and cry out after Mrs Owens – you met her once at the Cooper's. A delightful young lady. Disappeared from the face of the earth.'

'But people are coming and going all the time. You know what it's like out here – nobody asks any questions,' replied the Colonel uneasily.

'Different this time. I was to escort her to Letitia's last Sunday and she just upped and off from Carsons' with no reason given. There was a small child too. Brenchley's very upset about it. Like a dog with a bone, won't let it rest until he finds out what's happened to them.'

'Thought he'd come out here to marry Hester,' growled the rancher ungraciously. 'What's it to him?'

Revel told him about the accident out on Sutter's Slough. 'Very taken with her – and the child. And he won't let it drop. Wants me to put in a request for information in the *Tribune*. Says the West will never be civilised while it takes such a cavalier attitude to the safety of the weaker sex.'

'Oh, for God's sake!' exclaimed the Colonel in disgust. 'Why can't these namby-pamby Easterners see that things are different out here?' He chewed his lip angrily while he thought whether to say anything or not. 'Look here, Clive,' he said at last. 'You tell him from me, in confidence, that any hue and cry would be doing Mrs Owens a great disservice.'

'You can't expect me just to accept that!' objected Revel, looking at the Colonel in lively astonishment.

'If I give you my word that she's safe and well and wouldn't want anyone to concern themselves over her?'

'No,' said Revel flatly. 'Not that I doubt your word, but I think you ask too much. Besides, Brenchley doesn't know you ...'

'Damn him and his outmoded chivalry!' exclaimed the Colonel. 'Very well,' he sighed. 'In confidence, Clive, she's out at Tresco. She's doing the map for me – and the photography.'

Revel gave a low whistle. 'A remarkable woman!' he exclaimed. He mulled it over in his mind for a moment, then looked up at the Colonel. 'But if you don't want Lamarr to know, we can hardly tell them that. It'd be all over town in a day. And if you can't tell them you're employing her, then you'll have to say she's a guest of yours. Who's chaperoning her?'

'Oh, for God's sake, Clive! You know very well I haven't anyone out at Tresco but the hands and the foreman. Who the hell *could* be chaperoning her?'

'That'll go down well in Sacramento.'

'That's Sacramento's problem!' he snapped back. 'Damnation! Why couldn't you just have taken my word for it?'

'It won't do, Jack, really it won't,' said Revel with a shake of his head. 'People will talk. There's the note she sent to Letitia, begging her for help ...'

'The child was sick,' he muttered curtly. 'Of course, that's really the only reason she agreed to come, so Chen Kai – that's the Chinese cook – could look after the sick child.'

'What has the Chinese cook to do with it all?'

'I wish I knew the answer to that one, Clive,' Cornish confessed. 'But I do know that she's frightened of something or running from someone, so you see, Brenchley's hue and cry could be running her right into trouble.'

They argued the point round and round, getting nowhere. In the end, the Colonel, much to his chagrin, found himself

170

committed to bringing Mrs Owens in the following week to Letitia's soirée, time he felt they could ill afford with the rush to complete the maps and photographs.

'It's the only way to convince Letitia that you haven't kidnapped her!' insisted Revel.

What a pathetic creature they all seem to think her, thought Cornish. Beneath that pale, rather wan exterior there is a tough survivor, quite capable of chewing up effete Easterners and spitting them out in little pieces.

The camera Revel found for them was ideal and Cornish and Alicia spent the next few days going back over the ground they had already mapped. They went out alone, reluctant to take any of the hands lest word should filter through to Lamarr's informants in a drunken moment in a bar in Washington Town or Sacramento after payday. The heavy equipment had been repacked by Chen Kai — as Cornish always made a point of calling him now — in old sacking washed clean of dust or flour, and fashioned to sling across the saddle of a packhorse.

Cornish chafed at his demotion to the humbler role and attempted to be helpful, but Alicia brushed his proffered assistance aside.

'If I could have had Chen Kai, of course, it would have been a help,' she conceded, 'but he has his hands full with the house and Tamsin. And if I had to start teaching a new assistant from scratch — no, it would take up too much precious time.'

'Can't I just set up the developing tent for you? Set out all the chemicals?'

'Sounds fine in principle, but as I haven't the time to watch over you, it would be as dangerous as letting a child loose with Chen Kai's medicine box!' she said frankly. 'Have you any notion just how dangerous all these bottles are? No, of course you haven't!' She began to range the bottles at the back of the tray on a tripod over which the tent would eventually be thrown to shut out the light. 'Any of these chemicals could prove lethal in the hands of a novice,' she said crisply. 'This one, for instance, is an accelerator — fumes of chlorine. This is potassium cyanide, this one fumes of mercury. Many of these chemicals can poison or burn skin away. If we were

171

using the wet-plate method, with collodion, we'd have to contend with gun-cotton too — that means nitric acid and ether. That makes your eyes water just to coat the glass — and it's highly explosive too!'

'Now collodion I do know about,' he grinned. 'When the mine caved in, my back was ripped open. After the camp quack had stitched me up, they plastered me with collodion to keep the infection out. And every miner who came in to see if I was still alive seemed to have the end of a "ceegar" in his mouth. I was always terrified it would go out and they'd strike a Vesta to rekindle it and blow me and them to Kingdom Come!'

She looked at him with new respect. It was a brave man who could speak so casually of such heavy injuries. In her years in the mining camps, she had seen many men, adventurous beyond their technical abilities, dragged broken and bleeding from their burrow holes in canyons and hillsides. Medical assistance was rare, often non-existent, and most of them had died from horrific injuries, flesh hanging in flaps or limbs torn off where the earth had taken its revenge for the abuse they had meted out to her. Cornish had spoken quite casually about being stitched up; it was usually done with the viciously curved needles used to sew animal skins into hats or capes, and whatever mucky cotton thread happened to be about.

'I'll show you how it works when we've finished the job,' she said briskly.

'Yes, miss,' he said, touching his hat in mock deference. 'I think you missed your vocation : you should have been a schoolteacher!'

'I'll take that as a compliment,' she said with a short laugh. 'Although I doubt it was intended as one!'

The weather stayed fine and at each site she took photographs of all the boundary markers from a variety of angles. Cornish was intrigued to see that the paper she removed from the camera and took into the developing tent was quite blank. She explained to him that this 'blank' paper already contained the full image. Processing it in a solution which added silver proportionate to the amount of exposure each area had received, developed that hidden image into a master

172

negative. Once that had emerged, she could tell whether she had covered all the important aspects. The negative could then be used back at Tresco to print any number of prints, some to send to the Land Registry, others to be deposited where Lamarr could not get at them, an advantage which the one-shot daguerrotype could not offer.

She was delighted with the equipment — and congratulated him on the inspiration that had led him to Revel — but it came as a shock to her a few days later when he informed her that they were to make an appearance the following evening at Letitia's.

She turned away from the window embrasure, where she had been gazing down the valley watching the sun dip towards the rim of the mountains. 'But I thought we were going up to the Clearwater Lake to complete the mountain survey!' she protested. 'Surely socialising can wait!'

'I thought you would enjoy an evening of more elegant entertainment than Tresco can offer,' he suggested mildly.

'Of course. But I thought time was of the essence?'

'It is,' he conceded. 'But on this occasion I was left with no choice. Revel — and some easterner called Brenchley — were on the verge of launching a hue and cry following your disappearance.' He glanced sideways at her to see how she was taking the news. 'From the little Chen Kai told me, I knew that could cause trouble for you. The only way to stop them, it seemed, was for you to show yourself at Letitia's, fit and well. Nothing less would do. So — to Letitia's we must go!'

Later he wandered across to the arch that gave on to the verandah. She was sitting on the rim of the old fountain in the courtyard, listening to Tamsin's merry chatter, smiling fondly down at her; the rays of the sinking sun dappled her hair with golden lights.

He passed a hand wearily across his eyes and cursed himself for a fool. He should have told her of Revel's shock, prepared her in some measure for the censure that might be levelled against her — against them — but he had been too embarrassed, unable to find the right words.

173

He turned angrily away from the window, unbuckling his gun-belt and tossing his Adams revolver unusually carelessly to one side. To Hell with all small-minded hyprocrites, he thought savagely.

Chapter Fourteen

The dining room of the Orleans Hotel resounded to the clatter of busy knives and forks, the gruff tones of businessmen agreeing deals, the tinkle of feminine voices exclaiming over the latest fashion or scandal or shrilly telling their children, restless in the unaccustomed collar or tight sash, to sit still and hold their tongues.

'What the blazes is going on?' Colonel Cornish caught the head waiter as he sped past the doorway with a tray full of elaborate desserts.

George rolled his eyes heavenwards. 'Steamer in today,' he said. 'Brought a shipment of European furniture. Dunno how word got about, but I reckon half the population of Sacramento County – aye, and Solano and Yolo too! – was on the Embarcadero before dawn! Cleaned that ship out like a swarm of locusts – and now they're cleaning us out too. Booked a table, had you?'

He hadn't, of course, but he was a respected and regular customer and George swiftly found him a table by dint of sweeping two solitary diners on to a table with an elderly couple and promising them all a drink on the house for their trouble. He pocketed the coins Colonel Cornish slipped him with a knowing wink.

Alicia stood irresolutely in the doorway. Cornish reached her side just before George, relieved her of the parcels she was carrying and led her across to the corner table.

'I – I hadn't expected there to be so many people,' she stammered, suddenly conscious that a number of the diners were looking covertly at them.

'Nor I. There was a steamer in this afternoon. Furniture. Sure sign that the State is more settled when they start worrying about prettying up their homes. Myself, I'd always rather have a couple of good sound bulls or a sack of prime wheat seed than one of those rickety chairs the ladies rave over, that look as though they'll scarce take your weight.' He handed her the menu to peruse. 'Will you have wine?' he queried. 'Or soda? Or sarsparilla?'

She looked at the large glass of whiskey in front of him. 'I'd like a whiskey,' she said frankly. 'But that's not done, so I'll settle for wine.'

'I wouldn't,' he said. 'Thin, sour stuff they serve here. Used to whiskey are you?'

She nodded, remembering the days with Angelina.

He raised a quizzical eyebrow. 'Leave it to me,' he drawled.

'Soda for the lady — and another large whiskey for me,' he ordered, much to George's surprise, for the Colonel was normally an abstemious man and there was a full glass still in front of him.

When the order came — plates piled high with meat and vegetables in rich sauces in the fancy French style — he switched the fresh glass in front of her.

She took a drink and sat back with a grateful sigh. It was not going to be easy, coping with everyone at Letitia's without Chen Kai's herbs, and every little helped.

'Dutch courage?' he mocked.

She looked him straight in the eye and nodded.

'Comforting to know you have some weaknesses,' he observed drily, unobtrusively palming the glass back to his side of the table.

'You'd be surprised how many,' she said.

While George cleared away the plates and they ordered some of the desserts for which the Orleans was famed, he leaned back in his chair and observed her. She was wearing the simple grey silk dress, but whatever dress shop she had visited that afternoon had persuaded her to smarten it up a little. Delicate falls of lace had been stitched to the wrist bands and fell becomingly over her slim, work-reddened hands. The muslin fichu had been removed and an upstand

176

of lace trimmed the edge of the decolletage, revealing a modest amount of cleavage and emphasising the gentle swell of her bosom. In spite of himself, he found himself remembering the day at the *agua caliente* when nothing but a much-mended chemise had stood between them.

'Why didn't you buy yourself a new dress?' he demanded, more harshly than he had intended. 'If you didn't have enough money, you should have told me ...'

She raised her eyebrows. 'I have my wages, Colonel,' she said stiffly. 'I am entitled to no more than I have earned. And what I do with it is my concern, is it not?'

'Don't be so damned prickly!' he exclaimed angrily. 'I'll wager you spent it all on Tamsin. She's already a sight better dressed than you are. Silk petticoats while yours are calico ... When I was helping you out of the saddle ...' he ended gruffly.

Instead of being angry or blushing in confusion, he was astounded to see that she was actually giggling.

'So I stint myself to deck Tamsin out in finery?' she chuckled. She shook her head. 'Tamsin's finery is a relic of better days. What could no longer be patched or turned was cut down for her; sadly it all had to be replaced by calico. I can assure you that I am as fond of silk chemises and petticoats and ... whatever ... as the next woman.' She coloured. 'And this is a most improper conversation and we had better leave it there. If I fail to come up to your standards ...'

'A little old-fashioned, perhaps, but it suits you well.'

She raised startled eyes to his.

'Dammit!' he growled. 'That was supposed to be a compliment! I only meant – you're not quite as richly dressed as ...' He waved his hand generally at the few respectable ladies in the dining-room, elaborately dressed in bright silks and satins, mostly over-ornate.

'You forget, Colonel,' she answered quietly. 'I am a widow, and therefore expected to be more soberly dressed.' Her lips curved in a delightful smile. 'And now, since we have to go on working together, I think you had better leave the compliments and take me to the soirée.'

He could not remember ever being so clumsy with a

woman before and he had known many. But not under
such intimate circumstances: under the same roof, morning,
noon — and night.

He handed her into the gig and settled himself next to
her.

'Here.' He groped under the seat and thrust the little box
at her. 'Chen Kai asked me to give this to you.'

Wrapped in many layers of paper was a tiny flask of
perfume. 'Oh,' she sighed. 'What a lovely surprise. But how
did you ...?'

'He told me what to buy,' he said curtly. He preferred
women as nature made them and would rather have the
perfume of the herbs she rinsed her hair with than the heavy
drifts of musk and chypre so many society women wore.

When they arrived at the Coopers', Cornish leapt down
easily, handed the reins to Lucius, the Coopers' servant, and
hurried round to hand her down from the gig. As she stepped
down on to the raised sidewalk, she could not resist kicking up
her skirts to reveal a rustle of silken petticoats. 'The auctioneer
threw them in with the dress,' she murmured softly as she saw
him glancing down. He grinned sheepishly.

'Oh, Mrs Owens!' Letitia Cooper darted forward from her
brother's side as they were ushered into the hall. 'Alicia! Oh,
how my heart bled for you and the poor child when I read
your note! To be from home in your hour of need!'

'I was desperate,' admitted Alicia as she emerged from
Letitia's warm and friendly hug. 'I could think of nowhere
else to turn, but in the end, I believe it all turned out for
the best.'

'Oh, my dear girl! How can you say so?' wailed Letitia.

'But, ma'am, I assure you ... Tamsin is fully recovered!'

'All turned out for the best indeed!' The older woman was
near to tears, her face unbecomingly pink. 'To go out alone
to that place ... oh, Alicia, how could you?'

'I have Chen Kai ...'

'A servant!'

'A friend.'

'Everybody's talking about it.'

'Let them talk,' shrugged Alicia indifferently. 'What is it
to me?'

178

'Everything!' hissed the Reverend's sister vehemently. 'Everything! Your position in society ... You must leave Tresco, leave it immediately. You must both come here at once.'

'But you don't need any more servants!' exclaimed Alicia, her brow creased.

'Of course not!' replied Letitia indignantly. 'As my guests!'

'I know you mean it for the best, ma'am, but it isn't possible. I − I would rather not accept charity.'

'Friendship,' persisted Letitia obstinately.

'Charity offered with loving friendship is still charity. Thank you for your offer, but I believe I must continue my employment at Tresco.'

'Surveys! Men's work!' muttered Letitia darkly. 'Quite unbefitting a lady!'

Alicia looked around nervously.

'I know. Secrets. But Lamarr's not here tonight, nor expected. Though one never knows who may be on his payroll, obnoxious man. And that's another reason why I don't like it.' Letitia frowned. 'Lamarr is not a man to be trifled with. I told Colonel Cornish ...' She turned, as if expecting the Colonel and her brother still to be standing at her elbow. 'Oh, drat the men, they've gone!' she complained. 'Now we'll have to go in on our own.'

As they entered the drawing-room, a sudden hush fell on the assembled gathering. The Reverend Cooper was the first to step forward and greet Alicia, but even he seemed at a loss once the formal phrases had been uttered. Miss Letitia turned back into the room for a moment, casting an anguished look at her friends, gathered in little groups, but they all stood there as if frozen to the floor. The awkward pause seemed to Alicia to last a lifetime, although in truth it was barely a moment in duration. It was broken by Mr Revel, the newspaperman, who strode across the room to her side.

'Mrs Owens!' He bowed over her hand and kissed it with his cold lips. 'My mother was just expressing that hope that you and I would sing a duet again this evening.' He drew her across to his mother's side, leaving the older woman no choice but to follow her son's lead and greet Alicia.

Outside in the hallway there was the bustle of another arrival and the Leons, looking as ever like Beauty and the Beast, came in and began to greet their acquaintances. They professed themselves, without any hesitation, delighted to see Alicia once more. It broke the awkward moment and for that she was grateful, but she had been left in no doubt that her standing in this little society had subtly changed. There was a watchfulness in the eyes of the company that had not been there before. The initial inquisitiveness had been replaced by a slight, but palpable, condemnation — at least from the older ladies.

Across the room she could see Cornish chatting away quite calmly to Mr Revel Senior, as if nothing untoward had happened. If he could ignore the raised eyebrows, she could do the same. She stiffened her shoulders and lifted her head defiantly: she could be just as blasé as he.

Revel was at her elbow again, this time with another young lady on his arm.

'I don't think you have met Hester,' he said cheerfully. 'Hester — Mrs Owens, who delighted us with some decent singing at our last soirée. Mrs Owens — Hester Bryant, one of the few young ladies who does not put my teeth on edge when she sings.'

Hester smiled shyly and held out her hand. A rather delicate girl with a mass of fluffy fair hair and smoky blue eyes, she reminded Alicia of a little statuette, a Dresden shepherdess Mama had brought with her around the Horn and given pride of place on the mantelpiece in the little house in Yerba Buena.

'Hester, child, I want you!' called an authoritative voice from the other side of the room, where a stout, poker-backed figure was hovering anxiously.

'A moment, Mrs Bryant,' replied Revel cheerily, ignoring the look of panic in Hester's eyes. Alicia, ever quick to sense another's feelings, realised that the girl was very much under the domination of her mother and frightened of defying her.

'Now Hester,' Revel continued smoothly, as though there had been no interruption, 'Hester sings a beautiful rich alto. Wouldn't it be marvellous to hear the two of you singing together? We could get Edith to accompany you ... Letitia!' He turned to draw the Reverend Cooper's sister into the group. 'Can you think of something that Miss Bryant and Mrs. Owens could sing for us? Your knowledge of music is so much wider than mine.'

It was a challenge that few of the music lovers among them could resist and in a few minutes, Hester and Alicia were pouring their sweet voices into the air. Astonishingly, Hester had a truly rich alto voice, just as Revel had said, quite at odds with the delicate and submissive air which led one to expect a thin, breathy soprano. The two of them went on to sing 'Nymphs and Shepherds' with Mrs Revel. Then Alicia consented to sit at the piano and accompany Hester and Revel in a duet from von Flotow's popular opera *Martha*.

As the applause for the last duet died away, a deep voice behind Alicia murmured: 'Beautifully rendered, Hester.'

Hester drew her breath in sharply and two high spots of colour appeared on her cheekbones. Slowly she turned away from the piano and it seemed to Alicia that the entire room held its breath as the fair-haired girl confronted Augustus Brenchley, her former fiancé.

But they were to be disappointed. Hester neither fainted nor burst into tears, nor did she turn on her heel and ignore him.

'G-good evening, Mr Brenchley,' she said, with a fair assumption of calm, looking more delicate than ever beside the tall, well-built newcomer.

They stood stock-still for a moment, eyes locked, until the Reverend Cooper broke the silence with the offer of a glass of punch. Groups split up and reformed as the gentlemen handed round the cool glasses.

'What about you, Brenchley,' said Señor Leon jovially. 'Will you sing for your supper or have you some other talents?'

The lawyer in reply took up his seat on the piano stool that had just been vacated by Alicia and ran his fingers tentatively over the keys.

'It is some time since I have had the leisure to play, señor!' he replied deprecatingly. 'I fear the fingers have stiffened somewhat!'

He entertained them with a rondo and a minuet by Beethoven, played competently if not brilliantly. The final short piece he played he seemed to pour his heart into. When the last stirring chord had died away, there was a momentary silence before applause broke out. When they had finished clapping, he pushed the stool back from the piano.

'What was the last piece, Augustus?' demanded Mrs Revel. 'I do not believe I have heard it before.'

Brenchley looked past his friend's mother and locked Hester's eyes with his. '"An die ferne Geliebte",' he said deliberately. '"To the Distant Beloved".'

Hester looked for a moment as though she were going to burst into tears, but then her mother was at her elbow, drawing her away from the piano under the pretext of finding another duet to sing. Miss Cooper decided that the moment was ripe for supper and everyone broke up into small groups to exchange news and gossip. Alicia sympathised with Hester but at the same time she could not but be relieved that all eyes were now on her and Brenchley.

'We were sorry not to see you at the last soirée, Colonel Cornish,' chided Mrs Revel. 'Everyone was quite sure that you had gone to San Francisco to join the Vigilantes.'

Alicia, standing at a table laden with mouthwatering refreshments, suddenly found that her appetite had deserted her. What she would not have done for some of Chen Kai's herbs of oblivion! Blindly she allowed Henry Bryant to help her to a selection of delicacies, while straining to hear Cornish's answer.

'Because I was with them in '51? Oh no. It's quite a different kettle of fish this time.'

'How so?' queried Captain Sharples.

'We're no longer a frontier town, Captain. I'd rather fight for uncorrupted law officers. That's what the Vigilantes should be doing — and the Government should be working alongside them to achieve it.'

'And Gwin and Weller too,' agreed Mrs Revel. 'If they spent less time in Washington and more in the state that elected them ...'

'And what of Terry?' asked Mrs Pikeman eagerly. 'Will they hang him, d'you think, Colonel?'

'I think they dare not,' he answered frankly. 'The navy's under orders from the Governor to shell the city and declare martial law rather than let the Vigilantes hang a Supreme Court Justice.'

'And Hopkins?'

'His life hangs on a thread still. And I fear the future of law and order in California hangs there with it,' he said sombrely. 'Those of you who pray, better pray for Hopkins's survival.'

Brenchley was at Alicia's side with a glass of wine, taking her away from young Henry with practised ease and drawing her out on to the verandah, where they found a swing seat unoccupied.

'I understand from my friend Revel that you've had rather an uncomfortable time since we last met, ma'am,' he said with a sympathetic smile that sat well on his handsome features.

'I fear so.'

'And how is young Tamsin now?'

'Much improved, I thank you, sir. The air at Tresco ...'

'Why the deuce did you go out there, Mrs Owens?' he demanded in exasperation. 'You must have known how folk would gossip!'

She put her glass down with a snap. 'I don't give a damn what they say about me! And I'd be sorry, though not surprised, if you should join in their pettiness!' She took a deep breath. 'But – I owe you Tamsin's life, after all. The fact is, Mr Brenchley, Tamsin fell ill the day after you hauled her out of the Slough and they were threatening to put her in the Asylum. I never found starvation to be a cure for sickness.'

'I can't blame you for that. But the Colonel should have known better than to expose you to such gossip!'

'Perhaps he – like me – prefers not to run his life by what other people think!' she snapped. 'He needed someone to put Tresco to rights, a housekeeper if you like, and I needed the work. Employment is more important to me than social approval!'

He looked over his shoulder to be sure that no one else was within hearing distance. 'Don't fear, my friend Revel has told me why Cornish had need of your services. That's in my capacity as a lawyer, and I'm always discreet. I shall be calling on the Colonel to offer him my services in the forthcoming affair. It promises to be something of a test case.'

'You're not returning to New York?'

'No.' He bit his lip. 'Although my original purpose in travelling to California can no longer be served, yet I feel that the air here suits me well. I may even decide to hang out my shingle in Sacramento.'

The verandah was beginning to fill up now as more of the guests came out to savour the light evening breeze which wafted over the gardens, carrying the sweet scents of the native plants with which Miss Cooper had filled her garden.

'Have you seen the new production of *Camille* at the Forest, Mrs Owens?'

'It's not one that's come my way,' she replied.

'I — er — I have some tickets for a performance a week Saturday,' he began hesitantly. 'I wonder whether you would care to accompany me — with Miss Cooper, of course,' he added hastily. 'And perhaps the Reverend. It is Miss Hayne, you know,' he urged as she hesitated. 'Direct from performing the role in New York.'

'Hadn't you better consult the Colonel first?' came Mrs Bryant's sneering voice from directly behind them.

Alicia coloured angrily at the insinuation. Unfortunately for Mrs Bryant, Cornish himself had just come out on to the verandah.

'My dear lady,' he said in deceptively silky tones, 'Mrs Owens has no need to seek her employer's permission for anything she chooses to do in her spare time. What can you be thinking of?' His raised eyebrow made it quite clear that he knew *exactly* what she had been thinking of and was daring her to come out in the open and say it.

'My dear Colonel, how you do take one up!' she trilled. 'I assure you you quite mistake me, quite.'

'I believe Miss Pikeman is going to delight us with a sonata,' Cornish went on imperturbably, as though nothing had happened. 'Shall we go in?'

He held out his arm and Mrs Bryant, puffing and muttering, her face a faint shade of purple, was left with no choice but to take it.

'Can we not press you to play for us this evening, Jack?' demanded Miss Cooper later that evening. 'We've enough ladies for a country dance or a foursome reel. I know you did not bring your instrument, but there is always Octavius's violin ...'

'I fear no one would dance to my tune this evening, Letitia,' he replied ruefully. 'I could play you a fine lament and have all the ladies in floods ...?'

'No, no,' interposed the Reverend hastily. 'We're endeavouring to banish melancholy, not encourage it! But if you won't play, then you'll have to sing for your supper! You know Letitia's rules!'

By the time Señor Leon had finished, none too expertly and rather more *basso* than *profundo* with 'Rocked in the Deep', Miss Cooper had found the music she wanted.

'"The song of the Cornishmen",' she announced with pleasure. '"And shall Trelawney die?" Such stirring words, don't you think, Colonel Cornish?'

'Very moving!' he agreed gravely and Alicia wondered whether she was the only one to notice the curl of the lip as he spoke. Obviously not one of his favourite songs. 'What else have you there? Ah yes, Tom Moore's Irish Melodies.'

'"The Last Rose of Summer",' she said with a romantic sigh. 'Such beautiful sentiments so nobly expressed. Mrs Owens will sing with you − I shall accompany.'

Alicia felt the colour creeping up her throat to suffuse her face as she stood next to her employer, looking over the music, aware that all eyes were once more upon them. Damnation! she thought savagely. Why couldn't she have picked someone else?

Even as they sang the first notes, she knew that she was in the presence of a far superior singer. Cornish's voice was rich and splendid, soaring effortlessly over a wide range and encouraging her to an excellence she had not thought herself capable of. As the last liquid notes died away, there was a moment of appreciative silence before the listeners broke into enthusiastic applause.

Soon afterwards, the gathering broke up, the guests departing in their carriages or on foot, some to their homes in Sacramento and the nearby settlements, others who had driven in from farther afield to the various hotels where they would stay overnight.

'I wish you would stay,' grumbled Miss Cooper as the Colonel handed Alicia up into the gig. 'I don't like to think of you driving all that way back.'

'It's a fine moonlit night, Letitia,' he replied easily. 'And the road I know like the back of my hand. Besides, I can't afford to lose any more time if we're to finish the job before the Commission closes its doors.'

'Yes — but I don't like it, don't like it at all,' she complained peevishly. 'Taking on a man like Lamarr — it's just asking for trouble!'

'You wouldn't want me to let him walk in and take Tresco from me without a fight, would you?' He took her thin hand in his and kissed it gallantly. 'Trust me, Letitia,' he added seriously. 'And I'll take your advice on — the other matter.'

'I should hope so!' she replied grimly. 'And I'll do what I can at this end, never fear!'

A wave of the hand and they were away, heading down to the Embarcadero.

Chapter Fifteen

The steamboats were still plying across the wide, muddy river, fetching the gamblers back across the Sacramento from the brothels and hell holes of Washington town.

'You have a magnificent voice,' Alicia said softly. 'And you play the violin. Surprising talents – for a country boy.'

He negotiated the steep curve that took them on to the road to Tresco. 'Music has played a large part in my life,' he concluded.

'And yet you wouldn't sing that Cornish song for Miss Cooper,' she commented curiously.

'Ah! You noticed that.' He looked slightly sheepish.

'I'm not as easily diverted as Miss Letitia,' she observed drily.

'Pity.' He heaved a sigh of resignation. 'It's just that – I differ from the rest of the world in seeing a pack of bishops as potential heroes.'

'Why?'

'It's an unedifying story. I was a scholarship boy at a cathedral school – chosen for my voice, not my brains. I received my musical training there, and a good education, as long as it lasted. When the piping treble voice broke, they threw me out. Overnight. Out on the road to walk back to Cornwall. And when I got back, there was nothing for me but the mines.'

'And Trelawney?'

'A seventeenth-century Cornish bishop, imprisoned for his principles and threatened by the English with hanging. No doubt very heroic. But when they threw me out of the

Cathedral School, I could happily have imprisoned thirty Cornish bishops and seen the English hang the lot.'

They breasted the ridge. The ranch-house stood on the far side of the valley, bathed in silvery moonlight, magical and quite different from its daytime self. She drew in her breath sharply, realising with an ache in her heart how quickly she had come to regard Tresco as a refuge.

'Don't drive on yet,' she whispered. Her face glowed in the moonlight, quite stripped of its normal guarded expression. He let the reins fall slack on the horse's neck and leaned back on his seat, his arm casually along the back, turned slightly sideways to observe her.

'You knew what was going to happen this evening, didn't you?' she demanded abruptly.

'Yes.'

'Could you not have warned me?' Her voice was plaintive, like a child's.

'You might not have come if you had known what was waiting for you. And that would have caused even more gossip.'

'To Hell with them!' she exclaimed inelegantly. 'You hired me to do a job, and I'm doing it. I don't propose to take any notice of their small-mindedness.'

'Unfortunately, it's not that simple,' said Cornish gravely. 'Especially since we can't tell them just *why* I employed you.'

'But –'

'It's all fine and dandy for you to say "to Hell with them", Mrs Owens, and normally I'd join you, because I know there's no basis for their gossip, but I have to go on living here,' he said with a scowl. 'And it isn't just a case of offending Society : that society consists of lawyers, senators, men of standing like Cooper, newspapermen like Revel, all the people I'll need on my side to fight Lamarr, all the people whose support Letitia and Octavius and I depend on for our schools campaign. I can't afford to alienate them all just for the sake of a gesture.'

He saw her shoulders sag wearily.

'There is a solution.' She turned her face to him, ghostly in the moonlight. 'Letitia suggested it.'

'What?'

'You could marry me.'

He had expected a strong reaction to his words and he was not disappointed. 'Have you gone mad?' she whispered.

'It's not such a bad idea,' he said calmly, with the air of a man considering a business proposition.

'We hardly know each other, let alone ...'

'Let alone love one another?' he completed for her. 'Of course, there's no pretence of *that*,' he said scornfully. 'But calm down and you might see the sense in the idea. We're already as well acquainted − if not more so − than many couples who supposedly marry for love. We can rub along together in a fairly superficial manner, which is all I require. And what does the future hold for you otherwise? What future for you or Chen Kai or Tamsin in tramping about the state looking for work? Well enough when you had your camera, and no doubt you were very good at your work, but as the country grows more settled, the prospects of that kind of enterprise become less and less. Don't forget the state you were in when you first arrived at Tresco ... is that what you want for Tamsin?'

'You don't want a wife,' she protested.

'Not particularly,' he admitted. 'But I want to see Tresco flourishing. And you could put it in order. There's a great deal in what Letitia says.'

She twisted the ends of the shawl in taut fingers as she struggled to find the words. The prospect of staying on at Tresco, of a stable way of life after the misery of the last year, warred with the prospect of marrying again, of being at the mercy of a man, as much a man as Robert, or −

The unbidden memory hovered on the edge of her mind, eating away at the invisible defences she had thrown up and she knew with a dull certainty that she could not do it.

'I will do whatever work you have,' she said, in a voice so low that he had to crane forward to make out the words, 'but I am no hypocrite. I will not marry you.'

He ground his teeth audibly in annoyance. 'You saw tonight what the consequence of that attitude will be!' he snapped. He took a deep breath to calm himself. 'Look, we're both tired,' he said. 'We'll talk about it again in the morning.'

She shook her head. 'There's no point,' she murmured. 'The answer would be the same.'

He picked up the reins and urged the horses forward, driving down into the valley, over the bridge and up the slope to the ranch far too fast for safety, for all that the moon shone so brightly.

When he drew up in the stableyard, she gathered her skirts up to climb down from the gig, but he was before her and she had no choice but to accept his help in descending.

As she reached the ground, she tried to hurry away, but he held tightly to her wrist, gazing down at her in baffled silence. She met that angry green gaze for a brief moment, then looked pointedly down at his strong fingers curled painfully around her wrist.

'Damn your obstinacy!' he muttered, and as he relaxed his grip she slipped away, gliding soundlessly in the moonlight to her door where, like a wraith, she disappeared from view, leaving behind her only a faint perfume, like the breeze passing over a field of wild flowers on a spring morning.

There were only a few hours left of the night, but, despite her exhaustion, she could not sleep. She lay wakeful, alert to every little sound or sigh from Tamsin in the inner chamber. She would have given a great deal for a draught of Kai's herbs, but on her return from Pedro's, he had refused to give her any more.

'You have been dependent on them too long,' he had said firmly.

'But —'

'It's time to face up to life, Alicia.'

'I can't.'

'If you can't do it here, where can you do it?'

'Somewhere where there's no one to remind me . . .'

'Alicia, there are men everywhere in California. Unless you plan to join the Sisters of Mercy, you'll have to learn to face up to what happened and move on.' His heart ached for her, but he wouldn't let it show. 'After Robert, you managed to cope with the men in the *cantina*. Coping with the men in Sacramento society cannot be worse than that. You'll manage.'

As the first rosy fingers of dawn painted a glowing pattern

on her window, she gave up the struggle and rose to don a light shawl. She stepped into the other room to gaze down on the sleeping child, envious of her deep and serene slumber.

She remembered when Tamsin had tossed and turned night after endless night, often screaming out in her nightmares, times when Alicia would have given the world to see the little girl at peace with herself again. And now Alicia was planning to take her away from 'the pretty green place' and set them all back on the tramp again, to join that miserable band of failures who had proved incapable of making a living in the prosperous new state. It was madness, she knew, but she could do no other.

She was not the only one to have had a disturbed night. Cornish, scowling over a cup of coffee, barely acknowledged her greeting. Even Tamsin's sunny face did not bring the usual smile and pat on the head, but she had learnt at an early age to adapt herself to the behaviour of the adults around her, so she sat quietly on her chair and ate her bread.

Kai placed a plate in front of Alicia and she helped herself, with a slight grimace, from the leathery bread in the centre of the table, wondering whether there would be leisure in the day to come to do a decent baking.

'I'm sending Chen out with you today, Mrs Owens,' said the Colonel abruptly. 'There's a report of some broken stockading in one of the valleys where we keep cattle. Kerhouan and I will ride over and check it out.'

'But what about the cooking?' she asked.

'Juan or Luis can do it!' he snapped. 'Whatever they do, it can't be worse than we get now! The sooner Chen Kai is out of the kitchen, the better we'll all be pleased!'

'I let us in for that, didn't I?' murmured Alicia ruefully as they saddled up their horses.

'Not a good evening?'

'A fair number of unpleasant remarks and insinuations. Nothing I couldn't cope with.' It was only the proposed solution that worried her.

Kai did not refer to the matter again. On the way back, however, a chance remark about Tamsin, who had been left playing cheerfully with Josefa under Luis's watchful eye while

191

his father and brother cleared out one of the old outbuildings for expected stock, brought the painful thoughts of the dawn back to haunt her.

'What is it, Alicia?' he enquired.

'She's happy here, isn't she?'

'Of course.'

'And you too, Kai, are you happy? Or would you rather be back on the road again, with the picture wagon?'

'They were good days,' he nodded with a broad smile of reminiscence. 'But you can't live in the past. Those days are gone. I suppose we would have had to settle down in the end, for Tamsin's sake, and I can't think of many places better than Tresco. So much to be achieved here — though preferably not in the kitchen.' He reined in his horse and looked at her. 'The Colonel wants us to stay on?'

She shook her head, cursing herself for raising his hopes. She was almost tempted to pour out her troubles to Kai, but that was the coward's way.

That evening, when they returned to the Mission, they found Augustus Brenchley standing on the *portal* in animated discussion with Kerhouan and Cornish. He ran lightly down the steps and across the yard to help Alicia down out of the saddle.

'Mrs Owens!' he exclaimed. 'How delightful to see you again!'

He held on to her hand, bowing over it and brushing it with his lips. Aware of the Colonel's scrutiny, she found herself blushing.

'I've asked Brenchley to take pot-luck with us,' said Cornish stiffly. 'We have a lot to discuss — you'll join us for dinner?'

It was a command, not a request. She could hardly refuse.

'You'll want to change,' the Colonel allowed, casting an eye over her dusty clothes and dust-streaked face. 'Luis will bring water to — your apartment.' This with a sidelong glance at Brenchley.

It was Kai, not Luis, who turned up with the cans of hot water.

'Alicia! What on earth am I going to feed Brenchley?' he pleaded.

She almost laughed at the panic on his face, but she took pity on him.

'There are some lemons in the store,' she replied soothingly. 'Pick some herbs and make him a good cool drink. Then set Luis to build up the fire and prepare lots of vegetables. I'll be with you in ten minutes.'

The water was silkily cool against her skin, but she did not linger over her bath, for she knew Kai would never cope.

She wondered as she drew on her grey silk how Mr Brenchley would take to dining in such surroundings, though he did not strike her as one to stand on his dignity.

In the kitchen, chaos reigned. The fire had been stoked up high and the heat hit her as she walked in the door.

Luis was distractedly trying to clear the table of the accumulation of papers and Xavier was looking with deep suspicion at the contents of the store cupboard. Kai was just looking very unhappy.

With a sigh she picked up the sacking apron lying on the kitchen chair, issued her orders and set to.

Within moments, the sweat was running off her brow and her clean dress was sticking to her as she arranged trivets and pans over the heat. She thought longingly of the efficient closed range which Angelina had bought from the first batch shipped around the Horn, which could take twice as many pots, as well as having two ovens, and which had never, in the hottest summer, produced the stifling heat this fire did. And to think that so many stoves had been shipped in and glutted the market, that they had used them to fill the holes in San Francisco's main streets!

Despite the difficulties, she soon had everything under control. Before long she was able to leave Kai and his assistants to carry on, pausing only to set her apron aside and mop the sweat from her face. Her hair had slipped down from its knot, but she had no time to dress it again. She pinned it back with two high combs, took a deep breath to steady herself and marched in.

'At last!' growled the Colonel in exasperation. 'I've been waiting on you this half hour and more!'

Mr Brenchley rose from the settle and drew her across to sit beside him. 'But you'll agree it was worth the waiting, Colonel,' he murmured, with an admiring glance.

She accepted the compliment with a gracious inclination of her head, though it amused her greatly that they should think she had spent all this time on her dressing!

'I wanted to show Brenchley the photographs,' snapped the Colonel impatiently.

Clearly small talk was not part of his plan for the evening.

Alicia fetched the maps from her room and the prints from the windowless store cupboard which she had transformed into a darkroom.

'These are really very good, Mrs Owens,' said the young lawyer, glancing with shrewd blue eyes from photographs to maps and back again. 'Yes. These should hold up very well in court if Lamarr should be foolish enough to take it that far.'

'Sure?'

'Finished, cross-referenced and sworn, of course. You realise, Mrs Owens, you will have to swear an oath as to their validity?'

She nodded.

'Good. I can get Halleck of Halleck, Peachy and Billings — they specialise in land claims, you know — to come to my office privately and witness them. Halleck trained with me back east, and he's a good friend, so we can be sure Lamarr has not got to him. But you may have to swear them again in court.'

'In court?' Her voice shook.

'Yes,' replied Brenchley without looking up from the photographs. 'Land Commission Court. Sits in San Francisco until next month.'

At that moment Luis came in to announce dinner and they did not see the Colonel's hard, speculative gaze on her.

The dinner was simple but excellent. The lightly grilled fish was followed by well-dressed meat and succulent vegetables from the garden, and the whole was rounded off with a bowl of New England syllabub which Brenchley declared rivalled anything the Orleans could provide.

'Come back in six months time, Brenchley, and it'll be even

better,' said the rancher with a look of determination in his eye. 'I intend to undo the neglect of the past and make Tresco self-sufficient.'

Brenchley did not linger, as he had to ride back to Sacramento that evening.

'Will you take the first batch of photographs back with you?' asked Alicia.

'No,' he replied decisively. 'We don't want to do this piecemeal and run the risk of alerting Lamarr. He and his wife are back in town. Have it all prepared and I'll get the swearing organised in Sacramento in the next week or two. Then we can send copies to Washington and anywhere else they're necessary, all in one go.'

'Brenchley left this for you,' said Cornish, when Brenchley had gone. He drew a sealed letter from inside his waistcoat. 'Though what he has to say to you that can't be said openly, damned if I know.'

She made no move to open the letter.

'Why didn't you tell me you'd been busy in the kitchen?' he demanded abruptly.

She shrugged. 'If you'd rather believe I spend that kind of time thinking about my finery ... Besides, it's not my place to argue with my employer.'

'You're not a slave!' he snapped angrily. 'You're as entitled as anyone else to tell me when I'm talking through my hat!'

The anger died out of his eyes, but the look that replaced it made her feel uncomfortable. She turned away with the glasses and crossed to the door. His voice, warm and low, stopped her in her tracks.

'You should dress in a hurry more often,' he said with an appreciative chuckle. 'With your hair like that, you look more like Tamsin's sister instead of her governess.'

Kai took the photographic equipment from Alicia and loaded it on to the packhorse. Alicia checked the girths of her mare and gazed out across green meadows speckled with the jewel bright colours of wild flowers to the barely visible peaks beyond which were their destination.

The sky was pale, the rosy haze of dawn barely fled before the bright rays of the sun which had just topped the distant ranges of the Sierra Nevada; Tresco looked as though it had been new washed in the gentle dew.

'What is it, Alicia?' Kai left the horses and sat beside her on the steps. He took her hand in his. 'What is it?' he said softly.

'Oh, I'm just being foolish.' Then, as if she could not stop herself, she blurted out : 'This is the last survey, Kai! There's just today out at Lake Clearwater, then — then it's all finished.' And I'll have to decide, decide whether we stay here on his terms or set out again on that long, weary road that leads God only knows where.

'Alicia, you have your work to do — do it well. It is enough for the moment. Live a day at a time, my dear. The rest will sort itself out in its own good time.'

'Chinese fatalism?' she laughed.

'Better for the soul than New England melancholia!' he teased. 'When you are ready, you will find the decision will come quite naturally. And above all, you must not allow the past to colour what you do now.'

She looked at him suspiciously. 'Chen Kai! Did the Colonel tell you?'

'I am guessing. What else would take such thought, cause such anguish? And his attitude to you has changed ... It is something only you can decide. If you want my advice, you know I'm always here.'

'But — it is your business too! Kai, there's no reason why you shouldn't stay on, even if I —'

'Abandon you and Tamsin?' he demanded scornfully. 'Don't be foolish!' He gave her a quick hug. 'We managed before. We'll manage again.'

'When you're ready, Mrs Owens,' came a deep voice from the shadows behind them.

She rose swiftly to her feet and crossed to Rosita's side. Chen Kai, impassive as ever, helped her up into the saddle.

They had been riding for over an hour before a word was said.

As they emerged from a narrow defile into the more open upper hills, lightly dotted with a variety of trees, he edged his horse alongside hers and passed the water flask across.

'What did Brenchley have to say?' he demanded abruptly. 'Or was it private?'

'Not particularly.' She wiped the neck of the flask and handed it back to him. 'He just said that Miss Cooper was working on the Sacramento gossips and he was quite sure she would see them all off. He reminded me of our arrangement to go to the theatre. Oh, and he says ...' she blushed a little. ' ... he says that in order to allay suspicion from Lamarr, who's back in town, he has put it about that he comes to Tresco to − er − to see me.'

'You're not fool enough to believe Brenchley has any serious intentions?' he exclaimed. 'A man does and says some stupid things when he's been rejected by a woman. And although he'll do very well for Hester, I'd have thought you had more backbone than to fall for a soft easterner!'

'If a man doesn't wear a gun and talk about crops and cattle or mining, and if he's well-mannered enough to be polite to the ladies, then to a Californian he's soft and effete! You're so prejudiced! Anyway,' she touched the mare lightly with her heels and moved away, 'I'm quite aware that he's in love with Hester. And I've already told you that I have no interest in men!'

'Fine. Then we'll not mention him again,' he said indifferently. 'I grant he knows his stuff as a lawyer.'

'If you had seen him when he saved Tamsin's life you would not dismiss him so scornfully!' she snapped.

'Let's hope his efforts were not wasted,' he growled back. 'Take that child back on the road again and you put her life at risk as much as it was at Sutter's Slough!'

Clearwater Lake, when they reached it at last, was stunningly, breathtakingly beautiful and they both reined in their horses and gazed down in silence at the scene below.

The lake was situated in a depression, a sort of upland valley, set in a bowl of green hills whose lower slopes were carpeted with exotic wild flowers of myriad hues which tumbled down the hillside to lap the margins of the lake, a jewel in a perfect setting whose colour changed bewitchingly from jade to turquoise and back again. In all her travels, she had never seen anywhere so sublimely beautiful.

The water, when they dismounted to let the horses drink,

was crystal clear and swarming with shoals of fish of all shapes and sizes. While Alicia set up the camera and made her preliminary sketches for the survey, Cornish set lines to catch their midday meal.

When she was quite ready, he picked up the marked surveying staff, ready to move to left or right as she directed him, while she measured the angles and calculated the distances. 'The last time I'll have to do this!' he laughed.

The last time! The last day's surveying. After this, the rest of the work would be done back at the ranch house. She owed it to him to take as little time as possible with the drawing of the maps and the printing of the photographs, for he had to put his claim in swiftly before the Land Commission finally closed its doors to business. And then what? Don't think about it.

Her spirits rose as she set the camera up and looked through the lens. Always that strange energy surge at the magic of creation. If this one were only hers ...

She uncapped the lens and counted, knowing that the beauty of the scene would be, by her intervention, encapsulated and frozen for all time.

She would take several views, she decided, and the best one she would tint, recreating the full glory and splendour of the colourful scene before her.

It was soon done. There was no breeze, the light was perfect and this far from the ranch there was no fear of interruption. When she had finished, she set the camera in the shade of a huge spreading pine tree and went down to the water's edge to cool her face and hands. Greatly daring, she slipped her feet out of her buttoned boots and dipped her stockinged feet into the icy water, sending shivers of pure pleasure through her. Her hair had slipped out of the tight knot into which she had hastily twisted it that morning and she knelt down on the cool grass to pin it back up, unconscious of the hard green gaze fixed on her slim silhouette.

He joined her at the lake side a few moments later, his jacket discarded and his shirt sleeves rolled up. He plunged his arms into the cool water and held them there a moment before splashing his head and neck with great liberal handfuls.

'Come out of the sun!' he commanded, reaching down to

draw her to her feet. 'It's very exposed up here; you don't want to get sunstroke.'

In the great tree's shade he had set out a veritable feast. 'A celebration lunch,' he explained.

The ride and the work had given her quite an appetite and she ate heartily of the smoky flavoured fish, the remains of the meat from yesterday, sliced cold, and some choice fruit. There was even some wine, shipped all the way across the Atlantic and round the Horn to be drunk thousands of miles from the vineyard, in this beautiful spot on top of the New World.

'That was delicious!' she exclaimed when she had eaten her fill.

'Pleasant change to eat good food you haven't had to cook!'

She nodded sleepily, her eyes half-closed, languorous from the effects of the warm sun and the strong wine.

'Siesta time,' he murmured. And within moments, she was asleep.

It was a little cooler when she woke about an hour later. Cornish was still asleep, his face curiously young and vulnerable as sleep smoothed out the lines of worry.

He stretched and sat up and she averted her gaze. 'Where next?' she asked lightly.

'Nowhere,' he answered lazily. 'Not till we're ready to go back to Tresco, that is. And I'm in no hurry.' He propped himself up on his elbow and smiled at her. 'The last boundary. Look, over there. See that fold in the hills over to the right? That's where the Tresco flows out of the lake. Remember that waterfall we surveyed way back at the beginning? That's the spot. And over to the left a way, is the mountain where you found the cinnabar.'

He ran his finger around inside his cravat, tight in the heat of the afternoon. 'Would you mind ...?' he began, hand on the knot.

'Not at all.' Truth to tell, she envied him, for she was feeling just as stifled in her high-neck blouse.

It was as if he read her thoughts. 'Feel free,' he invited.

She shook her head. After a moment she rose and wandered down again to the lakeside. Leaning against the rough bark of a tall tree she gazed out across the water to the far shore, deep in thought.

'Beautiful, isn't it?' he said, pride and awe mixed in his voice. 'Like the Sierras before we spoiled them.'

She nodded her agreement.

'One day I'll build a cabin up here,' he declared unexpectedly. 'Nothing elaborate, just somewhere I can come to be alone.'

'Too many people at Tresco?'

'There will be eventually.' He shrugged philosophically. 'It's inevitable. You can't run a ranch this size with three men and a dog. And I want Tresco to be as self-sufficient as possible : blacksmith, saddlery, granaries, a proper bunk-house, a cookhouse and a decent cook.' He looked sideways at her to see her reaction. 'Yes, Tresco will grow,' he went on. 'And I'll be glad of it, but that doesn't mean I won't want to get away from it now and again.'

He narrowed his eyes and looked across to where the sun shone brightly on the peaks of the Coast Range.

'Show me how to make a plate?' he suggested unexpectedly.

'If you like,' she replied. After all, he was paying for her time.

She padded back across the cool green grass to set up the camera. Patiently she showed him how to place the sensitized paper in the light-proof holder, set it in the camera and then uncap the lens for the required time. In the bright sunlight, Alicia reckoned that about half a minute would be sufficient.

'Now you do it,' she told him. And he inserted the paper, slotted the holder into the camera and ducked under the hood to focus.

'Is that right?' he questioned.

'Let me see.' She pulled off her wide hat and slipped under the lightproof cloth next to Cornish to look through the lens. 'Perfect,' she confirmed gravely. 'Now, put your hand round to the lens cover. Here.' She reached forward to guide his hand round and he caught his breath at the feel of her pressed close up against him and the perfume of her in his nostrils.

'Once you have uncapped the lens, you must remain

perfectly still,' she instructed in a calm voice that betrayed none of the disquiet she felt coursing through her veins as their hands touched. Involuntarily she shivered. 'If you jar the tripod, you will ruin the photograph.'

As soon as she could, she withdrew from beneath the cloth, leaving him to take a few more plates by himself. He insisted on taking a picture of her leaning against the tree by the water's edge.

'Now I'll take one of you,' she suggested. 'Stand in the same position, but keep quite still. You can dream of your log cabin, if you like.'

He made no move to go down to the lakeside, but stood looking at her with a strange unreadable expression in his eyes. He reached out and took her hand and once again she felt that strange shivering sensation that she could not control. Yet this time it didn't feel like fear.

'Thought any more about my suggestion?' he demanded, hard green eyes challenging her.

'I – you see – I –'

'We could build some sort of understanding between us,' he went on as if she had not spoken. 'Think of Tamsin! Think how much happier she would be if she could stay in Tresco – the "lovely green place" she calls it.' He held her hand tightly between his. 'I'd care for her as if she were my own,' he said softly.

'Is this the man who said there was no place for women and children in the new state?' Her voice was brittle and high.

'I've said some foolish things in my time. I was very bitter then. I'm sure you've heard the story.'

'Is that why Lamarr is so against you?'

'I doubt it. If the roles had been reversed and he'd been rejected for me, then, possibly.' He smiled at her. 'And you're trying to change the subject. Answer my question: could we not work together to build Tresco, as we've worked together on this?'

She became aware suddenly that her hand was still lying, quiescent, in his and drew it away.

'If it's Belle – Mrs Lamarr – you'd have no cause for jealousy,' he assured her.

'Jealousy doesn't come into it.'

'The memory of your husband ...?'

'My husband? Ha!' Her laughter was slightly hysterical. 'Despite what the Mrs Pikemans and Mrs Bryants of this world would have you believe, not all women yearn for a husband to take their cares from their shoulders! Some of us prefer our freedom. Unlike you, I've tried marriage, Colonel, and I wasn't smitten by it. I have no plans to repeat the experience.'

Back at the ranch, all the photographs came out well. Cornish's photograph showed her very pensive, her head bowed down and reflected in the still water; hers showed him very stiff, a resentful expression frozen on his face.

Chapter Sixteen

In between working on the maps and photographs she tried to make some order out of the living accommodation at the Mission, whose shortcomings had been shown up only too clearly by Augustus Brenchley's visit. She hoped Cornish would not think she was exceeding her duties!

One sunny afternoon, she was passing by the stable as Luis led in Kerhouan's horse to be rubbed down and fed. She stopped to stroke Gwalarn's nose and heaved a regretful sigh.

'Oh, what wouldn't I give to be riding across the hills again!' she murmured into his glossy ear.

'You've only yourself to blame,' came a curt voice from the shadows. 'As long as you're here, Rosita is at your disposal.'

She jumped as Jack Cornish emerged from the stables, a saddle in his hand.

'I thought you were out riding the boundaries!' she said.

'Just come back. And I mean what I say about the horse.'

'But I − I have no right to be using your horses now the work is over,' she objected.

'I'll give you two reasons,' he said sharply. 'Rosita is eating her head off and getting fat and lazy again with no one to ride her and you're spending too much time indoors and losing that healthy glow.'

'I'll wager you're glad to be back out on the range again,' she said shrewdly.

'Yes indeed! Lamarr caused me to waste far too much time

that would have been better spent on the ranch. Not that there weren't compensations in travelling around with a beautiful woman – '

She looked up at him sharply.

' – but they were too few and far between,' he ended blandly. 'And I have to make up for last year's neglect.'

'And yet the land and the animals seem to be in good heart.'

'Thanks to Kerhouan,' he admitted. 'But my stock could be improved.'

She looked at him curiously. 'All those Longhorns we saw running in the valleys out towards the *agua caliente* – they're as good as any I've ever seen in California.'

'As Longhorns go, they're not bad,' he agreed. 'But I want Tresco beef to be the best there is. Longhorns are simply not good enough for me.'

'What's wrong with Longhorns? The Spanish ran them and the Mexicans; everyone out west runs Longhorns!'

'Oh sure, and if you want quantity, then the Longhorn is your best bet. All that open plain land in Texas now, that's ideal for running great herds. The Texas plains are not all that prime, but the Longhorn can survive and flourish on very little. The drawback is they don't mature in less than ten years, for the most part. With the prime and fertile grasslands we have here, why not aim for quality, instead of quantity? Sure, the cities back east are hungry for just about any kind of beef, but what about the cities here? Plenty of money about. And what does the man with money prefer in the way of beef? Even the Texas cattlemen? They go for Shorthorn beeves any time.'

'But there have only ever been Longhorns in California – haven't there?'

'Up in Oregon there are Devon, Hereford, Angus – been thriving up there since the settlers brought them back in the forties.'

'All right. I'm convinced. But how do Shorthorns in Oregon become Shorthorns in Tresco? They're not as hardy as Longhorns – they'll scarcely be good stock by the time you've marched them down over the Klamath mountains, always supposing that the Indians don't decimate them on the way.'

'They're already at San Francisco,' he said with a ghost of a smile. 'Just waiting for me to go down river and collect them. Captain Bateman reports that they've had good sailing weather and very few losses. By comparison, the trip up the Sacramento should be a holiday for them!'

'It must have cost a fortune to ship them all that way!' she exclaimed.

'Investment in the future of Tresco, m'dear. If you don't have faith in the future, you may as well not be in California. Besides, I won't have to wait as long for a return as my rivals with their stringy Longhorns: my Herefords will be ready for market at six years. Many of them will be mature already. They'll just need a good rest and fattening up and there's plenty of good grass here for that. And who knows? Next year, perhaps even some surplus grain if the harvest comes good.'

'And calves for breeding stock . . .'

'Of course. And a couple of good milch cows. Milk to fatten Tamsin up a little! So you see, I must get down to San Francisco very soon. Perhaps I'll take Chen Kai along with me.'

'No!'

'He'll be glad of a change,' he went on, as if she had not spoken. 'I've a deal of business to transact, so I'll need someone who's good with the figures.'

'He — he can do all that here,' she interrupted breathlessly. 'He — he doesn't much like San Francisco.'

San Francisco again! He remembered his earlier suspicions.

'I may take Kerhouan.' He shrugged and turned away, but not before he had seen the relief wash over her face.

The subject was not mentioned again; Alicia, spending every spare hour working at the maps, gave it no further thought.

Cornish was very tired when he returned to the ranch. He'd spent a long day down at the old Mission buildings, seeing how much work needed doing to make them habitable again. He arrived back just as Brenchley, Alicia and Tamsin rode into the stableyard, laughing, every inch a happy family group. There was a bitter twist to his mouth as he watched Brenchley jump lithely down from the saddle, turn to catch Tamsin by the waist and toss her up in the air before setting her down safely on the ground. Then he turned to hand Alicia down, a warm and admiring expression in his eyes.

'Colonel Jack! Colonel Jack!' cried the little girl excitedly as she caught sight of him. 'D'you know what I did today? I rode Mr Brenchley's horse — all by myself!'

'No! Really?' exclaimed the Colonel teasingly.

'Really! Really I did!' she squeaked, quite pink in the face with excitement. 'I holded the reins and told him when to go faster or slower and Mr Brenchley didn't do *anything* and please may I have a sugar lump for Star because ...'

'Hold on a moment!' exclaimed Cornish, laughing at her exuberance. 'Why don't you ask your mama? She knows where the sugar lumps are.'

'Oh, *I* know where they are,' cried Tamsin impatiently. 'But Lisha says they're your sugar lumps and we mustn't just help ourselves ...'

'She also said you weren't to trouble the Colonel, Tamsin!' chided Alicia.

'No trouble, ma'am,' drawled Jack Cornish, reaching down to scoop Tamsin up onto his shoulder. 'Good day to you Brenchley. C'mon, child. We'll go fetch some sugar lumps ... we'd better give Ross one too, or he may get jealous.'

Brenchley must have sensed something in the atmosphere, for he declined the invitation to dine and rode back to Sacramento. After the evening meal, the Colonel took Kerhouan and Chen Kai down to the levée on the Sacramento and Alicia, now that the maps and prints were finished, found herself curiously at a loss.

The sky was still quite light, for they had dined early, and she was not in the least tired. She decided to take the opportunity to explore the rest of the Mission.

There were four good-sized rooms facing on to the central courtyard, most of them empty, but one or two of them with old chests or the odd chair in them. In one was an old oaken table, more suitable for the kitchen than the one they were at present using. If she put the smaller table in the kitchen, the larger one could go into the spacious empty room next to the main room. With one of the chests as a side-board, it would turn the cobweb clad room into an excellent dining room!

It took her over an hour to sweep and dust the proposed new dining room to her satisfaction. Another twenty minutes with a damp cloth — she really must get some beeswax next time she was in Sacramento! — followed by a good buffing made the old oaken table quite fit to go into the kitchen. She knew that moving the large table was beyond her, but she had a great desire to see whether the oak table would look well in its new home and by dint of much pushing and pulling, she managed to manoeuvre it over to the wide doorway. It proved to be not quite wide enough, however, for it refused to go through and jammed, just as she heard the sound of voices in the courtyard.

'Bitten off a bit more than you can chew again, Mrs Owens?' queried Cornish sardonically as he surveyed the situation.

She became uncomfortably aware of her dirt-streaked face and the strands of hair that had slipped out of their coils.

'I'm sorry,' she muttered, wiping a grubby hand over her forehead and leaving more dirty streaks behind. 'I thought it would be a good idea ... and the long table from the kitchen in here ... but perhaps you don't want a dining room. And I shouldn't have interfered.'

'It's an excellent notion, m'dear,' he reassured her. 'But why the deuce you couldn't have got someone else to help, I can't for the life of me see.' He crossed the room to the outer door and hollered: 'Luis! Xavier!'

The boys, who had been scrubbing out the dishes across at the bunk-house, came at a run. 'Finished your chores?' demanded the Colonel. They nodded. 'Then give me a hand with this table.'

'But ...'

'Yes?'

'Should you? I mean, your arm ...'

She knew it was a mistake as soon as she said it and could have bitten her tongue for her folly.

He looked at her for a moment with narrowed, angry eyes, then said in a voice as cold as a Sierra winter: 'You concern yourself with your health, Mrs Owens, and I'll concern myself with mine.'

Without her interference he would probably have let the lads take much of the strain, for they were sturdy youths, but it seemed to her that he made a point of taking as much of the weight as they did.

In a few minutes the table was in place in the kitchen and looking very well there. Fortunately, as Jack Cornish decided to take the large table through, Kerhouan and Kai came in and took over his end smoothly, without a word being spoken.

'Anything else, Mrs Owens?' he asked icily. 'While we're all in the mood?'

'Nothing that won't wait,' she replied, still berating herself mentally for her folly.

'That old chest would make a good *buffet*,' rumbled Kerhouan. 'If Mrs Owens thinks it good, we will fetch it here, Chen and I.'

'An excellent idea!' she exclaimed, as if the thought had never before occurred to her, then wished she had stayed silent as she felt Cornish's cynical gaze on her.

Once the chest was installed, she began to rub it down.

'Make any improvements you like, Mrs Owens,' said Cornish softly from just behind her. 'But don't try to do them alone — I can't afford to have you sick before we've sworn all those maps and photographs.'

'Your concern for my welfare does you credit, Colonel,' she replied sarcastically.

'And yours for mine. But don't make the mistake Lamarr did and think me less of a man for a crippled arm.'

Brenchley had arranged for the documents to be sworn when Alicia came into town to visit the theatre. Sitting in the gig she was quite startled to see Chen Kai ride up alongside.

'But you can't come!' she exclaimed unguardedly. 'Who will look after Tamsin?'

'She's staying with Letitia,' the Colonel informed her laconically. 'The housekeeper will look after her while you are at the theatre.'

Before she could argue, Tamsin, grinning from ear to ear at the treat in store, came bouncing along on Kerhouan's shoulders.

'Chen Kai-Tsu and I are off to San Francisco,' revealed the rancher. 'Perhaps you and Brenchley could revise your plans and join us?'

'San Francisco? But Kai — you mustn't!' she cried in alarm.

'The arrangements have been made, Mrs Owens,' stated Cornish impatiently. 'Letitia is quite happy ...'

'But Chen Kai ...'

' ... is in my employ,' he reminded her harshly. 'I need him in San Francisco. And now, if you please, the horses are becoming restless.'

She looked at her friend with wide, panic-stricken eyes, but he shook his head very slightly and hooded his eyes. Biting her lip with frustration she took her seat and settled Tamsin between herself and Cornish.

Tamsin's bag was tossed into the back along with hers and, after a last word to Kerhouan, the little party set off.

'Sure you won't change your mind, Mrs Owens?' Cornish enquired with a sidelong glance. 'Come with us to San Francisco! I believe Edwin Booth is playing Hamlet.'

She steadied her voice with an effort. 'Thank you, but I believe we will stick to our original plan.' Another thought struck her. 'How long will you be away?'

'Only a couple of days. I've some freight to pick up in San Francisco and some more hands to hire on. I believe Captain Bateman can do the trip in a mere fifteen hours, but I have no intention of risking a boiler blow out like the *Pearl's* captain did by racing her.'

'You're travelling on by river?'

'A more tolerable mode of travel than the old overland pack mules. Yes, I guess we should be back within two or at most three days; long enough to get the jetty finished, I hope.'

'So that's what the men have been doing down by the river these last few weeks.'

'It'll be much more convenient. Necessary too, if Lamarr decides to elbow me out of the Californian Steam Navigation wharfs. Lucky I bought the old boat when I did, or he might have denied me the entire river.'

'You have interests in diverse quarters, Colonel.'

'I never did believe in putting all my eggs in one basket. Never did like anyone telling me what I could or couldn't do, either.'

The swearing of the various documents took place without a hitch in Brenchley's new offices, not far from the Wells, Fargo freight depot in the bustling business section of the city. Young Mr Halleck of Halleck, Peachy and Billings was there, inclined to be a little more fulsome in his praise than she was prepared to admit in so recent an acquaintance; more importantly, Brenchley had managed to persuade one of the judges from the Land Commission to attend and witness the oath.

'That should cinch it for us, having old Judge Kellett there,' declared Brenchley as they walked down the stairs and out onto the street again. 'Query the validity of our deposition, you question his standing as a witness.'

While he and the Colonel concluded their arrangements, Alicia slipped away to where Kai was standing with the horses.

'Oh, whatever are you thinking of, going back to San Francisco again?' she whispered distractedly. 'What if . . . ?'

He reached out a gentle hand to pat her cheek. 'Alicia,' he chided softly, 'we cannot live the rest of our lives on "what if?" But I will be very careful. No unnecessary risks. Wherever possible, I will stay on the ship.'

'But it's foolish! Why does the Colonel need you?'

'We shall see,' was all the answer he would vouchsafe.

She looked at him suspiciously.

'Yes,' he anticipated her question. 'I did know. But I saw no point in you worrying before you had to!'

There was no time for any more before they parted, she and Tamsin to be escorted to the Coopers, and Chen and the Colonel to drive down to the levée, where the *Tresco*, steam up, was waiting for them.

She slipped swiftly down the broad Sacramento, away from the oak-lined banks around the city until, as the sun set in a splendour of orange and gold, they reached the flatter landscape of the lower river on its approach to the delta lands that led at last into the broad expanse of San Pablo Bay.

She was a trim side-wheeler slightly under the average size. About her there was none of the fanciful trimming and gilding of the riverboats which were still the main transport for passengers between San Francisco and the Californian capital. She could carry passengers, but her main purpose was freight and she had been adapted to that end. There were two tiny cabins and in case of need the deck saloon, but that was all. Everywhere else there were cattle pens, racks and hooks for the transport of everything from livestock to carcasses, timber to grain, food or household goods.

Chen Kai nodded approvingly as Jack Cornish showed him around below decks and elaborated on his plans. So absorbed were they in their discussions that they did not realise how far down the river they had travelled until the buzz of the Delta mosquitoes, the most vicious insects on the Pacific coast, sent them scurrying below.

They made the city by the bay in the early hours, but the dock area was deserted and so they slept on. Shortly after dawn Captain Bateman knocked on the cabin doors and by the time the sun was fully up, the loading had begun.

It was hot, sweaty work, but the Colonel paid well and by noon the hold was almost full. Only the live cargo was still in pens on the wharves, and that would not be loaded until the Tresco was ready to sail.

Cornish and Bateman set off soon afterwards to dine in the city and pick up the latest news, but Chen was adamant in his refusal to join them. The less he was about in San Francisco the better.

He set a line out from the rail into the Bay, the Sundown Sea of the Californian Indians. Where the salty tide met the fresh water from the Sierras there was always abundant fishing; tom cod, rock cod, kingfish or striped bass — he wasn't too fussy. Dozing in the hot sun, his mind drifted back to Alicia and he wondered idly how she was getting on in Sacramento.

The evening for Alicia turned out to be one of unalloyed

misery from start to finish. It wasn't that the play was bad: Miss Hayne gave a superb performance with which the author would have been delighted, the supporting cast was excellent and the surroundings, an elegant theatre which she had never before visited, perfect. But from the moment the Lamarrs invited themselves to join Brenchley's party in the spacious box, all of her host's polite attentions could not make up for the uncomfortable feelings which they brought with them.

'You naughty man,' chided Mrs Lamarr with a pout as she took the seat nearest the front and next to Brenchley as of right. 'You should have *told* us you were coming this evening to see the *divine* Miss Hayne, and then we could have made up *such* a party! And to think I nearly told my husband we could not go! How *angry* I should have been if I had decided to go to Mrs Pikeman's *boring* soirée!'

Alicia felt quite sorry for Brenchley who was looking rather foolish, his handsome mouth fallen open as he desperately searched for something appropriate to say. He need not have worried, however, as Mrs Lamarr did not wait for an answer but rattled on regardless, in an affectedly childish voice, until the curtain rose and a party in the adjoining box, to Miss Cooper's eternal mortification, hissed at her to 'Cut the cackle there! We paid to listen to them, not you!'

As the lights went up in the interval, Alicia became aware of being watched. In a box opposite them sat Hester Bryant with her mother and the Crockers.

Alicia smiled, but received in return a look of positive dislike before Hester turned her shoulder pointedly on their box. She looked up to find Brenchley looking across the theatre with a look of such wretchedness on his face that her heart went out to him; she suggested that they should go and pay their respects in the interval.

It had seemed such a good idea, but she knew it for a mistake when the Lamarrs decided to join them.

The sight of Belle Lamarr hanging on Brenchley's arm and flirting outrageously with him was not calculated to soften Hester's heart. On closer sight, she was seen to be looking much less than her usual pretty self, for her eyes were red-rimmed and swollen; nobody believed Mrs Bryant's talk of a slight summer cold.

Attorney Crocker was talking to young Henry Bryant, and Miss Cooper and Mrs Crocker were deep in conversation about school charity foundations when Lamarr came to Alicia's side with a glass of chilled champagne.

How could his wife ever have preferred him to Colonel Cornish? An unprepossessing man, of no more than middle height, short-necked, with a heavily-jowled face red from drink, he looked more like an enraged bull than ever tonight. But not Beauty and the Beast, like the Leons, she thought, for Señor Leon's face always lit up when his eyes fell on his beautiful wife, whereas Lamarr's scowl was deepening until he looked as though he would happily have throttled Belle.

'Deserted by your escort, my dear?' he sneered.

'I was just going to join Miss Cooper and Mrs Crocker,' she replied coolly.

He pressed the glass into her hand. With reluctance she accepted it.

'Like the play?' he demanded abruptly.

'Miss Hayne is an excellent actress ...'

'Prefer the other one,' he growled. 'The buxom wench. Don't care for these die-away women, all airs and graces.' He took a noisy swallow of his wine and went on in deceptively sympathetic tones: 'So you're working for Cornish, are you? Don't get too enamoured of the job − or your employer,' he leered, 'because neither of 'em's going to last much longer. And you can tell him I told you so.'

Before she could reply, he slid his arm around her waist and pushed his face closer to hers until she could smell the spirits on his breath. 'Still, pretty little filly like you − you could find y'self another *housekeeping* job right easily. Might even have a place for you myself.'

The blood was drumming at her temples as panic flooded through her. She was going to scream, she knew she was, and then Miss Cooper was at her side and her voice fell welcomingly on Alicia's ears.

'Do come and join us, my dear Mrs Owens. Mrs Crocker is telling us of the excellent plan she has for raising funds for the new school.' She practically dragged Alicia out of Lamarr's grasp and over to the other side of the box.

'Odious man!' hissed Mrs Crocker. 'His behaviour is a

213

disgrace! Do steer clear of him, my dear Mrs Owens. That kind of man, when crossed, can act in a most unpleasant manner – especially when his wife is making a fool of him so blatantly.'

Alicia could barely nod, for she was still shaking with a mixture of anger and fear. Across the room, Lamarr and his wife exchanged a few angry words and then he strode abruptly out of the box.

Brenchley had managed to manoeuvre Hester into a quiet corner, but just as he began to speak, Belle Lamarr was at his elbow, laying a fragile hand on his arm.

'I really think we should return to our box, my dear,' she breathed softly, looking up at him through her long eyelashes. 'Otherwise our party will be holding up the curtain.'

Hester flushed vividly, turned sharply on her heel and stormed back to her mother's side. Belle Lamarr was really very clever, thought Alicia angrily. With just a few words, the spoilt beauty had managed to give the impression that Brenchley had got up the party specifically for her benefit.

The rest of the evening could only drag. She narrowly avoided being seated next to Lamarr at the supper which Brenchley had arranged at the Orleans – Belle Lamarr having left him no choice but to invite them too. Only Letitia's insistence that she change seats with Alicia – 'for I must take this opportunity to talk to Mr Lamarr about Mrs Crocker's fund-raising' – saved her from more of his unwelcome attentions. She wondered how Belle Lamarr could bear to see her husband behave so, but all *her* attention was focused on Augustus Brenchley!

As she collapsed gratefully into the soft feather bed at Letitia's, she almost felt it would have been easier to risk San Francisco!

Chapter Seventeen

Chinatown was expanding rapidly, but Chen Kai-Tsu still knew his way around and led Cornish along Upper Sacramento Street to Dupont where gradually the white faces turned more golden and round eyes became almond.

The free and easy attitude to racial mixing of the early goldrush mining community had long since disappeared; now San Francisco had its clearly marked ghettoes of Chinatown and Nigger Alley.

The breeze from the ocean had driven away the heavy mists that so often shrouded the City by the Bay in summer and the warm sun had broken through to sparkle on the waters of the bay, where steamers and sailing ships jostled for wharf space alongside the hulks of vessels abandoned by their crews in the mad rush of the gold years.

They strolled down Dupont Street, past the prosperous shopfronts with their display of exotic and strange delicacies, past the herbalist's kiosk and the fortune tellers' booths, the tall Westerner and his companion attracting no little attention, and then cut up a side street and down a gloomy alley, for it was not among the rich that they would find what they were seeking, but in the poorer back alleys, where families found themselves on the border line of poverty because there was just one too many sons to absorb into the family business or trade, and those down on their luck had not yet started on the downward slope of despair and opium that would render them unfit for any worthwhile occupation.

Here were the brothels and the opium dens condemned but still frequented by the sanctimonious Anglos who indulged in daily tirades against the 'yellow peril' they had imported; here too skulked those unfortunates who had fallen foul of the law and in accordance with San Francisco's notorious Pig-Tail Ordinance had their queues cut off an inch from the head, seeking to hide their shame in the shadows until their hair grew back again. Chen shrugged himself deeper into his American jacket and pulled his hat down over his ears.

He stopped in a doorway where a middle-aged Chinese lounged, watching the passers-by, and put a question to him in swift, fluent Cantonese. At first the man just shook his head, but the production of a handful of coins soon evinced the answers he wanted.

They ducked down another turning: here there were no houses, only shacks and lean-tos and, at the far end, shabby canvas tents.

In the first tent they came to there were three young men and an older couple. Three of them were busily making cigars in the corner of the tent, but there was not enough work for the other two. It was a common problem: the middle men were unwilling to let them have more tobacco, for as newcomers with no *tong* or association to vouch for them, they were not yet considered credit worthy.

With no ties to hold them to the City's Chinese community and little prospect of bettering themselves, they were happy to exchange the cocoon of Chinatown for the wide open spaces of the Sacramento Valley, particularly as there would be work there for the mother.

They gave Chen Kai a number of other directions and the two men moved from shack to lean-to to tent. Mostly Chen Kai would do the talking, but from time to time Jack Cornish would put in a question. They were looking for young men, fit and strong, to start a rice plantation down by the Sacramento, where the annual floods made the land unfit for anything else, but they took none who did not speak reasonable English. Usually the brief interview ended with a slapping of hands and instructions on how to find the *Tresco* by sundown, but occasionally Chen Kai would murmur that he was honoured to have made their acquaintance and that he would be in touch.

'What was wrong?' asked Cornish in surprise outside one

shack. 'They were fit and strong; the shack looked pretty clean and good ...'

'Too good,' stated Chen Kai drily. 'They're not poor – they're trouble. *Tongs*,' he enlightened his employer. 'One of the nastier kinds.'

By the time the sun was dipping down towards the glassy surface of the bay, they had all the workers they needed, plus the woman to help with the laundry and the housework. They had only one more call, to two young men who worked in a bakery and cookhouse nearby and slept in the rat-infested storeroom at the back. They shook hands enthusiastically on the deal, then the older one turned hesitantly to Cornish.

'You need house help too?' he asked anxiously. 'I know very good worker: do you cooking, laundry, anything you want.'

'We only need men at the moment, Li,' repeated Chen Kai. 'Planting rice fields and building houses.'

'She can work in the fields good as any man,' pleaded Li. 'If you can find a job for her – anything – I beg you –'

'When you've settled in and the work's underway, you can send for your woman,' Chen Kai reassured him.

'By then it is too late,' shrugged Li fatalistically. 'Mr Kweh has called in her father's loan and I know they cannot pay it.'

'A moment!' commanded Chen Kai and turned away for a hurried consultation with Jack Cornish.

'He can't pay this debt just on the promise of future work, surely?' objected the rancher.

'Probably not. But Li must have some money. I guess this is the girl he wants to marry.'

'Then why doesn't he?'

'Pride. While the family is still in debt, they won't consider alliances. And perhaps the father thinks a richer husband might pay the debt for him.'

'Let's go see.'

Down an even gloomier and shabbier alley they went, ending up outside a lean-to made of old planking scavenged from one of the old abandoned hulks.

In answer to Li's call an elderly man came to the front and bowed obsequiously to Cornish and Chen Kai. In answer to

Chen's brief enquiry in Cantonese, he gabbled a few excited sentences, then disappeared into the gloomy depths of the lean-to.

'Careful, Kai,' joked the rancher. 'He may see you as that prosperous husband and make you an offer!'

'He already has,' replied Chen Kai with barely concealed disgust. 'It seems his daught —'

His voice tailed off as Ho's daughter appeared in the doorway.

She was exquisite: a dainty figure dressed in an elaborately embroidered gown in red and gold which showed up the soft ivory skin, only faintly tinged with colour on the high cheek-bones. Everything about her was in perfect proportion, the wide-set almond eyes, straight nose and delicate rosebud mouth; the clinging folds of her silken robe emphasised the shapeliness of her neat figure.

Chen Kai-Tsu stood a moment with his mouth open in shock, then he pulled himself together and turned angrily to Li.

'I thought you said she was poor?' he hissed. 'She's dressed like a rich man's concubine!'

The girl, who after a first swift glance had dropped her eyes modestly to the ground, now raised her head, its elaborate crown of dark hair seeming too heavy for her slender neck.

'It is kind of you to honour us with your opinion, esteemed sir,' she began in a soft voice, slightly blurred with ill-suppressed tears, 'but if Li has brought you here to change my mind, he has wasted his time and yours.' Her English was clear and barely accented.

'Pearl! There could be work for you — a new start, up valley, on a farm!'

Li's voice was eager, boyish, but the girl he had addressed as Pearl just looked at him, her eyes filled with the melancholy of years.

'Li, it doesn't change anything. Tomorrow is Steamer Day, when all debts fall due. My honoured father cannot pay in cash, so Mr Kweh demands payment in kind. This morning he sent round this dress for me, so ...' Her voice broke.

'But your parents —'

'If they don't pay, Mr Kweh will turn the *tong* on

218

them, put them out of work, or worse. I owe it to them ...'

'You owe them *nothing*!' protested Li vehemently. 'After the way they treated you!'

'It will not be so bad, Li,' whispered the girl, struggling to hold back the tears. 'He will wipe out the debt and he will graciously permit me to send some of ... of my ... earnings to my parents until my mother is well again.' Her voice quivered piteously. 'Since my brothers died ... there's no one but me to look after them.'

'It's not right!'

'It is my duty.'

'This Mr Kweh,' asked Kai softly, 'he is not Kweh of Dupont Street?'

She hid her face in her hands. 'Yes,' she whispered brokenly.

Chen Kai drew Li aside. 'How can you let this happen, Li? This is the girl you were to marry?'

Li laughed mirthlessly. 'She is the daughter of Ho. He was a prosperous farmer in our country, before the floods came, and the famine, and his two sons died. He would not have a humble cook for a son. If I had the money I would pay the debt, but I thought ... if I could get a job for her ...'

Chen Kai turned on the girl.

'How much is the debt?' he demanded abruptly.

She looked at him with wide, frightened eyes. 'One hundred dollars,' she moaned. 'My father gambled with money he did not have.'

One hundred dollars. The price of a Paris hat for a rich Sacramento lady. The price of dishonour and shame for this family.

Stifling a sob, the girl turned to run back into the gloom, but Chen Kai reached out swiftly and grabbed her firmly by the wrist.

'Oh no you don't!' he exclaimed. 'You stay here!' He repeated his command in Cantonese in case she had not understood. 'Don't move, do you hear?'

Her eyes widened in surprise, for she had thought him an Anglo, like his companion.

'Corr-onel Cornish,' whispered Chen Kai urgently, 'at

home — at Tresco — I have some fifty, sixty dollars with Alicia. I need a hundred now. Will you cover my money and lend me the balance?'

'It's not your debt, Chen Kai!' protested the rancher. 'And has it occurred to you we may have been set up?'

'She is not lying,' replied Kai gravely.

'Come on, Kai, this is Li's problem, not yours. We don't need any more workers. And we'll miss the tide if we delay much longer.'

'Please help me in this,' Kai pleaded. 'If Alicia were here she'd beg your help too. I wish I had not become involved, but now I am, I can't just leave her to Kweh's mercies.'

Cornish sighed heavily. 'You're a fool, Chen Kai,' he warned, pulling out his heavy leather purse. 'Tell me, Li, her father, can he work? I won't take on three useless mouths.'

There were barely a thousand Chinese women in the whole of California, most of them prostitutes. He'd started out to look for one decent woman, and looked like being landed with three!

'Old Ho was very good farmer,' Li assured him. 'But they give all the food to Pearl this week, you understand.'

'To plump her up for Kweh? My God!' bit out Chen Kai. 'Sometimes my own people disgust me!'

The girl, who had followed the conversation with a puzzled frown marring the perfection of her pale face, shrank away at this outburst of anger.

'I'm not angry with you, child,' he reassured her. 'Tell me, your mother — what ails her?'

'She has a bad cough, master,' answered Li frankly. 'But only since she worked in the dusty factory. All day and half the night. Trying to pay off Ho's debt to Kweh.'

'So long as she's not consumptive,' challenged the Colonel. 'Deceive me in that and I'll send you all back! Now go fetch Ho.'

Li disappeared into the murky interior of the lean-to and they could hear the murmur of voices within. Cornish counted out the money. 'Hope you know what you're about,' he said grimly. 'You know where you can find this Kweh?'

'Everyone knows where Kweh lives,' ground out Chen Kai. 'At the Golden Dragon House — the biggest brothel in Dupont Street.'

Cornish looked at Chen Kai, his face rigid with shock.

'Now you understand, Corr-onel?' he asked softly.

'Now I understand.'

While the family packed their miserable possessions together, Kai went to Dupont Street, along with Li and a middle man for witness, and paid Ho's debt.

It was a long and elaborate transaction, for they had to propitiate the middle man with all necessary ritual in order to save Ho's 'face'. For the most part he left it to Li, partly because the superficiality of it all was distasteful to him, but more importantly because here, among the minor hierarchy of the Chinese underworld, he wished to avoid any reminders of that other westernised Chinaman whose companion had fallen foul of the Vigilantes.

They hurried down to the wharf, Li and his brother carrying Ho's wife in a wickerwork chair. Chen Kai slung Pearl's small bundle over his shoulder and automatically offered her his arm; he had lived so long among Anglos that he had forgotten how little physical contact there was between Chinese, even members of the same family. Pearl, dressed now in a more sober and shabby robe, smiled shyly up at him and took it.

Captain Bateman had loaded the two wagon loads of auction lots which the Colonel had bought, the cattle were all loaded in pens and the ship had steam up by the time the small party reached the quayside.

'All cargo battened down, Colonel,' he announced proudly. 'The coolies are all up on deck and Mrs Santana is waiting for you below.'

'Very well, Captain,' declared Cornish. 'Prepare to cast off.'

221

The sun through the portholes woke the Colonel early the next morning and he groaned as he straightened up from his improvised bed of two chairs in the deck saloon. The two cabins had been allocated to Mrs Santana and the two older Chinese women.

On the other side of the small table, Chen Kai, unusually, still slept on. The previous night, Kai had taken up his bedroll to join the new hands out on the deck under the mosquito awning, but Cornish had stopped him. He needed Chen Kai to oversee the work in the village and the clearing of the river margins where the new rice fields would be set out and it was vital that his status was made clear from the start. 'Face' was so important.

The rancher was already up on the bridge when Mrs Santana, a buxom lady in her fifties, with liquid brown eyes and jet black hair drawn back from her face in a knot, bustled into the saloon with a coffee pot and one cup. Chen Kai looked up from clearing away and stowing the bedding and inclined his head politely. She clicked her tongue in irritation and pushed past to start laying the table.

'Good morning, Mrs Santana,' said the Colonel from the doorway. 'I trust you slept well?'

Her face was wreathed in smiles as she nodded. 'But please, you call me Angelina, huh?'

'Angelina.' He returned her smile. 'Breakfast smells great.' He cast a swift eye over the table. 'We'll be two to eat in here. You've already met my deputy, Chen Kai?'

She opened her mouth to say something scathing, then thought better of it. She took a deep breath and said: 'Deputy, huh?'

The Colonel nodded as he took his seat and gestured to Chen Kai to do likewise.

'Looks like one of the hands to me,' she sniffed. 'Still, you the boss. I'll bring another cup.' She turned back in the doorway and looked scathingly at Chen Kai. 'That Chinee girl you was making cow's eyes at last night – she slep' on the floor of my cabin. Don't think it right she should stay out on the deck with all them men.'

Chen Kai thanked her gravely.

222

'Someone got to look after her,' she shrugged. 'Brute of a father, fool of a mother.'

'Perceptive woman,' commented Cornish drily, 'considering they only converse in Chinese!'

When the last of the dishes had been cleared away and the door to the galley was closed, Cornish looked up to find Chen Kai regarding him with a troubled expression.

'Corr-onel Jack ... what you said to her about ... being your deputy.'

'Yes?'

'Corr-onel ... you do me too much honour,' he declared, stumbling over his words — a rare occurrence for Chen Kai, usually so fluent of expression.

'I see your ability and I want to harness it to Tresco. Neither Kerhouan nor I can do aught but struggle with the books, and we know nothing about rice! I want you to stay with Tresco, hitch your fortunes to ours ... But there is a condition,' he went on with a grin. 'You call me Jack. I can't abide to hear you mangling the language every day with this "Corr-onel" nonsense!'

Chen Kai had to chuckle at that, but the laugh soon died. 'Corr-onel — *Jack* — I thank you ...'

'But?'

'But my first duty must always be to Alicia and Tamsin.'

'Then you must persuade her what folly it would be to leave Tresco!' Cornish replied harshly.

'One of the reasons we have never quarrelled in all the years we have travelled and worked together is that neither of us tells the other what to do. If I felt I could not stay at Tresco, Alicia would decide we had to move on. If she cannot settle, the same will happen with me.'

'Then we will have to make sure she never feels that way,' growled Cornish.

Later on, standing with Chen Kai by the rail, looking down at the girl settling her mother in a chair in the warm sunshine, running around after her cantankerous father, Cornish asked abruptly : 'Would she really have gone to the brothel for his debts?'

'She sees it as her duty. It sickens me.'

'I'm sure Kweh would rather have had her than the money;

she'd have been quite an attraction. Not my taste, though. Wonder where she picked up such good English? Old man Ho speaks very little.'

'From Li perhaps?' scowled Chen Kai.

Cornish's mind had moved on. 'Hope Kerhouan has the jetty finished,' he said laconically. 'Or I don't know how we'll ever get this load through!'

A few hands were still out riding the boundaries, but Pedro had left Manuel and Julia in charge of the sheep and come down to work with Lachie and young Calum and the rest of the hands, dragging the hardwood from up in the hills to finish the strong jetty that jutted out over the Sacramento's muddy brown waters and the tough cordwood road that meandered across the marshy river margins to connect up with the track to the ranch house.

In the hot steamy kitchen Alicia paused to brush her hair back out of her eyes. The air in the kitchen was hot and heavy, redolent of the smell of fresh bread. She longed to step outside and fill her lungs with sweet fresh air but there was no time.

Luis, fidgeting at her side, was supposed to be helping her, but he longed to be down at the river with his brother and the men.

'All right, Luis, off you go,' she said with a sigh. 'Tell Kerhouan chow is almost ready.'

She looked at the heap of loaves that had taken her most of the morning to make and knew a moment's content at her achievement, but most of them would be gone today and tomorrow it would be all to do again.

Wearily she went into the living hall and crossed to the window to look down the valley. She saw Luis — and there, trotting to keep up with him, were Josefa and Jorge! Before she could tell whether Tamsin was with them, they had vanished around the bend, towards the jetty and out of her sight. Even as she squinted into the sun, trying to catch sight of them again, she heard a piercing whistle and realised that the steamer had arrived.

She threw off her apron in agitation and hurried into the

224

courtyard. But Tamsin was not there, nor was she in their rooms.

'Damnation!' she swore out loud. The last thing she wanted was for the children to get under the Colonel's feet as soon as he arrived back. Josefa and Jorge were old enough to keep out of the way − that was all they had done all their lives! − but Tamsin ...

She contemplated running down after them, but she knew she would be too late. Better to be here when he arrived and be seen to be earning her keep; better to be sure there was a good meal and plenty of cool drinks ready.

She heard the wagons rattling down the cordwood road to the jetty and the sight of the horses brought another swift frown to her eyes. Tamsin often went to the stables to give the horses apples or sugar lumps. She had no fear, even of the great plough horses or Cornish's huge stallion. Alicia had told her time and time again not to go without her or Kai, but this time, with everybody busy elsewhere, might she have gone in alone?

She hurried out, through the kitchen garden and across the stable yard. As she entered the stables she heard a noise in the far corner and hurried towards it, her eyes straining to make out the shapes in the shadows after the dazzle of the sunlight outside.

'Tamsin!' she called softly. 'Tamsin! Where are you?'

She didn't see the man until he was right in front of her.

'The kid ain't here,' he told her. 'Saw her down at the jetty with the foreman.'

'With Kerhouan? Then I can stop worrying!' She laughed nervously, not so much for her unease over Tamsin, but because she had recognised the figure in the shadows as Jos Evans. He had been around the stables a good deal over the last few days, spending time hanging around the kitchen door; too much time for Alicia's peace of mind. He had not been insolent or forward but there had been a warmth in his eyes when he looked at her that she had found infinitely more disturbing.

'Well ... better get back to the kitchen,' she said airily. 'They'll be hungry when they get all those wagons back up here ...' Her voice trailed off uncertainly as she realised that he had placed himself deliberately between her and the door to the yard. Over to her left the horses went on eating, the sound of their jaws on the grass and the buzz of the insects in the shafts of dust-laden sunlight that slanted down from the overhead vents unnaturally loud as she strove to still the panic rising in her breast.

'No need to rush,' he reassured her with a lop-sided grin, showing teeth that were strong and white and even, not yellow and tobacco-stained like – like – She shook her head to clear it. She would not panic, she told herself. As Kai had said, she had coped before in the *cantina*. This was *not him*, this was just another lonely ranch-hand, too long away from his weekend spree, trying to make a little small talk with a rare female. 'Always rushin' about, ain't you?'

'The – the stew – on the fire,' she muttered, forcing a smile. 'The wagons ...'

'Plenty time till the wagons git here,' he said deliberately. 'I been waitin' a long time to speak to you. Just, like, the two of us. Must get a mite lonely, just you and the kid. Thought mebbe you and me could give each other a bit o'company of an evenin'?'

She was transfixed to the spot, like a rabbit mesmerised by a stoat, desperately searching for the words, the clever, evasive words, that would get her past him and back to the sanctuary of the kitchen, but they would not come. Her heart was in her mouth, choking her, and she could only shake her head, eyes wide in fear, trying, frantically trying to beat back the scream that was welling up within her.

'No!'

'Now ain't that just a mite unfriendly?'

Her brain told her to run, but her feet would not move from the spot. He was reaching out for her. Why had she thought of him as a little man? He was strong, far too strong, and now he was pinning her close and she could not free herself without a fight – and she knew she could not do it.

'No!' she cried.

'Ain't bin that long since you had a man, has it?' he mocked, and then his face was lowering to hers and suddenly it was Evans and Fisher, blurring into one another.

'No!' she said with a sob in her voice. 'Please – no!'

'The lady said no, Evans!' came a deep voice from the shadows and suddenly Evans was no longer there, his weight no longer pressing on her; she fell, sobbing, in the hay.

There was a snarl, some vicious swearing, and then the thud of bone on bone. She looked up in terror to see Evans measure his length on the hard floor of the stable; after a moment he rose to his feet, shaking his head, and fled.

Cornish stood a moment longer, fists clenched, his face drawn and angry. He turned back to Alicia, but she was still lying in the hay, her eyes blind.

He squatted down beside her, a puzzled frown on his face.

'It's all over now. He's gone and he won't be back. He'll not bother you again, m'dear, I swear it!'

He'd make sure Evans didn't bother her again, if he had to kill him first. He wished he could be as sure of himself. At the moment it was taking every ounce of self-control he possessed not to push her back down in the hay and take over where Evans had left off!

She began to gabble incoherently and he could barely make out what she was saying.

He caught her wrists and drew her up. 'Listen to me!' he commanded sternly. 'Tamsin is quite safe, Evans has gone, and the dinner can go hang! Calm yourself down! Chen Kai sees you in this state, we'll have him sticking a knife in Evans and that'll be the end of them both.'

'I thought it was *him*. I thought *he'd* come back again —'

'What?'

She drew in her breath in a shuddering gasp and raised tear-drenched eyes to him. With a light hand he brushed her hair out of her eyes and stroked her cheek as if gentling a nervous colt.

'Come on, Alicia. I've told you — he won't dare trouble you again. It's not the end of the world. Bound to happen some time, so many men who don't see a woman from one month to the next.'

She was silent still, her face frozen, her eyes unnaturally blank.

'You know, if you want to be safe from the

227

likes of Evans, there's nothing simpler, Alicia. Marry me.'

She looked down at the strong hands gripping her wrists: hands that were long and slender, a musician's hands, she reminded herself, but hands that were rough too with the heavy manual work of the ranch.

'No.' He had to bend his head to hear her words. 'No. You think I'm a good bet for Tresco, but I'm not.' She swallowed painfully and forced herself to go on. 'There are things about me that would ... you don't really know me at all.'

He drew her up from the hay but still held onto her wrists.

'Then tell me!'

'I – can't.'

'I know something – or someone – has frightened you very badly.'

'It's not just that! Oh God!' She began to cry again, helplessly. 'If that were all! You would turn from me in horror if you knew!'

'Really have to be something bad!' he said with a laugh. But then the laugh died as he remembered with painful clarity her reaction when he had spoken of prostitutes and camp followers. His mind once set on this track, other memories came crowding in; Alicia drinking whiskey in the Orleans, a casual remark she had made that she did not know the proper version of many of the songs sung at Letitia's.

She hadn't said what she was doing in the stables with Evans in the first place, and she had made no effort to fight him off. And then there was the vexed question of her relationship with Chen Kai-Tsu ... His mouth set in a thin, angry line as he demanded furiously of himself whether that was the sort of mistress he wanted for Tresco?

Oh, he wanted her all right, wanted her badly, more than he had ever really wanted Belle. But was a saloon prostitute the mother he wanted for his children, the children who would carry on at Tresco after he was gone? Morality was not as strict out here as back east – how could it be with so many men and so few women? – but he had found by bitter experience courting Belle that he demanded a loyalty in his wife that she for one had not been prepared to give.

The first of the carts rattled into the yard.

'Go and tidy yourself up,' he commanded harshly. 'We'll wait on you to eat.'

'I — I'm not hungry.'

'Chen Kai sees you with a face like that, m'dear, he'll have Evans's guts for a horse-halter,' he warned. 'I'll make your excuses. But make sure you show this evening.'

'And . . . Evans?'

'I'll deal with him. I've told you he won't trouble you n'more. But — don't tell Chen Kai. He's too ready with that knife of his and I won't see him hang to bolster your vanity.'

Chapter Eighteen

Chen Kai put Tamsin's supper in front of her and crossed to Alicia's side.

'Your head was bad?' he asked solicitously, placing a cool hand on her forehead.

'Much better now,' she smiled.

He looked searchingly into her eyes. 'You will tell me about it when you are ready,' he murmured.

'It was just a headache,' she insisted. 'Now, tell me the news from San Francisco. Are the Vigilantes still —'

'Alicia! Do you think I went about asking questions?' He smiled. 'You must ask the Colonel about that. I kept my head well down. But I can tell you some other interesting stories ...'

She was, as he had expected, suitably indignant when he told her Pearl's story.

'But this Kweh,' she asked anxiously. 'He won't suspect who you are? Don't forget, *he* had connections with the *tongs*.'

He patted her hand comfortingly. 'His contacts were all in the Hip Shing Tong, who control the gambling. And perhaps also in the Chee Kung, they specialise in blackmail and intimidation. But Kweh will be in the Hip Yee Tong. They control the brothels and import the girls from China.'

'I'm glad you paid off the debts,' she said with a shiver.

'I should have asked you first ...'

'If you had waited, it would have been too late.'

'It means we are penniless again,' he warned.

'Freedom is more important than —'

There was a curse and a sharp word from the *sala*.

'Chen Kai!' The Colonel sounded angry.

They hurried to the main room.

'Chen Kai, you'll have to give them a hand,' muttered the Colonel. He was rather white about the mouth, his left arm held awkwardly across his chest.

'It's nothing!' he snapped at Alicia, and she checked her instinctive movement across to his side. Turning away, she looked around the room, eyes wide in astonishment.

The old carved benches had gone, the piles of papers had been placed in a crate at the foot of the stairs and in their place stood a pair of large leather-covered stuffed couches and four brocade-upholstered chairs, two with arms and two in the latest fashion without, to accommodate the new wider skirts. A whatnot, a number of highly-polished knick-knack tables and a pair of ornate mirrors were stacked together in the centre and on the far wall, over by the foot of the stairs, strangest sight of all, was a small pianoforte.

She looked at the Colonel in surprise. He shrugged. 'There was an auction at the hotel ... Only I don't know where to put everything. Where do you want the piano?'

The men looked at her expectantly.

'Over here,' she said decisively. She spent a thoroughly enjoyable hour, organising everything into its place. To her relief, the Colonel left Juan and Chen Kai to move the heavy furniture : she guessed he'd met his match with the piano.

While Kai and the others were out of the room, she plucked up her courage. 'Is it bad?' she murmured as she passed him.

'I jarred it,' he replied with a scowl. 'I must have hit him harder than I realised.'

And then she looked so upset that he wished he hadn't reminded her.

They stood in the doorway and surveyed the results of their labours.

'That's grand!' exclaimed Cornish with satisfaction. 'Just as I'd imagined it.'

'It's still a bit bare,' considered Alicia.

'Next time you're in Sacramento, you can buy a rug and

some knick-knacks,' he suggested. 'I'll leave the finishing touches in your hands. Only one thing I beg — not so many frills and flounces and ferns that I can't move.' He grinned boyishly. 'I'm always terrified at Letitia's that I'm going to wreck the room if I turn around suddenly. And poor Captain Sharples — he just cowers in a corner!' She chuckled sympathetically. 'I want it to look smart,' he went on, 'but still be comfortable. Is that possible?'

'It's your house, Colonel. And the stores would be only too pleased to supply you on approval, so you can send back anything that doesn't suit you.'

'I have every faith in your good taste, Mrs Owens,' he assured her gravely. He raised her hand to his lips and kissed it. 'And every faith in you,' he added deliberately.

She blushed and lowered her eyes in confusion. Oh, glory! Now why had he done that? Totally overset her and made her want to burst into tears! It was almost easier when he shouted at her.

Uncomfortably conscious of everyone's eyes on her, she fled.

In the kitchen she was pulled up by the sight of a broad back bending over the stewpot from which was emanating a deliciously spicy smell.

She stopped in her tracks, Cornish right behind her.

'Mrs Owens — meet our new cook, Mrs Santana.'

The plump figure wiped her hands on the apron which covered her black dress and turned away from the fire.

'Not "Missus Santana",' she scolded. 'You call me —'

'Angelina!' shrieked Alicia and rushed across the room to be enfolded in a warm, spicy bear hug.

Cornish looked on in astonishment. 'I see no introductions are needed,' he quipped.

'Let me look at you!' exclaimed Angelina at last, brushing the ready tears from her eyes. 'Four years I don't hear from you if you alive or dead!'

'Angelina — I sent a note back with the mule!'

'And then nothing, huh?' Angelina held her at arm's length and looked at her shrewdly. 'You too thin still. That husband of yours still knockin' you about? *Ay de mi*, what a *malvado, heh*?'

232

Alicia looked nervously over her shoulder, but Cornish had disappeared.

'He's dead, Angelina,' she sighed. 'Died at Dry Gulch, in the cholera. After that, there seemed no reason to stay on in Sonora.'

'No reason, huh?'

Alicia flushed at the justified criticism. 'I'm sorry, Angelina, truly I am, but I wanted to make a fresh start and – '

Kai came through from the *sala*. 'Angelina – I'd like you to meet Chen Kai-Tsu. My business partner.' At least he was, she thought grimly, while there was still a business.

Chen Kai bowed politely.

'Him? Yes, we meet already,' said Angelina dismissively. 'But how you be in business with him? These Chinee, they make good coolies, that's all.' She turned her back on Kai, ostensibly to check on the stew. Kai shrugged, smiled wryly, then went on his way again. Outside in the courtyard, she heard Tamsin's excited voice calling to him.

'Angelina,' she said softly, 'for the sake of our old friendship, please be good to Chen Kai. He has been a good friend to me.'

'Friend? A Chinee?' She was scandalised.

'If it hadn't been for him, I wouldn't be here today. When there was trouble . . .'

'Trouble? A beeg man with a beeg beard and . . .'

'How did you know?' Her terrified whisper echoed around the room.

'He come to Sonora camp – looking for you,' explained Angelina. 'He come to Angelina's cook house one-two years ago, with some tale of big house back east left to you. Need to find you quick, *he* say.'

'Liar!'

'He don't look like no fancy-pants lawyer I ever met. So I say, you bring lawyers and papers, then I see if I find out where you gone. He get mad, break the place up a bit, but then at last he go away. He don't have very pleasant ride away from Sonora, I think. I put good herbs in his *tortillas* – give him belly ache for three days! Angelina slow him down real good!' She laughed, a deep rolling laugh that made her ample bosom quiver. 'So.' She set her arms akimbo. 'Why you stay where trouble is? Why you not go back east when your bastard of a husband he dead, eh?'

'There was no longer anywhere to go,' Alicia replied tiredly. 'That big house – it was my inheritance. But Robert gambled it all away.' She rolled up her sleeves and began to shape the *tortillas*.

'Angelina,' she went on softly. 'I – I don't allow myself to remember the bad times. Please don't make me relive them.'

'Perhaps better you talk it out with Angelina,' the cook suggested shrewdly.

'No! Oh, it isn't just the misery of those days with Robert. So much more has happened since. I – I call myself Mrs Owens now. There are still too many of the forty-niners who remember Robert.' She forced a lighter note. 'And you, Angelina, what brings you so far from Sonora?'

'I no want to leave Sonora. I have good *cantina* there, still much miners like Angelina's cooking, you bet!' boasted the older woman. 'But I don't get any younger. My son, he want me to come live with him and his new wife. Great wedding present for her, huh?' She guffawed as she swung the stewpot aside. 'So I take pity on his wife and say no. But my *cantina* is very hard work. He tell me his boss need good cook. I meet his boss in San Francisco and he give me good terms, so I sell up and here I am.'

'Your son?' Had she ever met any of Angelina's children?

'Pedro – my eldest – he work here at Tresco. He and Julia live over by Twin Peaks.'

Pedro Santana – the sheep man! Angelina's son! '*Now* I know why he always looked so familiar!' she exclaimed. 'He reminded me of you!'

'So you hadn't forgotten old Angelina altogether?'

'How could I?' she responded warmly.

'You think I be what the Colonel wants, huh?'

'Of course!'

'And you show me the ropes?'

'Gladly. As – as long as I'm here.'

It occurred to her suddenly, sickeningly, that there was no

longer any need for her at Tresco. Fool that she was not to have realised it before!

'I — I'd better go and see who's eating here tonight,' she said awkwardly. 'And — Angelina — I'm glad you're here.'

She eventually found the rancher sitting in the courtyard in the shade of the lemon tree, stitching a torn saddle. As she rounded the corner to speak to him, she realised she could hear Angelina's tuneless humming and the clatter of dishes through the high kitchen window! How long had he been sitting there?

'We'll be four to supper this evening,' he said blandly before she could voice her question. 'You, me, Chen Kai and Kerhouan. We'll eat in the new room, tell Angelina.' His eyes went back to the viciously curved needle with which he was stitching the new leather and he went on calmly: 'Quaint, you knowing Pedro's mother, wasn't it? A small world, this California of ours.' He looked her straight in the eye, his steady gaze unwavering.

'A small world,' she agreed miserably. She fixed her eyes on the gnarled branch of the tree. 'Once Angelina has settled in, Colonel, I assume you'll have no further employment for me.'

He set the saddle aside and stood up, so that she had to look up at him.

'I'll be needing Chen Kai for some time yet. He tell you I asked him to stay on as my deputy? I want him to sort out the accounts, keep the books, start off the new rice fields for me. And I guess if I want Chen Kai, then I get you too,' he said deliberately.

'But I've told you, I can't ... I won't ...'

'Marry me? I wasn't aware that I'd asked you again. Good idea bringing Angelina here, don't you think?' he went on blithely, ignoring her embarrassment. 'Don't you look forward to eating decent food again? I do. And of course, as a bonus the cook can chaperone the housekeeper and the housekeeper can chaperone the cook.'

There was a deep chuckle of delighted laughter as Angelina surged around the corner to find out whether anyone was planning to eat that night.

'Señor!' she chuckled. 'I am past the age of needing a chaperone!'

'As I am,' echoed Alicia. 'But – thank you, Colonel Cornish, all the same.'

Over Angelina's superb dinner they discussed the plans to start rice fields in the water meadows. Dishes and plates were moved around the table, knives, forks and salt cellars pressed into service to explain how ditches and dikes would be cut to drain the water and allow it back in through cuts and dams to flood the land in preparation for planting the young rice shoots.

'Diversification!' declared Jack Cornish enthusiastically. 'That's the only answer. Then the weather and the markets, the gluts and the shortages, won't bankrupt you.' He reached out for a plate with his left hand and stopped abruptly, his face drained of colour.

Kerhouan picked up the thread of the conversation again, but the optimism of the evening had faded and by the time Angelina's delicious desserts arrived on the table, Jack Cornish was growing morose and melancholy, drinking more and more heavily.

He leaned forward and pounded the table violently.

'Tell me, someone tell me, why we're making all these plans. So Lamarr and his crew of perjured bloody lawyers can snatch Tresco from us? God only knows!' He shook his head angrily. 'We should be locked up, the lot of us. Don't you agree, my darling Mrs Owens?'

'Go to bed, Jack,' ordered Kerhouan sharply.

'Me and my bottle,' muttered Cornish in a slurred voice, reaching out to pick up the whiskey bottle by the neck, swinging it gently. 'Go to bed with a bloody bottle ... G'night to you all.' He sketched a caricature of a bow and left the room.

There was an uncomfortable silence.

'I'm sorry, Mrs Owens,' said Kerhouan heavily.

'It's his arm, isn't it?' Throughout the evening he had used the stiff arm less and less but drunk more and more.

When she saw him again the following evening, he was full of remorse.

'An unfortunate baptism for our new dining room,

236

ma'am,' he apologised. 'Especially after you had gone to so much trouble. And I understand that my — language — left much to be desired in the company of a lady.'

She grinned wryly. 'This lady isn't easily offended,' she replied. 'Comes of working in *cantinas*!'

'But you should do something about that arm,' suggested Kai gravely.

'Cut it off, you mean,' snapped the rancher with a scowl.

'Nothing as drastic as that!' smiled Kai, refusing to be provoked. 'Almost certainly the nerves are pinched between the two broken ends. Let me break it and reset it for you.'

Cornish shook his head. 'We'll need every pair of hands for the harvest — even if they're only half a pair.'

Kai was not discouraged. 'Then I will do it in winter,' he stated equably.

The onset of harvest imposed its own pattern on the life of the ranch. Kerhouan was quite capable of running it, for in California there was not the urgency to get the crops in before the weather broke, but Cornish insisted on working alongside the men, even though it put a strain on his bad arm.

'It's a bad boss who can't do what he asks his men to do,' was all he would say.

When he wasn't working in the harvest fields, he was out in the far valleys where Juan and Xavier were settling in the new Shorthorns, or on the distant boundaries where Lachie and Evans, the latter still nursing a badly bruised jaw, were building line stations for the hands.

Chen Kai was busy from sun-up till sun-down at the river meadows bordering the Sacramento, organising the digging of drainage and irrigation ditches in preparation for the first rice plantings. In the early evening, when the hands were seeing to the horses and preparing the reapers for the next morning, he and Kerhouan would ride down to see how much progress had been made in repairing the village buildings for the new arrivals.

With Angelina cooking for the house and Li for the hands, Alicia found herself with nothing to do. After weeks spent in the saddle, mapping and surveying all day, rising early to suit her employer and going late to bed so that she could help Kai with

237

the baking, she found it a strange and unwelcome sensation.

'They're cleaning out the old buildings,' Kai told her, when she confided in him. 'Go and organise that. Tell Mrs Chang to take the laundry to the *agua caliente* with Juan. The rooms upstairs here — they are in a dreadful state.' He looked at her thoughtfully for a moment. 'It's for you to organise all this,' he chided her gently. 'You are the housekeeper.'

'But I don't want to overstep the mark.'

'You won't. Assert yourself. Earn your keep. His bark is worse than his bite anyway.'

And she knew that he was right.

Like the Pied Piper of Hamelin she set off that afternoon for the cluster of houses, followed by Tamsin and Josefa, Jorge, Xavier and Luis, all clutching buckets and mops and brushes.

Li pointed them to the third cottage, an adobe building with mended doors and shutters, its walls freshly whitewashed. Leaving the children to explore the overgrown gardens, she mounted the steep stairs and found the two women busily scrubbing the bare boards to the colour of pale honey.

'No, don't get up,' she insisted. 'I didn't come to disturb you, only to help.' She turned to the older woman who had risen to stand respectfully before her. 'Shall I sweep out downstairs? I'll set the children to clear the weeds and brambles in the garden.'

Mrs Chang turned to Pearl to ask a shrill question in Chinese.

'Mrs Chang says it is not fitting that one of the — that you should clean her house,' Pearl explained.

'Nonsense! Tell Mrs Chang that this "foreign devil" works for her keep, Pearl!' replied Alicia, who had recognised the phrase. 'You speak such very good English, Pearl. And what a pretty name — it suits you so well.'

For the first time since she had arrived, Pearl allowed the ghost of a smile to pass over her serious face. 'Thank you, ma'am,' she murmured humbly. 'The Sisters named me — and taught me my English.'

'But what of the name your parents gave you?'

'It is not the custom to give a daughter a name when the

238

parents do not intend to keep her,' she replied calmly.

'But they did – keep you?'

'Oh no, not then. They had two strong sons, what need had they of me? But my honoured father permitted my respected mother to offer me to the nuns and they had room in the season of my birth.'

'And if they had not?'

'Then they would have put me with the other unwanted babies, down by the river.'

'To *die*?'

'It is the custom.'

'It's a disgrace!' The bile rose in Alicia's throat. The girl's parents had abandoned her as a baby and yet she still felt a duty to her father, a duty that would have taken her to the Golden Dragon House. She turned angrily on her heel and stalked downstairs to start brushing down the walls.

Halfway through the day Pearl excused herself to attend to her mother. Alicia crossed to the window to watch her and her father carry Mrs Ho out in her wickerwork chair to sit in the warm sunshine. Pearl scurried about, fetching this and that for her father who rewarded her with a scowl, angry words and a blow aimed at her head which she, obviously from practice, managed to dodge.

A few minutes after Pearl's return, when they had almost finished scrubbing out the kitchen, the children called her in great excitement.

'Señora!' cried Xavier. 'A well! We've found a well!' He put Tamsin back from the edge as Alicia fought her way past the brambles to his side.

It was a splendid well, obviously the water source for the cottages, but blocked with choking weeds and broken slabs of stone which had once formed the well cover. It would be a hard job to clear it out, for only Xavier was really big enough to work around the well without danger of tumbling into it.

'Xavier, I'm going to get someone to help you,' she decided. 'Meantime, keep the others away, there's a good lad. Josefa?' She saw her picking wild flowers. 'Take Tamsin over by that tree. Clear a little space and let her sleep a little – she's tiring herself out in this heat. Jorge and Luis, you can carry the rubble away when it's got clear and take it to the end there. But you go no nearer than that. *Comprende*?'

She found Mr Ho sitting in the warm sunshine. His wife, he assured her, was much better. Before he could launch into an account of his own ills, she said with a deceptive smile: 'I'm glad she's well enough to be left alone. I have just the job for you.'

Unable to use his wife as an excuse, Ho shuffled grumblingly across the way and set to, clearing the well. Alicia decided to work at the back too, so she could make sure he was pulling his weight and not leaving it all to Xavier.

By the time evening fell, they had almost finished the second house. As Alicia gathered the brooms together and sent Luis to round up the children, Pearl came into the room and stood before her, hands meekly folded. Although she had worked as hard as Alicia that day, she still looked neat, not a hair out of place. From the tip of her dainty feet to the top of her glossy head, she looked exquisite and Alicia felt clumsy and grubby beside her.

'Yes, Pearl?' she queried.

'Mrs Owens,' she blurted out. 'Please — would you tell me who it was paid my father's debt? He will not tell me and it would be impertinent of this unworthy female to speak to the Colonel or to Chen Kai-Tsu unless they spoke first to me. I know one of them paid Mr Kweh — I must know who. I — I must thank him.'

'It's not a secret, Pearl, but they don't expect your thanks. Chen Kai-Tsu repaid the debt and the Colonel insisted on paying half with him.'

In fact there had been quite an argument about it.

'Hang it all, Chen Kai!' Cornish had said angrily. 'D'you think I'd have stood by and let her go to this Kweh if I'd known what was going on?'

'It makes no matter, Jack,' insisted Chen Kai stiffly. 'I undertook to repay you and I will do so.'

'Hundred dollars to me isn't a great deal; to you it's all your savings!'

'It is just as bad to trick the rich man as to trick the poor!'

'You aren't tricking me; I'm offering the money with my

eyes wide open. Hell! You think you're the only one wants to make a humane gesture?'

In the end, each had considered the other's stubborn pride and agreed to divide the debt between them.

'Once we've finished down here I think we'll start in real earnest up at the ranch,' said Alicia, 'so you'd better move up to Tresco.' It didn't really matter to her whether the girl was at the house or down in the village, but she hated to see her go in fear of her father. It made her remember all too vividly the black eyes and the bruises she had received at Robert's hands. 'Tomorrow we'll clear the room next to Angelina's,' she went on. 'Tonight you can sleep in our rooms. Get Li to fetch your bedroll and bundle up later this evening.'

When Li came to find her after the evening meal, she dragged along behind him, her face tragic and her shoulders slumped in misery.

He reprimanded her sharply. 'The way Ho treats you, I thought you would jump at the chance to get away,' he chided her.

Her eyes clouded and her mouth turned down at the corners. 'It's not that, Li,' she defended herself miserably. 'It's just that – oh, you could not understand.'

'We have been given a great opportunity,' he reminded her gravely. 'No more starving in Chinatown slums! We make a good place for ourselves here! We must show that we are worthy of it!'

She bowed her head meekly. 'I will do my duty,' she murmured.

It was late when Alicia found her bed that night, for she had stayed up late helping Angelina clear out the kitchen. Among the goods brought back from the auction was a new patent cast iron kitchener, a closed range sufficient for the needs of the large ranch house. It was to be set into the fireplace the next day so that food could be cooked, even on the hottest summer's day, without the cook being affected by the heat.

Pearl and Tamsin were already asleep by the time she retired and so tired was she that she fell asleep without any of the tossing and turning which usually plagued her.

She did not stir as Pearl rose from her mattress in the early hours of the morning and slipped noiselessly out of the room.

Chapter Nineteen

Kai was in a deep and dreamless sleep; he did not stir when the door opened and closed again noiselessly. A soft footfall sounded and he half opened one eye. 'Tamsin?' he muttered. Then, as his senses sharpened, he shot his hand under the pillow, drew out the razor sharp knife and whirled about.

There was a sudden sharp intake of breath as the moonlight gleamed on the wicked blade and the intruder stepped back nervously.

Too slight for a man, thought Kai, relaxing his guard slightly, but not Alicia.

'Please, master, put away the knife,' came a soft voice.

'Pearl?' he hazarded, confusion in his voice.

'Yes, master,' she whispered.

He laid aside the knife and jumped swiftly from the bed, clad in nothing but light cotton pants.

He grabbed angrily at her wrist and pulled her into the shaft of moonlight that slanted down from the high window. 'What in the name of all the devils are you doing here?' he hissed. When she did not answer, he shook her furiously and she stumbled off balance, eyes closed against the cold, revealing light. The silken wrap she was wearing parted to reveal small, delicate breasts.

'Dear God!' he breathed, dropping her wrist as if it were burning him.

Before he could properly gather his wits, she stepped out of the silken wrap. Beneath the robe she was completely naked, her skin glowing like a golden pearl in the moonlight and rich ebony hair rippling loose down her back.

The air quivered between them and Chen Kai had difficulty catching his breath.

Then Pearl lowered her eyes, as befitted a modest Chinese woman in a male presence, breaking the spell for Chen Kai, who in his years in Gum Shan had learnt to read emotions and intentions in the eyes of both friends and enemies.

'What the devil are you playing at?' he demanded furiously. 'Why are you here?'

'Master, where else should I be but here? I belong to you now.'

'You – belong – to – me?' He let out the words on a long exhalation of breath.

'Of course,' she replied. 'You paid the debt.'

With an effort he tore his eyes away from her body.

'And you are the repayment?' he demanded harshly.

She nodded.

'What am I supposed to do with you?'

'As you wish. I am your woman.' She stepped forward until they were almost touching. It was a struggle not to reach out and hold her.

'But what of Corr-onel?' chided Chen Kai, his voice deceptively soft. 'He paid half the debt. Does that not make you half his woman too?'

Her head jerked up sharply and she gave a little gasp. Then she murmured: 'Yes, master, if it is your wish, then I am his woman too. It is your will, master.'

His hand came up from his side and struck her, open-palmed, across the cheek.

'Whore!' he swore violently. 'You think I want a whore? You think Corr-onel wants a whore?'

Her head snapped back and her eyes looked into his for the first time. In them he saw pain – pain and confusion.

His rage died as quickly as it had come. 'I should not have done that,' he said gruffly.

She raised startled eyes to him, looking with shock through her long, silky lashes. It was unheard of for a Chinese man to apologise to a woman.

'Master, I am at fault,' she assured him. 'This unworthy person has offended you.'

'For God's sake!' His voice was raw with emotion. He had

been too long away from China and the Chinese people; he had all but forgotten the vast differences between the two cultures. 'Who put you up to this?' he demanded. 'Was it Li? Prostituting his own bride?'

'Please, master,' she stammered. 'I am not Li's bride.'

'Because your father thinks he can sell you to a higher bidder?' he queried bitterly. 'It was your father, of course.'

'I need no bidding, master,' she whispered. 'It is my duty.'

'Not your duty, any more than it was your debt!' spat Chen Kai furiously. He bent down and snatched up the robe from the floor. 'Put this on!' he ordered. 'It's Ho's debt and *he'll* damn well repay it! I can find plenty of ways for him to work off the debt! Tell him that!'

'Master,' she said frankly, 'if I speak thus to him, he will surely beat me!' Her voice quivered.

'You are right.' He held her robe for her to slip into and reached out a tentative hand to cup the cheek he had struck. The marks of his fingers still lingered. 'Enough violence for one day.'

'Thank you, master.'

'Don't call me that!' he insisted angrily, taking her by the shoulders and shaking her. 'Pearl, here in California there are no masters, no slaves! How will the Americans ever see us as equals when our women are prostitutes, with no pride and no value? You aren't my slave, nor your father's! You are yourself, Pearl, and unless you insist on that, you will be treated as a nothing, a nobody! Never forget that! When you marry Li, for God's sake bring your children up to be *free* men and women!'

He half turned away from her, angry, but also afraid lest his resolution waver.

He did not see the sudden rush of tears that filled her eyes. 'You do not want me,' she stated flatly. 'You do not find me beautiful or desirable as Mr Kweh did. You want only women who are tall and fair-skinned and can ride horses like men.'

With a hoarse cry of frustration he whirled and caught her by the wrist, drawing her roughly to him. For a brief moment she looked up at him wide-eyed, then she bowed her head submissively.

'Perhaps you are right, Pearl. Perhaps I have been too long in Gum Shan and forgotten my own people.'

He spoke with studied indifference, but he desperately wished that she would go, for he doubted he could control himself much longer.

In a voice so low he had to stoop to make out the words, she whispered: 'I am shamed.'

'There is no shame!' he shouted furiously, his fingers digging brutally into the soft flesh of her upper arms. 'You are still thinking like a coolie! You think if I accepted you as payment for a debt that was nothing to do with you, if I took you by force because I was your master and you were my slave, then there would be no shame?' She winced at the harshness of his words. 'Yes,' he ground out cruelly. 'Put like that it sounds a sight *more* shameful, doesn't it, even to a dutiful Chinese daughter!'

'It is the custom ...' she repeated stubbornly, like a child reciting its lesson.

'Very well,' he replied coldly. 'If you cannot break free of the shackles and take responsibility for your own life, then *be* a slave! As for ... all this ...' He made a gesture of distaste that took in the girl, her dishevelled robe, her very presence in his room. '*I* don't want you – and neither does the Corr-onel. A fine way to thank Li! You seem to have forgotten that if he had not brought us to your father, you would be at Kweh's now!' He pushed her angrily away from him. 'Get out!' he said through gritted teeth.

The door closed quietly behind her and he threw himself down on the bed with a curse. His jaw clenched and his brow creased. After a moment he passed his hand tiredly across his eyes and sighed heavily, then he reached behind him and drew out a bottle of whiskey.

245

Alicia and Xavier took the midday meal down in the buggy to the gang digging the drainage ditches. The men broke up into small groups around the buggy and Kai and Alicia squatted side by side in the welcome shade of a huge live oak.

'Where's Tamsin?' he asked her as he sank his teeth into one of Li's freshly baked loaves.

'With Pearl,' she replied through a mouthful of cold beef. 'Kai, just what's going on?'

He forced a nonchalant smile. 'Whatever do you mean?'

'It's not like you to drink alone,' she said deliberately.

Chen Kai looked at her sharply.

'I thought you were ill,' she went on frankly, 'until I saw the empty bottle.' And smelt that heavy feminine Oriental perfume, she thought, but she lacked the courage to say that to his face.

'Jack Cornish . . . ?'

'Knows nothing.'

'And you know too much — and see too much sometimes.' He smiled grimly; there was little humour in him today.

'Why, Chen Kai?'

She'd been trying to work it out all morning. Pearl had been like a different girl today — no chatter, no smiles, just silence and sniffs when she thought no one was looking. And once, when Mrs Chang had said something to her, she had started to cry! Li had been like a bear with a sore head when she went to fetch the bread and Chen Kai, directing the excavations, had been looking at Ho as though he'd like to strangle him and working him as hard as though he were a strong and healthy young man!

'Why? Oh, the usual reasons. Call it a clash of cultures. And leave it at that. Please?'

She looked at him for a long, still moment and then nodded abruptly. 'If that's how you want it . . .' She picked up the earthenware jars and began to pack them away. 'But next time, wake me. It's not good for the soul to drink alone,' she said sombrely.

He reached out a hand to her, knowing she was remembering those nightmarish days after her release when, bruised both in mind and body, she would steal and cheat to lay her hands on drink in a vain search for oblivion. He had sat with her then and seen her through the worst.

He handed her up into the buggy and as she reached down to take the reins from him, she caught a glimpse of Pearl's father, shuffling grey-faced towards the levée.

'Go easy on old Ho,' she suggested mildly. 'I know he's not a very admirable character, but you won't endear yourself to his daughter by driving him until he drops!'

'You are mistaken,' muttered Chen Kai woodenly.

'About her father?'

'About Pearl. She is spoken for. To Li. At least, in a manner of speaking.'

'In whose manner of speaking?' snapped Alicia angrily. 'Ho's? Li's? Yours? Has anyone asked *her*?'

Before Chen Kai could answer, she clicked her tongue at the horse and was on her way back up the bluff to the ranch house.

Cornish was modifying the piping which fed water into the boiler on the side of the new kitchen range when there was the sound of hooves and a cheerful shout from the yard.

Alicia hurried down to the kitchen to see Augustus Brenchley pause dramatically on the threshold, Clive Revel close on his heels.

Brenchley looked from the Colonel to Alicia until he was sure he had all their attention.

'The judgement will be handed down today — officially,' he said gravely. Then his eyes twinkled. 'Unofficially, they told me late last night!'

The atmosphere was so tense that it was almost snapping. Even Angelina and Tamsin, only vaguely aware of the reasons, held their breath.

Alicia had an almost overwhelming urge to cross to Jack Cornish's side, but she forced herself to stay where she was and willed Brenchley to say the right words, to produce the magic formula.

'You won!' crowed the lawyer triumphantly. 'Tresco is yours. That's final. The Commission's last decision before it closed its doors, so there's no argument and no appeal!'

The stunned silence lasted a bare moment longer and then Brenchley and Revel were pumping Cornish's hand; Angelina kissed Alicia and then the startled Revel, then Brenchley and Cornish in turn. Clive Revel, his face wreathed in a rare smile, planted a cool kiss on Alicia's brow, then Brenchley caught her by the hands and whirled her around, grinning like a schoolboy, and kissed her on the cheek before spinning her around and into Cornish's arms. It should have been the simplest thing in the world for him to have kissed her in similar friendly fashion on the cheek, but he held her a moment too long, his hands gripping the soft flesh of her upper arms. For what seemed an eternity, he held her gaze, staring gravely into her brown eyes as if he would read her mind.

At last, she moved to break the spell, reaching up to plant a chaste kiss on his cheek, anything to get out of that disturbing grasp. He made a move at the same moment, bending to kiss her cheek. As they both moved together, their faces brushed and their lips briefly touched. They both recoiled as if they had touched fire.

'The Commissioners commended the map and the photographs most highly,' Brenchley went on. 'They were the deciding factor – all Lamarr's perjured witnesses and bribed lawyers could not argue with the facts! He was livid! You should be very grateful to Alicia, Colonel,' he went on admiringly. 'I am sure she has saved Tresco for you.'

'*Mrs Owens* has my gratitude –'

'I did my job,' intervened Alicia swiftly. 'For which I was well paid.'

'The labourer is worthy of his hire?' asked Cornish.

'What else?'

'I must find Kerhouan and Chen Kai and tell them the good news,' grinned Cornish. 'Tell Chen Kai how right he was to trick me into taking on a female at Tresco! Clive, you'll ride with me? And you, Brenchley?'

'Willingly.' Brenchley answered for both of them.

She was tired, but it was not the tiredness she had once suffered from, exhaustion compounded of a worn out body and a depressed and desolate spirit, rather the pleasant tiredness of a job well done.

She and Pearl and Mrs Chang had finished turning a succession of dusty, cobwebby rooms, separated from the *sala* and each other by the previous occupants but never used by them, into a civilised upper storey with a couple of guest bedrooms and a few other spacious and airy chambers awaiting the rancher's decision on future use. While the hands carried upstairs the bedsteads and feather beds brought upstream on the *Tresco*, Alicia decided to take the opportunity to bathe in the shaded and sheltered pool upstream. Nothing would persuade Mrs Chang to join in such shocking behaviour, but Pearl agreed to come along and stand watch for Alicia, who wasn't prepared to risk a repetition of the embarrassing scene at the *agua caliente*.

The pool was deserted. While Tamsin splashed about in the shallows, Alicia slid gratefully into the cool, silky water and began to wash the dust from her face and hair. At last she lay back with a sigh of pleasure to let the water run through her long tresses. When she was quite satisfied she had removed all the dust and sweat, she walked out a little further and swam lazily up and down the river. She saw Pearl covertly watching her, her face dust-streaked and sweaty as Alicia's had been.

'Come on in, Pearl,' she coaxed. 'It's so cool and refreshing.'

'You come in, Pearl!' cried Tamsin from her spot in the shallows where she sat splashing happily. 'It's fun!'

In the end, Pearl was unable to resist the cool lure of the splashing water and she slipped shyly behind a tree and emerged a few minutes later to slide unseen into the water. Respecting her modesty, Alicia turned and swam a little downstream. Tamsin, however, had no such reservations and began splashing and playing and shrieking to Pearl until at last the two of them were playing like young puppies in the shallows.

They emerged at last, rested and refreshed. The water had invigorated Alicia, filling her with the exuberance she'd felt when her father had taught her to swim in the icy mountain streams.

Walking back along the bank towards the house, Tamsin chatting merrily between them, Pearl began to open up a little and chat about the progress down in the village and her mother's health.

Alicia looked about her in satisfaction, revelling in the splendour of the scenery, its majesty only slightly muted in the early evening sun. The sky was a paler blue than in the heat of the day, the sun a warmer gold and here, higher up than the scorching bottom of the valley, there was a playful light breeze. Her eyes fell on the solid outline of the old Mission house, its white walls shining, its red roof-tiles glowing warmly in the sun, with here and there a white dove, gently cooing. It looked so warm and welcoming, a haven offering security and peace; it was hard to remember that it was so short a time since she had been brought here, so grudgingly, by its owner.

'Chen Kai!' screamed Tamsin in glee, running and hurling herself at her friend, who had just come up from the village. 'Oh, Chen Kai! Where've you been? I hasn't seen you all *day*!'

He grinned and swung the child up into his arms, his eyes meeting Alicia's laughingly over the child's golden curls. 'Did you miss me?' he teased. 'Or was it only Beatrice?'

'We've just had a swim in the river, and d'you know, Chen Kai, Pearl didn't want to come in, but she did ... and d'you know, Chen Kai, she can't swim?'

'Come on, chatterbox, race you back to the house,' said Chen Kai. He swung her down and they raced ahead to the house, hand in hand. Alicia turned to say something to Pearl, but a shuttered look had come down on her face.

'I — I am sorry, lady,' she answered bleakly. 'I did not quite hear ...'

'My name's Alicia!' She looked sideways at the girl, puzzled by the change. 'I said Chen Kai looks as if he's had a good day too.'

'Excuse me,' muttered Pearl almost inaudibly. 'My father — I must see how my mother is ...' A brief bow and she was gone, leaving Alicia with the impression that she had been on the verge of tears.

She was not allowed much leisure to contemplate the problem, for she arrived in the bustling kitchen to be informed by Angelina that their two guests were staying not only to dinner, but overnight.

'What will we give them?' she asked anxiously, for she knew that Revel would be far less inclined to rough it than Brenchley.

But Angelina had stocked up before the installation of the new range, and the marble shelves of the pantry were full of pies and pastries, puddings and jugs of cool drinks.

'Colonel Jack, he is expecting you in the *sala*,' she informed Alicia. 'Soon as you join them, I start rest of dinner. Pearl will see to the little one.'

Reluctant to keep him waiting again, Alicia hurried off to change.

'Hmmm,' said the cook, looking her over with a critical eye as she passed through the kitchen. 'So you still wearing those drab colours to scare the men off? Never worked in Sonora, won't work here.'

'Mrs Owens!' Brenchley had been looking out for her and now came forward to offer her his arm and lead her across to one of the comfortable armchairs. 'I've been congratulating the Colonel on the changes he has made, ma'am,' he murmured politely. 'But it seems the credit should all go to you. Truly, you have wrought wonders to transform this outpost into a civilised home.'

'Colonel Cornish bought the furniture, sir,' she replied in some amusement. 'I merely arranged it. But I am delighted that our more civilised veneer has prevailed on you both to give us the pleasure of your company.'

'There's your flattery back for you, Brenchley!' laughed Revel.

'Thought we'd ride into Sacramento with them tomorrow,' suggested Jack Cornish. 'If it suits you. We need some more supplies and we – or rather you – could buy the rest of the furnishings.'

'As you wish.'

'Why not wait and go down to San Francisco?' suggested Revel. 'It's safe to venture there again.'

'Really?'

'We had news in yesterday that the worst is over. Hopkins, miraculously, has survived, so they won't hang Terry. If the Vigilantes have any sense, they'll just quietly let him go and then disband.'

'So demonstrating that if you're a Supreme Court Justice you can stab a man without fear of punishment?' protested Alicia bitterly.

Brenchley shrugged. 'I echo the Colonel's words,' he replied. 'California is no longer a jumble of frontier towns. Justice must be seen to come from the law and the Government, not from the mob.'

'Surely, Mrs Owens, you'll be glad when the Vigilantes have disbanded?' queried Revel with interest.

'Yes, I shall,' she replied; it was a struggle to keep her voice light and conversational. 'The Vigilantes are only human: what they call justice could as easily turn to mob rule and an awful lot of old grudges can be settled under that cloak!'

'May I offer you a drink, Mrs Owens?' asked Jack Cornish. His hand hovered over the whiskey, a twinkle in his eye as if he was daring her to ask for what she really wanted. Her eyes locked with his and held a moment longer.

'A sarsparilla would be very pleasant, thank you, Colonel Cornish,' she said at last. She didn't want to shock Revel.

'We'll stay on for Letitia's soirée,' suggested the Colonel casually. 'She'll be happy to hear our good news.'

'Lamarr might be there,' warned Revel.

'All the better. I'd like to see his reactions.'

And his wife's too, I'll wager, thought Alicia cynically.

Chapter Twenty

The dinner was excellent and they lingered in the comfort of the new dining room drinking, Alicia thought, far too much of the rich red wine. At first she protested when Cornish refilled her glass but after a while she permitted herself to relax, to enjoy the fact that for once someone else had prepared the meal and would clear it away afterwards. Above all she revelled in the illusion that she was at home here, secure, safe and contented. Reality would intrude with the dawn's light, but for now she no longer cared.

'Marvellous to relax at last!' exulted Jack Cornish, as if he had picked up on her thoughts. 'We've all worked at full pelt for so long we've almost forgotten how to enjoy our leisure!'

'Never heard there was much leisure in ranching!' observed Revel dryly.

'Oh, I grant you, at sowing and harvest and the cattle round-up we work all the hours God sends, but a well-organised ranch can run smoothly and allow time for leisure. With good deputies like Kerhouan and Chen Kai, the ranch can be left to run itself.'

They rose at last from the table, replete with Angelina's excellent fare and adjourned to the *sala*. They would not hear of Alicia withdrawing and leaving them to their whiskey.

'Perhaps you would delight us with some music, Mrs Owens?' suggested Brenchley, gesturing to the piano in pride of place.

'My fingers are a little stiff.'

'A poor excuse,' mocked Cornish. 'The piano is at your

disposal any time you wish to play. But perhaps you have had a little too much wine ...'

'Men have been challenged to fight for such slurs, Colonel,' she riposted icily.

'And you, of course, are a dead-eye shot?' he enquired with a mocking lift of the eyebrow.

He instantly regretted his teasing, for she seemed almost to crumple before his eyes. 'Forgive my strange sense of humour,' he apologised, drawing her swiftly across to the piano, away from the interested and speculative gaze of their guests. 'My sister always warned me that it would get me into trouble.'

Her attention was momentarily diverted. 'You have a sister?' she asked in surprise.

'Yes. I even had a mother and father. Why? Did you think I was a changeling?'

Clive Revel came up before she could answer and together they turned to select some music from the box which had come at auction with the piano.

She played for them for about half an hour and then pleaded tiredness of fingers long unaccustomed to playing.

'Perhaps Mr Brenchley would take my place?' she suggested.

Cornish rose from his comfortable armchair and set his glass down on a nearby table.

'You'll excuse me, Brenchley. I must give my orders for tomorrow.'

'Go ahead, Colonel,' replied Brenchley easily, running his fingers idly over the keys while Alicia leafed through the music. Revel followed Cornish out, to smoke a cigar on the *portal*, she guessed.

She hummed gently to the popular tune that Brenchley was playing. Looking down at his bent head, she thought to herself what a very handsome man he was. Golden curls, like Robert's ... What a fool Hester was! For it was obvious that the lawyer's good looks were more than skin deep and, unlike Robert, he was as pleasant in nature as in looks.

He glanced up from the keys and saw her looking at him, but seeing, he guessed, someone or something else. He reached up a gentle hand to touch her face.

254

'Come back to the present, Alicia,' he said softly.

'Of course.' She laughed shakily. 'And what does the present hold for you, Mr Brenchley? Will you go back east?'

'I guess I'm fixed here for good now. I may buy some land – nothing on this scale, of course! Perhaps a partnership.'

'There must be more work back east.'

'Surely,' he responded, strumming gently on the piano as he spoke. 'Too much, sometimes. I like it better here. I'd been thinking for some time of coming west, but I was too lazy to pull up my roots and do it. I'd probably never have got over the state border if Clive hadn't introduced me to Hester, but now I'm here, I intend to stay.'

'But if the reason for coming here has gone ...'

'I never give up hope, Mrs Owens,' he assured her quietly, his hands still.

'Why did you and Hester break off the engagement?' she asked curiously. 'Oh, it's none of my business, I know, and I shouldn't have said anything, but it does seem so sad.'

He hesitated for a moment, then rose and crossed the room to refill his glass. 'Between ourselves, it was Mrs Bryant,' he stated wearily. 'You know, you must have seen, how completely Hester is under her thumb?'

'But she thought you were such a *catch*! Mrs Bryant, I mean, of course. It wouldn't enter Hester's mind. But her mother couldn't talk of anything else!'

'My son-in-law, the New York lawyer?' he laughed jeeringly. 'My son-in-law the future Supreme Court Judge? Ever heard of a Supreme Court Judge from California?'

'Give it time,' she protested laughingly. 'We've only been in the Union a bare five years!'

'*We* know that,' he agreed wearily. '*We* can look to the future. But Mrs Bryant cannot see past the end of her nose and her whole life since she came out here so unwillingly with her late husband, has been devoted to finding a husband for Hester who will transport them all out of the savage wilderness and back to New York and civilisation.'

Just as her mother had done.

'But Hester *likes* it here!' Alicia objected.

'Do you think Mrs Bryant cares what Hester thinks?' he asked savagely.

'Then what will you do?'

He shrugged hopelessly. 'Pray that my sister can find an appointment for Hester's brother so he can take his mother back east. Pray that perhaps one day Hester will have the courage to defy her mother ... I don't know,' he sighed wearily.

'She was very unhappy that evening in the theatre,' ventured Alicia. 'When you escorted Mrs Lamarr – and me.'

'Good!' He banged his glass down with quite unnecessary violence. 'I'm glad!' He paused a moment, then went on a little more calmly. 'No, I'm not glad really. But it might help.' Absent-mindedly he took her hands in his and smiled down at her. 'I never set out to make her jealous, please believe that,' he explained earnestly. 'But I'm only human. It worries me, though, that I might have put you in an awkward position.'

'Is the whole town gossiping about me?' she sighed ruefully.

'A goodly number of our leading citizens won't hear a word spoken against you'

'Bless Letitia!' she chuckled.

'But against her, there's Mrs Lamarr and Mrs Bryant. I no longer have the influence over her tongue that I once had. And spreading the rumour that I was coming to Tresco to see you hasn't helped.'

'What have I done to incur Belle Lamarr's enmity?'

'If I saw Lamarr leering at you in the theatre, you can be sure she did too. She may turn a blind eye to his cheap women, but for him to be making up to a woman, who despite all she may say to the contrary, is a lady and moves in her own level of society ...? Besides, you're here with Cornish, and she still has ambitions in that direction, I'm told.'

'Yes. I've seen her at Letitia's, making up to him. I don't see how she can object when her husband does the same.'

He shrugged. 'Her kind of woman wears her beauty as a boon to bestow on a chosen man. He isn't expected to look elsewhere, even when she withdraws that favour. Both the Colonel and her husband have looked in your direction, and you're generally popular as she is not, so it's inevitable she'll

256

turn her tongue on you. Anyone with any sense will dismiss
her jealous attacks for the spite they are.'

'She'll have no competition from me,' riposted Alicia
angrily. 'Her husband is an unpleasant toad —'

'And the Colonel?' he teased.

'He is my employer, that's all!'

'Then why Angelina?'

'Because he needed a cook and she's a damned good one!'
she snapped back at him. 'And if you think —'

'All right!' he conceded. 'I'll say no more on that head.
I am quite sure that you are mistaken about Cornish, but I
don't want to fall out with you over it.'

The angry light died out of her eyes. 'It's forgotten,' she
agreed with a smile. 'Life's too short to worry about what
you can't change.'

'Still friends?'

'Of course.' Impulsively she took his hands.

'A good friend,' he murmured, putting his arm around
her shoulders in friendly fashion and giving her a hug. She
smiled up at him and he bent his head to drop a gentle kiss
on her cheek.

There was a noise from the doorway and Alicia turned to
see Jack Cornish standing there, a look of open disgust on
his face.

'I trust I don't intrude!' he ground out between clenched
teeth.

'Of course not,' answered Alicia calmly, stepping easily
out of the circle of Brenchley's arms.

To her relief Angelina came bustling in with a jug of
steaming coffee and the moment passed.

Revel's suggestion that Jack should entertain them on the
fiddle was curtly vetoed. 'It's time we all retired if we're to
come in with you tomorrow,' growled Cornish. 'Mrs Owens
will show you to your rooms.'

Alicia did not linger upstairs. It was an uncomfortable
situation, a young and unattached lady in the bedroom
with bachelors — whatever would Letitia have said! — but
she was, after all, the housekeeper.

Downstairs all the lamps had been extinguished except the

257

one over by the fireplace. She crossed the room and reached out a hand to lift the chimney and almost dropped it as a shadow in the corner of the sofa moved.

Cornish had taken off his boots and lay stretched out at his ease. He swung his long legs off the sofa and padded lithely across the room to her, glass in hand.

'Don't go, Alicia,' he said softly. 'Have a nightcap with me. There's whiskey here.'

She stood a moment irresolute. She could not estimate his mood and that disturbed her. As he pressed the glass into her hand, a remote part of her brain registered that he was swaying, so slightly as to be almost invisible, on his feet. She raised her glass and sipped at the whiskey, cautiously awaiting his next comment.

'Did you see to *all* Brenchley's requirements?' he asked suggestively.

Her eyes widened with shock. 'One more comment like that and the only use I'll have for this is to throw it in your face!' she flashed in a voice vibrant with fury.

'So bellicose!' he mocked. 'You didn't throw anything at Brenchley except yourself!'

'I didn't! It wasn't like that! He's just a good friend!' None of the fear, none of the threat she felt now.

'I thought you didn't like men,' he jeered.

'It wasn't that kind of kiss!' she protested. 'It's true!' she cried as he raised his eyebrows in mocking disbelief. 'He's a friend, like Chen Kai!'

'Ah, but we only have your word for that relationship, haven't we?' he said deliberately.

That hurt her more than anything. 'Why bring Angelina here if you're so set on driving me away?'

'I wouldn't drive you away, m'dear,' he replied frankly, holding her eyes with his. 'As Brenchley says, you've well earned your place here.' He moved closer to her. She wanted to turn and run from the room, but her feet would not move from the spot. 'Don't run away,' he said softly, hypnotically, as though he had again read her mind. 'If you can give Brenchley a friendly kiss, why not me?'

'Why?' Her voice was barely audible.

'Any reason you care to name.' There was the slightest

slur in his voice and he articulated his words with care. 'To celebrate saving Tresco, to thank me for keeping you on, just to be friendly — you choose.'

'If that's what it takes, you can keep your job!' she answered contemptuously. 'If you think —'

He pulled her into his arms before she could finish. She tried to draw away but he lowered his head and his mouth sought hers.

'No!' she gasped, tearing her face away from his and struggling ineffectually to push him away. 'No!' Her eyes widened in panic. 'Leave me alone!'

Her reaction sobered him as effectively and abruptly as a bucket of icy water. 'All right!' he exclaimed, hastily dropping her wrists and stepping away from her. 'I won't touch you again, I swear it!' But by now she was beyond reason, cowering against the wall like a trapped animal. As she had that day in the barn with Evans — but this time he could not help her.

'Alicia, please!' he pleaded.

'Leave it, Jack!' came Chen Kai's voice from the doorway. 'Get out of here! I deal with this.' There was compassion on his normally impassive face and his speech lacked its usual precision.

'I never meant to upset her ... She was all right ...'

'Is nothing you can see,' replied Chen Kai heavily. 'But the sickness of the mind will destroy as swiftly as any plague.'

He drew Alicia unresisting to her feet and into his arms, making soothing noises as if to a child. 'Come, Alicia,' he murmured gently. 'It's late. You must sleep.' She went with him meekly, eyes wide and blind. And when she began to weep quietly the sound cut him to the quick.

'I never meant to upset her,' Cornish muttered. 'I — I didn't realise she hated me so ...'

'She doesn't,' stated Chen Kai firmly. 'It's not as simple as that.' He stroked Alicia's hair gently. 'Don't cry, dear, or you will frighten Tamsin.' The sobbing gradually subsided. 'Was bound to happen sooner or later. If not you, then someone else.'

Cornish stood in the doorway and watched, white-faced,

as Kai led Alicia unresisting out of the *sala*, his arms around her, her head on his shoulder.

Kai led her across the courtyard and into her room, closing the door gently behind them. He did not see the pale figure of Pearl standing in the shadows watching them.

Alicia's chair was empty at breakfast, but Cornish could hardly ask Chen Kai about her in front of his guests.

He was harnessing the horses in the stables when he saw her in the doorway, regarding him with a wide, troubled gaze.

'Was I supposed to be going to Sacramento?' she asked hesitantly.

'I realise — after yesterday —' He hadn't felt so lost for words since he was a gangling youth. 'Would you like me to tell Revel and Brenchley you're indisposed?'

She didn't answer. Just stood there with that lost look on her face.

He tried again. 'I — apologise for yesterday. I misread the situation. If you'd rather not come ...'

She looked at him in some confusion. 'Don't you want me to come.'

'Better if you do,' he said ungraciously. 'Or there'll be more questions from Letitia.'

'I'll go and get my hat.'

As he turned away he caught sight of Chen Kai standing in the shadows and wondered irritably how long he had been standing there.

'What's the matter with her?' he asked, eyebrows raised. 'I tried to apologise and ...'

'She is not ready to talk about it. Please to say no more to her.'

'When might it suit her to receive my apology?'

Chen Kai's mouth set in an ugly line. 'If you knew the half of it, Corr-onel, then you would not sneer.'

'So tell me!'

'Is not for me to tell,' growled Chen Kai.

They were in Sacramento before the worst of the noonday heat and the party split up to go its separate ways.

Alicia, armed with her instructions, set off around the

stores. She felt strangely tired and drained today. She would normally have revelled in the purchase of the rugs, cushions and trimmings that would turn Tresco from a house into a home, but today she could not arouse any enthusiasm. There was something nagging away at the back of her mind, but she knew from hard experience not to dig too deep to bring it out.

Everywhere she went she was congratulated on Cornish's success. Word had travelled fast and it was clear that Lamarr was not the most popular man in Sacramento. Everyone was delighted to let her take everything she chose on approbation; they offered her credit, but she preferred to pay in cash, although the double eagles slipped through her fingers alarmingly quickly.

She met Señora Leon in the milliner's shop, where the Senator's handsome wife was trying on hats.

'Ah, Señora Owens! You will give me an honest opinion, I am sure. Which of these hats should I buy?' she demanded, her striking dark beauty marred by a frown as she tried on a wide-brimmed chip straw tied with clouds of white tulle.

'Show me the other.' Alicia picked her way around a heap of bandboxes and parcels. 'Oh no,' she said before Señora Leon had even tied the ribbons of the rosy pink poke bonnet under her chin. 'That colour makes you look sallow, and you're not.'

She removed a chip straw trimmed with vivid scarlet silk flowers from a stand. 'This one!' she insisted.

'I have the bonnet in an emerald green,' offered the milliner.

The chip straw with its bright glossy flowers was perfect, as perfect as the bright bonnet. On paler hair, or against paler skin, it would have looked gaudy and over-dressed, but against the raven's wing sheen of Señora Leon's luxuriantly waving hair and her glowing skin, it was stunning.

'Perfect!' she agreed. '*Exquisito*!' She turned to the milliner. 'I take this one and the other I will wear. And you please have my purchases sent around to my house?' She took Alicia's arm in a firm grip. 'And now, you come and take tea with me, heh?'

Alicia demurred, but was overriden. 'No, I insist. Otherwise I never find an opportunity to talk to you by yourself. Always there are the men, or those gossiping women. Even worse!'

Alicia bought the stockings she required and the lace for the petticoat she was altering, but she resisted all the milliner's blandishments and flattery to purchase a bonnet for herself. Her packages looked extremely meagre beside Señora Leon's purchases.

Back at the elegant house, the handsome brunette admired herself in the mirror. 'You are right. This colour is much better for me. Alicia — I may call you Alicia, I hope, and you must call me Consuela — you have so good feel for colour and style, so why ...'

'Why do I dress like this?' She looked wryly down at her grey dress, which even with the new lace trimming was plain. 'I am a widow, ma'am, and a housekeeper. It does not become me to dress smartly. A widow is expected to stay unobtrusively in the background.'

'In other societies, perhaps. But in California, even in these days, young and unattached women are still in great demand; if a pretty young widow like you doesn't remarry, it won't be for want of asking,' she observed shrewdly. Then, much to Alicia's relief, she changed the subject. 'Ah, here is Luisa with the tea-tray.' An elderly woman, almost as broad as she was high and dressed all in black, carried in a tray with cups and saucers of the finest china and silver teapots. Close on her heels came a mournful man with a tray set with delicate sandwiches and cakes of all descriptions. Alicia's mouth watered.

'*Que bonito!*' said the Señora with a sigh of satisfaction. 'This will refresh us. You look tired, my dear. It is the heat, of course. So trying for you *norteamericanos*. Quite enervating.'

Alicia could barely suppress a smile. She wondered what her hostess would say if she knew that the object of her sympathy had once panned for gold fifteen hours a day, waist deep in muddy torrents and icy waters, under lowering skies or pitiless sun, or that she had walked from San Francisco to Shasta and then on to Sacramento so soon after escaping the hangman. Perhaps it was just as well that she didn't know!

'I think there is a great deal more to you than meets the eye, Alicia,' remarked Consuela shrewdly. 'You and I might have a great deal more in common with each other than either of us has with those priggish gossips we mix with. There! I am being very frank with you, because I think we could be good friends.'

'A Senator's wife and a housekeeper with a dubious reputation?'

'I always ignore any gossip or slur which emanates from Belle Kingsley − Lamarr, I should say − and you'll find anyone worth knowing will do the same. As for my standing, well, appearances can deceive. Here I am the Senator's wife, leader of society. Only my husband and a few close friends know that my father was just a *peon*, a peasant, in Panama City. My husband was on his way back to California. He married me and brought me with him.' She gave an elegant shrug. 'Wife of the Senator or *peon's* daughter, I am still the same me.

'Now tell me,' she said as she poured tea. 'The Colonel Cornish, is he a good employer? Interesting, that one. My husband is always trying to persuade him to stand for the legislature. We could do with good *Californios* there, instead of these ambitious Washington politicians like Gwin, with their snobbish little wives. What a relief to us all that he won Tresco back! What a strange name that is, *por Dios*! Is it after one of your English saints?'

Alicia shook her head laughingly. 'I have no idea, señora,' she said frankly. 'I am more acquainted with the Roman Church's Calendar of Saints than with the English.'

'How so?'

'I was educated by a Jesuit.'

'*Madre de Dios*!' Consuela exclaimed, regarding her guest with narrowed eyes. 'Not a greenhorn *norteamericana* at all! And now you wonder if you were wise to tell me, heh? Do not worry, *querida*,' she said softly. 'What you say is between us two only. But it intrigues me greatly.'

And before Alicia had time for second thoughts, she found herself telling Consuela something − but not everything − about her life in California before the Gold Rush.

'There!' said her hostess. 'I knew there was a fascinating story. No, do not fear. I don't press you to tell me more than you wish. But perhaps one day you will tell me the rest, heh?'

They went on to discuss the latest news from San Francisco until the little gilt clock on the mantelpiece struck four.

'Now you must go,' she announced, 'for I am expecting another visitor, a politician.' She wrinkled her nose. 'Boring, but necessary. And here is Luisa with your bonnet and wrap. So, we meet again this evening at Letitia's, *si*?'

Alicia stepped out on to the dusty main street feeling that she had made a new friend and that there was one more person in Sacramento who cared whether she lived or died. It was dangerous, she knew, to become involved, something she and Chen Kai had always avoided, but at the same time, it was comforting and today she felt strangely in need of comfort.

Chapter Twenty-One

By the time she reached the Orleans the large purse the Colonel had handed her that morning was almost empty, in contrast to the little antechamber off the front hall of the hotel, which appeared to be alarmingly full of parcels and packages for Tresco. She hoped they would all fit in the buggy!

'Colonel's already in the dining-room, ma'am,' said the attendant, relieving her of her wrap.

She found Jack Cornish holding court at the centre of a constant stream of citizens who wanted to shake his hand and tell him they'd always known he would come out on top. She sat back, submitted to the endless introductions, smiled and drank far too much of the wine that Cornish kept pouring into her crystal glass.

'It's very pleasant to have everyone telling you they're as pleased as you are you've saved Tresco,' he said later as he handed her up into the laden buggy, 'and I hope I've discretion enough to sort the genuine from the favour seekers, but I'm still very uneasy.'

She looked a question.

'In the course of the day, I've seen all the big mining men or their deputies and not one of them reacted the way I expected. And I'd been so sure Lamarr was fronting for one of them.'

She wrinkled her brow. 'For the cinnabar deposits, you mean? But surely Lamarr has his own reasons for wanting to take Tresco from you.'

'Because of dear Belle?' he said with a warm smile in his eyes. 'That's true. But I'd be surprised if he had embarked on this without having a buyer already lined up. And I was sure it was one of the big mining companies.'

'Perhaps you'd better ask *dear Belle*,' she snapped. 'Señora Leon tells me the Lamarrs will be at Letitia's this evening.'

He looked down at her as he took up the reins, amusement glinting in his eyes; she flushed scarlet from the base of her throat to the roots of her hair.

He set the horses off down the street. 'You met Consuela today?'

'In the milliner's.'

'She persuade you to buy an extravagant new bonnet?' he enquired.

'Certainly not! I persuaded her to buy two, both very extravagant!'

'A pity. That drab grey does nothing for you.'

'On the contrary!' she snapped. 'It makes me look what I am — a housekeeper.' She bit her lip. 'You don't mince your words, do you?'

'And you're offended?'

'What do you expect? No woman likes to be reminded ... Anyway, Señora Leon has a position to keep up in society and the means to do it.'

'Tresco's flourishing,' he argued. 'I could run to a pretty bonnet.'

'That *would* give them all something to gossip about!'

'I wasn't planning to escort you to the milliner's!'

'The principle would still be the same,' she insisted. 'The labourer, as you say, is worthy of her hire, and what she chooses to do with it is her affair!'

'This foolish plan of yours to go back east?'

'East or west, only a kept woman would permit a man to buy her clothes.'

'Chen Kai bought you perfume,' he objected.

'Quite different!' she snapped.

'Only because you say so. To the casual observer the situations are identical.'

'To me Kai is like family.'

'Ah, yes, family. Consuela may have more pretty bonnets than you, but that's something she'd give all her wealth for: a child like your Tamsin.'

266

A warm welcome awaited Cornish in the spacious drawing-room as guests surged forward to offer their congratulations. Most of them were genuine, but a few had clearly waited to see which way the wind blew before making any move.

'Cornish!' called McLean, a man of small stature and equal social standing usually to be found at Lamarr's side. 'Settle this wager I have with Wilding! He insists those maps were produced by an Army man. Now I thought I knew all the Army mapmakers in California . . .'

'I'm sure you do, McLean,' replied Cornish sarcastically. 'And I'm sure they're all — ah — indebted to you for the acquaintance.' There were some sniggers, barely suppressed, at the inference, and McLean bristled. 'But I fear neither of you will win the wager.' With a grin he crossed to Alicia's side and drew her forward. 'Ladies and gentlemen, may I present to you my map-maker and photographer — army-trained, I promise you.'

There were gasps of surprise from those who had not been in on the secret and now she had to take her share of the handshakes and be chaffed on her hidden talents, but when her hand was grasped by Emory Lamarr and she saw the naked fury in his eyes, she knew that she had made an enemy.

'Clever as well as beautiful!' cried young Henry Bryant and, to his mother's ill-concealed annoyance, raised a toast to Alicia. She took the first opportunity to slip away from all the furore.

She and Brenchley were flicking idly through some of Letitia's new music when she saw Hester Bryant slipping surreptitiously out on to the verandah.

She touched the lawyer's arm. A swift glance around showed Mrs Bryant at the far end of the room. A second or two and Brenchley too had slipped away and out into the garden.

'Love's young dream?' Belle Lamarr's voice fell bitter-sweet on her ears. Alicia turned swiftly to see the beauty watching her from the door. 'What disillusion awaits them,' she went on, venom in her voice.

'Mrs Lamarr, I didn't see you there,' replied Alicia. She racked her brain for small talk to detain her unwanted companion a little longer, lest she follow Brenchley.

She registered the magnificence of the rose pink crinoline the other woman wore. Its hoops wide and swaying, its voluminous pink skirts heavily trimmed with mauve ribbons and rosebuds of a darker pink, the ensemble far outshone anything anyone else was wearing.

'What – what a magnificent dress,' she began.

The other woman preened herself. 'Paris, of course,' she said languidly. 'They make *toilettes* that no other city can come near to, certainly not in this benighted land.' She surveyed Alicia's dress with an insolent sneer. 'Tell me, Mrs Owens – it is Mrs, is it?' She looked pointedly at Alicia's bare hands. 'Tell me, why do you always dress so *very* drably? Did your mother never tell you how very important dress can be for a woman – particularly when she is blessed with such very *average* looks?'

A wave of irritation swept over Alicia. First Señora Leon, then the Colonel, now this unpleasant woman! If they had seen her in San Francisco, a wraith dressed in rags, they might allow her to be content with the way she looked now!

'Indeed she did, but my father always insisted that the *content* of the parcel is so much more important than the wrapping.'

'Oh yes,' sneered Belle Lamarr. 'Those mysterious parents who presumably taught you all your quite unfeminine talents – will you ever, I wonder, reveal their identity to us?'

Alicia had drunk several glasses of the Reverend Cooper's excellent punch, pressed on her by the young men – and the not so young – who always crowded round the few unattached women at these gatherings like bees around a honeypot. Together with the wine she had taken at the Orleans, it was sufficient to imbue her with a feeling of recklessness.

'No mystery, ma'am,' she replied evenly. 'They were persons of standing and discrimination. I don't believe you were ever likely to have met them.'

Belle Lamarr let out her breath in a furious hiss and looked at her through narrowed angry eyes, searching in vain for an answer. Just then Colonel Cornish passed close by them and Belle's face was suddenly wreathed in smiles.

'How delightful that dear Jack is to keep Tresco,' she cooed admiringly, fluttering her eyelashes as the Colonel passed by. Then, when he was once more out of earshot, she went on in a brittle voice: 'You really must allow me to congratulate you on your choice.'

'My choice?' echoed Alicia blankly.

'Of employer.'

Alicia's palm itched to slap that complacent, mocking face. 'Then you must allow me to commiserate with you, Mrs Lamarr, on *yours*.' She looked pointedly across the room at Emory Lamarr.

Belle's mouth twisted unpleasantly. 'You'll never catch him, you know!'

'Mr Lamarr?' Alicia's eyes opened wide in surprise.

'Don't play games with me, madam!' Belle hissed angrily. 'You know very well who I mean! Jack Cornish!'

'Oh, I'm sure we will, ma'am! Look, there he is ... if you wave, I'm sure he'll see us!'

'You choose to make a jest of it,' snarled Belle. 'But you know full well what I mean. He'll never offer marriage!'

Alicia smiled sweetly. 'Oh, you'd be surprised,' she murmured.

'You'll always just be a housekeeper, however *talented*,' she said pityingly. 'You're destined for the shelf, my dear woman. Better get used to it.'

'Hardly, ma'am,' replied Alicia coolly, more coolly than she felt. 'You forget, I am a widow. I was married ahead of you — by a good few years.'

She had struck a sensitive spot. Belle Lamarr had strung her rival lovers along for so long that the defection of Cornish had laid her open to similar sneers from other, less favoured, young ladies. She looked at Alicia with murder in her eyes, then she turned on her heel and pushed her way across to her husband's side.

'*Brava*!' came an amused voice from behind Alicia. Clive Revel stood a few feet behind her, leaning against a walnut cabinet, an appreciative grin on his face. 'I came to help you out when I saw the cat had her claws in you and I stayed on to enjoy the entertainment.'

'I shouldn't have said what I did,' she exclaimed rather guiltily.

'Nonsense! It was nothing but the truth.'

One of the clerks from the Steamship Company came up at that moment, excused himself to Alicia and whispered in Revel's ear.

After a moment Revel nodded and dismissed the young man.

'Mrs Owens,' he said, 'would you excuse me? It appears my presence is required in the garden.'

'Oh dear. Brenchley?'

He nodded. 'And I had such high hopes,' he sighed.

She linked her arm in his. 'Slowly,' she advised. 'Or you'll draw attention. I'll come with you.'

There was no one on the verandah, but they had no difficulty finding Brenchley: they simply had to track down the source of the noisy sobbing that racked the air.

In the shade of a heavily scented blossom tree, on an elegant rustic bench, drooped the tragic figure of Hester Bryant, struggling to stifle the sobs that racked her slim body. Bending anxiously over her, anger and concern warring for supremacy in his handsome face, was Augustus Brenchley. Hovering nearby was a portly figure, vaguely familiar, muttering distractedly: 'Oh dear, oh dear! This is most unfortunate! Most! I really had no intention ... Mrs Bryant was quite clear ... oh dear!'

Brenchley's face lightened when he saw Alicia. 'Thank goodness!' he exclaimed in a low whisper. 'Can you calm her down while I deal with this old fool?' he pleaded. 'I think she's beyond listening to me.'

'I'll do what I can,' she promised.

He turned to the other man. 'General Stokes? May I beg a moment of your time? There are some matters you and I must discuss.'

They walked away, but the General's voice carried across the garden. 'I assure you, young man, my suit was sanctioned by her mother! But if I have offended, I am prepared to offer satisfaction ...'

Hester flung herself at Alicia and grasped her painfully

by the wrists. 'Oh no!' she cried disjointedly. 'What does he mean by it? "Satisfaction", he said ...!'

'A duel, I imagine, if your honour has been impugned,' replied Alicia drily.

'Oh no!' shrieked Hester. 'No! He must not! He might be hurt!'

'The General?'

Hester looked scathingly at her. 'Augustus, of course!'

'Don't fret. I imagine Mr Brenchley will have more sense than to engage with a man old enough to be his grandfather!'

'Don't you care that Augustus may risk his life to protect my honour?' demanded Hester tragically.

'I shouldn't think that old fool would pose a risk to anyone's honour!' riposted Alicia, struggling to suppress her laughter.

'I never thought you could be so callous,' sniffed Hester, dabbing daintily at her eyes and nose with the handkerchief Clive Revel had pressed into Alicia's hand before retiring to a discreet distance.

'I find it hard to see anything to worry about in the entire situation!' chuckled Alicia. 'Laugh at, yes, but no more than that.'

'If you truly loved Augustus, you would do something about it!' cried Hester. 'You would throw yourself on your knees at the General's feet and beg him not to take his vengeance on Augustus! Let me pass! I must stop him!'

'Hester, you've been watching too many bad melodramas!' exclaimed Alicia in lively astonishment. 'If I let you do such a thing, Augustus would never speak to either of us again. Indeed, I would think it quite surprising if he ever showed his face in public again after such embarrassment! And that *would* grieve me, because I do care for him, you see, as a good friend. He is a sensible man, quite capable of getting himself − and you − out of far worse situations than this. I *don't*, however, care for him in the way you suggest. If you want to listen to the Sacramento gossips, the more fool you!' she said brutally. 'Between them and your mother, they're making an excellent job of running − and ruining − your life.'

271

'Of course you do!' stammered Hester. 'You want him — they told me!'

'I know it shows a lamentable lack of good taste, but I really don't want him.' Alicia paused. 'Nor do you, of course, for you terminated your engagement.'

'I wish I never had,' groaned Hester, subsiding on to the grass without a thought for her elegant pale pink robe, or the insects that might be hidden beneath the blades of grass. 'Mama said he — he would soon change his mind and take us all back to New York, but he — he isn't going to, is he?' she ended on a strangled sob, gazing up at Alicia with drowned eyes.

'No, he isn't. He's happy here. And would you have been overjoyed if he had done your mother's bidding?' she asked shrewdly. 'It would have been weak-willed and lily-livered, and I don't think you want to leave California any more than he does.'

'Yes, but Mama ...'

Ruthlessly she cut in on the girl's tearful protests. 'You're happy here, aren't you?'

'Yes, and so is Henry, but Mama ...'

'Mama wants to go back to New York.'

'Yes. It's her health, you see.'

'I can't think of a woman in more robust good health than your mother!' protested Alicia.

'You only see her society face,' explained Hester mournfully. 'When she is at home, she has the most dreadful palpitations ... and fainting fits.'

'I'm sure she does,' agreed Alicia. 'And if I guess aright, always when you or Henry decides to stand up for yourself!'

'Do you really think so?' Hester's eyes were round with surprise. It had clearly never before occurred to her to question her mother's claims of ill health, but Alicia could see her mentally going through the occasions and finding that they tallied. 'But why?' she demanded in an awed whisper.

'Power,' said Alicia bluntly. 'Over you, over Henry. But it doesn't just affect you, does it? I suppose you and Henry are entitled to ruin your lives to pander to her selfish whims, but now there's Mr Brenchley's life to consider too. And the girl, whoever she may be, with whom Henry will eventually fall in love. Think what a miserable time *she* will have if your mother is permitted to go on in this tyrannical manner.'

'But how can I stop it?' breathed Hester, awed by the vision Alicia was inspiring.

'You need only be firm,' advised Alicia.

'But she will have spasms and — and — palpitations,' she objected.

'In public?'

'You mean — tell her — here?'

'You'll find plenty of support, I promise you. And among the older women whose opinion she values. She'll think twice before throwing a fit in front of them,' she said unkindly.

'But what if she does . . .?' Hester's voice trailed away as she contemplated the prospect with horror.

'She's never come to any harm, has she?' asked Alicia cynically. 'Look, Hester, you've got to make the decision — whether to upset your mother or Augustus. But remember,' she went on casually, 'then there'll be nothing to hold him to Sacramento. He could go to San Francisco, or Stockton, or Marysville. You might never see him again.'

The girl went so pale that Alicia thought she might faint. Then a look of determination came over her pretty face. 'I won't let it happen,' she said grimly, rising to her feet and setting off up the garden.

'Even if it means Mama doesn't get to New York?' queried Alicia, hurrying after her.

'Let *her* marry General Stokes,' said Hester with a shudder. 'The old fool's going back east in a few weeks.'

Clive exchanged a look of shocked amusement with Alicia as they both followed Hester up the garden. On the verandah stood Brenchley, nervously smoking a cigar. Of the General there was no sign.

Hester tumbled up the steps and flung herself headlong into Brenchley's arms. 'Oh, Augustus!' she cried breathlessly. 'Tell me you won't fight the General!' Then before he could answer, she went on: 'Please, please, don't go to Marysville. You wouldn't like it at all, really you wouldn't!'

Brenchley, choosing the only option open to a sensible man, threw his cigar away and kissed her soundly.

'Think she'll stand to it when her mother starts on at her?' asked Revel as he and Alicia walked away arm in arm.

'I don't know,' she answered frankly. 'I hope so, but there's no more we can do. I feel totally drained.'

'You didn't mince your words, did you?'

'There's little enough happiness in the world. It makes me so impatient to see two good people wasting theirs because of a lack of guts to stand up to an emotional blackmailer!'

'I know. But it can become a habit, letting your mother make all your decisions for you.'

Alicia felt as though she had been at the soirée for half a lifetime, but when she came back into the saloon from the garden, she found that the evening was still not even half over, for the doors to the dining room were still firmly shut.

The Leons were entertaining the company with a spirited rendering of 'Drink to Me Only with Thine Eyes', Edith Pikeman accompanying them only half a bar behind. Over by the doors to the hall, on the far side of the room, the Reverend stood with Captain Sharples and his wife, benignly smiling on the assembled company; Letitia sat by the piano, nodding her head gently in time to the music, breaking off only to dart the occasional angry look at Belle Lamarr, flirting not too *sotto voce* with a thickset land agent with a raucous laugh. Beyond them sat Mrs Bryant and her son. He was amusing himself making eyes at Amy Pikeman, a precocious fifteen-year-old with shining dark curls and sparkling black eyes, the only one of the brood of eight not to have inherited her mother's plain and pasty looks.

The usual polite applause greeted the end of the song. As Señor Leon and his wife stepped away from the piano, they exchanged a look of such warmth and affection that Alicia felt a lump come into her throat.

'Touching, isn't it?' came a familiar voice from behind her. She turned to find Jack Cornish standing behind her, holding two sparkling glasses of wine.

She nodded wordlessly as she accepted the wine. She remembered what he had told her about the Leon's childlessness and her face clouded over.

'Life can be very unfair,' she murmured.

'Yes.' He paused and took a sip of the cool wine. 'Does

274

Tamsin remember her father?' he said unexpectedly.

'Her f-father?'

'Your husband.'

'He's n –' she began, then shook her head. 'He – no – I – he died in the big cholera outbreak in '52. He never knew Tamsin . . .'

'Jack! Do come and find something for Miss Clarence to play!' called Miss Cooper, as two of her guests struggled in with the ornate harp which customarily stood in the hall.

'Good God!' exclaimed Revel behind her. 'Letitia's been trying to dragoon someone into playing that wretched harp for as long as I can remember! Don't tell me she's finally found someone!'

'Miss Clarence,' Cornish informed him with the ghost of a smile. 'Of all things her elegant east coast soul has yearned for since her arrival in this benighted land, her harp heads the list. She is eagerly awaiting its arrival any day.'

'She tell you so?' demanded Revel.

'No. Her father. He also told me that her exquisite sensibilities make it impossible for her to accompany any but the finest singers and instrumentalists, although she realises this must be a limitation at such gatherings as these.'

'Good God!' Clive's face was a picture. 'And why haven't I met this paragon?'

'If you and Mrs Owens had spent less time in the garden and a little more in the saloon,' answered Cornish sharply, 'you would have.'

There was a bustle in the doorway and several of the young men nearby hurried forward to offer an arm to an attractive young lady with wide blue eyes and glossy black curls dressed in the latest fashion. An elegant tarlatan robe showed off her narrow waist and sloping shoulders to perfection.

Behind the newcomer bustled a rather stout and florid man in his mid-fifties, somewhat overdressed for his surroundings. He followed his daughter in and fussed around her, commanding the Colonel to shift the harp a trifle to the left and adjust the spindle-backed chair accordingly. At last, satisfied, he stepped back, running his fingers around the inside of his elaborate cravat and mopping his sweating forehead before subsiding into a nearby chair. Miss Clarence

275

permitted young Edward Sharples to hand her to her seat and began to tune the harp to the violin which Cornish had taken from the top of the piano.

'Do you suppose there's a Mrs Clarence?' asked Alicia in a whisper as they took their places.

Clive Revel's eyes gleamed wickedly. 'Perhaps she's following on, crated up with the harp!' he joked. Alicia, who had just taken a sip of wine, laughed, spluttered and choked. As the two musicians chose that moment to finish tuning, her choking fit earned her an impatient frown from Cornish and a dagger look from the icy Miss Clarence.

Assured that everyone's attention was on them, Miss Clarence began to play. The duet was pretty enough and the sound of the harp sufficiently unusual in their gatherings to be attractive, but the comments at the end, under cover of the applause, were very mixed.

'What a delightful pair they make!' exclaimed Mrs Sharples, smiling acidly at Belle Lamarr, sitting to the right of Mr Clarence.

'Exquisite!' exclaimed Mrs Pikeman.

'No it was not!' snapped Claudia Revel, fortunately at the back of the room and out of hearing of Clarence. 'Wooden!' she pronounced.

'My dear Mama!' whispered Clive ruefully. 'As ever, tactless, but right! Miss Clarence is technically competent, but quite devoid of any heart. It rubbed off on Jack too – never heard him play with less verve!'

Alicia's attention, however, had strayed, for Hester and her former fiancé had just slipped into the room and stood arm in arm, gazing happily into each other's eyes, oblivious to the rest of the world.

There was, inevitably, a clamour for an encore.

'The next piece calls for piano accompaniment,' declared Letitia.

'Edith!' suggested Mrs Pikeman, pushing her reluctant daughter out of her seat.

'Mrs Owens plays much better than me!' protested Edith. She had no desire to expose herself to Miss Clarence's critical appraisal.

'Then by all means let us have Mrs Owens,' requested Miss Clarence, bored.

Reluctantly, Alicia allowed herself to be led forward. She nodded politely to Miss Clarence before seating herself at the piano, but received no acknowledgement, only a cold stare.

Cornish stepped forward to set out the music for her.

'What the deuce is going on with Brenchley and Miss Bryant?' he muttered. 'Like April and May again!'

'I hope they may have resolved their differences at last,' she murmured.

'With a little help from you?' he asked shrewdly.

'And Clive Revel.'

'Whenever you're ready, Mrs Owens,' suggested Miss Clarence sweetly. Cornish grimaced, stepped back, took up the violin and counted them in.

It was not an arrangement she knew, but it was not too difficult, even though she was fairly sure that Miss Clarence had deliberately come in too early on several occasions.

She turned away from the piano at the end to acknowledge the applause then froze as Miss Clarence's voice fell on her ears. 'His housekeeper, you say? A housekeeper who plays pianoforte – how quaint! I had not realised one mixed socially with one's servants in California.'

Before she could react, the Reverend Cooper was at her side, by intent, she was quite sure. He offered her his arm into supper, giving the signal for the gathering to break up and drift into the dining-room where supper had been set out.

'Try to ignore her, Mrs Owens,' he said, glancing across the room to where Miss Clarence stood, surrounded by young men all demanding to be allowed to take her into supper. 'The novelty will wear off after a week or two and then they will judge her by her good nature, or lack of it. It is always so in a small society such as ours. And you have already earned your place.' He handed her a plate and recommended some choice dishes to her, until Clive Revel appeared at his elbow.

'I do believe, my dear Octavius, that you should wander over to our friend Mrs Bryant,' he murmured. 'She is about to be in need of your support.'

They followed his glance and saw Hester and Brenchley, pale but determined, bearing down on her mother, who looked as though she could scarce believe her eyes.

The minister almost dropped his plate in his haste to reach the far door before the young couple did. 'Someone has been very busy!' he said drily as he passed Revel.

It turned out just as Alicia had prophesied. In the face of general approbation, Hester's mother, who had been on the brink of a severe attack of the palpitations, was left with no choice but to accept the inevitable. Led by the Reverend Cooper, enthusiastically seconded by Henry Bryant, who had seen which way the wind was blowing, they all drank to the health of the couple and urged them to name the day.

With the wind taken out of her sails, Mrs Bryant could only make the best of the *fait accompli* and she greeted with enthusiasm Mrs Crocker's prophecy that Brenchley had a brilliant career ahead of him in this brave new state — she was, after all, married to a leading attorney who might, any day now, be a judge.

Alicia found the edge was taken off her joy when her employer spent the entire evening paying court to Miss Clarence, to whom she had taken an inordinate dislike. She watched him fetching and carrying dishes and glasses of wine to the arrogant young woman and her father until she felt she could bear it no longer. She willingly accepted Clive's invitation to move into the other room to choose some music for the second half of the evening.

'Not more music!' complained Miss Clarence languidly. 'What we really need to liven up the evening is some dancing!'

'Excellent idea!' cried the young man on whose arm she had draped herself. 'That is, if Miss Letitia approves . . .'

Letitia smiled. 'Of course. It is quite some time since we have had any dancing.'

'Dancing!' sneered Belle. 'Lamarr! You may take me home. Too rustic by far.'

The carpet was soon rolled back and the floor prepared. It was quite comical to see Miss Clarence's face fall as Jack Cornish picked up the fiddle.

'But can't Mrs Owens play for us?' she demanded pettishly.

'Of course not!' replied Henry Bryant, none too politely. 'We need all the ladies we can find to make up the sets. We certainly can't spare Mrs Owens!'

'Nonsense! There are plenty of women!'

'At the moment. But just watch all the older ones drop out! They can't go on all night, you know. And when they go, we'll have barely enough left to make a decent set.'

'Oh, *country* dances!' she denounced with a curl of her lip.

'What else?' enquired Clive Revel. 'This is the minister's house, after all. Did you expect waltzes and mazurkas?'

She was on the verge of uttering a sharp retort to this man who stood there mocking her, the detested housekeeper on his arm, but became aware that a number of people around were listening to the exchange in some amusement. She decided to let it pass.

Alicia loved dancing, remembering long evenings in Sonora when Robert was up in the hills and she and Angelina had danced late into the night on the many feast days. That had been in the early days, of course, before the bars and dance halls had opened and to dance there had been to brand yourself an available woman. Here, however, there was no such restraint and she danced the evening away happily to the cheerful strains of Jack Cornish's fiddle.

He played indefatigably: 'Turkey in the Straw' and 'Money Musk', 'Roger de Coverley' and 'Maypole Weavers', mixed in with unknown English tunes which the dancers still managed to follow with enthusiasm and agility. At last, Brenchley relieved him and played for them for the rest of the evening. As they changed places, Cornish couldn't resist teasing him.

'The pleasures of betrothal fading already?'

'Not in the least,' he replied with a grin. 'but take my word for it, country dancing's not the place to tell your girl what you feel about her: every time you get in full flow, you have to move up the set and find yourself pouring your heart out to her mother, or Letitia!'

'Seems to suit you well enough.'

'Try it some time,' grinned Brenchley. 'Might suit you too.'

It was late when the gathering broke up. Alicia, who had

been to fetch her wrap, came into the hall just as the Clarences were taking their leave.

'I look forward to seeing you in church tomorrow morning,' Letitia was saying. 'And in the afternoon we have a meeting for the ladies, with readings and sewing for the poor from three. And the gentlemen join us for tea. We'd be delighted to have your company.'

'A sewing bee!' exclaimed Miss Clarence. 'I thought they had gone out with the ark!'

'Now, Geraldine!' her father chided her.

'Oh, Papa!' she pouted. 'You know I can't sit and set stitches!' Out of the corner of her eye she caught sight of Colonel Cornish, lounging against the newel post.

'Shall you be at tea tomorrow, Colonel?' she asked coyly.

'We only rarely get into Sacramento on a Sunday, Miss Geraldine,' he replied, eyebrow raised and a half smile playing on his lips.

'We?' She saw Alicia in the doorway. 'You don't bring your housekeeper?'

Letitia stepped hastily into the breach. 'Goodbye, Alicia. My love to Tamsin, dear child. And come to see us again soon. We all miss you.'

As their buggy drew away behind the Clarence's, Alicia said with a chuckle: 'I don't give much for the likelihood of Miss Clarence appearing at Letitia's sewing bee if you're not there.'

Cornish looked mockingly down at her. 'Oh, but you are quite mistaken. Mr Clarence is very eager to find his place in Sacramento society. In fact, he will be dining out at Tresco a week on Thursday — business dinner, for about twelve. Think Angelina can cope?'

'Of course.' She stifled the urge to ask him why.

To her surprise the carriage turned away from the rutted path down to the ferry and moved a little further downstream. There, moored to the quay, steam up, was the *Tresco*!

She declined Captain Bateman's offer of a cabin, preferring to stay on deck, watching the moonlight on the broad waters of the Sacramento. When the horses were tethered and the buggy secured Jack Cornish crossed to join her at the rail.

'Clarence wants to invest in Tresco,' he informed her abruptly.

'His money or his daughter?' she enquired, raising her eyes briefly from her contemplation of the dark, oily waters beneath them.

He looked at her quizzically. 'Money, as far as I know.'

'Does Tresco need outside investment?'

'No. but at least through Clarence I've found out why Lamarr and his cronies wanted Tresco.'

'Why?'

'Railroad,' he replied sombrely.

'They want to bring it across your land?' she whispered, appalled at the prospect. 'Or do they want you to invest?'

'I'm not certain,' he replied brusquely. 'Perhaps both. There seems to be some scheme they're hatching to extend the Sacramento Valley Railroad across the Sierras and over the Rockies to the East Coast. If they can link down to San Francisco, they'll have an ocean to ocean link.'

'Sounds reasonable. Although if they could get through the Sierras, why didn't they do it when they built the Folsom line?'

'They had other problems then, starting out at the wrong time. They'd just got the grading underway and a good engineer in Judah when the dry winter touched off a run on the banks. Good object lesson in how not to invest your money. Those of us who had land, stock, some investments – well, we survived. Those who had everything in banks lost it all. Poor devils like Wilson, who'd ploughed all his money into his railroad dream, went broke before they laid the first rail. Folsom took over from him, but he's dead. Judah's good, and he may get the Government's permission to go ahead, but you can bet they won't put any finance behind it. Land grants aplenty though, to tempt the speculators in.'

'But won't it ultimately be good for California – to be connected with the rest of the States?'

'Sure. There's a deal to be said for an Atlantic-Pacific Railroad. Goods wouldn't have to be shipped round the Horn, so they'd be cheaper; the markets for California goods would open up. But for me – I don't need Eastern goods and I have all the markets I need right here. And I doubt Judah will be

281

any match for Stanford and Crocker, and if Huntington and Hopkins get in on the act they'll run rings round him. And if Clarence and Lamarr are supporting the scheme, they are right on the brink of legality. Before long, they'll have the politicians in on it, fouling it up, pushing for it go through their county, not the next one. And I doubt San Francisco will support such a scheme, for their prosperity depends on the trade around the Horn. Oh, it's a grand idea, but its time is not yet.'

'Why do they want your support?'

'Perhaps because of my contacts in San Francisco. Maybe they'll try to buy them off by giving them a good route first — after all, they would hate to see Sacramento the terminus for the overland trade! Ye-es,' he murmured slowly. 'In some way, I think Tresco must be the bait for San Francisco. And if I know Lamarr — and Clarence — it will be something illegal, or at best extremely devious, and planned to put the maximum amount of lining in their pockets.'

'Why don't you just refuse to have anything to do with it?'

'Because then I'd still be in the dark. This way I find out what they have in mind — and still have the option of staying out of it.'

Chapter Twenty-Two

The accident, when it happened, was as unexpected as it was shocking.

Li and his brother were repairing the roof of the largest house in the village, to be the new bunkhouse for the men, freeing the barn at the back of the yard for grain storage. Kerhouan and Juan rode into the village in the late afternoon to inspect progress and were exchanging jests with the men up on the roof when a thin, high-pitched scream came from the opposite cottage. All heads swivelled round to see what was going on.

The door of one of the cottages crashed back on its hinges and Pearl came staggering out, the left hand side of her face a livid red. Old Ho came behind her, raised his hand and cuffed her again.

Kerhouan jumped down from his horse and with Lachie ran across to separate them.

Cornish came out into the doorway to find out from Juan what was happening; Li, on top of the roof, craned forward with a hiss of fury, and relaxed the pressure on the heavy beam they'd been about to secure. Gathering speed, it slithered silently down the pitch of the roof, unheard and unseen by the small knot of men standing below.

Too late Juan turned at Li's hoarse cry of warning and it seemed that he must be crushed but Jack Cornish sprang forward and at the last moment managed to drag Juan out of its path. The end of the wood whistled past Juan's ear, caught Cornish a glancing blow down one side and crashed to the ground.

Juan went white as a sheet as he realised how close he had come to death.

'You saved my life!' he whispered shakily. 'But you have hurt yourself, I think!'

'No, I'm all right,' Jack Cornish assured him, his face a little pale. 'Just — jarred my arm, that's all.'

But by the time Pearl and Kerhouan got to him, he was gritting his teeth, the sweat pouring down his grey face.

Kerhouan ripped the shirt sleeve open without hesitation; there was no visible damage but as he gently probed the arm, Jack Cornish gave a strangled cry and his knees buckled beneath him.

They put him on a hurdle to carry him back up to the ranch house, for fear that the falling beam might have done other, unseen damage.

Alicia, podding peas in the kitchen garden, saw the little procession pass through the heavy gates in the nopal hedge. The bowl and the peas were scattered all over the herb bed as she gathered up her skirts and raced down the slope.

As she drew closer and saw the familiar dark lock of hair flopping forward over his face, sick panic welled up in her throat and lent speed to her heels.

'Oh God! He's not dead?' she cried despairingly.

Kerhouan began to speak, then Li burst in, white-faced, to excuse himself for his folly, with Pearl tearfully adding her mite, while Juan told her how Colonel Jack had saved his life — perhaps at the expense of his own.

Closing her ears to them, she slipped her hand inside his shirt. She could feel his heart still beating, although not strongly. With a sob of relief, she placed a cool hand on his forehead.

His eyelids flickered and he tried to speak, but a second later his head fell to one side again.

'Get him up to Tresco!' she ordered. 'Someone run ahead and tell Angelina to clear the big table.' Her heart lurched as she took in the unnatural angle of his arm and the jagged rip in his trouser leg. 'And water — lots of hot water — and ice from the cellar! And somebody ride down to the water meadows and fetch Chen Kai. Take a spare horse for him. And hurry! For God's sake, hurry!'

284

Angrily she brushed the tears from her eyes. No time for that now. She kilted up her skirts and walked alongside the hurdle, never taking her anxious eyes from the still figure beside her.

He was on the table and still Chen Kai had not come. She could not wait.

She took Kerhouan's knife and as gently as she could, slit the shirt from him. His arms and chest were criss-crossed with the old scars from the mine accident. She had forgotten about that and the sight of them, white against the tanned skin, came as an added shock.

His shoulders and chest were covered with angry red patches, some of which were already beginning to show the purple of heavy bruising, but nothing else seemed to be damaged.

'Did he strike his head?' she demanded anxiously.

Kerhouan shook his head. 'I don't know. We didn't see.' He clenched and unclenched his fists. 'If only he'd come round again ...'

'Best if he doesn't,' she replied crisply as she passed gentle fingers over his skull. 'We shall have to see to that arm and he'll be better off unconscious.'

The arm was beginning to swell now, red and angry beneath the raised criss cross of white scars. Li hurried in from the ice house in the cellar; she filled the fish kettle with ice and carefully moved the injured arm into it.

There was a swift intake of breath and she looked up to find two green eyes regarding her.

'Sorry ... disappoint you ...' he said through gritted teeth. 'Not dead – yet.'

Just then, Chen Kai came running in. Swiftly he looked around and saw what she had done. 'Good,' he pronounced. Then, more urgently: 'Your head, Jack – how is your head?'

The eyes flickered and closed, but no answer came.

With head injuries you just never knew; Alicia had never forgotten the cocky little Frenchman up at Hangtown who had banged his head on a protruding beam up at the diggings, been perfectly well for two days and dropped dead on the third.

'Alicia!' Chen Kai's hand was on her shoulder, gentle but firm. 'I need you.'

She gave herself a mental shake and hurried across to take Chen Kai's medicine box from Juan, peering nervously around the door.

'The little one is with Angelina and Josefa,' he whispered reassuringly. 'No worry.'

'Thank you, Juan.'

'And we all pray for heem.'

She hurried back to Chen Kai. His long, sensitive fingers probed a little more around the forearm, his eyes closed as if in a trance. 'Curious,' he murmured. 'The old break, which I think has never healed over properly, has opened up again.' Without opening his eyes he gave his orders. 'A handful of leaves from the blue bag in a small cup of hot water. Then add three drops of number one. Quickly. The arm is already beginning to swell.'

She hurried to do his bidding. She had occasionally worked as his assistant before, usually with those settlers too poor to afford what they regarded as a 'real' doctor, and they had devised the system of numbered phials and coloured bags to avoid confusion.

When the strong-smelling brew was ready, Kerhouan raised Jack's head and Alicia trickled it down his throat. He swallowed it automatically, a good sign.

'I'm going to manipulate the arm now,' stated Chen Kai.

'Manipulate?' exploded Kerhouan. 'Move a broken bone? That is to risk the bone coming through!'

'I can free his arm,' he insisted. 'No more pain too much to bear, no more fingers that won't work for him.'

'But the risk!'

'Is a risk just to be alive,' shrugged Kai. 'But here the risk is very small. I can do it,' he repeated confidently. 'You know him best, Ker-hwan. Is for you to say if he would take the risk ... the chance. But decide quickly. Or the swelling will be too much.'

Kerhouan hesitated only a moment. He thought of the frustration Jack lived with, the times when he had been so mad with the pain that he had taken to the bottle and in his drink had spoken wildly of finishing the surgeon's task and taking an axe to the damaged arm.

'Do it,' he said softly. 'It is what he would choose.'

Because of the swelling they had to start before the sleeping draught had properly taken effect. Kerhouan held the upper arm steady as Chen Kai, eyes closed, began to move the muscles around the break, flexing and straightening the injured man's fingers, adjusting the position of the lower arm. After a few minutes he stepped back from the table and wiped the sweat that was pouring down his face. Under his direction, Alicia applied poultices and fomentations to the injuries, alternating the hot and cold cloths until Kai's ragged breathing was once more under control.

They seemed to have been there for an eternity. As Kai once more folded the fingers into a ball and then straightened them out again, Jack's body gave a convulsive jerk and he groaned.

'Stop it!' he cried in a tormented voice. 'Alicia! Stop the pain!'

She stood irresolute, midway between the table and the fire, looking to Kai for guidance.

'Talk to him,' he said in a low voice. 'Distract him, but keep him still.'

She hurried round the table. As he groaned again, she leaned forward and stroked his face.

'It's all right, my dear,' she said softly, trying to keep her voice steady. 'It's nearly over. Hush now, my dear.' She was patting him, stroking him, murmuring absurd nothings, meaningless noises such as one uses to comfort a child or quieten a hurt animal.

There was a grinding noise that set the teeth on edge and he jerked and yelled with the pain.

'Keep him still!' exclaimed Chen Kai angrily.

She propped her right hip on the hard edge of the table and leaned the top half of her body over his. Out of the corner of her eyes she could see Kerhouan, strong calloused hands holding Jack's upper arm and elbow rigid. She leaned forward, pinning his shoulder with her right arm, her bosom on his chest.

He groaned again. 'Alicia!' he gasped, pain contorting his half-dazed features. 'Where are you, Alicia?'

'I'm here, Jack,' she soothed. She lay her face against his, feeling the sheen of sweat that glissed against her skin.

'Ready,' murmured Chen Kai.

'I'm here, Jack,' she repeated. 'I'm here, my love, I won't leave you,' she whispered, letting her whole weight fall on him, pinning him to the table.

There came a dreadful grinding noise and his lips drew back against his teeth as he screamed. His eyes rolled up in his head and he passed out.

The opiates had taken effect, somewhat belatedly, and he was still sleeping soundly as the dawn came up over the Sierras. Quietly she pushed back the shutters and breathed in the fresh air, drinking in the view of which she never tired. She guessed that he had selected this room of all the others just for that view. Once the Sierras were in your blood, you found it hard to forget them.

Chen Kai and Kerhouan had divided the night watch up between them, but ripe fields waited for no man and soon they would be on their way, one to the wheat fields, the other to the water meadows, criss-crossed now with irrigation ditches. She was still anxious, but she knew Kai would not have left him if there were any danger.

She turned back into the room, looking at it properly for the first time. It was a stern room, she thought, as spare and unfussy as its owner. There was a large, heavily carved fourposter, a relic perhaps of earlier occupiers, and a tall brass bound chest of drawers, but the bed had been ruthlessly stripped of all its hangings and the boards were devoid of any carpet or rug. Behind the door two jackets hung on hooks, providing the room with its only sign of habitation.

'Meet with your approval?' came a weak voice from the depths of the fourposter.

She hurried across to the bedside. She passed her hand across his forehead and found it cool. His face was pale, but that was better than the flush of fever which had been so obvious in the night.

'Thank God. The fever's gone. Does it still hurt? No, what a stupid question. Of course it hurts.'

'I can bear it,' he declared. He looked down at his arm and frowned at what he saw.

The splinting had not taken long, but Chen Kai was determined the bone should not slip before the new setting could heal, so he and Juan had spent half the night devising a leather sleeve for the arm. A layer of soft calfskin had been stretched over the muslin bandages and then over that had been moulded a tube of tougher hide, wetted, beaten and left to dry on the arm. It had dried stiff and tough and the whole forearm, from wrist to elbow, was held rigid and immovable.

'Is this damn thing really necessary?' he demanded. He tried to raise his arm. 'It weighs more than a ton of grain, I swear!'

'Only because you're not used to it, Colonel,' she reassured him. 'This time you want it to set true.'

'I told you, there's no stopping in a harvest month!' he exclaimed angrily, shifting his weight onto his good arm. 'Don't just stand there looking at me. Help me up!'

She sighed heavily, hooked her forearm under his shoulder and heaved him up. When he was sitting, propped up against the pillows, the room swam before his eyes and he lay back, eyes closed.

When he opened them again a few moments later, she was still standing at the bedside, her hands on her hips and an exasperated frown between her eyes.

'Go on,' he said silkily. 'Now say "I told you so"!'

She shook her head sadly. 'I never waste my breath. When they're as stubborn as you, Colonel, best they find out for themselves.'

There was a knock on the door and Angelina surged in with a tray. She exclaimed volubly over him and told him to get back under the covers before he caught a chill, then she surged back out again, leaving him staring with ill-concealed loathing at the array of dishes.

'No appetite?' she queried in sympathy. 'Never mind. Just try to eat the soup. Keep your strength up.'

He insisted on spooning the soup up by himself and she let

him, feeling he needed to assert his independence. He made a fair job of it, but then, he'd been all but single-handed ever since the mine accident. She'd noticed how much weaker the muscles of his left hand had been.

He must have read something of her feelings in her eyes.

'I'm not much more handicapped with this on than I ever was,' he said sombrely.

'At least it wasn't your right hand,' she said bracingly.

He smiled up at her, a mocking, lop-sided smile. 'I'm left-handed,' he said sweetly. 'They tried to thrash it out of me at the Cathedral School, called me a Devil's Brat, but until the mine accident, I never could use my right hand for much. After, of course, there was no choice.'

Before long he lapsed once more into a deep sleep. When he awoke again, it was to find Chen Kai leaning over him. Of Alicia there was no sign.

Kai began to renew the poultices he had bandaged on to Jack's left leg, which had been bruised and lacerated in the accident.

'How is Pearl?' asked Cornish.

'Very upset. She feels she caused the accident.'

'Nonsense! And I hope you've told her so. If anyone's to blame, it's old Ho. Chen Kai, what are we going to do with him?'

Chen Kai compressed his lips in a thin angry line. 'Ker-hwan and I have spoken to him already. We told him to pack his bags and return to San Francisco! He can go with the boat on Wednesday.'

'Seems like the best idea,' he agreed sombrely.

'But — he insists he will not go without Pearl.'

'Pay him off!'

'It won't work.'

'Why not?'

'Face, Jack. He says his family honour will be destroyed.'

'But if he takes her back, what guarantee is there that she will not fall into Kweh's hands again?'

'None. So Ker-hwan and I worked out a compromise. If she is betrothed to Li first, then he can leave her here. *Then* he will take his money and go.'

'And Pearl?'

'She has agreed. Why should she not?'

Cornish frowned. 'Don't know. Something I can't quite put my finger on ...'

'You're too tired to think about it now,' said Kai firmly. 'Try to rest.'

He woke again in the late afternoon to find Alicia sitting in the warm sunshine at the open window, hemming a dress which she was making for Josefa from an old skirt Julia had sent down. She was absorbed in setting her stitches and he watched her for a while from under half-closed lids.

At last she became aware of his regard. She smiled at him and set her work aside.

'Drink?' she offered.

'A large whiskey,' he answered promptly.

'Perhaps tomorrow!' she chuckled, pouring him some juice. She held it to his lips while he drank thirstily.

'How long have you been awake?' she asked.

'About ten minutes,' he admitted, watching her closely. 'I was just enjoying lying here watching you.'

She was annoyed to find herself colouring under his gaze. The thought that he had been watching her without her being aware of it made her feel very vulnerable.

'You're a very restful woman,' he said.

To cover her confusion she wiped his face with the aromatic lotion Kai had left and straightened the sheets.

She was relieved when a gentle knock fell on the door. Tamsin stood on the threshold with Josefa hovering nervously behind her. They had picked wild flowers in the meadow just above the house and arranged them in a rather haphazard fashion in a couple of stone jars they had cajoled out of Angelina.

'Why d'you have to wear a harness on your arm?' demanded Tamsin, placing the flowers on the chest.

'To make it better,' he replied gravely.

'But Chen Kai told me it was better than good-as-new!' she exclaimed with a furrowed brow.

'And so it will be,' smiled Alicia. 'But only if Colonel Cornish gets his rest. Off with you now. And be good for Angelina, both of you.'

'Thank you for the flowers, sweetheart,' he said with a

291

warm smile. 'They're just what I needed to cheer me up.'

Tamsin looked thoughtfully around the sparse room. 'Yes,' she agreed. 'It's not a bright room like ours, is it, Lisha?' She turned confidingly back to Cornish. 'You should ask Lisha to make your room bright like ours. Chen Kai says Lisha can make a palace out of a pig-sty,' she imparted proudly.

'And you can make a tired man out of a strong one with your chatter,' said Alicia with a forced laugh. 'Off with you now.'

'You shouldn't have sent her away,' he reproached her. 'She's a never-ending source of amusement to me. Last week she told me I was just like the Good Smartman!' he chuckled. 'Took me awhile, but I got it in the end.'

'Oh, the Good Samaritan! Yes, it's one of her favourite stories, but she never gets it quite right ...'

'Who's looking after her while you're looking after me?'

'Angelina.'

'I'd have thought Angelina has quite enough on her hands with all the cooking.'

'Now that's something I wanted to talk to you about, Colonel Cornish,' she said. 'If you're feeling strong enough, that is,' she added conscientiously.

'I can see this is serious,' he mocked. 'Sit down.'

'I've told her to stop the preparations for Thursday, but Kerhouan insisted I clear it with you first. So if you let me have the guest list, I'll send Calum into Sacramento with your regrets ...'

'My regrets?' he queried coldly.

'For being unable to entertain them on Thursday as arranged.'

'But I have no notion of being unable to entertain them! I shall be up from this bed by tomorrow at the latest, which gives me two days more to get over whatever fiendish potion you poured down my gullet.'

'But ...'

'The matter is not open to discussion,' he snapped impatiently. Then he slumped back against the bolster, his eyes closed, his face pale.

She hurried to his side, holding the smelling bottle under his nose until he reached out and pushed it away, wrinkling his nose. 'If you don't calm down, Colonel Cornish, you won't even be out of bed by Thursday!'

'Stop arguing with me then,' he replied silkily. 'No!' he held up his sound hand. 'I'll hear no more about it.'

She reached behind him to straighten the pillows and plump them up. 'And what's all this Colonel Cornish nonsense?' he demanded, reaching up to catch her wrist in his good hand. 'You can do better than that — you did yesterday.'

She drew back, colour suffusing her face. 'Please — you're hurting me.' Even sick he had a strength in his one good arm that she could not match. 'Colonel, please ...'

'Jack!' he insisted. 'Maybe you can't say the rest to my face yet, m'dear, but Jack you'll call me if you want me to let go.' In his agitation, the Cornish accent was very strong.

'Please — J-Jack,' she stumbled over the words. 'You're hurting my wrist. Let me go, please.'

He released her wrist so suddenly that she staggered.

There was a mocking smile on his face, but as he watched her, it faded to be replaced with something more disturbing. He patted the counterpane for her to sit down. 'And now, m'dear, it's past time you and I sat down and had a serious talk.'

On top of the agitation of the previous day it was all too much.

'No. Please.' She turned away to the window, trying to stem the tears. 'I'm sorry!' she blurted out. 'But I just can't.' She fled across the room to the door. 'I'll send Angelina ... or ... or someone ... to sit with you. Excuse me.'

She kept steadfastly away from him for the next twenty-four hours. And when he was up and about again, she made sure for a couple of days more that she was always either with Pearl or Angelina.

And there was plenty to occupy her. With Pearl she was busy cleaning out the rest of the upper rooms and some of the outlying buildings which had been tacked on, haphazardly, over the years, and turning them into suitable guest apartments, for it was not to be expected, after the heavy drinking which would inevitably accompany such an all male gathering, that many of the guests would be capable of enjoying a journey back to Sacramento, even in the comfort

293

of the *Tresco*, which the Colonel was putting at their disposal for the journey out from town.

'I can't see why you're putting yourself to all this trouble!' he exclaimed, pausing in the doorway of the dining-room to watch, in some exasperation, as she finished beeswaxing a floor which, to him, already looked cleaner than he ever remembered seeing it. 'They all know this is a bachelor household — they won't expect to see it gleaming!'

She paused only briefly from her polishing. 'Look like a one horse farmer and that's how they'll estimate you,' she said briskly. 'Coming up from the river, they won't see what good heart your land is in; their lasting impression will come from the house. That'll show them what kind of man they're dealing with.'

'But all the cooking ...'

She smiled a rare smile. 'Don't fret about that. Angelina could cook for twice that number single-handed, aye, and with half the notice.'

'She can have Xavier and Luis to serve.'

'I can cope.'

'You are not to show your face on Thursday evening!' he commanded roughly. 'Is that quite clear?'

'But that's ridiculous!'

'Consider it an order!' he snapped, turning sharply on his heel and striding away down the corridor before she could think of a retort.

She recounted the conversation to Kai in the kitchen, but he only smiled at her anger. 'It is not like you to be so foolish, Alicia,' he said with a slow smile. 'He is trying to protect you.'

'I can very well protect myself!'

'From suggestive remarks made by a group of men far on in drink? I doubt it. Better for you to steer clear of them.'

'Better still if she marry the boss, then he can have proper dinners with a proper hostess,' Angelina chimed in from her post over by the range. 'More comfortable for all of us.' She ignored Alicia's strangled cry of protest and went on serenely: 'That child sure needs a father and you sure need a husband.'

Alicia did not deign to answer, sweeping out of the

kitchen grim-faced, closing the door with an angry slam as she went.

Angelina looked across at Chen Kai. 'Don't you go thinking that was a knock against you,' she rebuked him. 'I see how good you are with leetle Tamsin. But it ain't a situation I approve of.'

He shrugged. 'You are only saying what I have said to Alicia, but she won't have him.'

'You mean he's asked and she's turned him down?' she demanded in disbelief.

'I think so. Yes.'

'She always was stubborn,' she sighed, with a shake of her head, 'but that is madness. *Loco*.'

'Yes.'

'As mad as you,' she went on smoothly. 'There's that poor child Pearl and all you can do is give her the cold shoulder, as if she didn't have enough problems with those *loco* parents of hers.'

Their brief moment of unity was swifty gone and with a scowl Chen Kai found himself following Alicia's hasty exit. Angelina just smiled serenely to herself and turned back to stir the contents of the huge pan on top of the range.

Chapter Twenty-Three

The day before the dinner, Cornish came to the kitchen to talk to Angelina about the last few details. His arm was greatly improved and he only used the sling when Chen Kai-Tsu or Alicia reminded him.

'Everything's just fine and dandy,' Angelina assured him.

'And you can manage tomorrow night? Need any extra help?'

'Alicia and I can manage OK.'

'Mrs Owens? She can help in the kitchen if you really need her, but understand this — she's to keep well out of sight from the minute those men set foot on Tresco. *Comprende,* Angelina?'

'A good servant should always be invisible,' said Alicia with a smile as she passed through the kitchen with a pile of linen. He held the door open for her with his good arm, and watched her pass through with a baffled look on his face.

The Sacramento Valley was shrouded in mist when Alicia awoke on the Thursday morning and, for once, as she slipped out into the courtyard to draw the water for washing, she was unable to gaze across to watch the sun tip the peaks of the mighty Sierras with golden light. Robbed of the distant prospect, it seemed as though Tresco were marooned, an island of fresh, dewy greenness, silent but for the plash of the river as it curved around below the bluff before hurling itself into the muddy brown waters of the mighty Sacramento. Even the cluster of houses beyond the nopal hedge was invisible. She found herself resenting the approaching invasion for the threat it posed to the peace and quiet of Tresco.

The silence was broken by a crash from the kitchen and a door slamming somewhere over by the bunkhouse. She became aware of the chill in the damp air and drew her shawl closer about her shoulders. She and Tamsin were both glad to draw close to the range in the warmth of the kitchen.

'Tomorrow I send Pearl with hot water for you!' scolded Angelina.

'Certainly not!' replied Alicia with heightened colour as the Colonel and Chen Kai took their seats at the table.

'Of course she will!' Cornish insisted. 'She already fetches it to Angelina. Anyway, you mustn't argue with Angelina today, or she'll curdle all the puddings!'

Angelina put her hands on her hips and laughed one of her rich laughs, her ample chin and bosom quivering. 'That's right!' she chuckled. 'And today, be sure no one comes into my kitchen unless to help.' She banged a plate of hotcakes and sizzling bacon down on the table in front of them and then she rounded on Kai. 'And you,' she wagged a finger at him, 'you I don't see until this evening. You keep those children out from under my feet. And don't come in the kitchen, not to see Alicia, not to make eyes at t'other one.'

Kai looked as though he would have liked to strangle her.

By mid-morning the mists that had swept up the valley from the sea had dispersed beneath the burning rays of the summer sun. At midday Luis was dispatched to the river meadows with the men's food and Alicia emerged from the heat of the kitchen to sit with Chen Kai and the children in the shade of the lemon tree, listening to the soothing music of the little fountain as they ate the tasty pies that Li made down in the cookhouse.

'I've persuaded Angelina she must take a *siesta*,' explained Alicia. 'She's not as young as she was and when she gets tired, her temper gets hotter than her pepper stew!'

'And you?'

'Oh, I'm not tired!' she asserted, brushing a stray strand of hair out of her eyes.

'So I see!' he grinned at her. 'You're a different woman from the one I brought here.'

'Thank God for it!'

'Tresco has wrought a miracle in you,' he said softly, reaching across to take her hand.

'It saved my sanity,' she agreed. 'But without you, my dear friend, there would have been nothing left to save.'

'You wanted to see me about the guest rooms, Mrs Owens?' came Cornish's voice, sharp and edgy.

He was standing at the corner of the inner verandah, his leatherbound arm for once in its sling, his face taut. Behind him she could see Pearl, face pale, eyes downcast.

'At your leisure,' he said sarcastically. Flushing, she released Kai's hand and rose swiftly to her feet.

She put Tamsin to bed early that evening, resisting the child's requests to be allowed to stay up to watch the visitors arrive. Then she hurried back to the kitchen to help Angelina.

There were to be six courses, each served with two removes, and although a great deal had been prepared in advance, Angelina's pride had made her include a number of more elaborate dishes which had to be prepared and served up straight away.

'Is goin' to be a hot night,' observed Angelina as she rolled out the pastry for the raised pies.

'Hot and sticky!' agreed Alicia. 'But think how much worse if we still had the open fire!'

'Phew!' the cook exclaimed, and they both laughed.

They heard the *Tresco's* whistle sound down at the quay. Alicia put more of the ice to float on top of the bowl of punch she had mixed earlier and carried it through to put it on the table in the *sala*. Xavier and Luis, scrubbed and clean, were sent to wait on the visitors.

'Goin' to be a night of hard eatin',' observed Angelina.

'And hard drinking,' agreed Alicia.

Everything went smoothly, as Angelina and Alicia had intended it should. 'If we could feed a hundred miners every night, ten gentlemen not goin' to bother us!' laughed Angelina.

Every time the boys came through the door, carrying fragrant dishes in or empty plates out, they heard the occasional brief burst of conversation and as the evening wore on and the pile of empty bottles grew, the voices became louder, gusts of

298

laughter greeting what were obviously ribald stories.

'Just like being back in the *cantina* again!' commented
Alicia wryly.

There were ten men altogether, the boys told them in
answer to Angelina's eager questions. Attorney Crocker, of
course, and his brother, Lamarr, and a fat man they didn't
know, except that he sent his compliments to the chef on the
excellence of the pies, of which he had apparently eaten more
than his fair share.

'And who else?' demanded Angelina.

'Well, Colonel Cornish, of course, and Mr Judah,' confided Luis. 'He's trying to persuade them all to build a
railroad all the way to New York! No wonder they all call
him Crazy Judah!'

'And Mr Hopkins and Mr Huntington, they're there too,'
chimed in Xavier. 'But Mr Hopkins is only drinking water,
and he's hardly eaten anything at all. Looks as if a puff of
wind'd blow him over!'

'And they've brought two other men with them from San
Francisco. They're directors of some railroad company.'

'And Mr McCann is *real* ugly ...'

'But Mr Olsen's worse,' interrupted Luis. 'He's little and
fat and his eyes are sunk into his cheeks just like a pig.'

'Yes, but Mr McCann – he looks real mean!'

'You don't get that food on the table before it starts to
cool, I'll get real mean!' chuckled Angelina, sending them
on their way with a friendly shove.

The *pièce de résistance* was a masterpiece of the confec-
tioner's art, concocted by Alicia. Cream, saved from the
milking of the two Shorthorn house cows, thickened and
flavoured with the best brandy, was piled between layers
of fruit and delicate pastry into a pyramid, decorated at
the last minute by thin cobwebby strands of spun sugar.
Xavier took the heavy silver platter from Alicia and, without
thinking, she hurried ahead of him to open the door into the
dining-room.

As he marched proudly through the door with the elaborate
dessert, she had a momentary glimpse through the opening.
She saw Cornish's profile and, to one side of him, a huge man
with a full beard and moustache. As he turned to speak to his

neighbour, she saw him full face. The left-hand side of his face from the hairline to the uneven edge of the beard was covered in puckered purple scar tissue which drew down the corner of his eye and twisted the corner of his mouth to give the whole face a frightful aspect.

She slammed the door and ran gasping down the hall to the kitchen. She collided with a startled Angelina, who grabbed her to prevent her falling.

'What is it, *querida*?' she demanded.

Hand to her throat Alicia gabbled something incoherent, her voice rising hysterically, then her head snapped back and she fell to the floor in a dead faint.

'I don't want your damned whiskey!' she shouted at Chen Kai from the floor where she was struggling to tie a bundle of clothes in a large Paisley shawl.

'I won't let you do it, Alicia!' said Chen Kai, ashen-faced. 'I won't let you take her out on the road like this!'

'Let her stay here with you then!' She looked up at him, her face swollen and tear-stained. 'You'll both be better off without me!'

'You're not going anywhere!' snapped Cornish, coming up behind her and taking the bundle unceremoniously out of her hand. 'Not until I have some explanations. Angelina told me some cock and bull story about someone wanting to put you *back* in prison?' Alicia slumped down on the bed as if every bone in her body had dissolved. 'Now I've had enough of these half-truths of yours, Alicia. I want the truth — and I'm not aiming to leave until I get it.'

'Please, Jack, listen to me,' began Kai.

'Kai, I'm sure you have another good yarn to spin, but not this time. This time I'll talk to her alone.'

Chen Kai opened his mouth to protest.

'That's an order!' barked the rancher.

Kai drew a small bottle from his pocket and placed it on the table. 'Call me if you need me,' he said quietly. 'And when she's had enough talking, that will help her sleep.'

As the door closed behind him, Cornish poured a small glass of whiskey, knelt and held it to Alicia's lips.

'Now,' he said softly, 'now I want the truth!'

She looked piteously at him, but his face was set. This time, she knew, she would have to tell him — everything.

'I was in prison in San Francisco,' she said dully. 'And Fisher knows — he put me there! And now he won't stop until I'm back in prison, until I'm dead!'

'Fisher?'

'The big man with the sc-scarred face.' Her voice shook. 'Fisher.'

'McCann. God's sake, he'll be gone soon, back to San Francisco. I don't think he saw you, the door was hardly open more than a few seconds. Surely there's no chance of discovery. Even the name has changed!'

'He won't let me go,' she said on a rising note of hysteria. 'If I don't do what he wants, he'll turn me in and they'll hang me!' She began to cry, hot, scalding tears flowing unchecked down her pale cheeks. 'You don't know what I did, what an evil thing I did.' She pressed her hand to her eyes as if to block out the vision. 'There's no point in running away. He'll always find me.'

'Tell me!' he urged her gently. 'Tell me what happened.'

She shook her head helplessly. 'I can't,' she sobbed despairingly. 'Please ... don't make me.'

From the inner room came a startled shout and the sound of Tamsin crying.

She started to rise.

'Stay there!' he commanded harshly. 'If she sees you in this state, you'll only make her worse.'

He went in and knelt by Tamsin's truckle bed, his broad shoulders blocking her view of the doorway and the outer chamber.

'What is it, Tamsin?' he asked softly.

'Colonel Jack?' she whimpered.

'Yes.' He caught her hand and felt her shaking. She caught her breath on a sob. 'I heard a lot of noise and I thought that the bad man had come to take Lisha away again. I'm so frightened!'

'There's no need,' he said soothingly. 'You know I won't let anyone hurt you.' He stroked the tangled hair out of her eyes and held her and talked to her until the sobs faded away and she began to drift back to sleep again. 'No one will ever frighten you again,' he murmured as her eyelids began to droop tiredly. 'You're quite safe at Tresco, you and Chen Kai and your mama.'

The heavy eyelids fluttered and she chuckled drowsily. 'Silly, Lisha's not my mama, though I loves her like she was.'

His eyes widened in shock.

Alicia's shadow fell across the doorway and he half turned to her.

'Shall I ask her about the big man?' he said in a half whisper. 'Shall I ask Tamsin why she's so frightened?'

He hated himself for doing it.

'Don't!' came the panic-stricken whisper from behind him. 'For God's sake, don't make her remember! Don't make her remember!' He laid the sleeping child back against the soft pillow and turned slowly.

She was leaning against the wall as if she could no longer depend on her legs to support her. 'I'll tell you,' she went on dully. 'I'll tell you all you want to know. Then you'll understand why I wouldn't − why I could never marry you.' She crossed to the bed and sat silent for a moment, gazing into the distance.

'It's a long story,' she began. 'I guess it started back in '50, in Hangtown.'

'You were already in California then?'

'I'd already been married a year. It wasn't a good marriage. My husband deserves a place in the history books,' she said bitterly. 'First victim of gold fever. We were at the first camp in '49. He was probably already in debt then, but I didn't know ... Fisher treated me, when we first met, with a kind of familiarity I had not suffered before. Perhaps he already thought he had rights, who knows? But I thought he was just − it was just − because there were so few women.' She held out her empty glass and he refilled it for her without comment. 'We had a miserable few years, but I always told myself that if it didn't work out, I could go back to my mother's home, Valley Hall in Connecticut. Soon after I inherited it, my husband gambled it away − to Fisher. And that was the end of that dream.'

'Go on.'

'He — Robert — talked of having staked me against the house. Said he'd left me to Fisher after his death. It was such a ridiculous thing to say that I took no notice. I was so furious about the house I could think of nothing else. Robert died while I was working for Angelina. After that, things got better. Chen Kai and I set up in business —'

'And Tamsin?'

'She was an orphan. From the picture wagon. We just — took her in.'

'Go on about Fisher.'

'We didn't come across him again until last autumn in San Francisco.'

'Chen Kai told me.'

'But he wasn't there when we met. Fisher came in to have his photograph taken with one of Belle Ryan's whores on his arm. He — he got me into a corner and he asked me if I wouldn't like to have Valley Hall back again. He said if I married him, I'd have my inheritance back again.' She shook her head. 'It was odd. He was insistent, almost obsessed. Kept saying I was rightfully his.'

She took a drink. The whiskey seemed to have no more effect on her than water. 'I should have had more sense,' she said tragically. 'God knows why I acted as I did.' She shrugged. 'I think inside I blamed him for Robert — for all the wasted years. I said that he was the last man in the world I'd ever marry. I said he could keep Valley Hall and welcome, and I hoped the society had been to his taste.

'He was furious, but I didn't care. Unfortunately the woman with him was not stupid. She scented a story — perhaps an opportunity for blackmail. She found out the story from one of his men — he surrounded himself with slack tongues.

'Seems he'd set himself up as the Squire of Valley Hall, with a houseful of his old New York cronies he wanted to impress. Of course, Connecticut Society shunned him, gave him the cold shoulder, the servants all left and he was made to look a fool in front of his gang. God knows why, but he convinced himself that it was my doing and that if Robert had paid the debt in full and he'd got me with Valley Hall, Connecticut Society would have welcomed him with open arms.

303

'It was too good a story to pass up. She told me — and half of San Francisco.' She shivered. 'That was when our troubles started.'

Outside the rain began to fall heavily, drumming on the tiles, but she didn't move. He crossed the room to put a shawl around her shoulders and sat beside her.

'I tried to find Monique, to stop her spreading the story, but she'd vanished from the face of the earth. His doing, I'm sure. And by then it was too late anyway.'

'The props and then the camera ...'

'And then the studio.' She took a steadying sip of whiskey, but her voice was shaking as she went on. 'When we nearly lost Tamsin in the fire, I wanted to go and see him, beg him to leave us alone, offer to kill the story. I don't know.' She shivered. 'But Chen Kai wouldn't let me. He said we must get away, out on the road again. For a while I thought we'd got free, but ...'

'He took the wagon. Chen Kai told me.'

She nodded. 'He won't have told you the rest.' She drained the glass in one gulp and rose jerkily to cross the room. 'We were in a shack just outside Coloma,' she began in a low voice. 'Chen Kai had gone to see an old man about a camera; I was printing some views I planned to tint and sell to raise some cash.'

The scene was as clear in her mind as if it had been yesterday.

'Tamsin always knew she had to keep away when the chemicals were out. She was over by the door playing with Beatrice. There was a crash and the door was kicked open. Fisher stood there, with two of his men behind him, all armed. Tamsin started crying and he — he knocked her across the room, stunned her.

'I screamed at him to leave us alone. He'd taken my inheritance, my livelihood, what more could he want?

'He said I'd humiliated him, that I was a haughty New England bitch! He said he'd dealt with Monique. Now it was my turn.

'He — his eyes were quite mad. I knew what he wanted.

'He was coming at me. I was terrified.' Her voice dropped. 'I reached under the bench for the gun and screamed at him

304

to keep away, but he just laughed. He said: "You won't use that, you whore!"'

She could see him now laughing at her, coming at her. His hand fell to his waist and he began slowly, so slowly, to unbuckle his belt.

She shook her head. 'I pulled the trigger. One of his men dived at me at the last moment and jogged my arm.' Her voice rose to a scream. 'I shot the wrong man! It should have been *him*!' Then, once more, that calm, monotone voice. 'He didn't care about his man. He just ... I tried to fight him — I couldn't stop him — he — he — all with the dead man lying there.' The gorge rose in his throat, nearly choking him. He wanted to hold her, comfort her, but somehow he knew it wasn't the moment. 'He was gloating, gloating ... In the fight, the bench had gone over and there were bottles, the chemicals, all over the floor. My hand knocked against one. I loosened the stopper and threw it in his face.' She turned back to face him. 'And I'd have watched it eat him away too, I would have! But they said they'd shoot Tamsin — until then I'd thought she was dead. I had to tell them how to neutralise it. They saved his evil face.'

'They took you to jail?'

'And Fisher came every day to gloat.' She came across to stand before him. 'I'd have swung to rid the world of him,' she said brokenly. 'But I never meant to kill the other man.'

'He was probably just as evil as Fisher.'

'Or maybe just an ex-miner, down on his luck, taking any job he could get!' she riposted angrily. 'Maybe some woman's man, some child's father. Whatever he was, he was some mother's son.' Her voice dropped pathetically. 'There wasn't a day passed in jail but I thought of that. Each day Fisher came to taunt me: he'd drop the charges, he said, if I'd marry him and go with him to Valley Hall. He was mad, obsessed, he couldn't believe I'd rather hang.' She shuddered. 'And every day I wondered why it had to be the other man instead of him.'

He drew her down to sit beside him and took her restless hands in his.

'How did you get out of jail?' he asked gruffly. 'The

Vigilantes didn't usually let people go except on a one-way ticket to the Sandwich Islands.'

'Or to the gallows.'

'Tell me,' he said softly. 'No more secrets.'

She closed her eyes in pain. 'The doctor – the doctor told Chen Kai I was sick. Kai ... guessed I was ... pregnant.' He let his breath out in a hiss. 'I – hadn't told him, you see, everything that had happened.' Blindly she held out the empty glass and he could not refuse her, knowing what it was costing her to relive the horror. 'If he hadn't had Tamsin to think of, I think he'd have killed Fisher then.' She gazed down into the amber liquid. 'He knew I'd kill myself rather than ...' Her voice trembled as she tore the memories painfully from the dark recesses in which they had for so long been hidden away. 'He brought me in a herbal draught. It worked, thank God, but I was very ill. In the end it was the doctor who saved me. He didn't like Fisher; he'd tried to bully him into handing me over. He also disapproved of the Vigilantes. Under other circumstances, he said, I'd get a fair trial and be acquitted on grounds of self-defence. So he drugged me again and told them I'd died.'

As she finished her story she was shaking uncontrollably. 'Oh, Alicia!' he said, his voice cracking. 'What a terrible time!' She began to shake and he slipped his arm around her shoulders and drew her towards him.

'I don't deserve your sympathy,' she muttered into his shoulder. 'I'm a murderess twice over. That man, and ...' She couldn't bring herself to say it.

He held her close to him as she struggled to control the shuddering that racked her slim body.

'The doctor bought you time,' he murmured into her soft hair. 'Don't throw it all away now.'

'I'd rather be dead than in his hands again.'

'The Vigilantes have disbanded – no one wants to rake up old scores again. And they'd hesitate to indict my wife for a dead woman's crimes.'

'Your *wife*?' She looked up at him, startled.

'If he tried anything – well, I've some influence still in San Francisco. You'll see. They'll prefer to leave Mrs Langdon dead and buried. Who's to say there's any connection with

306

Mrs Cornish? And there are plenty to back me up — Cooper, Revel, Leon. And if that's not enough, I'm sure money will persuade them not to see the connection,' he replied cynically.

'You'd use bribery to save me?' she exclaimed. 'When you wouldn't use it to save Tresco?'

'Not just for you!' he said harshly. 'What future is there for Tamsin with you in jail? Look, you must see you've no choice. If he finds you and you're out on the road again, away from Tresco, I won't be able to help you. They'll likely lynch Chen Kai, put you back in jail and Tamsin in an orphanage.' His voice softened. 'I can only help you if you give me the right to protect you.'

'Why should you take on our problems?'

He shrugged. 'I've told you before. Chen Kai and Tamsin fit in here, they're happy here. Tresco needs a woman and I need a wife.'

'A wife who's a murderess?' she said, her voice trembling on the word.

'I killed a man once,' he said slowly. 'Back in Cornwall. But I don't call myself a murderer. His death saved two lives and a lot of misery and suffering. You had the courage to do the same.'

'I don't want to marry you,' she sobbed. 'Don't want to marry anyone. I can't ... I ... couldn't ... You'll want an heir for Tresco. Even if I could ... after ... *that* ... in prison ...I ...'

He reached out and brushed the damp hair from her face. 'Let's jump that fence when we come to it,' he suggested. 'But for now you need to say whether I send for Reverend Cooper or not.'

She reached out for the glass, but he moved it out of her reach. 'Decision first,' he told her implacably.

To run away from Fisher again, to go on the road that led God only knew where, or to stay and with Cornish's help face him out, stand her ground. To stay and make a home for herself and Kai and Tamsin in the 'pretty green place', even if it meant taking on a husband she didn't want. And even as she thought it, she knew she was being unfair to him. This was not a man like Fisher, or even like Robert. He could be harsh and autocratic sometimes, but she was not perfect either. He was kind to Tamsin, a good friend to Kai. When they were not fighting, she enjoyed his company.

'Yes or no?'

She shivered and nodded her head slightly.

'Say it!' he insisted.

'Yes, yes, yes!' she yelled.

He poured a small measure into the glass together with the contents of the small bottle Chen Kai had given him and sat with her while it took effect. As her head began to nod, he slid his good arm round her and drew her closer until her head rested against his chest. He laid his cheek against her soft hair, breathing in the fresh, herby smell of it.

Only tonight, when he had been in danger of losing Alicia, had he realised how much he loved her. Over the past couple of months she had become so intrinsic a part of his life that he had not noticed how much she had crept into his heart. Even the revelations of her recent past had not changed his feelings, except to make him even more determined that she would not suffer again. How he would cope with Fisher in the morning, how he would manage to keep his hands from him, he didn't know. And yet, for Alicia's sake, he must.

In the inner room the little girl muttered in her sleep and he smiled softly. The three strangely assorted travellers had blended in so completely that it was hard to remember the time when they had not been part of Tresco.

Alicia stirred in his arms.

'Jack?'

'I'm here,' he said softly. He wanted to say more, to tell her the way he felt, but it would be unfair to burden her with his feelings when she had been through so much already tonight. It could wait.

As her breathing grew steadier, he swung her legs up, covered her with the counterpane and slid a pillow gently beneath her head.

He turned the lamp down low and slumped wearily into the chair. A Hell of a way to make a proposal! he thought. A Hell of a way!

He left her at dawn, impressing on Chen Kai the need for the three of them to stay out of sight until the last of the guests had gone. After a late, hearty breakfast, he deliberately took those of his guests who cared to come to look over the ranch. Angelina was nowhere to be seen, but Pearl was busy in the kitchen garden.

Inevitably, McCann — Fisher — made a coarse remark, but Cornish, who would have liked to kill him with his bare hands, forced himself to laugh it off. 'Pearl's betrothed to Li, one of the men working on the building,' he said casually. 'As for me, when I lost the lovely Belle to Emory, I renounced women!' Lamarr smirked.

'Who was that having hysterics in the kitchen last night?' asked Clarence casually.

'The cook and the maid fell out — you know how it is ... Cook burnt her hand on a dish and blamed the maid for it.'

'Servants!' exclaimed Clarence. 'Need a woman's hand to keep 'em in their place. No problems in our household — Geraldine sees to that. Make some man a good wife!' he ended unsubtly.

It was with a sigh of relief that Cornish at last saw his guests off on the steamer. He'd given Captain Bateman his orders earlier that morning, together with the letters he'd written during the night while Alicia slept. He turned back from the jetty and walked thoughtfully back to the ranch house.

Chapter Twenty-Four

Alicia struggled to lift her head from the pillow. Someone was shaking her. She wished they'd go away and leave her alone.

At last she managed to lift her head up. It was swimming. Hardly surprising, she thought, despising herself for her weakness last night — or was it the night before?

'Lady?'

It was Pearl.

'Pearl, how many times? My name's Alicia.'

'Colonel has brought the minister to see you,' she said softly. 'Here is fresh water. And Chen Kai-Tsu also wishes to speak to you.'

As the door closed behind Pearl she sat up. Despite what she'd drunk, her memory, for once, was not in the least fuddled. She knew exactly why the minister had come. And, surprisingly, today she felt none of the panic that had once washed over her at the thought of Fisher.

Hurriedly she rose and washed away the sleep and tidied her hair. When she opened the door to the Reverend Cooper, she was quite composed.

He took her hand in his. 'My dear Mrs Owens,' he said gently — and then seemed at a complete loss how to go on.

She sat down and waved him to the other chair.

'Colonel Cornish told you? My past finally caught up with me.'

'He told me something of the story.' He paused uncomfortably and cleared his throat. 'He wants me to marry the two of you. Of course, the Colonel's

310

a good match. If you're sure you want to marry him . . .'

'I don't *want* to marry anyone!' she said pettishly. 'Like Letitia, I'm much happier single.'

'Appearances can be deceptive,' he replied gravely. 'The young man Letitia was engaged to marry was killed in the Indian Wars and no one else ever measured up to his memory. A waste.' He paused. 'You know of course that if you need a home, a refuge, Letitia and I would be delighted to have you and Tamsin with us.'

Letitia had been quite blunt, 'Tell her to come to us if she'd rather. But mark my words, my dear Octavius, she's not as averse to him as she may think. They've a lot more in common than they've had a chance to find out. A marriage could be the making of both of them.'

'Cornish is a good man,' was all he said now. He crossed to the door, 'Let me know what you decide. Take your time.'

Her decision. That was what Chen Kai had said, when she had woken, groggy and disorientated in the cold dawn — yesterday's cold dawn, she realised — and blurted it all out to him.

He had declared his readiness to take them all back on the road again and to kill Fisher with his bare hands if he tried to stop them, and she knew he meant it but she also knew that it was not enough. Neither he nor the Coopers would stand a chance against the likes of Fisher.

She must have sat there for hours turning it over and over in her mind, but by the time Pearl came back, she knew what she had to do. At least this way Tamsin would have a home, whatever happened. And she was tired of running.

Like a sleepwalker she allowed Pearl to brush her hair and pin it back with two ivory combs and help her into the splendid amber silk dress that Letitia had sent as a bride-gift. When Angelina came for her, bubbling over with enthusiasm, she gazed blindly at her. When Pearl held a mirror up for her, she saw only a pale stranger.

In a daze she walked across to the house where the four men were standing in an uneasy knot by the door, talking in low tones. Tamsin would have run to her side, but Kai caught her by the hand.

311

'You keep your word,' grated Cornish roughly.

She nodded, looking round her at the minister in his starched bands, the altarcloth and candles on the table in the centre of the room. Kerhouan came down the room with a bunch of heavily scented flowers which he thrust in some embarrassment into her hand.

She stood in the shaft of late evening sunlight that slanted in at the window, her hand icy cold as Chen Kai placed it wordlessly in Cornish's. They made their responses and Kerhouan produced a slim gold ring which Cornish took and slipped onto her finger. Then, at last, it was all over.

'You may kiss the bride,' said the minister with a grave smile, and she felt Cornish's cold lips on her cheek. Then eveyone, wreathed in smiles, was kissing her and it was doubly hard to stay detached in the face of their enthusiasm. Tamsin was hopping up and down in her excitement.

The candles were lit as the sun went down and as the shadows fell, Angelina and Pearl served up a very creditable celebration supper. Only the conversation was stilted and she made no contribution to the discussion about the harvest and the prospect of an autumn rice crop.

Halfway through, Pearl carried Tamsin off to sleep in Angelina's room and the talk became a little freer. Chen Kai and Kerhouan were both drinking deep, but the rancher and his new bride had hardly touched their wine.

The Reverend Cooper decided to turn in early in view of the next day's journey, and as his host crossed to trim a lamp for him, Alicia seemed to come suddenly to her senses. 'All that clearing up!' she muttered. 'I must help Angelina ...'

Cornish stood frozen at the bottom of the stairs, his face devoid of expression.

'No, Alicia.' Chen Kai removed the plate from her fingers. 'We'll manage.'

'Chen Kai!' She clung to his arm in panic, but he led her firmly across to Cornish at the foot of the staircase.

'Be good to her, Jack!' he muttered fiercely, then turned abruptly on his heel and strode out of the room without a backward glance.

'Go on up, m'dear,' suggested Cornish, trimming up a night lamp and handing it over to her. 'I'll be a while.'

His hands were still busy trimming wicks, but his eyes followed her all the way up the stairs until she vanished from sight.

It was another half hour before he followed her.

She was sitting in the chair before the open window, still as a statue, an empty glass beside her; for a moment, he thought she was asleep, or drunk, but as he closed the door behind him, she jumped and started to her feet. As he set his lamp down on the chest, she skittered across the room towards the door.

'For God's sake!' he exclaimed wrathfully. 'Will you stop that? You'll frighten me out of a week's growth!' He turned his back on her to trim the wick. 'I thought you'd have been in bed by now.'

'No!' Her voice was raw. 'I couldn't − I can't!'

'Look, let's have an end to all this!' he snapped, striding angrily towards her. He stopped abruptly as she dived for the gun in the holster hanging on the back of the door.

His lips thinned in anger as he looked at the gun in her hand. Then his face went stiff and he turned away and coolly began to untie his cravat. Tossing it aside, he sank down on the bed, his back to her, and began to ease off his boots.

'I'm thirty-five years old, Alicia,' he said deliberately. 'I've never yet had to resort to rape to get a woman to go to bed with me and I've no intention of starting now.' His second boot fell noisily to the floor. 'By the way, I haven't left a loaded gun around the house since you and Tamsin first came here.'

There was a click as she opened it up, then she threw the gun down on the chest with an angry curse. He rose and crossed the room to hang his jacket on the hook. She stood in the corner by the door, her eyes large and shadowed in a pale face.

'Do I have to sleep here?' she whispered.

'No,' he replied tautly. 'If you really want to humiliate me, you can go downstairs right now, past Octavius and Angelina and Pearl, and go back to your old room.'

She stood, undecided, in the middle of the room. He paused in the complex task of shrugging himself out of his shirt, no easy matter with the heavy leather strapping on his arm, and smiled at her. 'Go to bed, m'dear,' he said unexpectedly. 'You're tired and I'm tired.'

313

Her eyebrows snapped together in a frown. 'You – you don't want me?' Surprise and relief were mixed in her voice.

He looked at her with a disturbing light in his eyes. 'Oh yes, I want you. I've never seen you look more beautiful than you do tonight. It was worth the wait. But when I take you, I want two good arms to hold you in and both of us with clear enough heads to remember it the next day, not half-sodden with whiskey as you are now.' He turned away again, 'Put the lamp out when you come to bed,' he said smoothly.

She crossed to the corner of the room furthest from the light and began to undress; he could almost sense her willing herself to ignore his presence. There was silence for a while, followed by the sounds of a struggle. Then a small voice from the far corner called out: 'I can't undo the dress.'

He had great difficulty keeping his face straight. 'And how can I be of assistance?'

'Would you undo the lacing, if you please?' she asked in a choked voice.

Out of the corner of her eyes she watched him cross the room. Like Chen Kai, he wore nothing but a pair of loose cotton pants. She closed her eyes and told herself that this was just the same half-naked body she had nursed.

'You'll have to come over into the light,' he said crisply. 'You've got it very knotted and my fingers are still a little stiff.'

He lifted the golden brown hair out of the way and laid it over her shoulder. She shivered at his touch.

'Hold still!' he snapped. 'Stop jumping like a scalded cat! Christ! No one would ever think you'd been married. Can't you just pretend I'm your first husband?'

'My husband was more likely to take his fists to me than help me out of my dress!' she said unguardedly.

'Dear God!' His fingers stopped abruptly. 'What a waste,' he sighed. 'Then pretend I'm some other man you once felt some affection for.'

She bowed her head. 'You are mistaken, Colonel,' she said, 'I have never – known – any man but Fisher.'

'You mean – your husband ... never?'

314

'No.'

Memory stirred. 'Langdon?' he mused. 'Not Lucky Langdon?'

'That's him. Failed in fortune, failed in everything.'

'That why he beat you?'

She shrugged. 'Perhaps. He saw it differently. He said I was frigid.' She heard him grind his teeth. 'I — I did warn you . . .'

As the lacings parted, the lace-edged amber silk slipped away from her smooth creamy shoulders. He should have walked away then, but in spite of himself, he was transported back to the day at the *agua caliente* and his body began again to betray him. He ran the tip of his thumb softly along the top of her shoulders and bent his head to press his lips to the silky skin at the nape of her neck.

For a brief moment she swayed towards him, unable to control her reaction, then he felt her stiffen under his touch.

He dropped his hands to his side, not holding her any longer than she was willing. 'He was wrong,' he said softly. 'You're not frigid. One day, you'll see that.'

She didn't answer, all her attention intent on stopping the unlaced silk dress from slipping. To her relief, he didn't wait for an answer.

She turned down the lamp and slipped into her old nightdress. She could delay no longer. She stood beside the bed listening to his deep and steady breathing. At last she climbed into the bed.

She lay there a long time in silence, hardly daring to breathe.

'You'll never sleep perched on the edge like that!' came an amused voice from out of the darkness.

She drew in her breath in a sharp gasp.

'Get this straight — I am not Fisher. Don't jump and gasp every time I come near you! We made a bargain down there today. I expect at least the appearance of a wife in public. Now turn over and go to sleep.'

315

She was dreaming. She was lying in the big meadow above Tresco, peering up at the sunlight filtering through the wildflowers, the golden yellow Californian poppies, the deep magenta shooting stars, the Indian paint-brushes and the multi-coloured clarkias. The sun was warm on her eyelids. Her eyes flickered open and she saw that the shaft of sunlight was coming in through a window in a wall.

Memory came flooding back and she rolled over to see Jack Cornish lying by her side. She waited as if from habit for the mindless panic to wash over her, but curiously, it never came.

He looked very young and vulnerable in his sleep, and not in the least threatening. Before she could examine her feelings any more closely, a knock fell on the door.

Pearl slipped in, bearing a pitcher of warm water, a woeful expression on her face.

She put the pitcher down on the chest and stood impassively at the end of the bed, her hands together.

'Good morning, lady. I hope you have had a happy and auspicious night,' she murmured.

Alicia didn't know where to look. As Pearl moved away to pour out the water, she turned to find Cornish with one eye open, regarding her quizzically. He dropped his eyelid lazily in a conspiratorial wink and she found it difficult not to burst out laughing.

The door closed behind Pearl. 'And did you have an auspicious night, Mrs Cornish?' he asked, brushing against her as he sat up.

She managed to control her initial impulse to recoil and smiled weakly. 'I — yes. A good night's sleep,' she conceded.

He grinned back at her and slid his good arm around her to give her shoulders a gentle squeeze. 'And that's something you've been sadly lacking of late,' he observed wryly.

She forced herself to return his smile.

'There!' he exclaimed triumphantly. 'Not too painful, was it?'

Before she could answer, he had sprung lithely out of the bed, swept up his clothes and left the room to her.

That set the tone for their daily contact. Alicia, who had

dreaded she knew not what changes at Tresco, found that very little had, in fact, altered.

Every day she organised the house and the feeding of the men, aided by Li and Angelina, while Kai was busy down at the riverside. The restoration of the village buildings was now almost complete and the men were gradually moving down there. The next plan was to convert the old outbuildings to store grain, although much of this year's harvest had already been shipped on to San Francisco on the *Tresco*.

Every day she found herself growing less and less awkward with the man who had become her husband. He made no demands of her and after a while she no longer recoiled when he touched her and she could even accept it when he occasionally put his arm around her shoulders. He made it seem so natural that it would have been pointless to fuss.

The day after their marriage he had a folding screen put into the bedroom, giving her some privacy, and moved Tamsin into a small room close to theirs. A few days later he had a couch put in the dressing alcove and often slept there when he was restless. His arm, he explained. She had to admit that she had no grounds for complaint.

Weeks passed with no sign of any threat from Fisher. She could almost persuade herself that she had imagined the whole affair, except for the wedding ring on her hand.

Cornish was sitting at the window one evening, watching the sun dipping towards the peaks of the Sierras, when Tamsin came creeping down the stairs barefoot, holding the hem of her flannel nightdress up in case she tripped and looking anxiously around her.

The movement from the window startled her and she looked as though she were about to turn and flee.

'What is it, Tamsin?' he asked softly.

The child hung back. 'Lisha said I wasn't to bother you,' she said anxiously.

'I'm not busy.' He crossed to the foot of the stairs and knelt down in front of her. 'Tell me.'

The words came out in a rush. 'I can't find Beatrice anywhere! I's frighted the wolves will get her!' Tears stood in her eyes.

317

'Ssshhh!' he soothed her. 'There are no wolves at Tresco. Not you nor Beatrice will come to any harm, I promise you. You're quite safe, you and Beatrice and your — and Lisha. Come along, we'll both go look for her.' He took her by the hand.

They found the doll out on the *portal* where Tamsin had been playing earlier with Josefa. She clutched Beatrice to her joyfully and gave Cornish an exuberant hug.

Smiling down at the child, he caught sight of Alicia in the doorway, looking rather anxious. Forestalling her rebuke, he bent his head to speak softly to the child. 'Don't ever be scared to come to me for help, Tamsin,' he said deliberately. 'I'll always find time for you, child.'

She looked at him with her head on one side. 'Am I your little girl now that you've married Lisha?' she demanded. 'Josefa says I must call you Papa now, but Lisha said I wasn't to trouble you.'

'I'd be honoured to have you for my little girl,' he replied gravely.

'But — what about Chen Kai?' she said with a wail. 'I loves him too!'

He reached out and took her in his arms. 'Sweetheart,' he reassured her. 'Chen Kai brought you up and looked after you long before I met you. I wouldn't ever want you to forget that. We all love you. Nothing has changed. You and Chen Kai and Lisha can stay at Tresco for as long as you want and we can all be happy together. Names don't matter!'

She seemed satisfied with that, smiling cheerfully as Cornish took her back into the house. Alicia had disappeared again, so he picked the little girl up and carried her up the stairs to the little bedroom where she now slept.

'I s'pose I'm very lucky,' she muttered sleepily. 'I've got two sort of papas and one sort of mama. If Chen Kai married Pearl then I'd have two sort of mamas too, but she's going to marry Li.' She snuggled down beneath the covers with a yawn. 'Will you sing me that Cornish song you singed me last week?'

The next morning Kerhouan came in with a report of broken fencing in the valley where the new Shorthorns were pastured.

Cornish swallowed his coffee hastily and rose to his feet. 'Round up a handful of men,' he ordered. 'We'd best ride over straight away and see what's about. Chen Kai, take whoever you need to finish the work in the water meadows. Up here there's only the sweeping out of the new storehouse; Luis and Xavier can deal with that. Anyone still down in the village?'

'Only Pearl,' replied Alicia. 'Mrs Chang is sorting laundry for the *agua caliente* tomorrow.'

'Fine.' He leaned over to ruffle Tamsin's golden curls and looked across to Alicia. 'Might be better if you don't ride out today,' he suggested mildly, 'Stick around the ranch.'

The light died out of Alicia's eyes and Cornish almost wished he had not spoken. 'It's not likely there'll be any problems,' he said, giving her a brief reassuring hug. 'But best to be safe. Chen Kai will be down at the water meadows if you need help.'

'I'll be all right,' she assured him. 'Plenty to do here.'

'Fine.' He dropped a chaste kiss on her cheek and released his grip on her. ''Til this evening then.'

Luis had saddled up Ross for him and as he put his foot in the stirrup, he reflected that living with Alicia was rather like being around a nervous colt. Patience was all. If he ever lost sight of that and allowed himself to be angered or irritated, he might lose all that he had gained. He had almost made that mistake just now, when she had stood there like a statue while he longed to kiss her warmly, passionately. No, tell the truth, he rebuked himself sternly. While he longed to kiss her, undress her, take her right there and then. But there was nothing new in that. It was a long time since he had seen her and *not* wanted to do that. Up to now, thank God, he had managed to control himself, but he did not know how much longer he could stay cool and detached. Even sleeping on the couch was not distance enough from her. He still lay awake for hours on end, listening to her breathing, wondering in the still small hours of the morning whether he should not risk it all and climb in beside her, his imagination running riot and seeing her holding out her arms to him, welcoming him, wrapping him in a warm embrace. Thank God reality had always intervened before he made a fool of himself. Up to now.

He realised that Luis was watching him with interest.

'Is it your arm, Colonel?' he asked solicitously.

'No, Luis,' he laughed, shifting the reins to the fingers of the left hand, just to prove it. The arm was still encased in its leather shield, but he was able to use it quite a lot now. Chen Kai examined it regularly and had confirmed that the bones were well knitted. He had never been so free of pain or had such mobility of his fingers in all the years since the mine cave-in. The last few evenings he had even been able to dispense with the heavy leather. However, he had promised Chen Kai that for the next month, whenever he was using his arm, he would keep the shield on.

Halfway through the morning, Alicia set off down to the village, leaving Tamsin and Josefa shelling peas with Angelina in the kitchen garden. She was determined to speak to Pearl that morning even if she had to go and find her, for she had hardly slept last night for thinking about the news of her forthcoming marriage.

Not that is was entirely on Pearl's behalf that she had lain awake every night these last few weeks. The relief she had felt when Jack had taken to sleeping on the couch had evaporated like snow in summer and she found herself these days lying awake in the cool hours before dawn remembering how comforting it had been when he had lain beside her, wishing that she could turn and he would be there, that he would take her in his arms and hold her tightly. Further than that her mind would not go, only that she wanted to feel his arms around her, feel the comfort of him holding her close, knowing that she was not alone. Lying there last night listening to his steady breathing, she knew she had to stop Pearl and Chen Kai – and Li – making the mess of their lives too.

The village was deserted. She walked along the path between the houses looking for a clue as to where Pearl was working, but she could see no dust flying, hear no brooms knocking against wooden floorboards.

At last she tracked her down in the little half-ruined church, still awaiting its new roof and open now to the blue cloudless sky. In front of the cross on the wall, where the altar table had once stood, someone had placed a pot of wild flowers and there, in the dusty shaft of sunlight, knelt Pearl, her face wet with tears, her lips moving silently in prayer.

'I — I'm sorry, lady.' She leapt to her feet. 'I will get back to my work again.'

There was no tactful way to put it, so she plunged straight in. 'Pearl, is it true that you are to marry Li?'

'Yes lady.' She bowed her head.

'Why, Pearl?'

'I am betrothed to Li.'

'But you don't love him!'

'I am betrothed to Li,' she reiterated stubbornly.

'And you'll wed him even though you love Chen Kai-Tsu?' demanded Alicia scornfully.

Pearl hid her face. 'Please — not to say such thing,' she muttered.

'I shall say it to Kai himself unless you can look me in the face and tell me you do *not* love him.'

Pearl looked up at her, her determination faltering. 'I — I shall marry — Li,' she insisted. 'I — do not love —' Her eyes filled with tears and she could not go on.

'I knew it!' Alicia exclaimed in triumph. 'But ... any betrothal would have been sufficient to save your father's face. Why Li? Why not Chen Kai-Tsu?'

The tears spilled over and ran down her pale cheeks. 'Chen Kai-Tsu said that I was to be betrothed to Li. And it must be so, for he paid my father's debt and so I must do his will.' She subsided onto one of the pews, sobbing as though her heart would break. 'I am unworthy of Chen Kai, but even though he sent me away, I am still his servant and must do his bidding.'

'This is folly, Pearl! He does not look at you like a servant!'

'He sent me away, I tell you! He does not want me. He likes only women like you, who can talk and ride like a man.'

'Pearl, listen to me,' she insisted. 'I have travelled with Chen Kai for five years and I know him very well, as a sister knows a brother, and the way he looks at you is not the way of a man and a servant!'

'Then why did he turn me away?' she demanded angrily. She raised her head. 'I shamed myself,' she whispered. 'I went to his room and offered myself to him.' She shuddered at the memory. 'And he told me to marry Li.'

'Oh, Pearl!' She realised what it must have meant, to both of them. 'It is not his way to − to take you as a payment of debt! He despises the old ways. And both he and Colonel Cornish thought you were betrothed to Li.'

Pearl looked up at her hopelessly. 'No. I was never betrothed to anyone. My father intended me to stay at home and care for him as he grew old.'

'You don't have to marry Li.'

'But my father will have demanded a dowry ...'

'Pearl, listen! Forget about dowries, forget about debts and duties! This is a free country and you don't have to marry at all if you don't want to.' The irony of that statement did not escape her. 'If Chen Kai and Li both wanted to marry you, would you choose Li?'

'To me Li is like a young brother,' confessed Pearl sadly.

'Pearl, in your country marriages are arranged by go-betweens, aren't they? Middle men?'

'It is true.'

'Well, I'm going to be your middle man!' Alicia decided. 'Now, wipe your tears. You must help Mrs Chang this afternoon, because I'm going to be very busy!'

When Luis heard the hoofbeats in the yard and saw Chen Kai swing out of the saddle, he sent up a silent prayer of thanks to his guardian angel. He had so almost been tempted, when he had finished sweeping out the old bunkhouse, to slip away down to the river where he knew a fine, shady pool where the salmon were jumping. Instead he had begun to put in place the rough hewn pieces of wood which would separate one storage area from another.

'Good work.' Chen Kai looked round him approvingly. 'A lad does what he's told to do, but a man does what he sees needs doing.' Luis glowed.

'Has the Colonel come back?' asked Chen Kai.

322

'Li thought he saw some riders coming over the bridge.'

'Nobody came up into the yard,' said Luis.

'Strange. He said one of them had a badge. I'd better go check down in the village. Xavier has taken the chow down to the men, but I thought you and I could take ours down to the river and see if we can tempt some fish to join us for supper.'

Luis grinned at the prospect. Chen Kai had a skill with fish, picking one with his keen eyes and then scooping it, seemingly effortlessly, out of the pools.

He tethered Chen Kai's horse in the stables and they made their leisurely way down towards the village.

Pearl lingered a few moments in the church after Alicia had left, trying to pull herself together. She splashed her face with some of the water she had brought to put the flowers in and felt better able to face the world. She was almost through the door when she saw the group of men.

There were five men and three of them were wearing badges. One was brandishing a sheaf of papers in Alicia's face, but Pearl was too far away to make out more than the odd word they were saying. Some instinct she couldn't explain made her step back into the shadows in the porch. Then one of the other men turned and she knew she had not been mistaken; it was the big man with the scarred face. It was not so much his size or appearance that had alerted her but the threat that exuded from him even as he stood there.

She flattened herself against the wall, straining to hear what they were talking about, but it was impossible. She must fetch help, even if it was only Luis. At least he could fetch a gun. But before she could make a move, she saw Alicia climbing meekly on to a horse, without a fight!

No time for further thought; she must go at once and hope she could alert Luis in time. She slipped out of the doorway and into the tangle of shrubs nearby. As she ran, crouched low, she heard one of the men shout out. There was a sharp retort behind her and she fell to the leafy floor with a muffled scream. She had jarred her arm in the fall, but she scrambled to her feet and pressed on towards the ranch.

The shot reverberated around the valley and Chen Kai,

with an oath, threw down the pack with the food in it and set off down towards the village at a great speed.

He could hear the sound of horses' hooves echoing back from the buildings; no time to go back for a horse. He veered off towards the gate in the nopal hedge, the last place he could intercept anyone riding off the ranch.

He drew out his knife and waited. He was only just in time. When the riders came into view, he saw with rage and not a little fear that it was Fisher. He was holding the reins of Alicia's horse tightly, so that she was forced to ride almost knee to knee with her enemy. And she was on the far side, where Chen Kai could not hope to cut her mount out. He cursed fluently.

Chen Kai shot out from hiding just as the group reached the gate in the nopal hedge. With a high-pitched curse he hurled himself at Fisher's horse and tried to cut Alicia's reins free.

Fisher drew back his boot and kicked him on the side of his head. As his body hit the ground, Fisher calmly drew his gun and shot him.

Luis staggered out of the trees, white-faced and breathless, just in time to see the posse disappearing in a cloud of dust.

Chapter Twenty-Five

Pearl staggered on towards the gate, her hair dishevelled and her dress torn and snagged by the clinging branches, struggling for every breath.

Her heart almost stopped beating when she saw Chen Kai lying motionless on the ground in the dust. As in a nightmare, she moved forward on legs that didn't seem to belong to her and fell on her knees at his side, sobbing and wailing in high-pitched Cantonese.

The side of his face nearest her was battered and oozing blood and on the other side, Luis was trying to staunch a stream of blood with his kerchief. He looked at her across the fallen body.

'I — I don't think he's breathing,' he said fearfully.

'He *must* be!' she insisted fiercely, tearing his shirt open to place a trembling hand on his heart.

She lowered her head to lay her ear on his chest. 'I think — I think he is still alive,' she panted.

A soft breath stirred the hair on the back of her neck. 'Always try the pulse in the throat,' came a weak voice from behind her.

'Oh, thank God!'

'Tamsin?' he asked fearfully, struggling to open his eyes.

'Up at the ranch with Angelina,' she reassured him.

He closed his eyes again, in short-lived relief. 'If you've finished undressing me,' he said weakly, 'I'd better get up.'

'But you've been shot!' she protested.

'I ducked,' he grinned, putting a hand to his ear where the blood was beginning to run again. 'Just grazed me.'

With Luis's help he drew himself up, taking Pearl's hand as he staggered slightly. Suddenly she winced and clutched her arm, looking down wide-eyed at the blood seeping through her fingers.

'He shot me!' she said stupidly.

'One more item to his account,' said Kai softly. 'Luis!' He turned to the lad standing beside him, pale-faced and anxious. 'Back to the ranch. Send Xavier down with the cart. Can you find your way to the *agua caliente*?' Luis nodded. 'Find yourself a good horse and fetch the Colonel back. Tell him to follow me through the woods on the Sacramento road. I'll leave him markers. I'll take spare horses and supplies. Fast as you can.'

Luis set off at a run and Pearl sat down again abruptly.

'Let me see.'

'It is nothing!' she insisted. He took no notice of her, kneeling beside her and ripping the sleeve apart.

'No, not serious,' he confirmed, tying his bandanna around it. 'The bullet passed straight through. But you've lost a lot of blood and that makes you light-headed.' He sat down beside her and took her hand. 'No time to waste. Tell me what happened.'

'I couldn't hear much,' she murmured weakly. 'I was in the church and I couldn't hear ... When I tried to creep out to fetch help ... this happened.'

'Tell me what you saw. And heard.'

'The man with the badge spoke of ... Coloma, I think. Yes and something about Park ...'

'Parker. Yes, it begins to make some sense. And Fisher ... Did he hurt her?'

'No.' A frown marred her smooth forehead. 'Chen Kai, she did not fight at all. I could not understand it. She just went with them – without a struggle.'

'I don't believe it!'

She snatched her hand away, deep hurt in her eyes. 'So! I am a liar as well as a whore!'

'Pearl, don't!'

She was crying silently, rivers of tears coursing down her cheeks, her shoulders hunched in misery.

'Pearl, I never meant it that way! It's just that you were Li's ...'

She would never have said it if she hadn't been lightheaded with the loss of blood. 'I was *not*!' she protested. 'Never! Not then, not now!'

'But — you're betrothed to him!'

'Only because it was what you wanted!' she said fiercely. 'And I wanted to please you. But you taught me well, Chen Kai-Tsu. You said that this was the land of free people. So I *will* be free! I won't marry Li, not to please you or my father!'

He gazed down at her with a strange look in his eyes, but before he could speak Luis galloped into the clearing, followed by Xavier with the cart.

Pearl had to be helped to the cart, but they were soon up at the house and she was delivered into Angelina's capable hands.

A bare quarter of an hour later, Chen Kai looked into her room. Pearl lay back on the bed, her face as pale as the bandage on her arm.

'Is she asleep?' he asked Angelina softly.

Pearl opened her eyes wearily and tried to speak.

He crossed to the bed and took her hand. 'We will talk when I return,' he promised. On impulse he bent forward and dropped a kiss on her forehead. 'And Pearl ...' She looked up. '*Ngo ho chung yi nei*!' he said softly.

'About time you told her,' said Angelina as he left. 'An' don't look so surprised! Tell someone you love 'em, sounds the same in any language!'

Out in the yard he checked the saddlebags on the spare horses: supplies, guns, ammunition, his medicine box and a variety of strange items whose purpose Xavier, who had been sent to collect them, could not fathom. He sprang into the saddle, took the reins of the spare string in his hand and, putting his heels to the horse's flanks, set off down the slope.

327

The sun had almost set by the time the Colonel caught up with Chen Kai. He had brought only Kerhouan with him and their horses were sweating and blown, for they had ridden directly from the *agua caliente*.

'Alicia?' he demanded.

'Safe for a while.'

'Your trail was good,' muttered Cornish. 'How far ahead are they?'

'Only a little way,' replied Chen Kai. 'But from here we go on foot.'

'How many?'

'Still only five. Three men with badges, besides Fisher and another of his men. And Pearl says they had papers.'

'Law officers? He's learnt a lot by his association with Lamarr.'

'Jack ...' he hesitated. 'Pearl says she did not resist him.'

'So he must have used some threat other than the purely physical.'

'Can't just kill Fisher then?' said Kerhouan regretfully.

'No,' replied Cornish emphatically. 'First we find out what hold he has over her. Then I deal with him, for she's never going to be secure while he's around. But Fisher is mine. Understood?'

They nodded.

He looked thoughtfully at Chen Kai's bloodstained face. 'Five to two,' he said heavily.

'Don't count me out, Jack!' said Chen Kai, eyes glittering feverishly. 'I know a few tricks worth half a dozen men. You'll see.'

Chen Kai led them forward through the trees. After about five minutes he motioned them to silence and dropped flat on his stomach. Down in the clearing below two men were gathered around a camp fire, cooking something in a pan. Two others were deep in discussion in the shelter of a poison oak. Nearby stood the fifth man, gun in his hand, keeping a keen eye on Alicia.

Chen Kai stopped Cornish's hand even as it moved towards the gun. 'Out of range,' he said swiftly. 'Be patient. Your moment will come.'

328

Alicia sat with her back against the trunk of a huge redwood. Her eyes gazed blindly into the distance, seeing not the men moving around the camp-fire, nor even Fisher looming on the far side of the clearing, but only the still figure of Chen Kai lying in the dust.

If she could only get hold of a knife or a gun! If she couldn't kill Fisher she could at least turn it on herself. Anything would be better than to be in Fisher's power again.

Her guard crossed the clearing with a cup of coffee for her but she would not take it.

'C'mon,' he urged. 'Drink the coffee.'

She shook her head stubbornly.

'What's the odds?' he shrugged. 'Might as well drink it as not. Make you feel better.'

She looked at him levelly.

'You know what he's going to do with me, don't you?' she asked.

'Look, I'm sorry.' He shifted uncomfortably, trying to avoid her eyes.

'You approve of his way of getting a woman?' she jeered.

'If I'd've known, I never would've ...'

'Then let me go!' she implored him.

'I daren't. Sheriff swore me in and I gotta do what he says. Sheriff, he could make things pretty tough for me − and my woman's carryin' ...'

'She'd be proud of you, pimping for Fisher!' she said disdainfully. 'Better hope his eye doesn't fall on her next.'

'Damn you, don't have the coffee then!' he exclaimed angrily, dashing the contents of the cup onto the ground. He strode back to the fire, but try as he might, his eyes kept returning to the huddled figure at the foot of the giant tree. When the food was cooked, he took a plate across to her, but she turned her head aside.

He turned away with a shrug to eat the food himself. Fisher ambled across the clearing, a ghastly leer twisting the scarred features, and sat next to the woman. He reached for her and she whimpered as she tried to move away from him. The guard growled angrily in his throat.

In the undergrowth nearby, Cornish raised his gun.

'*Non*!' whispered Kerhouan. 'Chen Kai is not yet in position.'

Cornish ground his teeth together in frustration and lowered his sights.

Fisher pinned her arms cruelly behind her back, openly enjoying the terror he was inducing in her.

The young deputy threw down his plate with a curse and his hand hovered suggestively over the holster on his hip. 'Leave her be!' he commanded. 'She's in the Sheriff's custody. Ain't no call for you to paw her around if she don't want it!'

'Kinda simple, your deputy, ain't he?' laughed Fisher. 'Better tell the kid who's runnin' this!'

'Lay off, Dave!' growled the Sheriff.

'But it ain't right . . .'

'Morgan! I said lay off!'

There was a small explosion and a blinding flash and the two men on the far side of the fire staggered back, coughing and gasping, their eyes streaming. When at last the acrid fumes had dispersed, they mopped their streaming eyes and looked up to find themselves staring down the barrels of two very businesslike Adams revolvers held rock-steady in Cornish's hands. Twelve bullets between them at close range. They put their hands above their heads without demur.

Alicia, who had looked away as soon as the flashes began, opened her eyes to find Kerhouan with his rifle at Fisher's neck. She scrambled to her feet and out of his grip and nearly fell over when she saw Cornish.

'Oh, Jack!' She shook her head in disbelief. She wanted to run across to his side, away from Fisher's evil presence, but she knew she must not distract his attention until all the men were disarmed.

The young deputy who had come to her aid stood irresolutely between the two groups, overwhelmed by the speed of the attack.

'Unbuckle your gun-belt, deputy,' commanded a quiet voice from the shadows behind. 'One hand.'

Alicia's eyes widened as Chen Kai strolled out of the trees.

'Oh, Chen Kai! I thought you were dead!' she cried. And

yet who else could have done that trick with the magnesium flares?

'Closer to it than I ever want to be again!' he grinned, never taking his eyes off the young deputy until the gunbelt had been kicked aside.

One by one, Chen Kai searched them for arms, drawing throwing knives from inside boots, emptying guns of their bullets with a flick of the wrist. Then he dexterously tied their wrists together behind their backs while Kerhouan and Cornish kept their guns trained unwaveringly on their captives.

'You're interfering with a lawful arrest!' blustered Sheriff Hooper as Chen Kai tied him up.

'The Supreme Court Judges are goin' to be real interested to hear what you've been up to,' commented Cornish casually. He crossed to Alicia's side and put a comforting arm around her. He took her left hand and ran his finger around the gold band. 'Like to tell me why you kidnapped my wife, or will you save that for Sacramento? Or no, perhaps I'll take you into San Francisco,' he mused. 'I know the Vigilantes were going to disband, but Hell, I'm sure William Coleman will open up again for an old friend.'

The mention of the President of the Vigilance Committee, an upright and influential man with a deep hatred of crooked law officers, was sufficient to break the sheriff's nerve.

'I never knew she was your wife!' he said hoarsely. 'Never meant her no harm! Just doing my duty. Serving warrants duly issued.'

'Only one doing his duty was your deputy here!' snapped Cornish. 'Now you've a decision to make — whether you're going to proceed against my wife or not. But I warn you, she'll have Crocker to defend her. You going to stand against her?'

Hooper said nothing.

'You won't get away with this, Cornish!' swore Fisher, struggling against the ropes that bound his wrists. 'I'll get her, I swear it!'

Cornish looked hard at the Sheriff. 'How about it? Tear up those warrants and I'll let you go. Or we go see William Coleman.'

331

'Good try, Cornish,' sneered Fisher. 'But they ain't his warrants to tear up. I took them out and I ain't going to drop them, not less I get the woman.'

'That's right,' said the Sheriff heavily. 'Even if I hand these over to you, ain't nothing to stop him swearing 'em out again.'

Cornish slipped his hand into the Sheriff's jacket and drew out the documents. 'This all of them?' he enquired.

Hooper nodded miserably.

Taking his time, Cornish opened up the papers and read through them. 'So, you want to charge us with bigamy?' he chuckled.

'Mrs Langdon was already married. To Robert Langdon.'

'But my wife was Widow Owens,' he said blithely. 'And you can't prove any different. You'll have to do better than that!'

'Sheriff Hooper said it would never stick,' volunteered the deputy. 'Nor the one about kidnapping the little girl. He said they might lynch the Chinee, but they'd never indict her for it. That was just to get her to come along without a fuss.' He looked shamefaced. 'Sorry, lady. If I'd known ...'

'That so, Hooper?'

'Yeah, that's so,' muttered Hooper. At his side Fisher snarled. 'Ain't no use, Fisher. You gambled and lost. And I ain't goin' down with you.' Once he'd started, there was no stopping him. 'All those names on the depositions are false,' he admitted. 'Any half-decent lawyer would overturn them in no time. Only thing he could get her on was the murder of Parker, and I guess even if he could prove she was this Langdon woman, who for all I know died in prison, she could get off with self-defence. 'Course, *he* didn't plan it ever to get to court.'

Cornish looked thoughtful for a moment. 'Then if I could persuade Fisher to drop the charges, you'd have no reason to proceed any further against my wife?'

'Just let me go,' begged Hooper, 'and you'll hear no more from me.' He knew what was likely to happen if the hanging mob in San Francisco got their hands on a crooked sheriff and the prospect was not appealing. 'That goes for my men too.'

That left only Fisher's man. 'And you?' Cornish demanded, cocking the hammer deliberately, so that only the lightest pressure on the trigger would suffice to discharge it. He levelled it at his head.

'Hey now, mister! Don't have no call to go pointing that thing at me!' he yelped. 'I just look after his horses ...'

' ... and tote his guns!' added Cornish sharply.

'Look, I won't trouble you nor your good lady no more,' he promised. 'I don't know nothing about all this court stuff. I only worked for him a month. Honest!'

'That's true,' confirmed Morgan. 'He's just a layabout from Coloma that Fisher took up.'

Cornish slowly let the hammer fall back and the man let out a deep sigh of relief.

'So that just leaves you, Fisher. Will you give up these papers and leave my wife in peace?'

'The Hell I will!' snarled Fisher.

'Then I'll fight you for them,' stated Cornish calmly.

'No!' cried Alicia.

'Guns or knives, your choice,' said Fisher, licking his lips in anticipation.

'Just fists,' said Cornish equably, ignoring Alicia's outburst.

Fisher looked at Cornish's arm with an evil smile, then across at Alicia. 'No holds barred?' Cornish nodded. 'I agree.'

'My companions will hold the ring,' stated Cornish. 'Hooper will be untied to see fair play. Kerhouan — keep your eye on him.'

She crossed to his side and took his arm. 'Jack, don't do this,' she pleaded. 'He's evil. He'll try to kill you, I know it.'

Cornish looked down at her enigmatically. 'Best if you don't watch,' he said. He began to strip off, laying his clothes on a fallen tree at the side of the clearing.

Chen Kai crossed to his side and drew out a little bottle. 'This will help kill the pain,' he said. Jack tipped his head back and tilted it down his throat.

'Kerhouan,' pleaded Alicia. 'Can't you stop him? This is madness!'

333

'You don't interfere,' said Kerhouan firmly. 'Jack, 'e know what 'e is doing.' She could almost believe that he was looking forward to the fight, for he was grinning from ear to ear.

Cornish stripped off to the waist, while Fisher kept on his jacket and a broad leather belt with a vicious-looking buckle.

She had always thought of Cornish as being a well-built man, but against Fisher's bulk he looked very slim. And with his arm barely healed and still in the leather support, she thought miserably, what chance did he stand?

A nervous Hooper gave the signal for the fight to start and Fisher charged in like an enraged bull, fists flailing.

Alicia gasped and waited for Cornish to be knocked to the ground, but by some miracle he managed to sidestep and the blows whistled ineffectively past his ear.

With a frustrated roar, Fisher turned and rushed in again and this time his massive fist caught Jack on the cheek, but as Fisher's fist travelled on over his shoulder, Jack reached up and jerked on it. The momentum of the attack was so great that Fisher could not reverse it and flew straight over Cornish's shoulder, landing on his side with a crash that startled the birds from the trees.

Curiously, Cornish made no move to grapple with him on the ground, but stood back. Fisher was on his feet again within a moment and moving in to try and land a heavy punch on his opponent, but he had winded himself badly and when he did manage to strike him, the punch did little damage.

For a few minutes more, they circled around each other, Fisher punching furiously and Cornish concentrating on agile footwork to keep out of range of the massive fists.

There was a sudden flurry of jabs, then Fisher moved in behind a punch and grabbed at Cornish's injured arm.

'His first mistake,' whispered Kerhouan hoarsely. Fisher wrapped his arms around Cornish and was attempting to hold him in a bear hug when Cornish hooked his hands in Fisher's belt and with a grunt, tripped him and threw him heavily to the ground.

Four more times Jack Cornish succeeded in wrestling his opponent to the ground in the same way and each

334

time Fisher got up there was less and less strength in his punches.

Both men were blown and tired. Cornish's face was scraped and bloody where Fisher's punches had connected, but Fisher was in an infinitely worse state. There was something badly wrong with his ribs and since the last fall, he was moving very awkwardly.

'Why doesn't he finish it?' muttered Chen Kai. 'A few good punches now while he's off-guard ...'

'He waits his moment,' said Kerhouan.

Next time Fisher punched almost drunkenly at Cornish, he ducked and closed in, coming up at the side under his fists. But this time, instead of catching Fisher's belt, he locked the arm with the leather shield around his opponent's neck and leant on it. Through the mists of his rage and pain, Fisher suddenly realised what he intended. 'Hooper!' he croaked. 'He's trying to ...'

The pressure on his windpipe silenced him. Fisher put every ounce into a last desperate effort to wrestle Cornish to the floor. Jack went down beneath the onslaught but just as it seemed that he must be flattened by Fisher's fall, he arched his body and with one fluid movement jerked his legs up into Fisher's stomach and flipped him almost effortlessly back over his head. Fisher seemed to hang a moment, suspended in space, then, as he began to fall, Cornish's leather clad arm somehow caught under his opponent's chin. As the heavy body crashed to the floor there was a sickening crack that echoed all round the clearing. Fisher didn't get up again.

Into the eerie silence rode three men, guns in hand. The sinking sun shone brightly on the stars pinned to their jackets.

Chapter Twenty-Six

'So you admit the charges?' asked Brenchley.

'Hardly deny it, could I?' said Cornish wryly. 'Not after the marshal turning up like that. The one thing I never calculated was that Fisher had more men. Thought he'd have all his guns with him.'

'You could hardly anticipate that the one man he left behind would be involved in a bar brawl and the marshal would be trailing him out of town!'

'Maybe it's best this way. At least I won't have to keep looking over my shoulder to see if Hooper or one of his men is going to try blackmailing me. I've seen what that can do to a person.' He drummed his fingers anxiously on the table. 'How is Alicia?'

'As well as can be expected. Angelina and Chen Kai are clucking around her like a pair of mother hens, of course.' He looked at Jack from under a frowning brow. 'You've taken a great weight off her shoulders,' he said slowly.

'That was the intention.'

'She wants to come in and see you. She can't understand why . . .'

'You think it would help her to come here?' he demanded. He gestured grimly at the barred windows and the locked door with its guard outside. 'It may not be as dreadful as San Francisco jail, but it'd stir unhappy memories. Besides, I don't want to remind the marshal of her existence. She can do without being dragged into this.'

'If they knew her history, there isn't a man on the Coroner's jury would blame you for what you did . . .' began Brenchley.

Cornish banged his fist angrily on the table. 'No! I forbid it, do you hear me? I won't have that brought up for the gossips' delight. She's suffered enough without being made to go over it all again for their delectation. I'll never forgive either of you if you even breathe it. Tell Crocker that!' He shoved back his chair with a clatter and began to pace restlessly up and down the small room. 'Of course, if our leading attorney and a smart New York lawyer don't think they can cope with a Coroner's jury ...?'

'Crocker anticipates no particular problems,' Brenchley assured him hastily. 'Just that it would have made it easier ...'

'I'm not concerned to make matters easier for you or Crocker – or me!' snapped Cornish. 'It's Alicia I'm worried about.'

'Jack – does she know how you feel about her? I mean, that was a pretty strange marriage you went through by all acounts.' He saw the scowl that settled on his companion's face. 'I don't mean to pry. I just wondered if someone should tell her.'

'Get me out of here and back to Tresco and I'll deal with my own private life!' he growled. 'But she will *not* go on the stand!'

'All right. But I promised Crocker I'd ask. Sit down, for goodness' sake! Prowling about like that, it wears me out just watching you.'

'How much longer are they going to keep me here?' he demanded.

'They start swearing in the jury tomorrow morning. With any luck, they'll get through evidence of identification tomorrow afternoon. You should be in court day after.'

'That wasn't what I asked.' He shifted his arm uncomfortably. It had been aching like fury since the night before, when Chen Kai's wonder potion had finally worn off.

'I know. But I can't make you any promises. I never thought Crocker would fail to get you out on bail. Still,' he looked around him at the sparse room, 'given over into the custody of the marshal is better than the jail.' He looked up at Cornish, leaning against the wall with his arms folded, brooding. 'Jack, I have to

337

ask you — is there something the court knows that we don't?'

He shook his head. 'Only I know why I did what I did.' His voice dropped. 'You might guess, but no one can prove it was anything but an accident.'

'That's what I thought.' He looked at his friend. 'Jack, about the Valley Hall deeds ...'

'God's sake, don't let anyone get wind of them, or that'll hand 'em a motive on a plate!'

'I'm not a fool. But I'm wondering if you are.'

'Because I'd return Alicia her rightful inheritance?'

'But a wife's property ...'

' ... is her husband's? Not in my book. Dammit all, man, that puts me in the same bracket as her first husband! No. Tresco's mine, by the sweat of my brow, and Valley Hall is hers by her rightful inheritance. What she chooses to do with it is up to her.'

'And if she chooses to go back east?'

'Then I don't choose to stop her.'

A discreet knock fell on the door and the City Marshal put his head round the door.

'Time's up, Mr Brenchley,' he said apologetically. 'And Mrs McAlpin's wishful to know if you'd care for a haunch of venison for your supper, Colonel.'

'Mrs McAlpin could make a bowl of hash taste like a dish for a king,' said Cornish with a smile, 'so I'll enjoy whatever she wants to serve up to me!'

'I'll pass the message on, Colonel!' he said, a friendly grin on his battered, suntanned face. 'Now — guess I got to search you again. Regulations.'

Cornish submitted to this with as much patience as he could muster; his lot could have been much worse if the marshal wanted to make it so.

'Lost track of the number of folk who've called by to see you,' McAlpin told him cheerfully. 'Couldn't let 'em in to see you though. Don't know who might be called to sit on the coroner's jury. Orders is only to let your lawyers in.'

'I appreciate all the trouble you and Mrs McAlpin have been put to.'

He shrugged. 'Town pays for it, Colonel. An' I see no call

338

to put a leading citizen in jail when it's only a matter of a coroner's jury. Oh, an' that Chinee servant of yours came by. Said he'd call back in this afternoon. Wanted to see to your arm, but I can easy fetch in Doctor Harrap for you.'

'I think I'll stick with Chen Kai, if you don't mind,' said the Colonel. His arm had been badly bruised in the fight and he could do with some more of Kai's pain-killing brew. And he would be able to find out more about Alicia.

The Marshal decided there was no harm in letting Chen Kai in, once he'd searched him and his medicine box thoroughly.

'You can change the dressings, but call me when you're putting that leather splinting back on.'

Jack grinned at Kai. 'He can't believe I don't plan to escape! Madness!'

'How are you, Jack?'

'Well, except that this arm is aching like the devil.'

'What can you expect?' he said, unwinding the bandages.

'How's Alicia? Is she — is she still at Tresco?'

Kai looked up in surprise.

'Of course not. She's here in town. To attend the inquest.'

'Damn!'

'There!' Kai drew off the last dressing. 'Heavily bruised,' he said gruffly, probing it as gently as he could. 'But the bone hasn't slipped.' He looked up. 'You took a big risk.'

Jack shrugged. 'It paid off.' He dropped his voice, 'Listen, Chen Kai. I don't want Alicia to go into the witness box. If she has to, then she must say as little as possible — only what happened yesterday. Make sure she understands that.'

'You underestimate her, Jack. You've lifted a great weight from her shoulders and she's like a new woman.'

The marshal came to check the leather casing before it was laced up. When Chen Kai was gone, Cornish threw himself down on the bed and thought longingly of Tresco — and Alicia.

339

Thirty-six hours later – hours longer than any he had ever experienced – Brenchley came to walk with him in the stifling mid-day heat across to Garrison's, where the Coroner's inquest was to be held.

'Murray's the Coroner,' he said briefly. 'Don't know anything about him, but I guess he hasn't any axes to grind. Evidence of identification was given this morning by Elzevir Kane. Crocker says you know him, he's one of Lamarr's sidekicks. Claims to have been Fisher's partner. They're trying to make Fisher out to be a respectable businessman.'

'Even respectable businessmen can be kidnappers and murderers,' replied Cornish softly. 'And I know a thing or two about Kane's businesses that'd make your hair stand on end!'

'We'll keep that up our sleeves in case of need,' counselled Brenchley. 'I've got someone up in Coloma watching Hooper in case we need to get him up in court, though I know you'd rather not use him.'

'Put him in the box and he'll spill all the beans,' advised Cornish. 'He'll tie Alicia in with Fisher and that's what I don't want.'

'If he volunteers a statement, we could be in real trouble.'

'And lay himself open to a charge of kidnapping? Not him. He and his deputy were in the saddle before Fisher even hit the ground.'

They went up the steps to Garrison's, the marshal behind them, wondering anxiously whether he ought to have handcuffed his charge.

The warehouse was pleasantly cool after the heat of the streets. It had been cleared of its goods and rows of chairs filled the room where the sacks and barrels were normally stacked.

There was not an empty seat in the place.

As he walked in, all the faces turned expectantly towards him and an excited buzz of conversation ran round the room. Clive Revel was sitting with Alicia, and Letitia and her brother sat to her right. He grinned at her. She just managed a wan smile in return.

As he passed down the aisle, a number of men rose from

340

their seats to reach out and shake his hand, turning it into something of a stately progress.

'Why can he not sit with us?' Alicia asked Revel anxiously, under cover of the excited chatter. 'Why has he to sit up there? He is not on trial, after all!'

'It's still open to the jury to bring a verdict of murder,' explained Clive Revel sombrely. He saw her turn pale. 'I told you you should not have come.'

As Cornish shook hands with Attorney Crocker, the conversation grew louder and more excited until the Coroner banged his table with his gavel.

'I'll remind you all that this is a coroner's court and not a raree show!' he said irascibly. 'Any more disturbances and this court-room will be cleared!'

At last the noise died down and the jury filed back in, among them Edward Spalding, who had smiled at her, and one of the Reverend Cooper's churchwardens. All of the jury knew her husband. Twelve good men and true who knew him for the fine man he was.

Why had it taken her so much longer?'

'Call Colonel Cornish,' intoned the county clerk. Jack stepped up onto the stand and took the oath, swearing to tell the truth, the whole truth and nothing but the truth.

God help him if he did.

'Now, Colonel,' began the Coroner. 'This here is an inquest on Josiah Fisher to establish the cause of death. It will be for the jury to decide whether there is a case for anyone to answer. You are not on trial here, nor at the moment is anyone else. I recommend you be frank and open in your answers to my questions.'

'It is my intention, sir,' agreed Cornish.

'Good. Now how long had you known the deceased, Josiah Fisher?'

'I first met the deceased a few months ago, when he came to dine at my home,' answered Cornish in a clear, strong voice. 'Incidentally, he was introduced to me as Joel McCann.'

There was another outbreak of speculation across the courtroom and Alicia could hardly disguise her satisfaction. Respectable businessmen did not run under aliases. Without any effort, Jack had effectively smashed that image.

The Coroner looked across at the marshal with raised eyebrows. 'The deceased was recognised under both those names, your honour,' replied McAlpin. 'We believe Fisher to be his real name, but ain't no one's certain about it.'

'Dear me!' He turned back to the witness. 'And you met him again after that?'

'Not until three days ago.'

'Now, as to the events of that unfortunate day.' He adjusted his pince-nez and looked down at the papers in front of him. 'I have before me a statement from Marshal McAlpin that, while in pursuit of a known criminal, in a clearing to the north of Washington he stumbled on a fight between yourself and the deceased.'

'I do not deny it,' replied Cornish when the coroner looked up.

'Dear me! And why was that?'

Tell him, Jack! she prayed frantically. Or let them call me and I'll tell them!

In a slow and gentle voice, Cornish began to tell them of the events of that fateful day while Alicia sat, hands tightly clasped in her lap, anxious thoughts scurrying around her mind.

' ... and when I heard that Fisher had kidnapped my wife and shot one of my foremen, of course I rode straight after them.'

There was an excited chorus of 'Oohs' and 'Ahs!' throughout the courtroom and she knew that every eye was turned on her.

The Coroner banged his gavel again. 'Silence in this court!' he demanded. 'Go on, Colonel.'

'We managed to catch up with him and surprise him. Once my wife was safe, there was a fight.'

'Cain't understand why you had to fight,' said the Coroner curiously.

'Your honour!' said Brenchley indignantly. 'The man's home was invaded, his wife carried off and his foreman shot, and you can't understand why he fought the man who did it?'

342

There was a rumble of support from the body of the court and even the marshal and the members of the jury seemed to think the comment ridiculous. Once again the Coroner had to bang on the table to call the room to order.

'I would remind you, Mr Brenchley,' he quavered, 'that this is not a trial, merely an attempt to get at the truth. If Colonel Cornish has nothing to hide, he will answer the question. Why did you fight this fellow?'

'Heat of the moment, your honour,' replied Cornish carefully.

'Why didn't you bring him in and hand him over to the marshal?'

'It seemed simpler to deal with the matter myself, on the spot. No offence to the marshal. Just that I had no desire to be a nine days' wonder.'

'An understandable emotion, I'll allow. And of course,' he suggested maliciously, 'if you hadn't been found with the body by the marshal, then no one would have been any the wiser.'

'With respect, your honour, you are forgetting Fisher's men.' Who, fortunately for him, had hightailed it in Hooper's wake as soon as they saw the marshal ride in. 'To do as you are suggesting I'd have had to kill them all. But I did not.'

'Hear, hear!' came a voice from the back of the courtroom.

'Thank you, Colonel Cornish. We may have you back again shortly.'

Alicia watched him return to his seat. Oh, why was he taking such a risk when he could so easily stop the whole thing by putting her on the witness stand?

They put Luis on the witness stand instead. He confirmed the rancher's story of the kidnap, although he succeeded in confusing the Coroner. Not a difficult thing to do, she concluded.

'And when Mr McCann rode off with Mrs Owens, and Chen Kai tried to stop him, he shot him. I thought he'd killed him.'

'This is all getting extremely complicated,' complained Murray. 'Marshal McAlpin, can you explain? Who are all these people?'

343

'Sir,' said the marshal patiently. 'We accept that McCann and Fisher are — were — the same person. And Mrs Owens is the widow who has recently been married to Colonel Cornish.'

'And this Chenky — he is the coolie who was shot ...'

Cornish was on his feet in a flash. 'Chen Kai-Tsu is my foreman, sir!' he protested. 'Not a coolie, but a free man! Free as you or I!'

'Any more interruptions of this nature, mister, and I'll hold you in contempt of court! Now call this Chenky, Marshal!'

The Marshal rose uncomfortably to his feet.

'That ain't possible, I'm afraid, your honour,' he said shuffling his feet. 'This here Chen Key Too dressed the Colonel's arm only yesterday and, er, well, they was alone together some time.'

'You mean to say you allowed a potential witness to speak to the defend —' He cleared his throat hurriedly. 'That is to say — to speak to Colonel Cornish?' he demanded irascibly.

'But this is ridiculous!' whispered Alicia indignantly. 'He's acting as if Jack were on trial!'

'If the Coroner had his way, he would be!' muttered Revel. 'Lamarr's man may not have cut much ice with the jury, but it looks as if he convinced the Coroner.'

'I hear Murray's running for the Senate,' said the Reverend. 'He's trying to make his name without offending anyone. An impossible task!'

McAlpin tried to defend himself. 'Your honour, I thought a Chinee couldn't give evidence.'

'That's with coolies. I guess free men may be different. Anyways, such matters are at the court's discretion,' growled the Coroner. 'And that means my discretion, mister, not yours!'

McAlpin sat down with a glower and the Coroner angrily gathered up his papers with a grunt and swept out of the courtroom. 'Court adjourned!' called the clerk. 'Reconvene in half an hour!'

Alicia hurried across the room to Cornish's side, but McAlpin stopped her in her tracks.

344

'Let her pass, McAlpin!' protested the Reverend Cooper. 'She just wants to see her husband!'

'Not till this case is over!' he snapped. 'I ain't a-goin' to get my head bit off again!'

Alicia could have wept as she watched Jack being led off to the office at the back. 'Clive, go and see him,' she pleaded. 'Ask him to let me go on the witness stand!'

Revel wasn't allowed to see Jack, but he managed to have a word with Crocker just before the inquest resumed.

'It's Jack's wife,' he said frankly. 'She's insistent that you should put her on the witness stand.'

Crocker rolled his eyes to the ceiling. 'Don't tell me,' he groaned. 'I had her in here yesterday with the same demands. Grew very heated. Plucky woman, isn't she? Damned me and my reputation from here to Texas!'

'I can imagine!'

'But it isn't in my hands,' he went on. 'Her husband won't have it. Ask Brenchley here.'

Brenchley nodded. 'Says if we go over his head, he'll dispense with our services altogether. But if we don't get the verdict we want tomorrow, we'll go for a retrial and put her on the stand.'

'The Devil you will!'

'He won't get away with this fiddle-faddle about a crippled arm once a good prosecuting attorney gets his teeth into him. But I hope it won't come to that. I have every faith in the good sense of the Coroner's jury,' insisted Crocker, knocking his pipe out as the runner called them back to court. 'I was watching their faces; they're with him all the way. Despite all that nonsense in San Francisco, he has the reputation of an upright citizen. And his new wife is well liked. As my wife said, everyone loves a good romance.'

When the inquest resumed, Cornish was called back onto the witness stand.

'Colonel Cornish,' began the Coroner, 'the jury heard allegations earlier that you deliberately set out, for reasons of your own, to kill Fisher. And I have a deposition here says you are a skilled wrestler.'

'Excuse me, Mr Murray.' Attorney Crocker rose to his feet. 'Perhaps Mr Lamarr is not aware,' he drawled, 'that

345

he is supposed to give all the legal representatives sight or copy of his deposition?'

There was an outburst of laughter from the body of the court, and a few of the jury were having difficulty keeping a straight face.

'You come perilously close to contempt, sir!' said the Coroner, red-faced and blustering. 'Court Clerk will arrange for you to have a copy, Attorney. Meanwhile I advise the defend – the *witness* – to answer the question.'

'Your honour,' said Cornish quietly, 'for the last five years I have been effectively one-armed, as anyone in California will tell you. Hardly the best qualification for a wrestler.'

'But you do not deny that it was your throw that killed the man?'

'No.'

'And you still maintain you did not intend to kill him?'

'With one arm against a man his size?'

'A fluke then, you would say?'

'An unfortunate accident.'

It went on and on. Kerhouan was called to the stand to give his version of the events in the clearing. It was growing hotter and more airless in the courtroom as Alicia waited to be called, but the call never came. Before she realised what was happening, the Coroner was summing up. She rose in some agitation to her feet, but Revel pressed her back in her seat.

'Leave it, Alicia,' he warned.

'And so, gentlemen of the jury, you have a difficult decision to make. There are two possible stories, quite distinct, and you must decide which you believe. Either you say that Colonel Cornish, believing Fisher to have made off with his woman and killed his servant –'

'My *wife*, damn you!' Cornish leapt angrily to his feet. 'Kidnapped my wife and shot my foreman!'

Crocker was pulling him back into his seat.

'Oh, don't, Jack!' whispered Alicia. 'Let it pass!'

Letitia's hands covered hers, clenched in her lap. 'Don't worry dear,' she soothed. 'Look at the jury. They're behind Jack all the way.'

'Sit down, sir! I will not be interrupted!' shouted the Coroner. 'You are in contempt of this court!' He turned

346

back to the jury. 'Either, I say, you credit that Colonel Cornish, having pursued and rescued his – ah – wife, was foolhardy enough to go on to challenge the deceased to a fight although he had an injured arm, and merely by accident managed to fell him so hard that he broke his neck, or you say that he deliberately murdered Fisher. In the first case you have accidental death, in the second case murder. Now you must retire to consider your verdicts. Is that clear? Any questions before you retire?'

There was a muttering and murmuring from the jury and the oldest member rose hesitantly to his feet. 'Some of us would like to know, your honour, if we could consider a verdict of justifiable homicide or self-defence?'

'No. Those are defences to the charge of murder. That's for a higher court to consider if anyone's indicted.'

The heat in the courtroom was becoming unbearable. As the jury rose to retire, the Coroner drew out his timepiece.

'In view of the lateness of the hour, the court will adjourn for today. In view of the possibility of serious charges being brought, Colonel Cornish to be kept in custody.'

'Give Pearl my love,' said Alicia. 'I hope she's feeling better.'

'But – surely you're going back?' said Kerhouan.

'No,' she said firmly. 'I'm not leaving Sacramento till this is all sorted out.'

'Staying with the Coopers?'

'No. I'm not in the mood for socialising. I have a room at the hotel opposite McAlpin's and that's where I'm staying.'

She was not in the least tired. She knew that she would not sleep that night even though she was free at last. Even freedom could be bought too high – at the price of another's liberty.

She knew what she had to do, but it was not something she could do alone. She waited until some of the crowds had dispersed from the sidewalks, then, wrapped in a black shawl, she slipped out of the hotel and headed for the Leons' house.

Jack Cornish had spent most of the evening pacing up and down the room at McAlpin's.

'Does no good!' Mrs McAlpin chided him, bringing him up his dinner before she and her husband went to join a party at the theatre. 'All it does is wear out my carpet!'

He wondered how on earth he was going to get through the night. For certain he wouldn't be able to sleep.

It was going to be one of Sacramento's hotter nights. He slopped water from the ewer into the china bowl that stood on the washstand, stripped down to his cotton pants and washed. Then he turned the lamp low and flung himself back on the bed, eyes closed.

There was a footfall on the stairs and the key turned in the lock. The deputy with his coffee.

'Join me in a cup, Johnson,' said Cornish wearily as the tray clattered on the table. 'I'm heart sick of my own company.'

'I didn't come for coffee,' said Alicia softly.

He sat bolt upright on the bed. 'What the Hell ...!'

'But I'll pour you a cup if you want one.'

She took off the black shawl that she had wrapped round her shoulders. She wasn't wearing the dress she'd worn to the courthouse, but a well-worn shirtwaist and a simple black skirt.

'What's McAlpin thinking of?'

She took the mug of coffee across to him and pushed it into his hands.

'He's not here. I persuaded the deputy to let me bring the coffee.'

'I didn't want you to come here,' he muttered.

'I know. But don't send me away, Jack. Not yet awhile.'

He put the mug down so abruptly that the coffee spilled on the table. 'Why did you come?' he demanded. She didn't answer.

'We won't discuss the inquest,' he said brusquely. 'That's in the hands of the jury now. But I want you to know that I've made provisions ...'

'Hush!' She moved towards him and put a finger on his lips. Before he could think what she was doing, she had pushed him back on to the bed and sat down beside him. She reached up a tentative hand and gently touched his face, tracing the bruises that still shadowed his cheekbones.

'I was so frightened for you,' she murmured.

'And I — when I heard you were gone!'

348

She slid along the bed until her thigh was touching his. Then she nestled closer and rested her head on his shoulder. Before he could think what he was doing his arms were round her waist and he was holding her close. Alicia turned her face up to his.

He lowered his head and kissed her softly on the lips, a kiss that started out gentle, tentative, and became more and more passionate. Then, as she relaxed into his embrace, he came abruptly back to his senses.

'You'd better go now.' He rose jerkily from the bed.

'No,' she said softly.

'But Johnson ...'

'Don't worry about Johnson. He's been well paid. Señor Leon saw to that. We won't see him until the dawn.'

'Alicia! You can't stay here! For God's sake, girl, I'm not made of iron.' He turned away from her and crossed to the window.

When at last he turned back to her, his hands clenched rigidly at his side and words of reason on his lips, her gloves lay on the table and she was unpinning her hat.

'Alicia, you'll regret this in the morning.'

'No,' she said softly. 'No regrets any more. You have given me back my life. I want to live it.'

'But not this way. You don't owe me anything ... I'd have done the same for anyone.' He swallowed hard. 'You have your freedom now,' he said with an effort. 'Didn't Brenchley tell you? Valley Hall is yours.'

She looked levelly at him, her eyes soft and warm. 'I don't want it. My home, my life, is here, in California.'

'Then sell it. Set up your own business again. You could be an independent woman.'

'Don't make me beg, Jack.'

She stepped closer to him and he had to fight the desire to touch her. With a boldness she had not known she possessed she unfastened the waist of the black skirt and, as it fell in a shadowed heap around her ankles, stepped out of it and into his arms. He bent his head to hers and kissed her with all the pent-up emotion of the months since she had first come into his life.

The feel of his half naked body against hers had a curiously exciting effect on Alicia and she responded with a passion she had not thought herself capable of. As his hand gently brushed against her breast, all thoughts of gritting her teeth and going through with it for his sake were forgotten and she was shaken to find how his touch aroused her.

Had he unbuttoned the blouse or had she? She didn't know. She didn't care.

He eased her back on to the bed. His lips left her mouth and travelled down her throat, her shoulders, arousing the most delicious feelings; when she leaned over and kissed his shoulder his flesh was hot and smooth beneath her lips.

With eager hands he slid the thin chemise down, then drew back for a moment, his lips parted, breathing erratic, to gaze down at her body, glowing golden in the soft lamplight. The moment he'd longed for ever since the day at the *agua caliente*.

'Alicia, love,' he muttered thickly. 'Are you sure?'

'Yes.'

'You don't *have* to do this.'

'I know,' she said, her words barely audible. 'But I want to. Oh, I want to ...'

It was true. She wanted him with a desperation she had never before experienced.

He gazed into her eyes a moment longer, then lowered his head and gently dropped a kiss on her soft breast. She shuddered.

'I'll try to be gentle,' he promised.

But it was not a night for gentleness as he unleashed the passion she had carried untapped within her for so many years. His mouth, moving from her lips to cover her aching body with kisses, lit a fire in her that matched the flame in him. In the rough wooden bed, there was no room any more for doubt.

In the cool of the dawn she had slipped out of the room with only a backward glance at the sleeping figure in the bed. She had not woken him. They had said all there was to say in the early hours of the morning, wrapped in each other's embrace.

Turning hungrily to her again, he had grinned that boyish grin and whispered: 'The condemned man ate a hearty breakfast.' She had shivered fearfully.

Now, head high, she crossed the deserted main street. Consuela Leon was waiting to let her back into the hotel through a side door.

They were first in the courtroom with Brenchley and Crocker. She sat with Letitia and Consuela on either side and Revel, the Senator and the Reverend Cooper behind. So many good friends, she thought, and tears prickled behind her eyes. But even they could not console her if she lost him now, lost him when she had only just found him.

She heard the bustle of arrival behind her and blinked back the tears in time to greet her husband with a smile as he took his seat at the front.

Crocker had only just got to his feet to address the Coroner when the clerk hurried in. The jury was coming back!

They filed in and sat down, all save the elderly gentleman at the front.

'Has the jury reached its verdict?' demanded the Coroner.

'We have, your honour.' He adjusted his watch chain over his ample stomach and the court seemed to hold its breath. 'Accidental death.'

A roar of approval went up throughout the courtroom and men and women alike rushed forward to shake Cornish by the hand.

Murray was banging on the table with his gavel, but no one took any notice. Alicia stood as if transfixed while the crowd ebbed and flowed around her. Before she could reach his side, Jack had been hoisted on to someone's shoulders and the mob rushed him out of reach, sweeping past her and out onto the street.

Revel found her standing in the deserted street with Letitia, like a leftover from a hiring fair that no one wanted.

'Come on!' he urged, dragging her behind him. 'If we hurry we can get down to the levée before them.'

He led her away from Garrison's and down to Front Street, then, at sight of the crowd streaming onto the Embarcadero, they ducked down a side alley and there was the *Tresco*, just beginning to get steam up. Revel pushed her up the gangplank and into the cabin just as the crowd appeared.

They carried Jack Cornish shoulder-high along the levée and up the gangplank. As he caught sight of Revel he shouted anxiously: 'My wife?'

'Safe on board!'

'Thank God! Thought I'd lost her again!' At last the crowd grew tired of shouting and cheering and lowered him to his feet. He waved to them cheerily. 'Ladies and gentlemen,' he said with a broad grin, 'I look forward to entertaining you all at Tresco and showing you my gratitude for your support — but not for a week or two, I beg of you. I'm planning a belated honeymoon!'

There was a great roar of approval as he leapt up the gangplank and shouted to Captain Bateman to cast off.

As the paddles began to churn their path through the muddy brown waters of the Sacramento, he stepped into the cabin.

They looked at each other for a long moment.

'You don't lose me that easily,' she murmured.

MARY MACDONALD BELL

THE DAYS NEVER KNOW

Already, at eighteen, Frances Rintoul resents the narrow poverty-stricken life of the small Fifeshire pit town. But now, as the express train thunders over the dizzyingly high girders of the brand-new Forth Bridge, the possibility of escape beckons. Not just Edinburgh, Liverpool or London, but beyond to a true New World: Canada and the wide-horizontal prairies.

Life in frontier Canada is to prove hard and uncertain. Frances has to grow into a strong, determined woman if she is to overcome the bitter blows the future holds in store for her but the vigorous energy and challenge of her new life offers the opportunities that are all she ever asked for.

'Tackling a big canvas, *The Days Never Know* is new-wave romantic fiction, tougher and more realistic than has been traditional. The author is terrific at evoking the pioneering experience. Frances is a tough, believable heroine.'
Elizabeth Buchan, The Sunday Times

HODDER AND STOUGHTON PAPERBACKS

DIANE CHAMBERLAIN

KEEPER OF THE LIGHT

When a woman is brought into Olivia Simon's surgery with a gunshot through her heart, Olivia recognises her as Annie O'Neill, the much-loved local stained glass artist – and the woman with whom Olivia's husband has been obsessed for weeks.

The first time Olivia meets Alec O'Neill and his children, it is to tell him that she was not able to save his wife. That evening Olivia's husband, Paul, walks out on her.

Seeking to come to terms with their separate losses, Alec and Olivia turn to each other for comfort and a loving friendship develops. Yet Annie left a legacy of secrets behind her which threatens to destroy Alec, Olivia and Paul. Only one person can set them free – the Keeper of the Light.

'An absorbing tale of romantic obsession and betrayal'
Publishers Weekly

HODDER AND STOUGHTON PAPERBACKS

VIRGINIA BUDD

SUMMER'S SPRING

Bet Brandon, recently widowed, decides to start afresh.

With a peculiar assortment of relatives, and her troublesome dog, she leaves Hampstead to embark on a bizarre house-sharing enterprise in Suffolk. Domestic quarrels abound but her deliciously wicked sense of fun helps her to adjust to the dramas of her new life.

However Bet finds life in the country fiendishly quiet – until she meets the recklessly charming, would-be writer, Simon Morris. And soon she has an irresistible desire to throw caution to the wind and follow her heart.

HODDER AND STOUGHTON PAPERBACKS

DINAH LAMPITT

THE KING'S WOMEN

France in the Middle Ages; torn by internecine strife, menaced by the might of England's King Henry V. At the country's head; a frightened youth, the Dauphin Charles.

Yet fate has decreed that it is he who will become the most victorious king of all, who will drive the English from French soil. And it is through the love of women that this prophecy will come true.

The magnificent Yolande, more a mother to him than the depraved Queen Isabeau; Marie, his plain but intelligent wife; Agnes, his exquisite mistress. All will play a part. Yet above all will be Jehanne, the un-blemished girl who will ride at the head of his army whilst swearing allegiance to the mysterious Knights Templar. The girl who will become known to legend as Joan of Arc.

'A meaty dish of lust and medieval intrigue'
Maureen Owen, Daily Mail

'Ingenious, long and highly readable'
Philippa Toomey, The Times

'Best writer of her kind'
Kent Messenger

HODDER AND STOUGHTON PAPERBACKS

EVELYN ANTHONY

CLANDARA

Despite the centuries-old feud between their two clans, Katherine Fraser and James Macdonald fall deeply and passionately in love. Defying the past, the magnificent, wilful, Lady Katherine confronts her father's wrath and declares her wish to marry their bitter enemy.

It's 1745 and Bonnie Prince Charlie arrives on the shores of Scotland calling for the support of the highlanders to help him stake his claim to the British throne. But painful memories of the 1715 uprising prevent the Frasers from joining the rebellion: re-igniting the Macdonald's suppressed hatred of them and causing events which will bring about a deeper rift than ever between the clans. And as powerfully as Katherine and James were drawn together, they are driven apart.

HODDER AND STOUGHTON PAPERBACKS